TIME
to
SAY GOODBYE

JANE HATTON

© Jane Hatton 2012
Time to Say Goodbye

ISBN   978-0-9554508-7-7

Published by RaJe Publications
Garth Cottage
Little in Sight
Mawnan Smith
Falmouth
TR11 5EY

A CIP catalogue record of this book
can be obtained from the British Library.

Book designed by Michael Walsh at
THE BETTER BOOK COMPANY
5 Lime Close, Chichester,
West Sussex PO19 6SW

and printed by
IMPRINTDIGITAL.NET
Seychelles Farm, Upton Pyne,
Exeter EX5 5HY

TIME
to
SAY GOODBYE

JANE HATTON

AUTHOR'S NOTE

There are many villages in Greece named Ayios Giorgos, but the Ayios Giorgos mentioned in this book is imaginary, a composite of many places. All the other islands, villages and towns mentioned here are real enough, there to be visited and enjoyed by anyone who wishes to see them. The quayside in Mykonos town was as described when I was there some years ago now, plans to tidy it up may well have been implemented by this time.

Flotilla sailing is a growing industry, and deservedly popular. For anyone who enjoys sailing, it is a wonderful way to discover a new country. It should therefore be stressed that the experience of Marina and Steve, "when they were in the Ionian" is the rule rather than the exception, and that Panther Sailing, with their trail of disasters and disappointments, are not intended to be taken as more than a mariner's tale. No reputable flotilla company would dream of condoning such flagrant and dangerous mismanagement, or at least we must hope not.

But imagine, if you can, what it might be like if they did...

For

COLIN and PAM, DAVE and PAT

and EVE and MALCOLM

and remembering

JOHN

with love to you all

HAMPSHIRE

March 2004

I stood by the window, the pile of books in my arms and the box at my feet, looking out at the sunlit garden and wondering how it would feel never to see it again, as very shortly would be the case. It had been part of my life for so long, I would miss it. The cats would miss it. I wondered miserably where the three of us might end up, somehow I couldn't bring myself to focus on the future. It was a future that had been too long in coming, whose inevitability I had tried to fight every inch of the way.

Now, I was wondering why I had bothered, the end to our romance had been written long ago. It was some time now since I had really wanted Jay, even longer since I had trusted him. We had tried, and we had lost, and what I would be missing wasn't the husband who had left me in spirit many years before, but the home we had built together, where our children had grown up, that I was about to lose and that seemed a sad epitaph for our marriage.

Behind me, in the half-dismantled room, the sound of my daughter Sally briskly packing and sorting more books, had slowly ceased. A silence fell, into which her voice finally spoke, hesitantly. 'Mum?' When I didn't turn round, she repeated it, more urgently. '*Mum?*'

Only then did I summon the strength of mind to move, placing the books carefully in the box and straightening up, turning to face her. 'Hullo?'

'Are you OK?' She took a quick pace towards me and stopped, hands at her sides. 'Only, you had gone so still...'

'I was thinking,' I explained.

'Not surprised,' said Sally, relaxing. 'Dad is being a bastard! Do you really have to have this man intruding in your private affairs?'

'According to my solicitor, yes. I agreed to divide the value of the house down the middle to get your father off my back, it's entirely my own fault that I didn't realise that would mean the value of everything in it too. I thought he meant, half the house and he would take what he wants from the furnishings and things, and I would take what I want, and we'd sell the rest and just divide that. My mistake.'

'It's nit-picking, Mum. It's punishing you to make himself feel better, he doesn't really want any of it. Just tell him he can have the lot, and take the money yourself.'

'Unfortunately, it doesn't work quite like that. And there are some things I would like to keep.'

'Then just don't let the bastard know which they are.'

I sighed, but I couldn't help silently agreeing with her. Then I it said, anyway. 'Do stop calling your father a bastard, Sally. It doesn't really help.'

She gave me a belligerent look. 'Well, he can't touch your personal things.'

'That's why we're packing them away, before the valuer gets here.'

My soon-to-be-ex husband, Jay, had insisted that everything we owned between us should be valued, down to the last spoon in the drawer, and that the value of anything I took should be included in the settlement he had finally agreed: a sum equal to half the value of the house to me. I hadn't wished to be reminded of him by regular alimony payments and had fought for a lump sum. Now, it seemed, he was going to make me pay dearly for the victory. But that wasn't Jay, I told myself cynically. That was the grasping woman who presently had her claws in him, and I had little doubt that she would, very shortly after she haled him before the registrar, have the shirt off his back and move on. She had done it before, with other men. Poor, besotted Jay was the only one who couldn't see it. She was his worst mistake yet, and I found it hard not to feel that it served him right, and she was also one of the reasons I had stood out for half the house. When he was flat broke, as he probably soon would be, Jay would be in no position to make alimony payments, and I couldn't be bothered any more to argue about the exact terms of the agreement. Any furniture I would wish to take wouldn't be that valuable anyway.

Know thine enemy. Only he wasn't. I had loved him once, or believed that I had. It wasn't until we went to Greece that fateful summer, almost ten years ago now, that I had learned differently and every day since we came back I had been working out a self-inflicted penance for a betrayal that had never gone further than my own heart. I had thought I owed it Jay to try. Only, he hadn't tried at all in spite of all his promises. And here we were.

'You've gone off again,' Sally accused, staring at me. 'Mum, are you sure you aren't upset? I know you say you're not, but...' She fell silent again.

'Of course I'm *upset*!' I told her. 'Who wouldn't be? This is my home.'

'Well, said Sally, 'time to say goodbye. Where will you go, think about that. It's a new beginning for you, and probably the end for him, the –' She coughed instead of ending her sentence, and we both laughed.

'I haven't decided,' I told her.

'You could go and live near Marina,' Sally offered. Marina had said the same thing, but I didn't think so. She is my dearest friend, but she would try to run my life, and anyway I didn't want to live in Essex. Nor did I want to live too close to either of my daughters, I had done my share of bringing up little children and they both had young families, it would be a mistake to make myself too available and I could read the sub-text. If I was to have my freedom back, as both Sally and Stephanie kept assuring me I was, then I wanted to be free to enjoy it, not at the loving beck and call of my family or under the eye of my best friend So not Essex. Not Devon. Not West Sussex. That still left a wide field of choice.

'You don't want to be on your own in a strange place,' Sally assured me, but I rather liked the idea myself. I was still nearly two years off fifty. There was a lot of time left to enjoy. New surroundings, new friends, new things to do; it all looked very appealing from the springboard over nothingness where I stood now. I changed the subject.

'We should get on. I don't want the valuer arguing over whether I own things or whether I don't, and he's your father's recommendation.'

'Ouch!' said Sally. 'Better get on, then. When's he due?'

'Three o'clock.'

She glanced at her watch. 'Full steam ahead, then.'

Unfortunately, we didn't steam quite fast enough.

The valuer arrived punctually, and seemed a pleasant enough man, in fact I found I already knew him slightly from some of Jay's Lions' Club dinners. He was a man of around fifty called Maurice Hardacre, solid and reliable-looking, and came from a reputable auction house who surely had too much at stake themselves to play silly games with people. I had wondered if I might be wise to get a second valuation on my own account, but once I had met Jay's candidate, decided that I had been being paranoid. Moreover, as I walked round the rooms with him, he talked to me about the items he found interesting, and what he said made sense. For most of it, as I would have expected, he recommended a house clearance sale if neither of us wished to keep the things; for those of any worth that we had each already specified he gave sensible valuations. It was all going remarkably well until we reached the sitting room.

There was a picture hanging over the fireplace that Jay and I had bought together when we were first married; it was by a local artist, reputed at the time to be going places, and Jay had always referred to it as "our little investment." He said, always with a laugh and perhaps a little too often, that it was good to have an asset that we could appreciate while it appreciated, and it was on his list of desired objects. This, I had no problem with; I liked the picture, a pleasant street scene, but not as much as he did. He had obviously already mentioned it to the valuer, and I was careful to point it out, because if it was really valuable, half that value was due to me since we had bought it between us, and I would need it. However, things didn't work out quite as either Jay or I had expected.

'Oh yes,' said the valuer, giving it a cursory look. 'Edward Minton.' He peered at the signature in the corner. 'Yes, he looked like a coming name twenty, twenty-five years ago, but I'm afraid he never really made it. Three to five thousand, maybe, if it went to auction and somebody really wanted it. Say three and a half, realistically.'

'Jay thought it would be more,' I said, and Maurice Goodacre said he realised that.

'A good artist in his time, but not popular today. He had good reviews when he first started out, but he was a bit of a one-trick pony and it all fizzled out, I'm afraid.' He made a note on his pad and turned away, patently uninterested, and then his eye fell on a small watercolour hanging above the bookcase by the window, and he stiffened like a bloodhound on the scent. His previous polite interest in our modest worldly goods suddenly metamorphosed into a burning flame of interest. He crossed the room in three strides.

'I'm seeing things,' he muttered to himself, as I followed him. We ended up together in front of the bookcase looking at the picture of a small harbour crowded with boats tied under a high stone wall, and the curve of a Mediterranean quayside beyond , white in the strong sunlight with bright shops and strolling shoppers under a clear blue sky. It was vibrant for a watercolour, the paint laid on thick and bright so that it appeared to glow off the wall.

'Hydra,' I told him, helpfully, and he said, 'I can see.' He reached out almost reverently and touched the simple wooden frame. 'May I lift it down, have a closer look?'

'Of course, ' I said, bewildered by his manner. 'It isn't anything, you know. A friend gave it to me, years ago.'

He wasn't listening. He had taken out a glass and was studying the signature in the corner – no, not the signature, exactly. Just three initials, and a date. A date in a year that was graven on my heart and in my head. I swallowed, and even after nine years or more felt the tears pricking behind my eyes. He didn't notice. He let out a long sigh as he looked up, and asked, 'Wherever did you come by this?'

'I told you,' I said, more impatiently than I had intended. 'It was given to me.'

'Who on earth by?' He sounded stunned.

'Someone we met on holiday,' I said defensively. He narrowed his eyes at me.

'To you, personally? Or to both of you?'

'To me personally,' I said.

'You're sure of that?'

'Of course I'm sure. Is there a problem?'

'Not if you can prove it's your personal property, no.' He tapped the picture with his fingers, but gently. 'Do you know who painted it?'

'I told you. Someone we met.'

'Come over here.' He carried the picture over to the window where the light was better. 'See this in the corner? O J N, and just under it, a date back in 1995. In the early-to-mid nineties, long before he became known, a now very prestigious and desirable seascape painter named Oliver Nankervis was out in the Med, bumming around and getting what work he could, and sometimes, when times were hard and he ran out of money, he would pay a bar bill or for a meal in a taverna with a small painting like this one. He doesn't sign his work like this today, and because they are therefore hard to recognise, these early pictures turn up very rarely, and they fetch high prices since they have a scarcity value. Your friend probably bought it for peanuts in some waterside bar somewhere, and now here it is. I can't believe it!' He gave me another hard look. 'The friend who gave it to you will presumably confirm that it was given to you alone? Because this little picture is worth anything up to eighty thousand pounds today, and your husband may make an issue of it.'

I swallowed hard, and my voice came out as a squeak. He had no idea of the shock he had just handed me as I tried to pull myself together and make some sense of what seemed utter nonsense. 'I haven't seen him in years. I wouldn't know where to begin looking.'

'That's a pity.' He looked sorry.

'But it's mine. It's no business of Jay's,' I said, and knew already what he would say.

'I only have your word for that. Unfortunately.'

'Jay knows it's mine,' I said, knowing that I was fighting a rearguard action here. Once Jay got wind of this, he would swear blind, and to give him his due, probably believe, that the picture was a gift to us both.

'He may not remember,' said Mr Hardacre, diplomatically. 'I'm sorry, Mrs Starkey. Without proof of ownership or someone to corroborate what you say, I have to mention this to your husband. If I do not, and he finds out later, I could end up in trouble myself. Of course, he may well confirm what you tell me, in which case there will be no problem.'

I knew that if he once heard the magic words "eighty thousand pounds" Jay's memory, on purpose or not, would default to convenience mode and in order to resolve the argument the picture would have to be sold. I couldn't afford to pay him forty thousand pounds from my share of the present settlement if I was to live in any sort of comfort thereafter, and I would have to if I wanted to keep it.

I did want to keep it.

Mr Hardacre was looking at me, not without sympathy. He said, 'Is there no way you could trace your friend, do you think?'

I felt him to be on my side, even if he was watching his own back and I couldn't really blame him for that. Jay could be a real bastard, just as his daughter had said. I said, with regret, 'We met out there. I never knew where he came from originally.'

'A pity. Where were you staying, how did you meet? You might trace this person – this man –' he had spotted the giveaway pronoun, and what else I could only guess – 'that way.   If it's only nine or ten years, they may have a record still.'

'We were on a flotilla holiday,' I said, slowly. My mind was whirling with new ideas; I could hardly bear to think. He said, 'Then I suggest you start with the flotilla company. After you have phoned your insurance company.' He gave me a sympathetic smile, and repeated, 'I'm sorry, Mrs Starkey,' as he handed the picture back to me.

But I thought I might have no need of the flotilla company if what he had told me was true – and if they were even still in business, which might be debatable after what happened. After he had gone, I rehung the picture and went into the study to switch on my computer.

I felt numb, but slightly sick too as I watched the screen come to life and went on the net, called up a search engine.

Then I entered his name and sat there, staring at it with blank eyes that saw only the past.

HAMPSHIRE

March 1995

L ife is a bugger.

I sat in front of the dressing table staring at my face in the mirror and pondering this unoriginal thought. Why, I asked myself, when I appeared on the surface of things to have everything, should I suddenly have this frightening feeling that in fact, I had hold of mist?

List the plus points: two lovely daughters, some good friends. Lovely home in the country, active social life, two cars (that's one each, of course), yacht, quite a tally, and I wasn't even forty yet – not quite; the big Four-O was within touching distance, no worse. No financial worries. As I said just now, everything.

Or no. I had forgotten to list one handsome, successful husband.

Hmm...

The trouble wasn't anything that I wanted to put my finger on. Fear is a great deluder; my charming, good-looking husband, that, yes, I still loved after twenty years of marriage was fond of telling me this, often in connection with large spiders. For the first time, I wondered if he might possibly be right. In the past, I had always argued that fear sharpened the wits, the trigger for self-preservation in fact.

Self-preservation can take many forms.

Happiness is nobody's inalienable right, I told my reflection glumly, and then pulled a face. It was such a trivial incident that had triggered this dark mood, I should be ashamed of myself.

The previous Saturday had dawned bright and fair. Cool – it was only March, after all – but blue and sunny and lifting the spirits with the apparent imminence of Spring. Our eldest daughter, Sally, was coming home from university for the weekend to help celebrate her father's birthday the following day – our younger daughter, Stephanie, was at boarding school, and as yet uninterested in adult jamborees – and in addition to that Jay and I had planned to spend the afternoon prior to Sal's arrival down at the yard, fitting out our yacht *Foxtrot* ready for the coming season. I had been looking forward to both these things.

'I'm taking the whole day,' Jay said, over breakfast. He was his own boss, and could afford to do these things occasionally. 'There's a lot to do. I'll see you and Sal this evening. I know you're going to be busy anyway, with the party tomorrow.'

'OK.' I reached for the toast, sublimely unaware. 'I can slip down later in my own car, meet you for lunch and give you a hand for a couple of hours, maybe.'

'There's nothing for you to do, really. You'd only be bored and get in the way, and I'll probably just have a quick sandwich in the club. Why not just stay here and wait for Sal? She might be early. You wouldn't want not to be here.'

I wondered for a second whether to take offence. Getting in the way isn't something that anybody wants to be accused of. I asked, 'Why? What are you planning to do?'

Jay grinned at me. 'Scrub out the bilges. You know how you love that job.' Well, he had a point, that's nobody's favourite, which is why it often got overlooked.

'How virtuous,' I said. He grinned at me, irresistibly.

'You can do it if you really want to. I can wait in for Sal.'

'No, no – count me out. Please.'

So in the end, I didn't go down to the yard for a sandwich with my husband, and instead I stayed at home, got ahead with preparations for Jay's party tomorrow, and had a long conversation with my friend Marina on the phone. If I felt disappointed, well I was a grown-up and didn't brood over it, and anyway, just after my solitary bowl of soup, just as Jay had predicted, Sally arrived early.

Sally was then eighteen, in her first year at University, studying law. She was, and is, bright, pretty and endearingly scatty, which was permissible at that age. Although she had officially left home to live most of the time with two girlfriends in Reading, where she was studying, in practice we suspected that she was seeing rather more of someone called Peter. In between lectures, partying and enjoying her emergent freedom, she occasionally flitted home to see us, bursting through the door like a breath of brisk salt air in order, she said, to let us know that she was still alive. She would stay for a few hours, making the house ring with laughter, and then vanish again to her own life. Home and family no longer satisfied her. We hoped we could trust her, and so far she hadn't let us down. Given the times in which we live, anyway.

'Hi Mum, where's Dad?' she demanded at once.

'Down on the boat.'

'Really? So why aren't you with him?'

'He's scrubbing the bilges.'

'Goodness!' Sally stared at me, round-eyed. 'Is he ill?'

'Rude child, have some respect for your dad! Of course he isn't ill.'

Sally's grin was a reflection of her father's. She glanced at her watch, always a creature of impulse.

'Let's go down and drag him out. We can buy him a drink at the club, I bet he needs it!'

'They won't be serving drinks at this hour. It's the middle of the afternoon.'

'Oh Mum, don't nitpick! A cup of tea, then.'

It was a beautiful spring afternoon. We went. When we arrived at the small boatyard where *Foxtrot* spends the long, cold months of winter laid up ashore, the yacht was wrapped and silent and Jay nowhere to be seen. We went across to the Yacht Club, but he wasn't there either. We had a cup of tea anyway, looking out over the still waters of the river and enjoying a pleasant mother-daughter chat about everything under the sun except Peter.

'I expect Dad got fed up and went home. You can't blame him,' said Sally, as we left.

I had assumed the same myself, but as she spoke I found myself wondering. There *are* two ways to go from our village down to the riverside, but they diverge only at one point, just for a couple of miles, and are really two variations of the same route. It seemed odd, though not necessarily incredible, that Jay should have passed by one lane as we took the other, all in a space of five or ten minutes, the more so since the second route was by a very narrow lane that we rarely used. Odd too, though, and definitely incredible to wonder if he had ever been at the yard at all, which had to be the alternative.

He was at home when we got back, smiling and with his arms held out to Sal.

The rest of the weekend was good fun.

Yes, I know what you're thinking. Mountains out of molehills. Smoke without fire. The long arm of coincidence. Or maybe you're just a cynic, wiser than I. But up until then I had never consciously been a jealous woman, or a suspicious one.

I wonder now if I had instead been a stupid and complacent one.

The silly incident must have been preying on my subconscious. I awoke in those dangerous wee small hours of the night and lay in the dark, thinking. Beside me, Jay slept the deep sleep widely supposed to be the prerogative of those with a clear conscience. I lay on my back with a growing, but unsubstantiated uneasiness.

It isn't that Jay and I had a perfect marriage, I don't think there is such a thing. We married young – I had Sally when I was barely twenty – and we've been through all the usual things: happy beginnings, the arrival of our girls to much pride and joy, followed by accusations of "you're no fun any more", in our case from a husband for whom a sense of responsibility has never been top of his list of desirable virtues. But anyway, a lot of married men are a bit like that in my opinion, it's in their genes. At bottom they are all, even the mildest of them, still the same old primeval hunter/warrior, out on the prowl. It's women who seem to have lost their way, their sense of fulfilment. I blame washing-up machines myself. And vacuum cleaners. And probably disposable nappies too. Technology has removed most of the point from staying home to look after the kids and tend the fire in the cave, and not all of us want to go out to work like the men and farm the children out with carers

So OK, I sound like that modern anachronism, a domesticated woman, but it isn't that I love housework, never think it. It's just that, where's the point of having children at all if you're forever going to dump them on somebody else, unless you absolutely have to?

But anyway, what I am trying to say is, we came through all of that. The children grew up, and we were still together at the end of it with the rest of our lives in front of us to enjoy. But now, as I lay awake in the darkness with Jay snoring gently beside me, I began to wonder if, without the girls to hold us together, we were maybe drifting apart.

Here I have to say that Jay was always a bit of a ladies' man, prone to casual embraces and intimate teasing, some of our female friends (notably Marina, as a matter of fact, who has little patience with wandering hands) had needed to give him a pretty firm brush off once or twice. There never seemed any harm in it, it was all quite above board, and, I assured myself, not intended to humiliate.

I believed that, too. I really did. He always was like that, I knew it when I married him and I still went ahead with it.

Sometimes, too, he stayed late at his office – that old chestnut. He is an architect, and he would claim that he had sometimes to meet with clients who themselves worked during the day, which sounded reasonable then, and actually, still does, or up to a point anyway. I daresay it was often true, but with my present new wisdom, probably not every time. And anyway, his secretary was a competent older woman with a husband of her own and three grown-up children. I could never take seriously the idea that he might be having it away with Olwen, she just isn't the type. We used to joke about it.

So I didn't really know why I lay awake that night, although I am wiser now.

Then on Monday evening he stayed late at his office again. If it hadn't been for Saturday, I wouldn't have thought twice about it.

He came back just after ten, silent and preoccupied, and kissed me lightly on the cheek.

'Sorry love, didn't realise how late it was. He got on the net and stayed on for hours, sending forms and requisitions and things. Took hours over it. You know how some of them are.'

'Of course. You know I don't make a fuss.'

'You're a good girl Sue, you know that? No – I don't want any supper thanks. I think I'll just turn in.'

I scraped his uneaten meal into the dog's bowl, and not for the first time. The dog wagged her tail and looked at me sympathetically before settling herself down to tuck in, Boeuf Bourguignon doesn't often come her way. She is a nice mutt, but her sympathy, for some reason, upset me that night. Did she know something that I didn't?

Wednesday, that is the day before my communion with the dressing table mirror, a strange thing really did happen. I am ashamed, for once again, if it hadn't been for Saturday this might have got past me too. Olwen rang me at three in the afternoon asking to speak to Jay. I know, I know. But it's easy when you're on the outside, looking in. Like a lighted window after dark. I know that. Now.

'I thought he was at the office,' I said, cursing Jay for making me say it. Even to me it sounded lame.

'He went out to view a property and then on to lunch with a

17

prospective client,' said Olwen. 'I thought he must have gone on home. He didn't look very well, I thought he might have had flu coming on or something, it's going around right now.'

'He'd have told you, surely. Or at least, I would have when he got here.'

'He must have gone on to another appointment, or perhaps the lunch was a long one,' Olwen sounded puzzled. 'I wouldn't have bothered you, only he has an appointment here in ten minutes – the client is already waiting.'

'Perhaps you'd better tell him the flu story,' I suggested. 'You know how he is – if something interests him, he forgets about everything else.'

'All right, I'll do that, and make another appointment. Thank you, Mrs. Starkey.'

'Just hope he doesn't turn up before you get this man off the premises.'

Olwen had sounded quite satisfied. I put the phone down and stood with my hand resting on it, staring at the wall.

How long does it take for the tide to come in? From the moment it turns, far out in the oceans, to the moment it comes lapping round your feet on the shore? I stared at the wall in front of me and knew that I had felt the pulse of its turning long since, gone with its flow, watched our progress over the ground with complacence, not realising ... never realising... that we were being swept onto the rocks.

Rocks? Or safe harbour? I had no idea. No idea if anyone was actually navigating, steering the ship. Or where the lifebelts were stowed.

A moment later, the feeling had gone. I laughed at myself. There would be a perfectly simple explanation, there always had been in the past.

Jay came home at his usual time, and said nothing about his afternoon. I thought of asking him, but then the oddity of knowing what he thought I didn't know made me pause and think again. If he had something on his mind, he would tell me soon enough. I just hoped it was only business.

He went out that night to fish down by the river. It was three a.m before he came back, but that was nothing unusual. Very occasionally

I would go night fishing with him, on a warm night and with a good moon it can be fun. We would take a flask of coffee and a few cans of beer and some sandwiches; we had some good nights, so there was nothing in that to make me wonder. Sometimes, Jay even caught something, although I never did – but not that night. He came home empty-handed.

Which brings me back to where I started. Thursday morning.

I stared at my reflection and my own face stared back at me. A thin, freckled face with pale, winter skin. Hazel eyes with dark shadows under them, the shadows were new. Mop of unruly light brown hair, tight ringlets, impossible to style; the best I could do, now I was getting too old to get away with wearing it loose on my shoulders, was to scrape it back with combs or a scrunchie in the nape of my neck. A face neither outstandingly pretty nor particularly plain, just average. And thirty-eight years old.

Jay was five years older. Just ripe for the famous mid-life crisis.

But who was she?

Just asking the question was a knife in the heart, but it happens. Everyone knows that it does.

She might not even exist, except in my own imagination. I had no real evidence for her. And then, even as I thought this weasel thought, right on cue the front doorbell rang. I went downstairs to answer it, and there on the doorstep was Dawn.

Dawn...

She isn't – wasn't – precisely a friend. More of an acquaintance, a neighbour from down the lane who we had met when her lawn mower had run amok with her and crunched into a tree in her garden, and Jay had been the only man available (or so she said). Me, I would have sorted it out for myself and run it to the local garage for first aid, but that's not Dawn's style. After that rescue mission, we felt we had to invite her to our bigger parties, mainly because Jay said we should because she was a newcomer, and had made no friends as yet, and she and I had the occasional cup of coffee together in each other's kitchens, should we happen to run into each other in the village. Apart from that, we had little in common and had never been intimate. She is, I suppose, a few years younger than me, a thin redhead, slightly scruffy in appearance and given to wearing very short skirts and tight tops that don't quite meet in the middle, and chunky trainers without socks, as if she was fifteen or twenty years younger, and a lot of dramatic eye make-up; she has the sort of face, with a small, beaked nose and a little mouth, that I always thought, but never said, made her look like a rather bad-tempered chicken. Everyone in the village had deduced why her husband must have divorced her, she has quite a reputation given the short time she has been among us. Her story was that he left her for a younger woman.

'Sue!' she said, now.

I really wasn't in the mood for her. My greeting must have sounded lukewarm. 'Oh... hullo, Dawn.'

'I need to talk to you.' She was already over the threshold. I stepped back to avoid being trampled in the rush, and followed her to the kitchen. Automatically, I reached to switch on the kettle.

'What's the problem?'

She stood beside the kitchen table, hands clasped in front of her like a little girl about to recite her catechism.

'Your husband thinks he's in love with me,' she said. 'I thought you should know.'

For a long moment, we stared at each other. Her eyes, which are pale blue, never wavered from mine. For a second there, she almost looked scared.

I found that I had no instant reaction to this outrageous statement. If this had been a soap, no doubt I should have leapt on her and tried to scratch her eyes out, but to me, this didn't seem an option, so instead I just stood there while my world crashed about my ears. It would serve no useful purpose, anyway, to scream at her or shake her until her teeth rattled and I wasn't going to give her the satisfaction of seeing me so hysterical. When I thought that I could trust my voice, I said, 'Perhaps you'd better explain that.'

'I think he's close to a breakdown. He was round my place last night. He lay on the sofa and cried, and said that he couldn't go on, that there was nothing left...' She had the grace to let this sentence die on her lips.

No wonder he had looked washed out when he got home. I said, coldly, 'What was he doing in your house in the first place?'

20

'He often calls round. We're good friends.'

News to me. 'Apparently,' I said.

'Oh, don't be like that!'

I sat down slowly on the nearest chair. 'I'm sorry, did I miss my cue? What would you like me to say?'

'You could at least help me. I am telling you, after all.'

A lot of confused thoughts tumbled through my head, none of which made any sense. Dawn put on an air of injured innocence that this time, really did make me want to hit her.

'I don't *want* him,' she said, as if that made it better.

'A bit late to say that, from the sounds of it,' I replied angrily.

I remembered that I had seen her in town last week, in the shopping mall; she hadn't seen me and I hadn't drawn myself to her attention. She had been with an older man who had a smooth, dark, fondant-filled look to him. At the time I had thought nothing of it, now I found myself wondering whose husband he was. No doubt to have two of them on the go at once was too tiring for her: maybe that explained her present visit.

Our conversation seemed to have ground to a halt. Behind me on the worktop the kettle boiled and switched itself off, but coffee seemed too civilised for this occasion. Dawn, still standing, fidgeted on her feet.

'Well... I thought you ought to know. You ought to talk to him.'

Where exactly *had* he been on Saturday, on Monday afternoon? When he went fishing, had he caught himself a barracuda? I felt cold, if I hadn't clasped them tightly, my hands would have been shaking. I heard myself saying, 'He could have talked to me.'

She shrugged her shoulders. The gesture made me feel shut out, deliberately excluded. After almost twenty years of marriage, he took his troubles to this woman, not to me. She was blatantly sexual. I wondered what form her comfort had taken before things got out of hand. Dawn, I felt, didn't deal in sympathy and the sisterly pat on the hand.

I asked the question to which I didn't want to hear the reply. 'How long...?'

She shrugged again, the gesture irritated me. She really didn't care, except for her own inconvenience.

'He started dropping by about six months ago. Just a drink or a chat. We watch the telly, have a cup of tea maybe, that's all. A couple of times he's taken me out to dinner – just as a thank you.'

The betrayal was breathtaking. All those late nights in the office. All those lovingly cooked dinners in the dog's bowl. Even if I believed what she told me, it was too much. I swallowed, but remained unable to speak.

'I just thought you ought to know,' repeated Dawn, righteously.

'My voice worked only with difficulty. 'It never occurred to you to send him home, and just shut the door in his face?'

Dawn said nothing. I saw the twitch of the beginnings of another shrug, but she thought better of it, luckily for her. It might have been a shrug too far. I wondered why she had told me this now. Perhaps Mr. Fondant-Fancy was more worth her while than my husband? Better dinners, bigger presents, not so close to home. The bitterness of it was scaring.

'I'd better go,' she said, and did.

After the door had closed gently behind her, I still sat on my chair beside the kitchen table. Everything looked the same, which seemed odd when it was suddenly so different. The friendly, familiar room looked alien, but it was still the same room. The ceramic chicken from Italy, full of eggs, still sat on the worktop, the familiar potted cacti cluttered the window sill. In the sink, the washing up waited; Jay's mug, Jay's plate, Jay's knife and spoon. I drew a deep breath, and the slow, hot tears began to run down my cheeks. Grief, humiliation, misery... any or all of those burned my skin and dripped onto my hands.

The phone rang. I went to answer it, moving like a robot programmed to react to a given signal and scrubbing at my cheeks with the back of my hand.

'Hi Sue!' cried Marina.

I must have replied on autopilot. I can't remember saying anything at all, I can only deduce that I must have done by the fact that Marina went blithely on. 'How d'you fancy grease?'

Grease? Grease? The jump was too great for my already reeling brain to make. I felt as if I had run into a wall.

'Er...' I said. 'What sort of grease were you thinking of?'

'Sue?'

'Yes?'

'Are you sober?'

The impulse to confide in Marina, to spill it all out, swept over me like a flash fire and left me with the ashes. I couldn't do it. She may be – is – my dearest friend, but my pride hurt too much right then. Mangled as it was, I dragged it out of hiding to help me.

'Sorry. I've just this minute seen one of my neighbours off the premises, my brain wasn't in gear. Run that by me again.'

Marina laughed. '*Do not engage the mouth until the brain is in gear,*' she quoted derisively. 'I hope it wasn't that frightful Dawn. Steve says she looks as if when the bus stopped, she didn't! Listen, dozo, what we were talking about at New Year, remember? The flotilla?'

It all fell into place, then. Not grease, Greece. Sailing. And yes, I did remember. Another time, another place, another life, when everything was safe and certain, or seemed so.

An east coast winter evening, wind howling in the chimney and sleet spattering against closed windows. The four of us huddled around the telly in Marina and Steve's sitting room, watching a tempting travel programme promising exotic destinations, bathed in perpetual sunshine. We had almost felt the warmth, smelt the heady scents of unfamiliar flowers, heard the whisper of the tideless sea. The fire crackled and leapt in the grate, and in the springing flames the dreams began to form.

'I could really fancy the Med,' Jay said. 'It would make a nice change from Brittany, or Belgium and Holland.' He didn't mention France, because none of us is that keen on the Channel coast, we try to miss it out of our cruising itineraries. Dunkirk, for instance, is too brash and new, its lost heritage too full of ghosts – although the piped chamber music in the marina showers is some compensation, if you have that type of humour. I'm afraid I have.

Marina heaved a regretful sigh.

'It sounds a wonderful idea, but Steve only gets a month, he doesn't have the privilege of being his own boss like some. Even if we did it all in one go, even your *Foxtrot* would be pushed to make it there and back and have a holiday too in the time.'

'She wouldn't have to,' said Jay. 'I wasn't thinking of flogging our way across the Bay of Biscay, or wriggling down through the canals, thank you very much. We could charter. Then we'd be flying out.'

We discussed it for most of that evening, on and off. The four of us had covered a lot of water together in the years since we had first met. That was on the visitors' pontoon in Fowey harbour, Jay and I were on our first long sailing trip in our thirty foot dream cruiser. Steve and Marina Philipson, seasoned mariners, had sailed their twenty-six foot light displacement cruiser/racer *Koala* round from the east coast. We had got to talking, Marina and I at least had found a lot in common, Steve and Jay became good drinking mates. For five years now we had been cruising together, to Holland and Belgium on *Koala*, to the Brittany harbours in *Foxtrot*, round the Channel coast of England in company. We knew each other's strengths and weaknesses, tolerated each other's faults, were invited to significant birthdays and anniversaries, met, as now, at each other's homes for long weekends. And yet, between these occasions we seldom saw each other, hardly wrote, and Jay and Steve at least barely telephoned. The miles that lay between their home in Essex and ours in the New Forest kept us apart, but also, in a different way, they kept us together too. Had we lived closer, Steve's easy assumption of superior seamanship (justified, but that's not the point) would have got on Jay's nerves more than it did already, Marina's claim to be clairvoyant might have irritated instead of amused me. Anyway, I'm not sure I like the idea of clairvoyance.

Poor Marina, she really hated her name. Once, she said, it might have suited her, it had held the delicate suggestion of a sea nymph, a spirit of the waves. Today, one might as well be called "Municipal Car Park". Jay said that Marina hadn't the figure for a sea nymph these days, but not in her hearing. Too much making out to be a sea nympho in her wild youth, he said, resulting in marriage, childbearing, and a certain loss of style. Now she is chunky but rounded, with a bright, alert face under a mop of dark curls less unruly than mine, and more elegantly styled. She looks as wholesome and normal as brown bread. She is brave and funny and not at all the kind of person you would suspect of dabbling in the supernatural, which makes her claim all the more disconcerting.

By the time we left for home the next day, we had the whole thing roughed out. We wouldn't bareboat charter, said Steve. If we were only out there for a fortnight we wanted to make the most of it, we would get more out of a flotilla. He and Marina had been on one before in the Ionian, when their children were younger. They had all had a great time.

Jay wrinkled his nose in distaste. 'Don't they make you all sail together? Mother duck and all the little ducklings?'

'Good God no.' Steve looked amused. 'They haven't been like that for a long time.'

'It may have been like that in the very beginning.' Marina leaned forward eagerly, the light from the fire played across her bright, interested face, her eyes glowed sapphire. She should have been talking of the road to Samarkand, not a package tour in the Mediterranean. 'It's all different now, much more free and easy. There's a lead boat to help you with the language and the port officials, and things that go wrong, and a hostess to tell you about all the best places to eat, and the beaches, and where you can change your travellers' cheques, and of course they do look after the beginners. But there's lots of free sailing, you can go where you want within the sailing area, and there's a terrific social life because you're always meeting the other flotilla boats in harbour in the evening – you don't have to, I mean, except now and then, but there's usually one or two gone to the same place. It's fun to meet friends. And they arrange things – beach barbecues, and social evenings –'

'Charter boats aren't allowed to sail after dark in Greek waters, anyway,' said Steve, as if that settled it.

We had talked some more. Steve and Marina were off to visit the Boat Show in the coming week, they promised to collect all the leaflets they could find and have them sent to us, too. And until this inopportune moment, that was the last we had heard of it.

'Ah,' I said.

'We meant to do something about it ages ago,' Marina went on blithely. 'But it's been such a year so far, you wouldn't believe – but anyway, Steve went into the travel agent on Monday in his lunch hour, and he got a cancellation. Early to mid-June. Are you up for it?'

A good question. If she had asked it only a week ago, I would have given an immediate 'yes!' Today, I knew that a great many things could have happened by June, still ten weeks away.

'I'll have to talk to Jay, of course.' About many things more important than our summer holiday.

'But does the idea sound good in principle?'

'Wonderful. Brilliant.'

'You don't have to jump overboard,' said Marina mildly. Sometimes I wonder if her claim to clairvoyance is justified, for she went on to ask, 'Is everything OK down there with you, Sue?'

The honest answer to that was, of course, 'no'. I took a deep breath.

'Don't be silly! You caught me on the hop, that's all. Can you send us the details?'

'Put them in the post last night, you should have got them this morning. They're holding it for us until Saturday, that's the day after tomorrow. Can you let us know by tonight or tomorrow morning? Just to be sure?'

'Whee! That's quick!'

'Otherwise, there's nothing until October. Bit chilly by then.'

The front door rattled and the day's junk mail delivery fell onto the mat. A large brown envelope stuck together with green tape lay among the debris. I said, 'I think your letter has just arrived. Green tape and a re-use label?'

'That's the one. Take a look and let us know what you think. Must rush, 'bye for now.'

I put the phone down slowly. The brief, sunny interlude had set me a step away from Dawn and her bombshell, I no longer wept. But Jay and I were going to have a busy evening – if he bothered to come home.

He was late, but not that late. I wondered if he had gone to see Dawn, and if she had taken up my suggestion and shut the door in his face. He had a weary, defeated look that was unlike him, taking a beer from the fridge without kissing me first and carrying it into the sitting room. I followed him, and sat down in a chair facing his.

'We need to talk,' I said. He made a tired gesture with his free hand.

'Go on, then.'

I had spent all day wondering how best to approach it, but in the end it came tumbling out without finesse. 'Dawn came over after you'd gone this morning.'

He sighed. 'Oh. D'you want a drink?'

'No. Alcohol isn't the answer to this one, is it Jay?'

'Listen, darling –'

'Please don't.' I interrupted him. 'Call me darling, I mean. Not right now.'

He sighed again, heavily, and placed his glass on the small table beside his chair. 'What d'you want me to say? It happened. End of story.'

'No. Tell me why.'

'Why?' He smiled drearily. 'She was there, I was lonely.'

'No you weren't. You had me and the children, lots of friends and things we did together, shared. Tell me the truth, Jay. I deserve that much, at least.'

'I don't think I know it,' he said. A silence fell between us. We were in soap territory again, I thought, and I wasn't going to go that road. I waited.

He wouldn't meet my eyes. I watched him and felt cold, he looked a million miles away, shifty and unfamiliar, someone I no longer recognised.

'Does she matter?' I asked, eventually. He shrugged, an echo of her morning gesture. I felt anger beginning to stir beneath the fear.

'Was she the first?' I pressed. He stirred uneasily.

'Sue…'

She wasn't the first, then. I wondered who the others had been, and if I knew them too. The cold spread.

'Jay, *why*?'

'Look, Sue, I've had a hard day. Must we hold a post mortem right now?'

'Is there a better time, more convenient for you? I've had a fairly awful day too, come to that. What's gone wrong, Jay, you must know – you must be able to talk about it. Otherwise there's no point… to us. To the last twenty years. We can't have grown that far apart, and me not know about it.'

He looked at me then. 'You didn't want to know about it.'

'Dear God, Jay, I didn't know there was anything to know!'

'Well, you do now.'

This was worse than anything I had ever imagined. I held my breath against the pain, afraid that if I let go it would come out in a long howl of despair. The fact that he was making no attempt to defend himself was, I think, the worst thing about it. As if I no longer mattered.

'Jay...' It would sound like pleading, but if our marriage had ever meant anything, it had to be said. Only the truth – my truth as well as his – might rescue us now. I paused, choosing my words with care. 'I love you. We've come a long way together and shared a lot of fun. I don't want to lose you, but it wouldn't be worth it if you didn't love me, too. That would be too humiliating.'

He didn't move. I swallowed.

'I love you, Jay. But if you want a divorce, I'd sooner that than this... wondering all the time where you were, who you were with, what I'd done...'

'Oh Sue, of course you haven't *done* anything! And I don't want a divorce. I love you too – in a funny sort of way.'

'Thanks for nothing!'

He glared at me. 'I'm trying to explain. That's what you want, isn't it?'

I really wasn't sure any more. I looked down at my hands. 'Perhaps I'd better have that drink after all.'

Silently, he got up to fix me a rum and fresh orange juice, walking to and from the drinks cupboard and the kitchen gave us both time to find our balance. Finally, he sat down again and picked up his beer. He raised it with a ghost of a smile.

'Here's to us.'

I made a gesture with my glass that he could take as a response if he wished, but I had no heart for the toast. I wasn't even certain there was any "us" any more. I had to prompt him before he spoke again.

'You were going to explain.'

He drank, and pulled a face.

'It sounds so easy when you say it. I'm not sure that I can.'

'Try.'

He thought for a moment, and came up with, 'Life had got so dull and predictable.'

'Thanks,' I said, with pain.

'Look Sue, I'm doing my best. You could at least try to understand.'

'That I'm dull and predictable?'

'Not just you.' I could have managed without that word "just". 'Everything. Work, life generally... everything. All those years you talk about, and what have I achieved?'

'A good business, all your own. Two happy children. A lovely home and a wife who still loves you after twenty years. *Foxtrot*. What more do you feel life owes you?'

'Please try not to be bitter, Sue. Please.'

'And a dull marriage?' I flung at him. It was a mistake.

'Yes,' he agreed. 'A dull marriage. Now the children are growing up and beginning to live their own lives... and work seems to have drifted into a dead end, there's nowhere new left to go... I'm really sorry, Sue. It isn't anything you've done. It's my fault.'

I spoke past a lump in my throat. 'If you feel like that... then it makes a mockery of my life, too.'

'I do see that, believe me.'

I wondered if he did. It seemed to come out too easily to be convincing, but perhaps I was being over-sensitive? There really didn't seem to be anything more that could usefully be added to what we had said, I certainly didn't feel like digging any deeper... into *who* and *when* and *where*. That way, total disaster must lie. So we sat in silence for a while, drinking together and thinking our own thoughts, and eventually Jay said, 'What are we going to do, Susie?'

'Dawn –' Her name caught in my throat. 'Dawn said she thought you were heading for a breakdown.'

'Perhaps I am. Perhaps that's what it's all about.'

I wanted to ask, *how many years, Jay? How many women?* but if we were to survive intact, I knew that I mustn't. I must leave him with the easy get-out. So I said, 'How about a holiday? Somewhere new, something adventurous. Would that help, do you think?'

'We could get to know each other again… yes, that might work.'

I thought that we already knew each other as well as we were ever going to, but at least his face had brightened at the suggestion. I wished that my heart felt less leaden.

'What had you in mind?' Jay asked. I picked up Marina's green-taped envelope from the coffee table.

'Have a look at that. Steve and Marina sent it this morning.'

He took out the bright-coloured brochure and began to read it. Our talk was over, a truce declared, even if not in so many words. So far as I could see it had achieved nothing, leaving me feeling that I had drawn back from a precipice only a second before disaster. Only time would show if we had achieved anything, only time would prove if there was anything left to salvage.

And for the next week or two, he really seemed to be making an effort. Tension, which had kept me brittle and fragile as glass for days after our talk, began to ease. He stopped working late, he gave up night fishing, and with the yacht on the water again, our weekends became full of activity and the company of our sailing friends. Then one Saturday, as we lazed in bed with an early morning cup of coffee, the telephone rang beside the bed. Jay picked it up.

'Hullo?… oh, hullo there!… Yes… oh hell, that's a bugger… yes, of course I can. Yes… yes…give me ten minutes, I'm not up yet!… OK. Ten minutes. See ya.' He put the phone down, and pushed back the duvet without meeting my eyes. 'That was Dawn. Her car's broken down, and the child has a dancing class. I said I'd run them into town.'

I forgot to mention that Dawn has a daughter, a miniature reproduction of herself. A pert child, too knowing for her years, whom I try to like without much success. A wave of rage swept me. How *dared* she, after what had passed between us? I said, trying to sound reasonable, 'Can't she call a taxi, like other people?'

'Come on Sue, it won't take long. The poor kid's got an exam coming up. It's not easy for Dawn, living out here in the sticks on her own with a child to look after.'

'She's got a nerve, asking. And presumably it was her choice to live here!'

'I'll be back soon, I promise.'

'We were going sailing...' Even to myself I sounded like a disappointed child. I bit my lip, caught wrong-footed and unable to see what the alternative might have been.

'There'll be plenty of time for that – look, I haven't time to argue about it, I said I'd take them, and that's it.' He was gone, dashing on his way to the bathroom, avoiding further argument. Sir Galahad, rushing to rescue the damsel in distress. Our lazy, comfortable start to the weekend, our precariously rebuilt companionship, lay in pieces around me.

He didn't come back until lunchtime, with profuse apologies and some downright lies about having to slip into the office and see to something since he was in town anyway. By then, we had missed the tide.

GREECE

June 1995

Day One: Monday, 5th June

The heat hit us as soon as we stepped onto the tarmac at Athens Airport, dry heat vexed with a warm wind like a blast from a hair drier. Marina lifted her face to the sun and sniffed, audibly.

'Smell that air! Like nectar scented with spice!'

'It smells just like aviation fuel to me,' said Jay, giving her an affectionate push forward. 'Get along with you, you'll have us at the end of the customs queue if you insist on standing around inhaling diesel with a silly smile on your face.'

Not that it would have mattered. Ours wasn't the only tour party on our charter flight, and it seemed as if everyone but us was being scooped up and hurried away to start their fortnight in the sun. Small, disconsolate groups , all toting luggage bearing Panther Sailing's leaping black cat logo, drifted around the Arrivals hall like iron filings in search of a magnet, trying to avoid each other's eyes. Nobody seemed to want to know any of us. We did see the occasional Panther Sailing courier, skulking around in the crowd clutching clipboards and appearing not to know quite what to do, or huddling together in muttering conclave, but it was quite some time before one of them approached any of us.

'Are any of you for the Cyclades cruise? Please wait outside the airport building' Like an anxious sheepdog, she filtered out some of the groups, including our own, from the crowd and herded us outside to stand in the blazing sun – whereupon she promptly disappeared again.

Like good little sheep, we obediently stayed where she put us for a while. There was nothing to sit on, and it was very hot. We shifted uneasily from foot to foot, watching the Greek police drive past in armoured cars, machine guns at the ready, daring us to step out of line. A young woman standing close to me broke a brooding silence.

'Have they forgotten about us? What would happen if we just walked away, do you think?'

'Where to?' asked Marina.

The midday sun beat down on us, and a cloud of discontent began to gather; unfortunately, it didn't shield us from the glare. One or two of the hardier spirits among us picked up their luggage and set off in the wake of luckier tours, round the corner of the airport building. They didn't return.

'They've been gunned down for mutiny,' suggested Marina, and the girl beside us giggled nervously. Steve began to lose his sense of humour. He shouldered as much luggage as he could reasonably manage, and gave an authoritative jerk of his head.

'Come on. Let's move!'

He strode off towards the corner. He had only been addressing ourselves, but relieved to have a leader, the entire group straggled along in his wake. I didn't suppose for an instant that he knew where he was going, but that's Steve. He has this effect on people.

Beyond the corner, a spacious car park bustled with activity, coaches arriving, departing, waiting, taxis wriggling expertly through the ranks of bigger vehicles, it looked chaotic. Our courier sudden reappeared, smiling too effusively and trying to look crisply efficient but only succeeding in looking flustered. Scurrying into the lead ahead of Steve, she managed to be the first arrival at our coach, supervised the stowing of the luggage, and then hurried off again to resume her interrupted conversation with a colleague. The rest of us now sat in our seats, getting steadily even hotter due to the greenhouse effect of the windows, waiting again. It grew stuffy and close and nothing seemed to be happening. Steve began to get dangerously restive, he gave a distinct impression that at any minute he would be taking the wheel and driving us away. Marina, used to him and so relaxed and calm, wriggled back more comfortably in her seat to look out of the window.

'Oh, my God! Do watch this!'

Alongside us, a middle-aged Greek of piratical aspect was trying to back his car out of a tight space, and for lack of any other entertainment, the whole coachload crowded across the aisle to watch, exchanging bets on the outcome as we watched him edge forward, back, forward – a fifty-three point turn executed with style and, from the look on his face, swearing. Finally, striking our coach a triumphant glancing blow as he went, he drove away to the accompaniment of cheering from the back seat where a group of four, much our own age, were sitting together. We had noticed them first at Gatwick, they were a noisy crowd, already having a good time at seven in the morning. At this point, our driver, who had been loafing around outside in the fresh air, leapt into his seat, slammed the door, and drove off. We had no idea where to, and our courier had been left behind.

'Hijacked!' cried Marina. 'Isn't this fun?'

Our early start that morning, and the long wait in the sun, had made me sleepy. I closed my eyes, shutting out the moving picture of modern Athens passing outside the window and let my thoughts run free. It naturally didn't occur to me that the incident in which we had just played our part would have any bearing, however tenuous, on my future, and I had already put it out of my mind.

In the five or six weeks since Jay had made his brief sortie into the taxi business, we had arrived at an uneasy truce. *So far as I knew* it hadn't happened agin, but Jay had managed to make me appear to have behaved so unreasonably that I wondered sometimes if I was deliberately looking the other way. But we had rubbed along somehow and even, now and then, seemed to make progress towards a new start – or at least, a better understanding, which was the same thing maybe, and if our relationship had occasionally felt stifled and barren, time and effort might alter that. The prospect of our Greek Island cruise had helped, of course. Confirmations, flight schedules and tickets had begun to arrive in the post, and one morning an exciting fat envelope had fallen on the mat, forwarded by Steve and Marina, from Panther Sailing themselves.

Panther Sailing – a leap into the unknown! They didn't advertise themselves like that, but with hindsight, they might as well have done. They were a comparatively small company, operating in the Adriatic, the Ionian, and in the Saronic Gulf. Twice in each season, they ran a flotilla for more experienced sailors that also took in the Cyclades as well as the Gulf, and it was on one of these that Steve had booked us all. We spread the papers out among the breakfast plates and looked through them. These included, we found, a comprehensive inventory for the boat we would be sailing, a stapled sheet of advice as to what to pack, instructions on care of the engine and how to moor up bows-to, and little diagrams showing how to sail.

'A bit late for that now, surely,' said Jay, studying it with the academic interest of one who already reckoned he knew it all.

'I thought people on that flotilla were expected to have done that bit already,' I agreed. The Cyclades aren't exactly the nursery slopes in sailing.

'That's what I mean. Oh well, I expect they just bung it out as part of the package.' Jay tossed it aside and picked up the next sheet, which was a list of the boats on the flotilla and the names of those who would crew them. Our own particular yacht, we saw, was named *Phaedra*. Steve's name was on top of the crew list. Jay made a face. 'Trust Captain Steve.'

'Well, he did make the booking,' I pointed out. Steve is also a qualified Yachtmaster, and in addition a Yachtmaster Instructor, but it wouldn't do to say so. Jay is sensitive on the subject.

The lead boat was named *Eleni*. There were three names listed.

CAPTAIN   *Paul Gregory*

HOSTESS   *Emily Lewis*

ENGINEER   *Andy Miller*

'I bet Emily has fun,' commented Jay.

'She sounds like somebody's maiden aunt.'

'Bet she doesn't behave like one.'

The rest of the fleet had romantic-sounding names like *Aphrodite* and *Ariadne*. The people who were to sail them were called things like Janet and Ken. That's life.

Anticipation and planning had given us something to talk about until our departure date, and kept the communication lines open, and now here we were. Make or break time. We had just a fortnight in which to rediscover each other, and if we couldn't do that, I had no idea where we could go from there. Jay seemed to think there was no real problem but that *was* the problem to my mind. He had ceased to think about me to the point where my happiness was no longer a consideration, and I wasn't at all sure that the situation was reversible.

The prospect scared me. Whether because I had been blind or he had been clever, I wasn't sure. As you must have realised by this time, I hadn't seen it coming. I had lived all the years of our marriage believing that we had something good, that we were following a life plan that would last for ever, and suddenly it had all shivered and turned to sandstone. Not just sand, not quite yet, but one good storm might sweep it all away. And what came after that?

Emptiness, that's what. Without Jay, there would be things to do, of course there would, but they would be empty consolation. I was knocking forty. I had married young and from then on had always been the kind of woman that men seemed to like as a friend, rather than consider as a putative lover. Come to that, I had never wanted another man, Jay had filled my horizon since I was seventeen years old; that was a long time. I had spent all the best years of my life with him, building a home and a future together, loving him and thinking we were happy, and in the end he apparently valued me so little that he was quite prepared to throw it all in my face and walk away to a future that he had taken time to plan for himself, quite coldly excluding me, the middle-aged wife. With Dawn, maybe – if she would have him. Well, why not, she had apparently had just about everyone else.

Why? What had I done that was so wrong? I think that just not knowing was the worst thing of all.

The only twig I had to cling to in order to keep afloat was Dawn's comment about a breakdown. It was small comfort, because I didn't really believe in it. I suspected that what Jay was mainly suffering from was a guilty conscience.

Marina leaned forward from the seat behind me.

'Isn't it gorgeous? Aren't you excited, Sue?'

I opened my eyes. Beyond the window, Athens had disappeared. We now drove through a golden-brown, sunbaked landscape, spiked with dark cypress trees and relieved only by the silver-leaved groves of olive trees, with their nightmare-twisted trunks, that bordered the road. The village we were passing through looked unromantic and poor, clusters of flat-roofed houses around the inevitable taverna: there seemed to be a lot of corrugated iron in their construction. Goats and chickens wandered about and unidentifiable curs barked at the passing coach. So this was Greece, the birthplace of democracy, the land the poets raved about.

'It looks... alien,' I said, after a pause.

'You'll love it!' Marina assured me.

A taxi overtook us in a flurry of dust and pulled up ahead, skewed across the road, making our coach driver curse and stamp on the brakes. Our courier tumbled out of the back seat and ran towards us, scrambling breathlessly aboard. She sank into the front seat and, without a word spoken, we continued on our way.

There is no need to dwell on our journey, except to say that it was long, there seemed to be several hours of it. We had all started out irritated and bored and overheated, and after a while the sun-scorched, repetitious landscape began to pall even on Marina. We had travelled, on and off, in sight of the water at first, but towards the end we cut away inland. The air-conditioning wasn't working properly and the heat was becoming unbearable. I closed my eyes again and tried to escape into sleep. There seemed nothing else worth doing.

'Oh look!' cried Marina, disturbing me for the second time, 'The sea!'

'*Thalassa, thalassa,*' Jay muttered – showing off his classical education, probably to annoy Steve, who didn't have one. But I had no time for political in-fighting now, our destination was in sight. The whole dozing coachload was suddenly alert again. It was an enchanting sight.

First, there was a curve of golden-brown cliff top, leading the eye down to the unbelievable lapis-lazuli of the Saronic Gulf, ringed in distant hills of a dry dun colour, then, as the road swept down in a series of sharp hairpin bends, a little bay opened up below, smooth and still as a pond, dotted with the white sails of dinghies that seemed to be drifting rather than sailing. Around the bay, a scatter of square Greek houses dripped scarlet and purple bougainvillaea in luxuriant profusion, glowing red geraniums pushed through delicate balustrades, sunflowers blazed golden against the cracked white or cream-washed walls. The whole place was vibrant with colour and heat, the contrasted black shadows hard-edged and cool-looking.

Ayios Giorgos. Panther Sailing's home base.

The coach switchbacked down towards the water, and now we could see the village itself. To the left, there was a long white beach, to the right, a tiny harbour with bright-painted Greek caiques and a line of white yachts moored to a dusty quayside like a litter of piglets suckling a sow. There were at least three tavernas on the quayside too, so far as I could make out from this distance, and a tight cluster of pale, colour-washed houses rising up the cliff behind along steep, narrow streets, stepped in places and in deep shade between the close-packed buildings. Behind the beach lay a big white building, raised slightly above the road, black wrought-iron railed balconies and shady archways leading into a dim, unseen interior. Bright towels hung over the rails, and people sat around in long chairs. Our courier spoke for the first and last time.

'That's Panther Sailing's Yacht Club,' she said. 'You'll be having your first meal there this evening.'

We drove finally onto the waterfront and stopped in a swirl of dust and a scatter of cackling fowls. Stiffly, we all climbed out.

After even the uncertain air-conditioning of the moving coach, the heat hit us anew, freshened this time by the nearness of the water. Our boats lay stern-to along a quayside deep in fine white dust and puddled here and there with water from a leaky hose. And there, too, they waited greet us: Skipper Paul, Hostess Emily and Engineer Andy. We assumed...

'My God!' said Marina, in my ear. 'Aren't they young?'

They certainly seemed so, but that was only because they weren't that much older than our own children, two young men and a girl, brown and friendly, smiling at us. They wore brief red shorts, and cream T-shirts with a great black panther leaping across the left breast over the legend *Come Sailing in Greece with the Black Panther!*

'More like the Pink Panther, so far,' muttered Steve, but not so loudly that they would hear.

One of the young men stepped forward. He had a shaven blonde head, smooth as cat's fur, bright blue eyes, and spoke with an Australian accent. The contrast between very fair hair and burned brown skin was striking. Perhaps it was because I was hot, thirsty and tired, but I received a distinct impression that he knew it.

'Hullo everyone, I'm Paul, your skipper for the next fortnight. Welcome to Ayios Giorgos. I hope you had a pleasant journey.'

There was a murmur from the crowd, not entirely friendly since, on the whole, we hadn't. Paul gestured to the girl at his side.

'This is Emmy, your hostess. Emmy will look after your domestic problems and your social life, where to shop, where to eat, where to get water. You have a problem with anything of that kind, Emmy's your girl!'

Emmy was tall and slim, with enviable legs that seemed to go on for ever. She had a thick French plait of dark hair that began on the crown of her head and hung down between her shoulder blades, dark brown eyes under well-defined brows, and a freckled brown skin like an egg. She looked like nobody's maiden aunt, and I had no doubt at all that she did have fun. Very probably with Paul.

'Hi,' she said, with a friendly waggle of her fingers.

'And this is Robin,' Paul went on; his teeth gleamed white in his brown face as he smiled. 'Robin is our engineer, he's the one who keeps you afloat. A glitch in your engine? Send for Robin! Loo won't flush? Robin's your man. Missing a screw somewhere? Robin will have one. We couldn't function without Robin!' His hand fell affectionately onto the engineer's shoulder. The engineer noticeably didn't respond. He had light brown hair and a narrow moustache that framed his lips; his eyes were grey and intelligent, his smile more guarded, less open, than Emmy's or Paul's. He wasn't a tall man, the golden Paul topped him by nearly a head, but neatly made. He nodded casually to the listening group, and I wondered what had happened to Andy Miller. Paul went on smiling.

'Well, we won't keep you standing around, I expect you'd all like to unpack and have a cup of tea after your trip. If you go to your boats now and start settling in, Emmy will be round to you in turn to check the inventory, and Robin will come to give you the lowdown on the engine and the holding tank. Tonight, we'll be going to the Yacht Club for a group meal, and to get to know each other, and we'll assemble by the taverna over there at seven-thirty, but I'd like all the skippers to meet me on the quay here at six o'clock and I'll tell you all what you'll be doing over the next fortnight. Until six o'clock, then!'

We were dismissed with another easy smile, and our luggage now being unloaded from the coach, we trailed along the quay looking for our particular boats. *Phaedra* was about halfway along the line, and it was just our luck that her narrow gangplank rested in the largest of the puddles.

She was big – bigger than even *Foxtrot* by five feet, which made her very spacious below decks. She had a neatly planned galley adjoining a comfortable saloon, two double cabins aft, running back under the cockpit, and a fore cabin divided from the saloon by the heads and shower, a fairly standard layout for a yacht of her type. Exploring further, we found that under the galley sink was a larder unit that slid in and out like a drawer, which looked an excellent idea until later on, when we found that it had a faulty catch. It would slide out unexpectedly whenever there was the slightest angle of heel, and if anyone happened to be passing at the time it would catch them a glancing blow on the thigh, just where it hurts the most. So not such a good idea after all.

Steve was poking about in the bilges, he likes to get to the bottom of things. Marina and I stepped round him as we tried to stow the baggage.

'There's an awful lot of water down here. Hope we haven't got a leak.'

Jay peered over his shoulder, completely blocking the companionway. Marina, a bag in each hand, heaved a heavy sigh but they took no notice.

'Been there a while from the looks of it, it's green and slimy,' said Steve. He dipped a finger, sniffed at it, and took a cautious lick. 'Fresh. Surely they haven't had that much rain since the last time she was pumped out?'

Then Marina edged Jay out of the way, and we left them pumping out while the two of us went back down below to start checking the inventory. Apart from the fact that our grill had no grill pan, the domestic part of it seemed OK.

'You can't expect miracles from a charter boat,' I suggested, unwisely since it gave Marina her cue for the first of many reprises of *When we were in the Ionian*. The company under whose flag they had sailed there had apparently been a model of how a flotilla should be run, if she and Steve were to be believed. This would have been a lot less irritating had it not been becoming obvious that this one… well, wasn't, to put it bluntly.

Phaedra would have been a good boat if she had been properly equipped. There was no boathook on board, although there was one listed on the inventory. One of the cockpit lockers had the hinges broken. Our chart table had no navigation instruments and the first aid box contained a pair of scissors, a tube of antiseptic cream, one aspirin and a light bulb – the last perhaps in case somebody felt a bit dim, Marina offered. When Emmy came aboard to check that everything was in order, Marina challenged her about it.

'Yes, well, stocks are a bit low,' Emmy explained. 'But don't worry, the lead boat has a full kit if you need anything.' Presumably, if an accident happened on the water, or worse, while we were free sailing, we were required to lick the wound. On such short acquaintance we hardly liked to ask why she hadn't just slipped into the nearest supermarket – we could see one on the quay, conspicuously labelled SUPRMAKT – where presumably they at least stocked sticking plaster.

Emmy went off, promising to see what could be done about navigational instruments: the last crew had probably taken them as souvenirs, she speculated blithely. I remarked that it was a good thing we had packed the first aid kit from *Foxtrot*, and Marina said, what about a cup of tea unless anyone fancied a glass of duty free in the middle of the afternoon.

'Coffee would be even better,' Steve said, but there wasn't any.

'When we were in the Ionian,' said Marina, as she rummaged in the box of stores that Panther Sailing had provided, 'our starter pack had coffee as well as tea, fresh bread and a bowl of fresh fruit, and they even threw in a bottle of wine. All we seem to have here is a packet of rusks.' She tossed them onto the table.

A thud on the deck and a lurch of the boat announced the arrival of Robin, come to tell us about the engine. This didn't take long as Jay and Steve are both familiar with marine engines, and in any case, Steve manages two garages, both of which belong to him; one of which, the one he loves the best, specialises in vintage cars, both servicing and buying and selling.

'What about the holding tank?' asked Marina. 'There seem to be about a hundred different levers.'

'As many as that?' I thought there was a smile behind his eyes, but it reached no further if so. 'I can show you how I think it works, but I've only been with this flotilla a few days, and the boats on my last one were different.' I saw Marina's head come up and wondered if she had heard what I thought I had heard, a note of reservation in that level British voice.

A shout outside took Jay up to the cockpit to see what was going on; it turned out to be the boat next to ours offering the use of a hose to top up the fresh water tanks.

'They should be full,' said Robin, stepping precariously across to the next boat in line. 'Best to check, though.'

Jay leapt up onto the deck, knocking his shin on the broken catch as he went.

'Shit! Steve, did you think to ask about this bloody catch?' He rubbed his shin, painfully, smearing it with blood.

'He said he was sorry, he didn't have any spares,' said Steve, in an expressionless voice. There was a short pause

'When we were in –' began Marina, but Jay told her to shut up. He apologised a moment later, and Steve said, 'He did say he'd try to find us a boathook.' The two men exchanged a speaking look.

Our water tanks turned out to be almost empty. Jay filled them while I made tea, and then Steve pushed me out of the way to lift up the cabin sole. The bilges were full of water again.

'Some bloody set-up, this is!' he said, and began to throw things out of the forepeak into the saloon, which Marina had just that moment finished clearing. She opened her mouth to object, then closed it again and instead, took the seat cushion that Steve was pushing at her and propped it, without comment, against the table. Steve lifted up the locker lid that had been revealed beneath it, and a half-deflated water bag met our eyes.

Jay and Steve, strangely subdued for the beginning of an exciting holiday, did the tightrope walk ashore into the puddle and went off to the skippers' meeting armed with a long list of things we wanted put right before we sailed, and Marina and I showered in the cramped shower compartment with what remained of the water, and changed into cotton trousers and loose shirts before going to sit outside. Even this late in the evening, it was still baking and our shirts stuck to our backs.

'Isn't it glorious?'

The speaker was sitting on the cabin roof of the next boat. I recognised her as one of the Back Seat Gang. She smiled and waved a bottle at us. 'Fancy a drink?'

Marina leapt to her feet. 'I'll get some glasses.'

'Don't bother, we seem to have plenty. Step aboard.'

Janet and Sylvia, much our age, much our kind. Their husbands, Ken and Bill, had gone to the skippers' meeting. The four of us became friendly over duty-free red wine.

'This is a completely new thing for us,' Janet told us. 'We – Sylv and me – aren't sure we're going to enjoy it all that much, but the men had set their hearts on it. They've both done some dinghy sailing and of course, there's the lead boat to look after us.' She sounded doubtful, and Marina raised her eyebrows.

'Aren't the Cyclades a bit ambitious, in that case?'

Sylvia looked surprised. 'It's only island-hopping, isn't it? And the Mediterranean doesn't get rough, or anything.'

Marina and I exchanged a glance.

'Do you know what "Cyclades" means?' I asked. They shook their heads innocently.

'The Windy Isles,' said Marina. 'Think of "cyclone". Didn't you read the brochure?'

'It said the Saronic Gulf was easy for beginners,' said Janet.

'The Cyclades aren't in the Saronic Gulf,' I pointed out.

They looked unconvinced, and it was true, the brochure had said that – about the Gulf. What I didn't realise then, and what it turned out that Panther Sailing didn't realise either, was how many people there are who don't read the small print properly.

'You'd better stick with us,' said Marina. 'We can cruise in company when we start free sailing – if you'd like to, of course.'

'That would be nice.' Janet sounded unconcerned, what we had said, mild as it was, had made no impression at all. She went on, 'Our holding tank doesn't seem to work, we're a bit put out over that. It's only because of the holding tank that Sylv and I agreed to come.'

A holding tank, for the uninitiated, is a sewage management system that enables one to use the heads in port. Nobody is allowed to pump raw sewage into Mediterranean harbours, and quite right too – although Marina claims she has known places where the Greek authorities do it themselves – when she was in the Ionian, of course.

'Our Skipper is a bit tasty, isn't he?' said Sylvia, changing the subject for a more savoury one. 'I could really fancy him – if it wasn't for Bill, of course.' She gave a delicious little shiver as she spoke in tribute to Paul's golden machismo. Marina grinned, rather wolfishly I thought. Perhaps she was thinking of empty water bags, and Jay's bleeding shin with nothing but a light bulb to put on it.

'I'm really looking forward to seeing their club,' said Janet. 'There's a swimming pool, and everything, it sounds really nice.'

Marina cast a wistful glance at the tavernas, with their shady canopies and climbing morning glories, ranged along the quayside.

'I love Greek food. When we were in the Ionian a few years back, we had the first night group meal in a taverna, and the lead-boat crew sat with us and helped us through the menu with all the strange food. It was good fun. We learned a bit about the people and the country, and how to eat things like tzadziki and Greek salad, and we had a good laugh together too. Bonded, you might say.'

'I expect it will be the same tonight,' said Janet blithely, but we were beginning to wonder. Marina would say that the whole thing was beginning to have bad vibes, I thought – and in fact, later on she did say it.

Our four husbands came back from the meeting together. They were discussing holding tanks, it seemed to be a popular subject.

'Ours sort of half works,' Jay was saying. 'You can't pump directly out, but it seems to go through the tank all right.' Ken looked gloomy. He had a good face for it; dark and saturnine, with peaked eyebrows.

'Ours is the opposite, it only pumps straight out to sea,' he said. 'The tank pumps out all right or it would if there was anything in it, but as nothing goes through it, it doesn't help. It means we can't use the heads at night, and the girls aren't at all happy.'

'Be thankful,' said Sylvia, smiling up at him as he climbed aboard. 'On one of the other boats, *Pasiphae* I think it is, the holding tank doesn't work at all, it won't fill and it won't empty, and it's still full up from the last cruise.'

We all sat in respectful silence for a moment, contemplating a fortnight spent sharing a confined space with somebody else's waste products, however tightly sealed.

Right at that moment, I think we all took it for granted that the snags would be quickly ironed out. Missing boathooks, jammed seacocks, leaky water bags – these things happened to everyone from time to time, even Steve. It was just bad luck for the lead boat crew that they had all happened at once. It wasn't for some time that we discovered that they hadn't.

We said a temporary goodbye to our new friends and returned to *Phaedra*, where we broached our own duty free and sat around the saloon table, discussing the cruise. Steve produced a sheaf of notes from the meeting.

'There's going to be another meeting in the morning to run through the day's sailing and check on the gear,' he said. 'You two can go and stock up in the village. We sail at midday, or soon after.'

'Cooks to the galley,' I said wryly. It appeared that we were now in a man's world; we women, like Sylvia and Janet, weren't expected to understand or care about seamanship and navigation. Well, we would see about that. Marina and I exchanged a significant glance.

'But what did they tell you tonight?' asked Marina. 'You can't have talked about nothing all that time.'

Steve spread out his notes.

'Paul gave us a rough outline of the cruise area – tomorrow is a short shake-down, about twelve or thirteen miles across to Aegina. Poros the day after, then Hydra, a longer day's sail to Sounion to see some old ruins – there's a temple or something – then it's off to the Cyclades, when we've all had a chance to get used to the boats. Siros first, then two days for free sailing, Tinos, two more days free sailing we can use for Andros and Kithnos or Kea, or back to Sounion as we choose, then another long leg back to a rendezvous at Perdika – that's Aegina again – and a round-the-islands race back to Ayios Giorgos on the last day. Sounds as if it'll be good sailing.'

I wondered how Janet and Sylvia would enjoy it, and hoped that the weather would stay fine for them. Sylvia had confessed to being seasick, but she had brought pills with her. I hoped she remembered to take them. I was once sick the whole way across the North Sea from the Blackwater Estuary to the Roompotsluis in Holland, and it hadn't been funny. It's quite true what they tell you, first you're afraid you're going to die and then you're afraid you're not. It's only a joke to those who have never been seasick.

The remainder of the day was oddly unsatisfactory. The Panther Sailing Yacht Club was base for another flotilla besides our own, one which was known as the Shore/Flotilla – one week ashore in rooms in the village, with day sailing in order to learn the ropes, and then one week's cruise with a lead boat in close attendance. It was designed for complete beginners, and Marina and I thought, might have been a better option for our neighbours. There were also the dinghy sailors and the windsurfers, who actually stayed at the Yacht Club. Our own flotilla, only eating there two nights in fourteen, was catered for with a second sitting for dinner, and we had to wait until everyone else had finished and the dining room had been cleared and reset. The food, when we finally got it, had been kept hot for too long and suffered thereby, and it was English food, not Greek. It was also very overpriced for what it was. There was a certain amount of restiveness among our group – who were not all sitting together, as Marina had described it, but scattered at separate tables. Janet, Sylvia, Ken and Bill had gravitated towards us and we had pushed two tables together in order to sit as a group, which hadn't been well received. Sylvia, just like Marina, was a news-gatherer, and she had kept her ear to the ground while we waited our turn to eat.

'Everyone's very disappointed about the barbecue,' she said.

'What about it?' I asked. The barbecue was mentioned in the brochure, a group gathering on a beach somewhere with the crew cooking up a feast. But -

'A good question,' said Sylvia. There isn't going to be one.' Steve and Jay had said nothing about this, and Marina looked a question.

'Something about the weather,' said Jay. 'It might break, or something.'

'Somebody said there weren't enough chickens,' offered Janet.

'Enough chickens, where?'

'Wherever they were meant to come from, I imagine.'

'That's mad! The place is crawling with chickens!'

'Don't shoot the messenger, we're only telling you what was said,' said Ken.

Janet had the cruise notes in her bag, she took them out and began to hunt through the pages.

'I think we were meant to meet up with the other flotilla,' she said. 'Here we are – *the well-known Panther Sailing barbecue, a treat not to be missed!* You've been on a flotilla before, Marina. Did you get everything they promised?'

'We certainly did.'

Bill said that he was still hungry and grabbed at a passing Panther Sailing sweatshirt. 'Any chance of seconds?' he asked. The girl shook her head.

'I'm sorry, the staff all have to eat now.'

The staff were all eating together, Emmy, Paul and Robin among them. I remembered Marina's description of the first night meal in a taverna, with the lead boat crew sitting among the punters, making friends and giving advice, and I found myself wondering who had charge of Panther Sailing's Ayios Giorgos operation, or if this segregation was deliberate company policy. It wasn't only Bill who was hungry, none of us had eaten any lunch and our second sitting had made this meal very late; several envious looks were cast at the heaped plates at the staff table. It was a curious manager who let the clients go hungry while his staff ate like kings. They had seconds, I wasn't the only one who noticed.

It would be too much to say that Emmy and Paul were ignoring us, that would imply an awareness that we were there in the first place. Rather, they were wrapped up in their own friends and oblivious to us. Only Robin went casually from table to table, asking if everyone was all right. None of us was impolite enough to be honest, we all murmured that we were fine, thank you.

We drifted back to the quay in small, silent groups, vaguely disappointed. We had no idea that for most of that day we had been watching the seeds of disaster quietly germinating, how could we have? Even Marina and her clairvoyance couldn't have guessed what was to come.

Steve and Jay had to repair the lights before we went to bed that night, but as I lay beside Jay in the starboard after cabin, I was conscious, for the first time all day, of a small spark of pleased anticipation. We were here in Greece, with the exotic flowers and the warm sun, just it had been on the travel programme. We were going to have a wonderful holiday. We would see new places, make new friends... the hot, sun-filled days and the dusky, sweet-scented nights would breathe new romance into our middle-aged marriage and we would have fun, just as we had done so many times before. Everything was going to be all right.

I could hear a faint buzz through the bulkhead, proving that Steve, at least, was already asleep. My own eyelids felt heavy, my body relaxed -

Oh yes, I forgot to mention the dogs. There were several of them skulking around the quay, thin, rangy looking creatures with suspicious yellow eyes. Between them, they had fifteen or so assorted puppies. At night, it now transpired, they howled. If anything disturbed them, they began to bark.

And bark.

And bark.

But *Phaedra* was comfortable, for all her maintenance problems, and I was very tired.

Day Two: Tuesday, 6th June

The following morning we all slept late, waking to find the sun shining from a clear, blue sky, already hazy with heat, and the water in the sheltered bay shining like glass. Steve and Jay tied the awning over the cockpit and we sat outside in its welcome shade, eating our breakfast of rusks and apricot jam and idly watching activity going on around us. Our neighbours were either still in bed or already out exploring the village, but there was plenty to see without them.

'Hustle, bustle, bustle, hustle,' said Jay, stretching lazily in the warmth. 'What's the matter with them all? Don't they realise they're on holiday?'

'We're going to be doing a bit of bustling ourselves as soon as you've finished that cup of tea,' Steve told him. 'We've got that water bag to take out. Robin said he had a new one, we don't want to waste time.'

'That's what time is for when you're on holiday,' objected Jay, but Steve, who is less laid back to the point where I would describe him as hyperactive, at least at the beginning of a cruise, was adamant.

'If we've taken it out, he'll *have* to give us the new one,' he said. 'I wouldn't put money on it, otherwise.'

'Oh, surely...' I said.

Marina yawned, and said, 'Remember the slime. They haven't been in a hurry to do anything about it so far.'

'True.' We all fell silent for a moment, thinking about that.

When Robin came past half an hour later, he looked rather surprised when Steve hailed him and gave him the leaky bag, but thus presented with a fait accompli, he promised to be along later to fit the new one, and in due course he came. He wasn't talkative, Robin, not then. He completed the job briskly and confined his comments to replying to ours, and left with unceremonious haste. Almost as if, said Marina thoughtfully, he was afraid of what we might ask him – or possibly of what he might answer, if once he got started.

'What, have you been casting the tarot again?' I asked, grinning at her. Jay snorted.

'Don't be so stupid, Sue!' Considering that I had spoken purely as a joke, the force behind the words was unnecessary. I saw Marina blink in surprise, and turned away so I didn't meet her eyes.

'Not stupid at all,' she said, but lightly. 'There's bad vibes around. Can't you feel them?'

There you are. I warned you she'd say that. The only problem was, I wasn't quite sure of her reason.

'It's probably lack of a proper breakfast,' said Jay. 'Who's going to do the shopping, then?'

He and Steve tossed a coin to decide which of them would refill the water system and attend the skippers' briefing, and so it was Steve who came with Marina and me to the village. Armed with travellers' cheques and bags we made our way into the maze of little streets and steps that lay behind the quay. We knew where the "suprmkt" was, of course, but Marina wanted to find a proper bakery and, if possible, some decent fruit. She had transformed with ease from clairvoyant witch to the expert on Greek shopping, but I sensed that the subject wasn't closed.

We found one or two tourist shops, not very good ones, and then our noses as much as anything else identified a bakery. We bought bread hot from the oven, and some cheese puff things for our lunch, which Marina said were called tiranakopitia, what a language! There was some mis-shapen but sound fruit outside a dark little greengrocer. In the time we spent in Greece, we never saw glossy fruit of uniform size and appearance such as we're used to at home ; the oranges, for instance, were all sizes and shapes, often knobbly and with twigs still attached, and with greenish skins – but their flavour was sublime! Tomatoes were invariably the big beef tomatoes that at home often taste a bit disappointing, but here had the deep, intense flavour of fruit come straight from the vine. Marina showed me how to choose them from boxes piled high, all in various stages of ripeness to last over several days. There were huge melons, just ready for eating, crisp, squarish, pale green grapes, tight-packed in the bunch and tasting of honey, huge peaches with coarse, sweet flesh and with a flavour that I remembered from my childhood. I had always thought that it was my taste-buds that had deteriorated with the passing years! Nothing out here seemed to have been cultivated for uniformity of appearance or quality, which lost a bit on texture and looks, but paid dividends on taste. We loaded up with enough to last for a day or two, we didn't want to be forever shopping for stores. We finished up with a visit to the Suprmakt – not exactly Sainsbury's, but it provided butter and some rather peculiar tinned goods, wine and ouzo and bottled water and some fragrant goat's cheese.

We staggered back to *Phaedra* loaded down with our purchases and found Jay pottering about taking down the awning and removing the cover from the mainsail. The briefing had presented no problems.

'Just a more detailed run-down of the cruise area, and how things work on the boats – batteries, reefing, radio, nothing we don't already know.' Jay reached across to take the bags from us and sling them aboard. 'One or two of the other skippers looked a bit worried, I thought, but it was all pretty straightforward really. Oh, and if we have any problems, the answer is a bowline.'

'I beg your pardon?' said Steve. Jay grinned.

'There was a bowline-tying lesson as part of the briefing. We're to use it for everything, from mooring the boat to tying our shoelaces.'

'Bollocks,' said Steve. Jay grinned and continued,

'Mooring bows-to, we drop the anchor four or five boat lengths from the quay,' he went on. 'Would you believe, seven in deep water?'

Steve's eyebrows vanished into what is left of his hair. *'Seven?'*

'I thought it was a bit over the top myself,' agreed Jay, still grinning. 'I can only hope that Paul knows what he was talking about.'

'When we were in the Ionian,' said Marina, predictable, 'we were told three boat lengths were enough, except in the deepest harbours – but perhaps the harbours round here are deeper than deep.'

Steve shrugged. Like Jay, he was prepared – for the moment – to allow Paul credit for knowing his own sailing area, but he obviously had reservations as deep as the putative harbours.

Jay had found the peaches, and now perched himself on the cabin top and sank his teeth into one of them. He spoke through a mouthful of juicy flesh. 'As a matter of fact, there were a few grouses aired,' he told us. 'It seems that some people weren't prepared for the distances we're going to sail. They were only expecting five to ten miles a day.'

'Didn't they look at the chart before they booked?' I asked.

'Apparently not. Four crews have very little experience, three or four of the others just sail dinghies – like our friends from last night.

Some of the women, particularly, were a bit unhappy about it. One boat even asked if we could skip the Cyclades and stay down here in the Gulf.'

'And?'

'Paul said that we had to make the advertised cruise because some of us wanted to, and that was what we'd all booked. But there was definitely an atmosphere.'

Right on cue, the crew of the neighbouring yacht, *Hippolyta*, arrived with their own shopping. They had been to the briefing en masse, as apparently quite a few of the crews had done, and since then Sylvia had kept her ear to the ground again. She was full of news to add to what Jay had already told us.

'It seems that the flotilla after this one, which was the normal Saronic Gulf cruise, was over-booked,' she told us. 'The late bookings were offered places on this one instead, and nobody in the company's office in England even noticed that it was the long cruise. Can you believe that?'

'Unfortunately, I'm beginning to think I can,' said Steve, with dry humour.

'So some of the grumblers have a case,' I commented.

'They all had the full brochure, and presumably they can all read,' Jay pointed out.

All the same, it had made it awkward for Paul. I remember, we felt quite sorry for him.

Jay had finished his peach. He slid down into the cockpit, licking his fingers.

'We can leave whenever we're ready,' he said. 'We meet on the quay at Aegina at seven o'clock, there's to be a Skipper's Punch Party at seven-thirty sharp. So let's stow all this stuff and get the show on the road, shall we?'

Phaedra was first boat away; as we motored from the quay I looked back and saw Paul standing there, legs braced apart, watching us. When you come to consider it, it must be a big moment for a flotilla skipper when the first unknown quantity takes around forty-thousand pounds-worth of yacht to sea. In our particular case, after what had been said both of and by some of the women on this cruise, it must have been made even more nerve-wracking by the fact that Marina was on the helm.

We went on motoring for a while, just glad to be out on the water, but soon after midday the wind filled in (as advertised – it was comforting to see that something at least was conforming to the brochure), about force 2, and we were able to reach across towards Aegina under sail. The yacht seemed slightly under-canvassed for her size, having a rather small genoa, but no doubt this was deliberate company policy rather than an oversight by her designers. It gave her a lot of weather helm in this light wind, and Steve spent some time walking round the deck and twanging at shrouds and stays, staring up at the mast, busy making tiny adjustments and driving Jay mad. Steve is always like this to begin with, he gets so strung up during the course of the working year that it takes him a while to wind down, and this is his way of dispersing tension. At first it had irritated me, too, but over the years, although Jay is sometimes less than tolerant, I have come to understand and just ignore it. Today, when he had finished playing tunes on the rigging, he set about swabbing the dust of Ayios Giorgos from the decks.

We made good time across to Aegina – according to the electronic log, indeed, we were fairly tazzing along, it registered a maximum speed of 99.4 knots! As if we had struck a brick wall, it dropped immediately after that to 4.8 knots, which was at least a lot more realistic. Steve remarked that it was lucky most of our navigation was likely to be by line-of-sight, or we could have some quite interesting problems in checking our position. He was beginning to sound less amused by this time, some of the faults with *Phaedra* were emerging as potentially dangerous, and Robin may have tried, but hadn't succeeded in finding us a replacement boathook.

Armed with information provided by Emmy, we cruised along the coast of Aegina and dropped anchor to the north of the tiny island of Moni to have a swim. The water was warm as a bath, clear and still. We could see right down to the bottom in places, and more to the point, we could also see the barnacles on *Phaedra*'s bottom, and weed a yard long. No wonder the poor girl felt a bit sluggish!

'Pity we can't put her ashore for a scrub,' said Jay regretfully. Marina giggled.

'Ninety-nine knots not fast enough for you?'

I floated on my back, splashing the water with my hands to watch the rainbow spray flying, trying to make myself relax, and also trying to avoid being alone with Marina. A couple of other boats, both from our own flotilla, had sailed quietly in during the afternoon and anchored off while we were swimming. It was peaceful here, and none of us was in a hurry to move on.

Marina swam up beside me and stayed, treading water.

'Isn't this fun? Are you enjoying yourself, Sue?'

'Of course I am, what d'you think?' I turned on my front and dived away from her, but when I came up for air she was there again.

'Only you seem a bit subdued, for you,' she said.

'Rubbish! The dogs kept me awake last night, that's all.'

'And the night before?'

'We got up early.'

'Hmm.'

'What's the interrogation about, anyway?' I snapped, and heard myself, and winced. Marina stared blandly at the intense blue of the sky, her face innocent.

'Don't bite my head off, Sue. It was just a friendly question.'

I immediately felt mean. 'Sorry. I didn't mean to.'

She waited, as if for further explanation, but I swam away.

I never know if Marina is really clairvoyant, or just very sensitive to other people. Whichever it was, this time I didn't want her getting too close. I knew that if she was the smallest bit sympathetic I would spill everything out simply for the relief of not having to carry my fears alone – and yes, I also think I was afraid, truly afraid, of what she might say. Airy-fairy Marina might seem, but she has a way of going straight to the heart of things, and my personal pain was too private.

I had always been scornful about those *My man, right or wrong* kind of women you see on the telly sometimes, battered or betrayed or neglected, and still going back for more. I had found it impossible to believe that any half-way intelligent woman could go on loving a man who did any of that to them... well, I was on a learning curve now, all right. I could do without Marina's comments.

Shortly after six o'clock, Paul's voice began to haunt the airwaves, urging his charges to come home. The three of us left more or less together and arrived off Aegina harbour the same way. It isn't a big place, we could all clearly see Paul standing on the quay with a hand-held radio, if he had shouted we would probably have heard him, but for some reason he wouldn't rely on his eyesight – or ours – and insisted on radio communication as we berthed. This presented no particular problem to our crew of four, but was decidedly awkward for one boat that only had two on board. One of them was permanently below listening to Paul, while the other tried to steer, man the anchor, and look after the warps all at the same time. Even for us it was a cumbersome way to do things – Jay was on the foredeck with the warps, Steve on the helm and in charge of the anchor, Marina on the radio down below, while I sat at the top of the companionway and relayed instructions to Steve.

'Why can't he just stand and wave us to where he wants us to go?' wondered Steve, just as Marina spoke from below.

'What?' I asked, thinking I must have misheard.

'He says to drop the anchor ten boat's lengths out,' said Marina. I passed this on to Steve, who looked startled, as well he might.

'Good God, is this harbour bottomless?' he asked, but still at that point working on the principle that Paul was the expert round here, obediently dropped the anchor where he was told. Chain and warp snaked all over the bottom of the harbour, just asking to be overlaid by anyone else doing the same thing.

'Thank goodness we're last boat home,' said Steve, looking at it in disbelief.

We were last, but it now appeared that Paul hadn't been keeping a tally, and he had asked us twice which boat we were before we had even tied up. These were all such small things taken separately, and even Marina, for all her claims, couldn't really see into the future – at least, I didn't think she could – but Jay was frowning as he came aft, and Steve had a sceptical look on his face as he peered down through the clear water at the kedge warp.

'I just hope to hell nobody comes in and picks that up on his hook,' he said.

By the time we had tidied the ship and had a wash and change, the party on the quay was already in full swing. As we came ashore, Paul greeted us with a grin. He had a good line in facial contortions, everything from the disarming smile, via the deprecating simper to the friendly all-good-pals grin we were seeing now.

'You're late. They've nearly drunk all the punch up there.'

Sylvia seemed to have drunk most of it. She was bubbling with high spirits and had collected quite a crowd. Everyone had enjoyed the comparatively short and easy sail and the general mood was optimism, a complete turn-around from this morning's doom and gloom.

With everyone now safely accounted for, Paul came to join the party and it was noticeable that Emmy immediately gravitated to his side. They made an attractive pair, he so fair and she so dark, but it seemed to me, made over-sensitive perhaps by my own situation, that he treated her very casually. It was far easier to see what her feelings were for him. I felt a twitch of fellow feeling, but it was dangerous to start drawing parallels. Some people do have trouble in showing how they feel, and couples reach their own compromises. Such compromises are seldom equal, but making allowances is what they're all about. While you can go on doing that, the relationship will live and breathe and flourish... but when is it time to stop? I shivered in the warm evening.

'Emmy's got it badly, hasn't she?' said Janet, close to my ear. I turned, she was critically watching the pair by the punch bowl. 'It's almost indecent, the way she looks at him.'

'It's the propinquity that'll do it,' suggested Marina. 'Stuck together on a small boat all summer, they'd be bound to end up either loving or hating each other, wouldn't they?'

'Pretty rough on Robin,' said Janet.

Robin, however, seemed to be doing all right. He had got together with somebody's pretty teenage daughter, and was actually laughing. I was feeling pleased about this, for his sake, when Marina jogged my elbow.

'Watch,' she said.

'Watch what?'

'Robin. Watch his eyes.'

So I did, and I saw that they followed Emmy around even while he laughed with the pretty teenager. I thought that a love-triangle on a thirty-five footer would be a bit grim, and I said so. Marina gave an amused grimace.

'They're young, they'll sort it out.' She spoke lightly, as one to whom it was of little concern, but after that I watched our lead boat crew more closely, and it seemed to me that here was yet another potential spanner in the works. Emmy obviously worshipped Paul, who from what I could observe, took it as only his due. And Robin... there was a quality of patient doggedness in Robin that might have covered hurt, resentment, jealousy – who could guess? We hardly knew any of them, after all.

We arranged to meet *Hippolyta*'s crew for dinner, but we must have been a lot hungrier than they were, as at eight o'clock they were still making merry on board. Jay said that he couldn't wait any longer, so we told them we would see them at *that* taverna over *there*, the one with the three trees outside it, but after Panther Sailing's punch, it seemed they couldn't count up to three, so we enjoyed souvlakia and soggy chips with crisp Greek salad on our own. We met up later for coffee, however, and there was a certain amount of noisy fraternising with a party of Dutchmen from another yacht in the harbour, with singing and a fair amount of drink flowing. It was late when we finally began to drift, in ones and twos and groups, back to the boats and our bunks.

Taken all in all, it had been a good day. Almost like old times, I told myself, and nearly made myself believe it. I rolled towards Jay in the close darkness of our cabin and snuggled into his shoulder as we had habitually done when we still loved each other, before Dawn. And others? He shifted.

'God, it's hot, isn't it? Can you shift over a bit?'

'Goodnight,' I said, and turned my back.

Later that night, something on board *Phaedra* was going *slap, slap, slap,* followed by a gentle rocking motion as someone on board went *prowl, prowl, prowl.*

Admiral Steve was at it again.

Day Three: Wednesday, 7ᵗʰ June

Marina said that she hadn't come on holiday to be forever preparing meals and washing up, when eating in tavernas was much more fun and almost as cheap. Since none of us was about to argue with this viewpoint, we went ashore in the morning to a handy taverna that was serving a simple breakfast of eggs, bread and jam and coffee, with bacon in one-inch strips for those who fancied it – and felt they could afford it, the price was a bit steep. We sat out on a terrace over the water, savouring that indefinable magic of being abroad in strange places.

'It's so lovely and quiet,' said Marina, almost whispering herself so as not to break the spell. 'And it's so beautiful too – but I do miss the cicadas. When we were in the Ionian, they made a terrific racket, and even at night the night shift took over from the day shift – last night, I hardly heard a chirp.'

'Apart from Steve snoring,' I suggested, grinning at him. He had rendered the night-time hours fairly hideous once he had finally got to bed.

'Speak for yourself,' said Jay, instantly, but Steve returned my grin, taking the sting from the unnecessary rebuke.

'It's because the west side of anywhere is always that much more lush than the east,' Steve said. 'But taking the swings with the roundabouts, you get less mosquitoes for the same reason. Even Marina won't miss them, I know.'

'There's quite enough though,' said Marina, scratching.

Jay got up and went over to the rail that restrained clients from falling into the harbour. There was a drift of cloud across the sky this morning, and a ripple on the water.

'Going to be a bit more wind,' he said, with satisfaction. I thought I heard Marina mutter something about "a lot of hot air" but when I looked at her, she was sipping coffee and looking innocent. She didn't meet my eyes.

Ken and Bill arrived to join us. "The girls", they said, were feeling a little fragile, they had opted for black coffee taken on board in the comparative dimness of the cabin.

'We're going a bit further today, I believe,' said Ken.

'Was Sylvia OK yesterday?' I asked, sensing a reservation behind the comment.

'She enjoyed it – she said she enjoyed it, anyway,' said Ken. 'She spent most of the time down below with a book, but it *was* hot – wasn't it?'

We agreed that it had been, and didn't press the point. If Sylvia was about to discover the difference between sailing about twelve miles in an almost flat calm and twice that distance in a stiff breeze, there was nothing that anybody could do about it. It was Ken and Bill's problem in any case, particularly Bill's – or Paul's maybe, certainly not ours.

I had them worked out by this time. Janet and Ken went together, and Sylvia and Bill. They weren't hard-core yachtsmen like ourselves, but Bill and Ken had done a lot of dinghy sailing and they knew that there was nothing they shouldn't be able to handle with the support of the lead boat, which of course is what flotillas are all about, and they were looking forward to the challenge. Reading between the lines, Sylvia hadn't really wanted to come on this trip, she had only agreed to please Bill. About Janet, I didn't know. She seemed quite happy.

Ken was picking Steve's brains about navigation, and Bill turned to me with smiling eyes.

'Are you two swooning over our flash Skipper like Janet and Sylvia?'

'Not so that you'd notice.'

'The girls think he's the best thing since sliced bread. We say it must be the big blue eyes.'

'And what do you think?'

Bill lifted his shoulders and allowed them to drop, an oddly negative gesture.

'The big blue eyes cut no ice with me. Handsome is as handsome does.'

'He seems OK,' said Ken, turning from Steve to join our conversation. 'Young Emmy obviously thinks the sun shines out of his arse, anyway.'

'That's the big blue eyes again,' I said. Jay caught the words and turned his head.

'All you women are suckers for a big blond blue-eyed boy, but looks are nothing to go by.' It sounded dangerously close to a sneer.

'Give me credit for more sense than being a push-over just for his looks,' I snapped.

'He thinks enough of himself without our contribution,' added Marina, soothingly. 'Anyone can see he believes he knows it all.'

'Oh, and don't you think he does?' asked Ken, narrowing his eyes at her.

I awaited Marina's reply with quite as much interest as Ken and Bill, for so far Paul hadn't made a very impressive showing – particularly if you chose to hold him responsible for the administrative shortcomings too.

'You can't blame him for everything,' said Marina, fairly.

'So what do you blame him for, then?'

'Let's say, there are obvious gaps in his knowledge,' suggested Steve. 'I daresay he's done a fair amount of sailing, but I suspect it may have been mostly as crew – either that, or he's the kind that doesn't think maintenance matters, so long as nothing actually falls apart.'

'But some things *have* fallen apart,' Marina pointed out.

'Exactly my point.'

'Sylv was talking to the crew of *Pasiphae* last night,' Bill said. 'Apparently Robin told them that he had been transferred to this flotilla from one based over in Zakynthos because the previous engineer had left rather abruptly. He was apologising, I believe, for the lack of spares.'

Well, that was interesting.

Marina said, 'When we were in the Ionian, the lead boat carried a whole engine in the spare bunk. Among other things, that was, and they were smaller boats than these, too.'

Bill gave her a curious look, but before he could speak, Steve got to his feet;

'Briefing time. Who's coming?'

All four of the men went off together, and Marina and I set out to explore the shopping possibilities of Aegina. There were some nice shops, a great improvement on those in Ayios Giorgos, into which Marina plunged with the delight of the dedicated shopaholic, pointing out museum copies of Minoan pots, and pseudo-ancient bronzes, greened with the patina of simulated age, alabaster carvings of considerable grace and charm – beautiful things that she seemed ready to buy up wholesale until I reminded her that we were meant to be buying fresh bread for lunch. Reluctantly, she replaced a pair of leaping dolphins and followed me to the shop door.

'Steve will never forgive me, anyway, if I spend out this early in the cruise,' she remarked, falling into step beside me. 'Why is it, Sue, that when men get together in groups, they pretend to believe that all women have flittery minds that can only contain shopping, children and *Eastenders*?'

She was angling, I realised, after Jay's and my brief spats in the taverna. Perhaps too about other small incidents. If we couldn't do better than this, we were going to end up being psychoanalysed by our friends, and I didn't think I could face it.

'It's a defence mechanism,' I suggested, pretending to take an academic interest. 'They need to do it, because it usually means the women are getting into a gang too, and they need to keep their end up.'

'Women don't put men down, though – or do we?'

'Perhaps women don't need to.'

'Ooh, nasty,' said Marina, and allowed the subject to drop.

Once again, our noses located a bakery, and Emmy had told us that fruit and vegetables were to be bought from caiques down at the harbour, so thence we carried our baskets. Jay and Steve had made considerable inroads into yesterday's supplies, particularly the peaches – and the beer, but that was their responsibility. At the harbour, Jay met us with the information that we had been advised to stock up with the basics for at least one meal in the store cupboard, since some of the places we would visit later were short on tavernas. We sent him back into town for more eggs and some tinned sausages and luncheon meat, while Marina bartered with the women on the vegetable caiques. I was content to leave this to her; it probably comes of being too British, but I prefer to know the price of things and just pay it.

We left Aegina soon after, bound today for Poros with me on the helm, a reach nearly all the way if the wind held, so it would be a fast trip, if a bit bumpy. Yesterday had just been a shake-down sail, now we were cruising properly. The single column rearing skyward on Cape Kolona, that is all that remains of the ancient temple of Aphrodite, was like a landmark pointing the way to adventure. I felt a deep stirring of satisfaction as I watched it grow smaller behind us, born of a sudden, possibly unreasonable conviction that there were better times ahead of us.

'Oi, Sue!' called Steve. 'Watch where you're going, not where you've just been! Or would you like me to take her?'

'Perhaps you should,' said Jay. 'She seems to be away with the fairies these days.'

'Oi oi, lay off!' said Marina. 'You've been chipping at her all morning, give it a rest!'

'Have I?' asked Jay, apparently in surprise. 'Well, it does get a bit much –'

'– and so do you,' said Marina, as politely as such a thing can be said.

My mood of happy optimism was shattered, but it was great sailing anyway and I settled down to concentrate on my stint at the helm. The sea was lumpy but in no way could it be described as really rough, sheltered here in the Gulf, and *Phaedra* was going like a train, heeled well over and tramping along at around six and a half knots. Marina went to sit on the foredeck to leeward, legs dangling over the side, bare feet trailing in the flashing leap of the bow wave. From the cockpit, it looked as if she was singing. Steve and Jay had deflated the front section of our inflatable dinghy so that it would fit lashed down on the cabin top, and Steve now lolled in the back end in sybaritic comfort, head back and arms flung wide to embrace the sun. Alone now in the cockpit, Jay and I exchanged a glance. He looked shamefaced .

'Sorry Susie, but you were dreaming, weren't you?'

I looked at him coldly.

'I don't know what you were making a fuss about, we were hardly going to be wrecked on the rocks.'

'You should try and keep your mind on the job. It's true, you've been scatty as a cat in the wind lately. I don't know what's the matter with you.'

Oh yes, you do!

'It's you that's meant to be having a breakdown,' I reminded him, without sympathy. Jay sighed audibly and turned away. I thought

I heard him say, 'This isn't working, is it?', but I wasn't certain and I didn't ask him to repeat it, and it occurred to me that there were a lot of things I hadn't asked in the last twenty years. Perhaps I should have done.

The fact that it was true, I had let my attention wander, had once again put me subtly in the wrong, although there is no particular harm in the odd flutter of a genoa, however amateurish it may appear to others. We were not, after all, either sailing a race or trying to impress anyone, and there was no other boat near us. There was no reason why Jay should have made such a big deal of it, and I would have taken odds that Steve was wishing he had never opened his mouth. A feeling of hopelessness swept over me like a wave. However much I didn't want to see my marriage fail, was there anything that I could do to save it if all Jay wanted was an excuse to run after Dawn?

Maybe if I had thought that all Dawn wanted was Jay, I might have felt differently, how can I tell? But I knew – and Jay knew too, although he was choosing to pretend he didn't – that Dawn had a reputation for breaking up other people's marriages almost for the fun of it, it was probably one of the things that had broken her own. Gossip, and circumstantial evidence, both credited her with encouraging the men, ignoring the wives, and then taking the poor suckers to the cleaners before discarding the husk and moving on to pastures new. The female spider, sucking the juices from the male. Why I had never thought she would do it to us, I couldn't now imagine.

Except that she had told me about Jay. I had to be fair.

I remembered the smooth character in the shopping mall, he looked as if he would eat Dawn for breakfast if she started anything of a financial nature. The recollection failed to comfort me, although I would, of course, have liked to see her thus consumed. But if she failed with him, she might turn to Jack as easy game, and in his present frame of mind she would have a walkover.

I felt cold, in spite of the sun. I was glad we were a thousand miles away from her, and at the same time I wished we hadn't come. Marina and Steve deserved better than to be involved in our private problems. I resolved, for their sake, to put the whole thing on the back burner and enjoy myself in spite of it, and in fact it was such a wonderful sailing day that it proved easier than I expected. As we crunched our way across the short seas towards Poros, we saw several large ferries to which I gave a wide berth, and quite a few boats from the flotilla heading on the same course as ourselves. Some came close enough to wave to us, and Jay was busy with his camera, but if one of them was *Hippolyta* she didn't sail close enough to identify, and I spared a thought for Sylvia. But it wasn't bad weather – not that day. Just brisk and bright and invigorating. We ate fresh bread with sweet unsalted butter and goat's cheese, followed by some of the square green grapes for lunch, sitting in the cockpit while the spray flew past the hull. The grapes were warm from the sun and running with juice. Marina spread factor 8 sun cream on her reddening arms and heaved a sigh of satisfaction that could have added half a knot to our speed.

'The only way to live"' she said, closing her eyes against the light and smiling like the Cheshire Cat. 'Isn't this fun?'

A crackle came from the radio below. It had been jabbering on and off all morning, but none of us had taken much notice. Now, Steve sat at the top of the companionway, listening with interest and passing back titbits of information as he drank his coffee.

'Sounds like some kind of an argument, but it's all Greek to me... pity, it sounds lively! *Ariadne* is calling the lead boat... strange people! Can Emmy recommend a good taverna for this evening, will you believe? And the lead boat is answering, too. A bit of back chat between Paul and what I take to be the lead boat from another flotilla – last week's shore/flot, I think it must be – oops!' He grinned, broadly.

'What?' cried Marina. 'Come on Steve, do let us in on the joke!'

'Some joker interrupting,' said Steve appreciatively. 'Sounds as if he got out of his bunk the wrong side, too. *Panther Sailing, Panther Sailing, this isn't a bloody phone-in, you know!* Can't say I don't sympathise.'

'They use that thing like a CB,' said Jay. 'The coastguards back home would have 'em on toast for breakfast, but maybe the Greeks aren't so fussy.'

'Pretty slack of Paul & Co, just the same,' said Steve. He jumped to his feet. 'That babystay looks a bit slack to me, I wonder if it will tighten up a bit.'

We sailed down the north east coast of Poros and then gybed and hardened up again past Modhi. There was more traffic about now as we headed for the entrance to the harbour, and after a while Steve suggested that we took the sails down and motored in.

'The wind is falling light now we're close to the land,' he said. 'Anyway, the cruise notes tell us not to manouevre under sail in harbour, so let's be good – hullo, you don't see many of those around in these waters.'

We all looked where he pointed, half-expecting to see a square-rigger that we had somehow overlooked, but it was a big dive-boat, the air compressor and winches on her deck betraying her trade even if the legend ANGLO-ITALIA DIVING on her plump blue flanks hadn't done so. She was bustling busily in the opposite direction to ourselves, intent on her own affairs.

'Looks pretty commonplace to me,' Jay said.

'Now, that's where you're wrong,' Marina told him. 'You can only dive with a mask and snorkel in Greek waters, because of all the antiquities on the bottom of the Med. The Greeks get paranoid about it, and seal the bottles if you bring SCUBA gear in.'

'I can't say I blame them, after the Elgin Marbles and all that,' said Jay, watching the rapidly-diminishing boat with new interest. 'So presumably, they'll be on official business. I wonder where they're going? I'd be interested in that kind of thing.' He turned to Marina and his eyes crinkled up as he asked, 'Did you see any antiquities on the bottom when you were in the Ionian?'

If Marina recognised this as a dig, she ignored it. 'No,' she replied tranquilly.

'Anyway, they might just be salvage divers,' I remarked, before I could stop myself. Jay gave me a scornful look.

'Trust you!' he said. I had seen it coming the instant I had spoken, and ducked my head against the rebuke. What I had said was true, of course, but what on earth had made me say it?

Reason answered that there was nothing to say I shouldn't have, but reason had nothing to do with this. If Jay and I couldn't find the brakes, I thought in sudden panic, we would career downhill and fly off the edge of the cliff into oblivion.

I wished Steve had never mentioned the wretched boat, which just goes to prove that unlike Marina, I am not in the least clairvoyant. The dive-boat, too, was to be part of the slowly emerging pattern made by the events of this flotilla holiday, and indeed, so far as Jay and I were concerned, of our lives, but how could we tell that it would be the catalyst that was going to change the balance for ever? Just a ship that had passed in the night, I thought, except that of course it was daytime. And then, I forgot all about it. I can't believe that now.

The approach to Poros is described in the Pilot Book as *possibly one of the most beautiful in Greece*. I wouldn't argue with that. A wide, sandy bay to the right of the harbour entrance has white houses spilling round inside the bowl formed by low cliffs; to the left, a wooded slope – olives and cypress trees – climbs to a near horizon. The entrance to the harbour is guarded by a lumped green island with an old grey fort sprawling across it. Beyond this, a knobby headland studded with bushes divides the bay from the harbour channel, beyond again there lies a strip of low-lying land, part wooded, part scattered with buildings. Going up the channel, on the right lies the town itself, houses of grey and white, pink and blue, rising to the skyline with shady tavernas strung out along a wide quayside. Dark alleys dive into gaps in the bright commercialism of this waterfront, leading to who-knows-where, and begging to be explored. The Pilot Book warns to look out for unexpected ferries – we had seen plenty of those during the day, big ones that one could hardly miss, and we didn't quite appreciate at first that we were now looking out for small ones. They came at us from all sides.

We let the engine kick *Phaedra* slowly up the deep channel that runs up the starboard side of the waterway, looking around us and searching for a possible berth and the lead boat. A tiny church, jewel-bright in the early afternoon sun, stood on the shore and there were a lot of colourful caiques moored alongside the quay. There was so much to look at that it was difficult to know where to look first, and Jay's camera clicked incessantly.

'Cats,' said Marina, meditatively. Steve and cats have a natural affinity and gravitate towards each other seemingly by osmosis. We could see several already, prowling the quay or sitting on stacks of wooden boxes. Feral, most of them – nobody's fireside mog. It is another of Steve's more endearing traits that he takes even the mangiest and most unattractive to his lap, and I suspect to his heart too although he would never admit to it.

We passed the ferry berth and rounded the bend at the end of the channel, entering a circular bay. Here were fewer shops and tavernas, more houses, cream-beige, peach and white, piled one on the other up the hillside. Only a few gift shops straggled along this north quay, a hairdresser's, an ice-cream shop, and a store that appeared to sell nothing at all but touristy T-shirts. The mooring rings were empty this early in the afternoon, except for *Eleni*, but of Paul, Emmy and Robin there was thankfully no sign, we must have been too quick for them. We chose a position at random, directly opposite the OTE (*you may telephone from here*) and crept in bow first, relieved to be without radio-control, which made it all much simpler. A friendly shopkeeper came to take the warps, oblivious to Steve's yell of 'Windward warp first, Marina !' so that we drifted inartistically sideways. But not very far – thank goodness, for there were rocks along the edge of the quay, close in. We had been warned that the Greeks dredge them out of the middle of the harbours and just dump them anywhere around the edge – yet another factor that, unbeknown to me, was going to play its part in my life. For now, though, we were simply glad to remember that *Phaedra* carried a gangplank for just this sort of situation.

Jay killed the engine, and the sounds of the town rushed in. There were people strolling along the road, talking and laughing in the hot sunshine, from the T-shirt shop there poured out Greek music from a cassette player, outside the hairdresser a crimson parrot in a cage squawked at us in what we took to be a friendly way. Occasionally, a van or car drove past, honking at the straggling pedestrians. Jay went ashore for some ice-cream, and we sat eating this and drinking chilled ouzo, watching the world go by.

We could have paused on the way and anchored off some handy beach for the afternoon, of course, and probably a lot of the others had done just that, but by coming straight here we had left ourselves time to explore the town of Poros properly, and to relax before another leisured taverna meal under the stars. At first glance, the place lacked the charm of Aegina, being more obviously dedicated to the great god Tourism.

'The Blackpool of the Saronic Gulf,' observed Marina, a little unkindly, I thought. Jay grinned.

'More like Bournemouth – all those posh houses up there.' He gestured with his arm to the area beyond the quay. Marina got to her feet.

'Whatever you call it, I want to go and look. Who's coming?'

We wandered around the town for an hour, dodging from shade-patch to shade-patch in the burning sun, peering into shop windows and confirming Kipling's theory about mad dogs and Englishmen. Jay's camera came out, and he and Steve vanished up a flight of steep, narrow steps in search of a view, but Marina and I wandered into a cool, white-walled shop that sold – incredibly – thick furry sweaters! Hand-knitted designer ones in angora and cashmere with scraps of leather and fur stitched on, enormous shoulder-pads, and price-tags to match. Just for the hell of it, Marina tried one on, a luscious white jacket with magenta patches like blood spots among the fur. I looked at her critically.

'No darling – you look like a cross between a road accident involving a rabbit, and a Sumo wrestler,' I told her. She signed regretfully.

'I've always longed to be tall and willowy, but I suspect that even if I was, you have to be a very *expensive* person to carry off something like this.'

She slipped the disaster from her shoulders, visibly sweating, and handed it back to the shopkeeper with a shake of her head. We drifted back out into the narrow street with its slashes of deep shade and eye-dazzling sunlight and ran straight into Robin, striding along with a grim expression on his face that melted abruptly when he saw us into a rather forced smile.

'What, here already? No swimming today?'

'We had thought we might swim in the harbour,' Marina told him. 'And then, when we saw the state of the water, we thought we might not. Too many oily ferries.'

'Very wise.' He hesitated, obviously anxious to move on and resume his own private thoughts, but afraid of seeming rude. I took Marina's arm, pushing her forward.

'We're just looking for Jay and Steve. I don't suppose you've seen them?'

Robin said he thought he might have passed them on the quayside, and pointed back the way he had come. We parted from him then, and walked on up the alley, down a short flight of steps, and out onto the glaring sunlit road that ran beside the water.

'Not a happy man,' I suggested. Marina looked pensive.

'He can't have fallen that madly in love with Emmy after just a few days.'

'I don't think it's entirely that.'

'Some of it is.'

'It doesn't take long to fall in love sometimes – but Robin's got something else on his mind. I'd stake the cost of your traffic accident on it.'

Jay and Steve were ahead of us, Steve surrounded by cats and Jay squinting through his viewfinder. Marina said, 'Well, I can't think what else it can be,' lightly, because Robin's troubles, like those of *Hippolyta*, weren't our problem.

I was glad, as we strolled towards our men, that we had resisted the temptation to tie up among the caiques. Picturesque though it was here, not to put too fine a point on it, it smelt! A rich mixture of sewage, cats and rotting fruit, with overtones of very dead fish. But we might have been trapped there indefinitely by its photographic possibilities had we not suddenly seen *Hippolyta* chugging slowly up the channel, Janet and Sylvia coiling warps ready to throw and Ken on the helm. They saw us and waved.

'Let's go back and be there to take their warps,' Marina suggested. 'Steve, if you get fleas, I'm not sharing a cabin with you...'

We must have been among the alleyways and steps longer than we had thought; when we got back to the north quay, several of the flotilla were already there, and two or three other boats as well. It was coming up to the time of day when anyone who wants a comfortable berth heads for the harbours, and Paul was there with his hand-held radio, directing the traffic.

Sylvia came ashore smiling, but when Jay asked her if she had enjoyed the trip she confessed that she had once again spent most of it below with a book.

'I hate it when it tips over like that. I'd sooner not look.'

'It's designed to,' Steve told her.

'My ears aren't, though. It makes me feel peculiar.'

But she hadn't actually been sick, I thought. Scared, was probably nearer the mark. I wondered if Emmy realised it and if so, what she would do about it. But Emmy, standing beside Paul with his arm about her shoulders, smiling at a group of young Canadians from *Penelope*, seemed oblivious to anything but her own obvious content. It was Robin who came across to ask, 'There, that wasn't so bad, was it?'

Sylvia just smiled vaguely, and Janet said, 'She drank coffee and read all afternoon. I've caught the sun.'

'You want to watch that. It's easy to get burned out here.'

Sylvia was dissembling well, if she really had hated the day, and after a moment or two Robin walked off to take somebody else's warps as they came in. Paul had his radio to his ear, another of our flotilla was just coming round the bend from the main channel. Steve turned away.

'Let's have another ouzo. You too,' this to *Hippolyta's* crew.

This time, *Phaedra* played host. *Pasiphae* was one of our neighbours, and her crew was on deck tidying up. There were three of them; Carol, her husband Charles, and her brother-in-law Richard, and they, like ourselves, were one of the very few more experienced crews, along with the young Canadian lads down the quay. A few years older than us – most of the crews seemed to be either middle-aged or just-left-college. The in-between groups, presumably, were waiting for the school term to end so they could bring their kids.

'Wonderful sailing,' said Carol, over the gap between us, as we all climbed aboard *Phaedra*. 'Our only real problem is the holding tank.' She pulled a face. 'Every time we hit a wave, a great gust of noxious gasses came aft and nearly asphyxiated us.'

'You mean, it's still full?' asked Marina, in disbelief.

'We can't use the fore cabin at all, except for stowing the luggage, because of the smell. It's a good thing she's an eight-berth boat.'

'What does our skipper say about it?'

'They haven't got the right sized spanner.'

Into the short silence that followed this statement, Steve spoke. 'We've some sloe gin down below. It sounds as if you might need it, come aboard.'

Steve's sloe gin is famous. Rich in colour, full in flavour, and calculated to blow your head off! He had thoughtfully included two bottles in his baggage, and the whole crowd of us – eleven in all – sat in our cockpit drinking as we watched the remnant of the flotilla straggling home. Jay invited Paul and Emmy to join us when the last boat was in, and Emmy looked as she would have liked to accept, but Paul refused, saying they had things they must see to. They returned to *Eleni*, and Jay speculated as to what the things might be until Janet told him to shut up in case they heard him.

'That's the thing I find so different about this flotilla,' remarked Marina, addressing the company in general.

'What is?' asked Carol. 'I mean what *particularly* is, or do you keep a list?'

Marina smothered a laugh, but said, 'This business of *after seven, we're off duty.* When we were in the Ionian –'

'– here we go,' interrupted Jay, with a grin.

'– the lead boat took a couple of days off while we were free sailing, with just a couple of set times in the day when we could call if we needed, but the rest of the time they were there if we wanted them, any time of day or night. After all, it's in the evening when you want to ask questions – or perhaps just get to know them a bit.'

'Working twenty-four hours a day?' queried Charles, raising his eyebrows,

'But they don't,' Marina pointed out, 'Think about it. They don't see us all day, not unless something goes wrong that is – and in fact, the way this lot work, they hardly see us at all. Instead of their being an important part of the flotilla, I don't know about you, but I get the feeling that we're interfering with their private life.'

'I know what you mean,' said Carol, thoughtfully. 'There are very definite off-limits signs. But I don't see...'

'When we were –' began Marina.

'Just say W3ITI,' suggested Jay. 'It'll be quicker.'

'OK. W3ITI, the lead boat crew just asked us to leave them alone on the lead boat itself, except in an emergency, but if they ran into us in the evening, they didn't try to avoid us although technically, I suppose, it was their time off too. They didn't labour the point like Paul does, and they were... well, friendly. People liked that, and it was fair, I think. This lot...'

'... consider us just as a rather unwelcome job of work,' finished Carol.

'I think it'd be truer to say they don't consider us at all.'

We all brooded on this statement for a minute or two, then Charles broke up the party by setting aside his glass and getting to his feet.

'It's early days, perhaps we'll all settle down in a little while. And I'm for a wash and some food, I don't know about the rest of you.'

It signalled the break-up of the party and our guests departed, leaving us to clear up the empties and wash the glasses. If nothing else, said Steve, the conversation had clarified one or two issues; Carol, Charles and Richard obviously shared our views, but Ken and Bill still wanted to believe in fairies. As for Janet and Sylvia, they needed to be able to trust the lead boat crew, and that was that. He thought it might be a good idea if it wasn't discussed in front of them again, and we all agreed.

'But we'll keep an eye out for them,' he added.

As the sun went down and the air grew cooler, the little town began to come alive with people, all talking, jostling, and looking for food and drink – eating in tavernas is the only evening recreation in large areas of the Greek Islands, although there were rumours of a disco somewhere in the town here in Poros. We ourselves, together with the crew of *Hippolyta* who we met with on the way, chose a taverna on the waterfront whose forecourt was shaded with trees: a mistake, as they turned out to be home to large numbers of hungry mosquitoes. We had to push two tables together to accommodate us all, to which nobody seemed to object here, and ordered wine and tzadziki (yoghourt flavoured with garlic, cucumber and mint) and Greek salad, with swordfish and chips to follow. The usual gang of cats came slinking up to find Steve, which rather annoyed the taverna's owner. He kept coming over to shoo them away, saying they had fleas, which no doubt they did. They kept coming back though – scrawny, pathetic creatures that took swordfish skin gently from Steve's fingers but seemed far more to value the kind words and caresses that went with it. And yet, the lives of these cats are reputedly much better since tourism came to the Mediterranean. Whatever can it have been like for them before the British, so sentimental over their animals, appeared on the scene?

As we had already decided between ourselves, the talk at the table covered every subject under the sun but that of our lead boat crew's shortcomings, and it was possible to see Sylvia visibly unwinding. It couldn't help but occur to me, and no doubt to the others as well, that if Paul neither recognised nor accepted responsibility for the less experienced, it was going to put a burden on the rest of us that he was being paid to bear, but fortunately the Saronic Gulf in this weather was kindergarten stuff, and Bill and Ken were neither fools nor completely unskilled. If the Cyclades blessed us with easy weather, all could yet be well, and Sylvia would have a few more days yet to get used to sailing before we set out for the Windy Isles. The meltemi, the prevailing northerly wind, doesn't blow in its full strength until July and August, which of course was why the long-haul flotilla was timed for early June.

All in all, it was a pleasant meal. I began to appreciate the attraction of flotilla sailing for Marina had been right about one thing: it was pleasant to come ashore in the evening and sit among friends after a pleasant day sailing, and one accusation you certainly couldn't level at Paul, looked at from the other side of the argument, was that he nannied us!

The swordfish disposed of, Steve, whose metabolism seems to require large amounts of sugar, wanted pudding, but all that was on offer in our taverna was water melon. The four of us therefore left the rest of the party fishing mosquitoes out of their wine and ranging them round the sides of their empty plates, and went in search of sticky cakes and coffee.

Which was a mistake, because it was then that the evening came unstuck.

The kafeneion that we elected to honour with our patronage was a pleasant-looking place, full of people drinking coffee and eating sticky cakes beneath flowered awnings. It was crowded, and as we stood trying to spot a table, another of the crews from our flotilla hailed us and waved us over to join them. *Aithra* was crewed by a cheerful gang of young people led by a girl of about twenty-three or -four, who, like Ken and Bill, had considerable experience in dinghies but had never handled a bigger boat before. The rest of the crew, three tough young rugby-players and a dreamy girl called Elspeth had seldom been nearer the water than a rowing boat on a boating lake, as they cheerfully admitted.

'We look upon it as a mind-broadening experience,' one of the young men confided. 'We propose to drink our way round the Aegean, and Jenny will keep the boat pointed in roughly the right direction – I make the qualification because we nearly ended up in Hydra this afternoon.'

'It wouldn't have muttered much,' said Jenny, captain of this laid-back crew, with a lazy smile. 'We could have sat and waited for the rest of you to join us tomorrow. But we did rather want to see Poros, so we changed course.'

'We thought there might be a wild time on offer,' remarked a second young man, 'but the disco doesn't seem to get under way until midnight, so we decided to stuff ourselves with baklava while we waited – all the sugar will help to take us through the night!'

'You've no worries about coping with just a rookie crew then, Jenny?' asked Jay. He was sitting beside her, which round such a small table meant close, and as he spoke he laid his arm casually across the back of her chair.

'Women drivers, and all that rubbish, you mean?' asked Jenny, giving him a wide-eyed look that made him laugh. 'No, the only thing that might make me hang back a bit is the engine – and that doesn't work anyway, so where's the problem?'

'What do you mean, it doesn't work?' asked Steve. Jenny shrugged.

'Sometimes it does, and sometimes it doesn't. Don't ask me, I'm not mechanically minded.'

One of the men grinned, and said, 'Ten horse-power diesel – ten dying horses. We do it under sail.'

'What, like surfers do it standing up?' asked Marina, with interest, and Elspeth blushed. Jay clapped Jenny on the shoulder and roared with laughter.

'You don't find a problem with the harbours?' I asked.

'Of course she doesn't,' cried Jay. 'She's got guts, this one!'

Jenny moved a little to put some space between them.

'So far, so good,' she said. 'While we maintain a steady one knot max with the engine, we can't come to much harm. So long as it doesn't die altogether, then we might find we had a problem.'

Jay, as work is reputed to do, seemed to expand to fill the space available. 'We'll keep an eye on you, don't worry,' he said.

Jenny caught the eye of the young man opposite to her and they rose to their feet simultaneously.

'Come on, team,' she said. 'Let's go and paint Poros red!'

They said goodnight to us and left, in one entwined pair and a cheerful group of three. Jenny and the two young men were laughing, I had a feeling it might be at Jay – and indirectly at me, too. It doesn't seem to occur to anyone with no personal experience of it, but a husband who can't keep his hands to himself in front of his wife, by implication makes her look small. I had put up with it for years, I told myself miserably, so why start complaining now? But in spite of this, I heard myself saying, 'Well, you certainly got rid of them pretty smartish!'

Marina, who had opened her mouth to speak, closed it abruptly and Steve went still. Jay glared at me.

'Now what are you accusing me of?'

'It isn't compulsory to fumble every woman under forty that you meet! Particularly with me looking on, and in front of our friends"'

Did I really say that? I must have done. Marina looked down at her hands, loosely linked on the table in front of her.

'Why not with you looking on?' asked Jay. 'It might give you some ideas.' He got to his feet. 'I'm going for a walk. I don't like the company round here.'

He stalked off. I covered my face with my hands and heard Steve's chair grate on the concrete as he pushed it back.'

'I'll take him somewhere for a drink,' he said quietly. 'See you back at the boat, you two.' His hand squeezed my shoulder in passing, and between Marina and me a great silence fell.

After a while, I managed to say, 'I'm so sorry.'

'Well…' said Marina. She paused, and then went on, 'Look, Sue, it's been obvious from the start that something is very wrong between you two. If you don't want to tell us about it, that's fine, but you might remember it's our holiday too.'

'I've said I'm sorry. I didn't mean to spoil everything.'

'I'm not sure it's you that is,' said Marina, slowly.

I took my hands down and looked at her. She met my eyes, her own serious. I think she had expected to see tears, but it had all gone too far to think that crying would mend it now.

'You know our neighbour, Dawn,' I asked, on a sudden impulse.

'Oh God, I might have guessed! Don't tell me, she's decided he's next on the menu.'

Her reaction startled me, and for the first time for weeks I felt slightly better.

'Not exactly,' I said, and then I told her about Dawn's morning visit and its sequel when Jay came home. She rolled her eyes to the awning over our heads, and said, 'Let's have a proper drink. This is beyond coffee.'

She grabbed a passing waiter and ordered two doubles of Metaxa, the fierce Greek brandy. Two star strips paint but the five star is agreeable, particularly if, as now, the right mood is there. When it came, she pushed mine across to me and said, 'So what did you decide at this talk of yours?'

'I asked him if he wanted a divorce. He said not.' I added, slowly, 'He said he still loved me.'

'And what about you?'

'Me?'

'Yes, how do you feel about it? Do *you* want a divorce? Do you still love him?'

'No...' I said, slowly. 'And yes. But nothing has been the same since that night, and I'm not certain that it ever can be.'

'I'm not surprised. I don't think I could ever forgive Steve if he behaved like that – but then, Jay does a lot of things that I could never forgive Steve for.'

I stared at her in surprise. She said, 'Knowing what Jay can do when he's with you, have you ever wondered how he behaved when he wasn't? I have – and he's not my husband.'

I considered this.

'I never thought – until now – that it meant anything.'

'That depends on what you want it to mean. But Jay made quite a pass at me when we first met, and believe me, he wasn't in love with me. Perhaps he isn't with Dawn, too, but a woman like that... you can't trust her, either.'

That *either* wasn't lost on me. 'Oh God...' I said. Marina went on.

'Perhaps he does love you – more than anyone else, that is. But don't kid yourself that he's been faithful to you, there'll always be three or four Dawns who won't say "no" for every Marina who says it.'

I think,' I said carefully, because putting it onto words would make it true, 'that I have always known that, somewhere deep down. I just didn't want to see it.'

'Well, come to that I never took you for a fool.' said Marina.

'I think I've been one, just the same.'

'Whether that's true or not depends on what you wanted to achieve.' She paused to consider this profundity, and then laughed at herself. 'Listen to me! Anyway, aren't we all, fools I mean, when it suits us? What are you going to do now?'

'I'd still like to save our marriage... if it's worth saving. I'd still like to believe it is.'

Marina waved to the waiter again and ordered two more Metaxas. My head was beginning to swim. 'Well, I expect Steve has been lecturing him like a Dutch uncle while we've been talking here,' she said. 'We do like you both, you know, we're on your side.'

'But we're still spoiling your holiday.' I sighed. 'We don't mean to. I hoped that being right away from it all we might have a chance to get together again. I don't know any more what Jay hoped.'

'He's here, isn't he? Well then!'

I hadn't told her about the smoothie in the mall, and I didn't tell her now. I sipped my brandy slowly. 'We'd better not have another of these. The world's beginning to spin.'

'That's what the world does best. Go on – be a little devil!'

'But not a double.'

'All right then;'

After the equivalent of five Metaxas each, the world was beginning to look rosier as well as spinning merrily, and as by this time it was getting quite late, we began to stroll slowly and not that steadily back to the north quay. The evening was warm and still, moths dived around the lamps along the roadside and cats slunk in the shadows, watching them. The town was still buzzing around us, the tavernas were full and the streets acrawl with pedestrians, all the shops were open and doing good business. Bouzouki music poured into the night, fighting with itself from taverna to taverna.

Jay and Steve were already on deck, rather more sober than we were, waiting for us. They didn't seem to have much to say to each other, and as he gave me a necessary hand across the gangplank, Jack ruffled my hair – which I hate, but I have never been able to make him stop doing it. It was a gesture at least of affection tonight, however, even if not precisely love.

'All right?' he asked.

'She's drunk,' Marina told him cheerfully. 'We both are.' She posed in the centre of the gangplank, suspended in midair over the rocks, and Steve grabbed at her so that she fell into his arms, laughing.

'Coffee,' he said firmly. 'You two are a disgrace!'

Thanks to Marina, I had managed to get away without answering Jay, and we all went down below away from the mosquitoes and behaved, all four of us, as if nothing had happened. But after the coffee, when we were in our cabin, Jay took me very gently in his arms and kissed me.

'I'm sorry, Susie,' he said. 'I didn't mean... it's just that it's all so very difficult.'

'It's OK,' I said. 'Only, we must try to stop it, we're spoiling things for Steve and Marina. And ourselves. Can't we just give ourselves a break?'

'I am trying. You just seem to take offence so easily. I love you.'

'I love you, too,' I said. The tried and tested formula had served us throughout our marriage. I wondered now what it meant – or if it had ever meant anything. He kissed me again.

'Go to sleep. You're pissed as a newt.'

He turned over in the dark space and fell instantly asleep. But me, I lay awake and wished that he had made mad, passionate love to me. It might not have meant any more than the ritual words, but it would have helped.

It would have helped a lot.

But it was already tomorrow, and every circumstance was now in place that would change my life, Jay's life, many lives for ever. The players waited in the wings. The curtain was about to go up.

Day Four: Thursday 8th June

Poros woke very early in the morning, and in spite of the Metaxa, so did we. We seemed to have parked right beside the bus stop, and the buzz of talk as people waited for buses, and the grinding of gears from the buses themselves, acted better than an alarm clock. The weather looked threatening today, a heavy sky ashen as an unswept grate hung low over the town, and a few spots of sullen rain plopped into the water. Marina said she had a headache, but without arousing much sympathy.

'Serves you right,' said Steve.

We moodily scratched last night's crop of mosquito bites and looked at the day without enthusiasm. Breakfast in a well-sheltered taverna seemed like a good idea, and we went off to find one.

'Wind's gone round a bit from the north,' said Steve, as we walked along. He licked a finger and held it up. 'North-easterly, what there is of it. Hope it doesn't hold, it'll be dead on the nose tomorrow for Sounion if it does.'

We sat under an awning right by the water, the owner of the taverna was going round turning up the cushions on the unoccupied seats and the sky was growing blacker and blacker. There was hardly a breath of wind now, and there didn't seem to be enough air to breathe: the day had a thick, waiting feel about it. We dawdled over our coffee before going off to replenish the ship's stores – bread, and more fruit, cheese and spinach pies for lunch, sweet biscuits because Steve had eaten them all. It had begun raining in earnest by this time, big sullen drops from the leaden sky, and we dodged in and out of shops, postponing our souvenir and present shopping until a drier day. Steve found somewhere where we could buy a huge block of ice to help our cold box along – not suitable for drinks, it was for freezing fish and had some additive in it, but fine for keeping things cold. In the end, it lasted us almost four days!

Then it was time for the morning briefing, and we all went together for once to the appointed taverna. The glumness of the weather seemed to have affected us all, people sat in silent groups or clustered around Paul, Robin and Emmy, talking earnestly. We sat down beside Ken, Sylvia and Janet. They didn't look happy.

'It's only a bit of cloud, for God's sake!' cried Jay, unreasonably happy by contrast.

Ken said, 'But the forecast is a north-easterly for at least the next three days, force 4 – some of us don't want to go to Hydra if it means slogging thirty miles to windward to get to Sounion on Saturday. We'd sooner go back and have another day in Aegina, and go on from there.'

Marina looked disappointed. 'But Hydra's supposed to be lovely!'

'It would be too much for the girls,' said Ken.

Paul called the meeting to order, and everyone drew close to listen to what he had to say.

'We seem to have a bit of a split in the camp this morning,' he announced. 'We've all talked it over, and we've decided that the best thing to do is to call today a free sailing day, then those who want to can go on to Hydra, those who don't fancy the beat to windward tomorrow can potter back to Aegina when the rain stops, and meet us in Sounion on Saturday evening. I suggest that if you don't want to go back to Aegina harbour, the best place to head for is Perdika, there's good shelter from this north-easterly, some good tavernas and provisions are available, and you should get a good reach across tomorrow if this wind holds, as it seems it's going to. Emmy will give you a quick briefing later on if you ask her. Now then –'

'Where will the lead boat be?' interrupted Bill.

'We shall be going to Hydra, keeping to the planned cruise.'

Steve muttered, 'A bit of lateral thinking going on there, wouldn't you say? Shouldn't he stay with the less experienced crews?'

'It must be difficult for him,' Janet excused her current hero. 'He can't be in two places at once.'

'That's exactly what I meant,' said Steve, but let the subject drop. He exchanged a glance with Jay, who pursed his lips in a soundless whistle and stared up at the lowering sky.

The meeting broke up with very few people, it seemed to me, having decided exactly what they were going to do. We went back to *Phaedra* to prepare for the short voyage to Hydra, but by this time the heavens had opened and it was fairly throwing it down. We sat in the cabin listening to the rain hissing onto the cabin roof and watching it cascading into the cockpit; when it rains in the Saronic Gulf, it puts its whole heart into it. There was a squall or two, fierce but of brief duration, some brilliant flashes of lightning and the odd rumble of thunder. Great sailing weather, I don't think! Then quite suddenly, it stopped. The grey sky split over the mountains to reveal a streak of pale, duck-egg blue. Everything began to steam like a sauna, and Jay rose to his feet with a sigh of relief.

'Let's get out of here,' he said.

We cast off and chugged under engine back down the long, narrow channel to the open water, back past the moored caiques with their brilliant colours, the bad smell, the cats, the taverna with the tree full of mosquitoes where we had eaten last night. The little ferries were still bombing around in all directions, mostly empty at this minute. Low-lying cloud lay against the hills in solid-looking chunks and tatters, and everywhere looked grey. A burst of raindrops spattered into our faces, and after the downpour the faint breeze off the land smelled of wild thyme. There wasn't enough of it to make it worth hoisting the sails; we chugged on over the grey, heaving sea towards Hydra, and although we had no idea of it then, we were now on a collision course with a most alarming adventure... but not quite yet. This was only Act One, after all.

The voyage to Hydra was unremarkable to the point of dull. We met several ferries – the large kind – on our way, or maybe they weren't all ferries, but you get used to seeing a big ship and shouting *ferry on the port bow*, or wherever it happens to be, and most of them were certainly ferries. Because we had set out late due to the weather, we didn't get into Hydra until two o'clock, and we found *Pasiphae* there before us; she must have started out in the thunderstorm. The harbour was very crowded, and there was no sign of our lead boat.

'There's that dive boat,' said Jay suddenly. 'You remember, we saw it yesterday? There – stern-to on the end.

Steve, on the helm, scanned the packed quayside with narrowed eyes, looking for a space where we might squeeze in. 'We'll go alongside her,' he said. 'There's just about room, if we breathe in.' He throttled back the engine and headed in, while the rest of us got fenders and warps ready. A man standing on the dive boat's bow raised a hand to acknowledge that he had seen us coming, and strode swiftly aft along her deck to leap onto the quay, ready to help with our warps. We were glad of him, for it was quite a performance to moor up here. The quay was built very high, more of a sea wall really at this point, and it was necessary to climb down onto yet more unwelcoming-looking rocks and boulders to make fast – which, with an eye to an easy departure tomorrow, we did by slipping the ropes through the rings and bringing them back to the yacht to cleat them on the foredeck, never mind Paul and his sacred – and often inappropriate – bowline. The water that sucked up and down on these rocks looked slimy and unwelcoming, and rubbish of various kinds bobbed along the edge, it didn't do to study it too closely. All in all, not a good place to slip off the gangplank, which soared airily above the mess so high that it had to be balanced on the pulpit rail. I have no head for heights, and the mere sight of it made me feel sick.

'You laid out enough kedge,' observed our helper, with a lift of an eyebrow. 'Expecting a particularly high tide, are you?' He was young, which perhaps excused such tactlessness, and he stood on the rocks where he had done us such yeoman service and laughed up at us. I thought that the laugh had friendliness in it, but Steve had a flash of anger behind his eyes. He kept his voice level, however.

'Just following instructions. We're strangers here.'

'Whose instructions, for God's sake?' But he didn't pursue it, turning away with a briefly sketched salute to return to his own boat. Steve scowled at his retreating back. Up until that moment, I suspect that he had been rather pleased with the way he had berthed *Phaedra* in that crowded harbour.

No bells rang out. No trumpets sounded. The small incident happened and was over, and within ten minutes, we had all more or less forgotten it.

Carol, Charles and Richard came running along the quay, belatedly, to help us and as there was now no need for all that, we all sat in a row on the low guard wall overlooking the open water, in increasingly bright sunshine and growing heat. The clouds were clearing nicely and the wind beginning to fill in a little. Those on the way back to Aegina should enjoy good sailing. *Hippolyta* would be among them, as we already knew. Also, we now learned, six more out of the total flotilla of twelve yachts plus the lead boat. Thirteen in all, a significant number.

'One of the women on *Persephone* is recovering from a slipped disc,' Carol told us. 'She's only been out of hospital about a month. She only came because she thought it would be nice, gentle sailing down here in the gulf and her husband had set his heart on it. She's dreading the Cyclades, but anyway, she'd never have managed the beat back to Sounion.'

'A bit stupid of them to book this cruise then,' suggested Jay, but of course, like a number of others, they hadn't realised that they had.

'A bit of a muddle altogether, isn't it?' said Charles, and Marina asked if Emmy knew.

'I suppose so, everyone else does. It isn't a state secret.'

'And on *Calliope*, that couple and their son brought the son's girlfriend with them and she's most desperately seasick, added Charles. 'She threw up all the way from Aegina to Poros yesterday, and from Ayios Giorgos to Aegina the day before. There's no fun in that, is there? Not for anyone.'

Marina added her contribution. 'That group of kids on *Aithra*, only one of the girls has ever sailed before.'

'And their engine doesn't work properly,' Jay added.

A silence fell. These were the ones our lead boat, now coming merrily in between the moles to join us, had left to their own devices. Steve looked at his feet.

'It's not our business,' said Marina, watching him.

'Maybe not, but it ought to be somebody's,' he replied.

We sat there in the sunshine, and I thought about *Hippolyta* and wondered if her crew were having a good time. I wished they were here with us now for Hydra is a lovely place, quite different from the equally beautiful Poros, and Sylvia and Janet would have loved it. The harbour lies in a steep-sided bowl in the hills, golden rock and grey and white walls and red roofs climbing to the skyline. It seems to trap all the sunshine going, and I had already fallen in love with it.

At the briefing that morning, Emmy had told us that the old village (the present one is an artists' colony, she had said, disparagingly) lay over the hump of the hill, about three-quarters of an hour's walk away. There was an excellent taverna there, but the ones in Hydra itself, though good, were pricy. It was possible to take a water taxi round there if you didn't fancy a long walk in the dark. The seven of us now decided that this evening we would do this, but Steve and Marina elected to walk there now and see what it was like in daylight. Jay wanted to take pictures of the town.

'You go with Marina and Steve,' he said to me. 'You know how boring you find it when I get my camera out.'

85

I would have gone with him in fact, just for the chance to see the shops, but he obviously wanted to be on his own, and perhaps after Steve's lecture last night he needed to be. Certainly, things between us had been much better today, but obviously it wasn't going to be that simple. Before I could answer, Marina said, 'Yes, do come with us, Sue.'

But they, too, deserved some time to themselves, and come to that, so did I. Anyway, I'm not very good in the heat, even the thought of that long walk full in the blazing sun made me wilt.

'Thanks, but no thanks. I'll stay under the awning with a good book and a cold drink until it gets a bit cooler, if you don't mind.'

'Good idea,' said Jay. 'I'll come and find you when I've done the town, and we'll go for a swim.' He went off with his cameras, waving cheerfully as he went, and Steve saw me safely back on board before he and Marina too set out on their travels.

I scrambled down into the cockpit, grateful now for the shade of the awning, for the sky had cleared completely by this time and the sun was burning straight down into the bowl of the little harbour. The town rose high around it and the heat beat back from its pale walls, but it would be shady and cool early here, for the sun would go behind the hills. Then, I decided, I would venture out and explore the town, and perhaps Jay would be happy to come with me. For now, a quiet hour with my book and that cold drink I had promised myself would be very pleasant. I brought up the cockpit cushions and settled myself comfortably to enjoy my solo afternoon. I was, in any case, in need of a quiet interval for some constructive thinking. Last night had shown me one thing, whatever else it had or had not achieved; matters couldn't stay at stalemate any longer. You can progress – backwards if you must, sideways or forwards, but staying still and hoping for miracles is never an option.

My eyelids grew heavy in the warm air, and I let them close the better to think. Maybe Steve had shocked Jay into a realisation of what he was doing – to me, to our marriage, to our holiday together. Maybe it was what he had needed, an outside view. I wondered what he had said to Steve, for of course he had a point of view as well as me, he must know – as I did not – what had made him wish for something new in his life… or was Marina right, and he just had a roving eye that had always roved further than I had wanted to believe? If so, I had lived with it for twenty years without realising, in theory it should be possible to continue in the knowledge of it... or was the knowledge itself the rock on which we were doomed to founder? I did so hope not. I valued the life that I had with our home, our friends, and above all our children. I realise now that I clung to it like a downing man clings to the proverbial straw, but then, at that actual moment, it seemed like a justification. And loving Jay was the foundation stone. Unfortunately, loving someone can't be turned on and off like a tap. I know this to my cost, and I am not alone.

In spite of these sombre thoughts, I must have drifted into a half-sleep, for I was suddenly startled back to full wakefulness by somebody speaking almost in my ear. Not to me – not even in English – but on board our neighbour, the big blue dive-boat. I sat up hurriedly, grabbing for the book as it slipped off my knee. I hadn't intended to fall asleep.

The young man who had helped with our warps, I now saw, was sitting on the deckhouse roof, just above the level of my eyes, talking over his shoulder to somebody out of my sight. In Italian, I supposed, or it could have been Greek. It sounded like Greek, but either is Greek to me. His English accent had been irreproachable – a pity really, considering what he had used it to say, but that didn't mean he *was* English. I pushed the cockpit cushion more comfortably into the small of my back and considered him idly. He seemed to be drawing something, sketching the town perhaps, his face now withdrawn and absorbed. It was a face worth watching, too, dark and intense, oval in shape with good bones underlying a clear brown skin and a long, straight nose slightly blunt at the tip. He had dark hair, thick and straight, and long limbs, and his movements all had that graceful economy of effort that tells of perfect co-ordination and fitness. An archaeologist? Or maybe they were ordinary salvage divers, as I had speculated myself. His eyes, downcast on his work, would be brown, of course... he must have been around twenty-five, I supposed, certainly younger than Robin or Paul, so he would most likely be a technician or a diver rather than a scholar, since he was here... too old for a student, too young for a learned professor... my mind went free-wheeling on a journey of its own, half-stupefied by sleep and the heat, and then suddenly, maybe feeling my attention so intent on him, he looked up and straight at me. His eyes weren't brown at all, but grey like clouds in a storm, appearing light in his olive-skinned face, fringed with black lashes under flying dark brows. It occurred to me that he was beautiful. Appropriate enough in this land of old gods.

'You'll know me again,' he said, but he smiled as he said it. I stretched myself lazily, like a cat, responding to some instinct that I didn't care to think about too closely.

'Anywhere. But I didn't mean to be rude.'

'How could such open appreciation be rude?' he asked, outrageously. When he smiled, he had deep creases in his cheeks that in a woman might well have been dimples. Men have no right to be quite so attractive as this one, but he wasn't in any way effeminate. Nor, in spite of what he had said, did he seem more than peripherally aware of his own attraction. His tone mocked, but I felt it was himself, not me, who was the target.

I smiled back at him, with a fleeting and absurd wish that I wasn't pushing forty and the mother of two almost grown-up children. Where the more obviously handsome Paul had left me unimpressed, this dark beauty moved me strangely. And then I brought myself abruptly back to earth, because even if I had been twenty still, I was married to Jay and this wasn't the moment in our marriage to let my thoughts run so dramatically amok. In any event, our conversations all seemed doomed to be brief. He jerked his head towards the harbour.

'You've got company. Better give them a hand, they're going to need it.'

I scrambled untidily to my feet, to see a small yacht flying the Panther Sailing house flag hovering uncertainly off our transom. There was no space on the quay at all now, latecomers were having to come up on the sterns of us lucky ones. The couple on board hailed my appearance with relief.

'May we come in behind you, would you mind?'

'Be my guest.' I picked my way through the scattered cushions and climbed onto the after deck. *Phaedra* rocked as someone came aboard, but I couldn't see who it was because of the awning. My dark-haired Adonis had returned to his sketching and had no further interest in me, so it wasn't he. The woman on the bows of the newcomer stooped down, coiling warps, as the boat made a slow circle, dropped her kedge with a rattle of chain, and surged up on our transom as if she intended to sink us.

'Oi, take it gently!' Jay appeared beside me. 'Give her a touch of reverse – quickly – throw the rope – no, that one – put it under the wire. That's it.' The rope came flying through the air and he caught it neatly and made it fast to the cleat on our transom. The second warp followed, missed, and slipped into the water. Flushed and flustered, the woman gathered it in again and flung it haphazardly in our direction, I grabbed it in a muddle of untidy wet coils and made it fast. The throb of the engine died, and the man on the helm began to come forward to thank us.

'Haul in on your kedge first, I would,' remarked my new acquaintance on the dive boat, without looking up, and the man turned and hurried back. The woman stood on the foredeck, holding onto the forestay and smiling at us shyly.

'It's really kind of you – do you mind awfully?' Then she added, 'It's only the second time we've come into a harbour, and our lead boat isn't here.'

Ours was, but Paul and Emmy took their free sailing seriously. This, I surmised, must be the shore/flotilla lot, or part of it at least, and so it proved. Ben and Diana had never done any sailing before the condensed boat-handling course of their first week's holiday, so they had done pretty will in the recent delicate manouevre. They invited us aboard their little twenty-five footer to take a look round and share a cup of coffee. The rest of their flotilla had gone to Porto Kheli, they told us, but they had elected to come straight here and wait for the others, they were due in tomorrow.

Steve and Marina arrived back and announced that they were off for a swim. There was a swimming place – not a beach, exactly, Marina said – just a short walk away. And the old village was lovely, we must certainly go there this evening.

We were all feeling sticky after the heat of the afternoon, so we decided to have our swim with Steve and Marina and go round the shops afterwards when, hopefully, it would be a bit cooler. The swim was a unique, and slightly weird experience. Hydra has no beaches, it is simply a lump of rock sticking out of the sea, so to make a bathing place the Greeks have built a maze of steps into the rocks to get down to the water. There is a tiny taverna, complete with showers, and concrete platforms built above the deep water, and rusty iron ladders going down at intervals, or if you feel brave enough, you can dive off these platforms into the shadowy water, where a steady swell, like the breathing of the sea, heaves silently up and down. It is weedy and dim down there, and scattered refuse from passing ferries, some of it best not studied too closely, bobs on the swell. The cliffs rise steeply above you as you swim, rather eerie but cool and refreshing. We swam for half an hour or so before getting dressed, and all four of us together then walked into the town.

The main shopping centre is grouped around the harbour. There is a wide quayside that looks uncommonly as if it has been paved with marble, and tavernas in strategic places, and the most mouth-watering shops we had yet seen. Vivid paintings of mountains, windmills and caiques, more of the tempting pottery, beautiful rugs made of goats' hair, jewellery, you name it and they sell it in Hydra. Jay and I bought a picture together, a pepper-pot Greek windmill shining like a pillar of salt against a blue sky and bluer sea, and Marina fell for a Minoan amphora with an octopus and strange sea-anemones and snails painted on its fat sides. Not genuine Minoan, of course, but it did have a lead seal on the handle, stamped with the legend *This is a real copy*. Only the Greeks could phrase it just like that.

We enjoyed ourselves immensely, but walking back to the harbour we found out why our lead boat had been so keen on coming to Hydra, for obviously now, they had already arranged to meet friends here. Paul and Emmy and another young couple were sitting on *Eleni*'s deck with wine glasses and bottles as we walked past; Emmy caught sight of us and waved and smiled, but I don't think Paul even registered that we were there.

'About par for the course, so far,' remarked Steve.

'Forget it,' Marina advised.

Ben and Diana had to come ashore via *Phaedra* of course, and when we were all changed and clean to go out for the evening we returned their earlier hospitality and invited them aboard for a sloe gin before we went in search of the water taxi. It transpired then that they were planning to do the same thing as ourselves, and in the end we all went together, collecting Carol, Charles and Richard on the way. Walking to the taxi, we passed Paul and Emmy and their friends, now sitting outside a taverna around a table already well-laden with empties. Greek waiters in general seemed to leave the empties to pile up instead of keeping a tab, at the end of the evening they just count the dead men. Simple, but it appears to work.

'Having a good time?' asked Paul lazily, as we went past.

Out of politeness, we had to stop and chat. Emmy and Paul held hands and smiled, and for the first time since we made their acquaintance seemed to take a real interest in us. Their friends asked where we all came from and made envious noises when Jay and I mentioned the New Forest.

'How beautiful! You lucky people! So do you have a boat tucked away there in some gorgeous south coast harbour?'

'We've a thirty-footer lying in the Beaulieu river,' said Jack. They knew Beaulieu, and Bucklers Hard where *Foxtrot* lived, and we talked for a minute or two before moving on. It was unreasonable, I suppose, but that brief, friendly interlude had made us more tolerant towards our lead boat crew. Perhaps they were doing their best between a rock and hard place, and perhaps we were judging too hastily.

Too much sun can affect the brain, they say.

The water taxi turned out to be a speedboat with a tiny cabin for the passengers to sit in, out of flying spray. There was a smelly fish box on the foredeck, but it hardly had time to become offensive as the trip only took about two minutes. We tore at high speed over the water, bow wave sparkling prettily in the evening sunlight, and before we had time to get settled, we had arrived. Our taxi driver agreed to come back at nine- thirty to collect us – we had said nine o'clock, but he insisted we would be longer than that, with much arm-waving and in execrable English, before charging off, spray pluming out on either side of the hull, to head back to the town and more business.

We forgot about him immediately. Once again, we sat by the water, and two dogs and three cats came to join us – the dogs were a novelty, but of course it was the cats again that got the four-star service. We ordered our meal, going into the taverna to pick the fish we wanted to eat from a chilled display at the counter. Those of us who wanted a change from fish could choose from a limited menu, and the food, when it came, was simple and delicious,. As we ate, we learned a few more interesting details about Panther Sailing's Aegean operation, and our temporary amnesty with Paul began to waver, for the shore/flotilla, it now appeared, was a bit of a joke too. If that kind of thing was really amusing.

'Our inflatable only has one rowlock still attached to it,' Ben told us, 'and one of our oars only has half a blade.'

'And we're lucky,' added Diana, with a grimace. 'One of the other boats has a dinghy that doesn't even inflate properly.'

'Good God!' said Charles, staring.

'Oh, that's not the best bit,' said Diana. 'We've had real drama! Our hostess had a blazing row with the Skipper on the first night out from Ayios Giorgos, she caught the bus to Athens in floods of tears and nobody's seen her since!'

It seemed we had yet something to be thankful for. Nothing so exciting had happened to us.

Yet...

'She might as well have stayed, as it turned out,' said Ben. 'The Skipper has gone too, now – it appears that last week they had to leave two boats in Ermioni for some reason, and he's gone off to sail them home – one at a time, of course. It's likely to take him the rest of the week.'

'So who's in charge of the flotilla?' about four of us asked in chorus.

'Well, our engineer hasn't jumped ship yet,' said Diana. 'And the Skipper's mum and dad had come out for a holiday, so they're looking after us until he gets back.'

Steve looked as if he couldn't believe what he was hearing, but unfortunately it was all too believable. We mentioned some of our own horror stories, and all enjoyed ourselves shaking our heads and predicting doom. It hardly seemed real, that evening on Hydra. For that matter, looking back now with hindsight it still hardly seems real, and yet I know now what happened. We all laughed, I remember, although the laughter did trail off uncomfortably, for it wasn't really very funny. We speculated for an idle moment as to whether Panther Sailing's head office back home knew what went on out here.

'What did you think of their so-called "yacht club"?' asked Marina, for of course Ben and Diana had seen a lot more of it than we had. Ben shrugged.

'Apart from the fact that it seemed to be run as a social club for the staff, you mean?' he asked. We exchanged glances, interested to have our own brief impression confirmed unprompted.

'It was a bit like being an unwanted visitor in somebody's private house,' said Diana. 'In the evenings, they all crowded round the bar and positively ignored us.'

'Ah yes, the great off-duty time,' said Steve, nodding. 'We have the same problem.'

'I suppose they have to be off duty sometimes,' said Diana, but we all agreed that it should be away from the paying clients, and not all together. There should always be somebody whose business it was to make people feel welcome and answer any questions.

Steve fed fish heads to the waiting cats, and then, since a chilly wind had sprung up as the sun went down, we decided to have our coffee inside. We had our ears on the stretch at half-past nine and heard our taxi arrive all right – but by the time we got to the door, he had gone again. We stood indignantly among the tables.

Our old table was now occupied by a crowd of men and girls, among whom I spotted my acquaintance of the afternoon. There were a good many bottles, both full and empty, on the table by this time and the party was fairly rowdy. My acquaintance hailed me exuberantly.

'If that was your taxi, darling, he's gone! He came in, looked round and went off again, all in about a minute. You need to be quick off the mark around here.'

'The saucy swine!' said Steve. 'We've been waiting for him for half an hour as it is – and come to think, it was him insisted on the time.'

'They charge extra after nine o'clock.'

One of the other men stood up and began to pull more chairs into the group.

'You ring for another, and come and drink with us,' he advised, in a rich Italian accent. 'Any friend of Oliviero is our friend also.' Oliviero, if that was his name, stood up too and helped with the chairs, arranging that I should sit beside him with a casual sleight of hand that left Jay open-mouthed at the far end of the table.

'We're old friends,' he informed my astonished husband, and then, to me, 'What's your name, darling?'

He was drunk, a little, but his manner was easy, feather-light, romantic under the lamps. I felt myself opening out like a flower in the sun under this treatment, and settled down to enjoy the evening. When the chill wind made me shiver, I remember, he moved closer and put his arm around me to shield me. Close-to, he smelled of soap, and the clean, fresh tang of salt water. I leaned back into the hollow of his shoulder, feeling the hard strength of him against me. It was all curiously right, in a shadowy way that I couldn't analyse. Not that I tried very hard. Charles had gone to ring for another taxi, I hoped it would be a long time coming.

It's hard to remember now what we all talked about. We were a very mixed party, Italians and Greeks and ourselves, and a couple of the girls were American, no doubt picked up in the town (like me?). The beautiful Oliviero seemed to speak all three languages, although I suspected his Greek was more fluent than his Italian, which told me nothing more about him. We did learn, however, that all the men and one of the girls were divers, on charter to a big museum in Athens. Five of them were also archaeologists, and there were two Greek professors of archaeology among those. They were recording wreck sites among the islands – of which it appeared there were a fair few, but some of the accents were a bit thick, and it was often hard to follow the plot so I may not have that quite right. Yesterday, they had come up from Santorini, tomorrow they were headed for Delos. But they didn't want to talk about themselves, which was a pity for they all seemed to have at least a working knowledge of antiquities and some among them knew a great deal and it all sounded fascinating.

Jay had decided not to mind about my trilingual admirer, wisely since he was considerably younger than me. Instead, he had annexed one of the American girls, which I reminded myself that I had no right to mind on this occasion – and indeed, tonight I really *didn't* mind, what is sauce for the goose should also be sauce for the gander – or do I mean that the other way round? The girl was less laid-back about it, although she played up nicely to Jay, I caught one or two looks from her of a resentment so deep as to be flattering. But if she made the mistake of thinking that this charmer, Oliviero, intended to be taken seriously, I was in no danger of doing the same. In fact I began to wonder if the annexation of myself had been a deliberate ploy to warn her off. Whether I liked him for it or not would depend on how far the affair- if there had even been an affair – had gone, and that I would never know.

The taxi, as I had hoped, didn't hurry itself, but all good things come to an end, and of course we had to leave eventually. Oliviero kissed my hand when we said goodbye, and we planed back to town in a boat that this time smelled of diesel rather than fish, and paid a small fortune for the privilege just as we had been warned we would. We said goodbye to our friends at the quayside, but there was a disco blaring out into the night close by the harbour, and we sat around in the cockpit for a while, drinking wine and quietly talking.

'So who was your dangerous friend?' Marina asked me, eyes alight with interest.

'Oliviero? Not exactly a friend, we just got talking this afternoon while the rest of you were all off exploring.

'Just take care you don't burn your fingers.'

'I'm not likely to.' I spoke with regret, but my behaviour that evening had worked miracles with Jay, who now sat with his arm around me in a rare gesture of possessive affection. Perhaps, I thought, I should have given him a taste of his own medicine before this, but then again, opportunities for doing so were not exactly thick on the ground. And I couldn't see that, in the long run, it would have got us anywhere for both of us to play away. I added, 'Why dangerous, anyway?'

'I'm not absolutely sure,' said Marina, sounding surprised. 'Perhaps because he's the sort that when he breaks your heart, it stays broken for a long time.'

'These Italian men!' said Jay, tightening his hold and grinning at me.

'I think he may be Greek.'

'Don't you know?' He sounded amused.

'Well no. I know nothing about him.'

'And that's the way it always will be,' said Marina, with finality. Steve yawned.

'I don't know about all of you, but that disco sounds to me as if it's dug in for the night. It's after one o'clock now, and there's no sign of it stopping, and I'm ready for my bunk. It's going to be a long, hard sail tomorrow, remember.'

We collected up the glasses and went below. The disco went on thumping out music far into the early hours, but after a while it seemed to fade into the background; I suppose we got used to it. The wind was rising, I could hear it sighing through the thickly-clustered masts in the harbour... and then I slept. There was a major disturbance when our next-door neighbours came back – it must have been around three in the morning I suppose – loud shouts and laughter, followed by elaborate shushing sounds, and a splash that could have been someone falling over the side. I turned over, half-awakened, and then slept once more.

Day Five: Friday 9ᵗʰ June

Of course, I wasn't so naïve as to set any store by the events of Thursday evening. Whatever Oliviero had intended by his behaviour, it had been directed to his own ends, and whatever they were only he could know. Even so, it had a bearing on my own dilemma, and in two completely different ways.

First of all, and perhaps most importantly since it began to reshape my thinking, it brought home to me how very long it was since I had felt attractive and desired by my husband. This went back long before Dawn and, I now realised, had crept on me so subtly that I had become used to it without even realising. A hardened cynic might claim that all marriages are like that after twenty years or so, but I didn't want to agree, there was too much evidence around me to the contrary. Steve and Marina, for instance, who still talked and laughed and flirted with each other, my own parents, who held hands under the table after fifty years or more. Jay and I, on the other hand, seemed to have dwindled into mere friends over the years, and if I was being objective about it, sometimes not even that. There had been times, particularly recently, when I had wondered if he disliked me. This couldn't be right. Marriage, surely, should never degenerate into just a habit.

The other way in which it affected me was in that it put a new weapon into Jay's hands. He hadn't liked being given a dose of his own medicine, and although in the beginning, when we were all still under the influence of a pleasant evening, it had reawakened his interest, by morning this transposed itself into a reason to put the blame for all our troubles onto me. He was very gentle about it, and very cruel. I could see the relief in his eyes because he had found a way to make everything my fault and ease his own conscience.

'I didn't want to say anything before,' he said, in the quiet privacy of our cabin when we awoke. 'I know how easily hurt you are these days. But honestly Susie, you made yourself ridiculous last night, throwing yourself at that young man.'

I had woken feeling unusually happy and content, this unexpected attack left me momentarily speechless, allowing Jay to continue. He spoke kindly, which would have been an improvement had his words not taken my breath away.

'But-' was all that I managed. I had begun to say that the initiative had been all Oliviero's, but Jay didn't wait for me to find the words.

'We need a serious talk,' he said. 'I mean, *serious*. I know you like to blame everything on Dawn, but she told you herself, and so did I, that she's just a friend. I needed someone to talk to, that's all. You've been so moody and difficult... look, I know that it's only your age and you can't help it, but you must understand how hard it makes it for the people who have to live with you. You must have noticed, even Sal prefers to spend as much time as possible in Reading.'

I stared at him with my mouth open. So now I was a menopausal hysteric, was I? The sheer injustice of it was like a blow in the face, but every woman of a certain age must learn that there is no answer to it. The implication that my own daughter couldn't live with me was a sword to the heart, when we both knew that it was Peter, not me, that kept her away. He put his arm round me, cuddling me to him, and I could feel myself stiffening in his embrace.

'I think you ought to see the doctor when we get back,' he said. 'Truly, Susie, I did hope that this holiday... but last night, you were behaving so out of character, I was appalled. Steve was quite shocked. You couldn't see his face from where you were, but I did.

This was clever, as I realised only later. You can say what you choose about something that the person you are accusing can't possibly have seen, and there was obviously no way that either I would ask Steve, or that Steve would tell me if it was true. For the moment, however, it made me feel about six inches high.

'Jay –'

'No, Susie, I'm in the chair for once. Listen. I love you very much, I know you're going through a difficult time. But there's no way that I can handle it any more unless you get help. Valium or something, it would make a world of difference. Or HRT, isn't that supposed to help with these things? Isn't our marriage worth it?'

His voice was so tender and loving that for a moment there he had me wondering if I really was hysterical. I had noticed before that, along with time-of-the-month, "menopausal" is an accusation that some men find very convenient for keeping their wives in their place, but I had never visualised it being hurled at me, certainly not before I even hit forty! And my hormones have always been singularly well behaved, and anyway, surely everyone is entitled to be a little bit out of temper now and then? Particularly if they have a husband who is playing away with a Dawn, I now thought. I found my voice, and a space in the conversation in which to use it.

'You're talking utter rubbish!' I said indignantly. 'You might just as well say that Dawn is the result of your own mid-life crisis!'

He kissed me then. The Judas! When he was busy cutting the ground from beneath my very feet.

'Just give it some thought, Susie, that's all I ask. And no more glamorous toyboys. It makes you look a fool. Promise me? It's for your own sake, I should hate to see you a laughing stock.'

'And will you promise me that there will be no more nubile young yachtswomen?' I asked tartly. He sat up then, and began to disentangle himself from the light duvet that covered us both.

'There's no reasoning with you at all when you're like this!' he exclaimed, and went out into the main cabin to put the kettle on for some tea. I lay in our bunk and stared at the deck close above my head and seethed with impotent fury. I was too angry at that moment even to fear the void of parting. I just wanted to strangle him.

The day echoed my mood, when I finally crawled out of my bunk to face it. The wind had continued to rise during the night, and by this time it was obvious that we were all going to have a very lively trip to Sounion. Marina and I cleared away breakfast as quickly as we could and then set about making a heavy-weather stow below, so that things wouldn't fly all over the cabin as we sailed, while Jay and Steve took the cover off the mainsail and prepared the ship for sea. We hadn't gone ashore to eat breakfast today, Steve wanted to be out of harbour and on our way as early as possible. Paul's laid-back habit of holding his briefings at nine, or even half past, was yet another of the things that Steve found annoying about him, since it wasted half the morning every day.

As soon as we were ready, we hailed Ben and Diana, for we would have to warp ourselves out past them, allowing them to slip into our berth. A couple of the divers were on the deck of the dive boat, looking a bit the worse for wear, but of the beautiful Oliviero, perhaps fortunately, there was no sign. Still sleeping it off, no doubt: he looked like a man who knew how to party. I felt a small regret that I wouldn't ever see him again, but Jay had spoilt it for me and it soon passed. Anyway, it was quite true, I was far too old for him, he couldn't be more than twenty-five or six at the very most.

Getting out of Hydra gave me something else to think about, as a largish ferry decided it was a good time to leave just as three yachts, including our own, were manoeuvring for the harbour entrance – but this is all part of the fun and games of sailing out in Greece. We cleared the mole without actually colliding with anyone, hoisted the main, unrolled the genoa, and settled down to the long slog upwind to Sounion.

'*Anatolikos*,' murmured Marina, as we slipped round the end of the mole. 'Who was he, Jay?'

'Not a person at all,' said Jay, pleased to be asked to show off. '*Anatolikos* is the east wind.'

'How chilly!'

'Not out here. The east wind is a warm, friendly wind. It blows from Arabia, not Siberia.'

'Why do you want to know?' I asked curiously. It isn't like Marina to explore the realms of classical knowledge.

'It was the name of your friend's boat.'

My dangerous friend, Oliviero... obviously, Marina felt no embarrassment in teasing me about him, and I began to feel better. But even so, I gave myself a mental prod in the back, for a married woman like myself had no business to go all moony about a man who could almost be her own son, if she had been very precocious that is. Jay was unanswerably right about that, if about nothing else.

'You know everything,' Marina was saying, admiringly. Jay grinned.

'No. I just read it in the Pilot Book.'

Owing to our having to wait for Ben to get dressed before we could get out, we hadn't made quite the early start that we had hoped for, and it was nine-thirty before we had settled down on the first long tack up to the north east, we were going to have to sail all out to meet Paul's deadline of six-thirty. To begin with it was quite fun, a hard breeze and spray flying everywhere, and one of our fellows just far enough ahead to make catching her interesting, but bashing into a force 5 dead on the nose is a pleasure that soon loses its edge, and as the day wore on, volunteers to take the helm were in increasingly short supply. Jay went below to catch up on some sleep that he claimed he had missed last night through worrying about me, Marina had appointed herself chief caterer and coffee-maker, and only Steve and I seemed to want to sail *Phaedra*, and I freely admit that after the first few hours I was quite happy to leave it to Steve, too. There was an island ahead of us, called on the chart Nisos Ayios Giorgos – shades of Panther Sailing! – that never seemed to get any closer, although it subtly changed shape as we sailed; I began to hate the sight of it. We had plenty of time to view it from new angles and it never became noticeably more interesting, just a boring lump of rock stuck out in nowhere. As we became progressively more tired from the constant bashing over the waves, it also began to feel cold. There was no pleasant, warm sunshine today, just a rather grey and overcast sky overhead. Marina went below to fetch sweaters and didn't bother to come up again. I could hear her striking matches and cursing the larder unit, which had leapt from its home to smack her where it hurt. Steve caught his shin on the broken locker catch twice – when we finally reached Sounion, he unscrewed it with the blade of a knife and threw it away. It was very loosely attached.

By late afternoon we were pushing *Phaedra* along under main and engine, hustling her against a stiffening wind and a short, uncomfortable sea. It was sailing of the most soul-destroying kind, a wet and miserable bucket to windward that never seemed to get us anywhere. It justified the decision of Ken and Bill to go back to Aegina as nothing else could, Sylvia would have loathed every minute. We could see several boats behind us in the distance, heading our way, but if they were our own flotilla they were going to have to shift some to make the deadline.

As we approached Sounion, the radio began to crackle into life. *Calliope* had arrived in the bay and was wanting to know where she should anchor. The lead boat was presumably already there – they motor-sailed almost everywhere in order to arrive first – we could hear Paul answering, giving advice on how much chain to lay out, and I remembered that gibe about the putative height of the tide and stole a glance at Steve to see if he remembered it too. Really, Paul had an obsession about anchoring, he must have had a very unfortunate experience somewhere along the way to account for it.

We made the bay with twenty minutes to spare, sailing in under the headland which bears the ruins of the ancient temple to Poseidon, god of the sea, and dropped anchor close inshore, astern of *Eleni*.

'It's quite shallow,' commented Steve, from the bow where he was peering over into the clear, green water. 'About seven feet I should think, no more.' The bow anchor bit and we dropped back, paying out chain until we swung clear of the lead boat. Paul, in the cockpit gave a lazy wave.

'You've not got much chain out,' he accused. Steve took another look over the bow.

'There's yards of it,' he called. Paul lifted a hand in acknowledgement and turned away. They still had the two strangers on board the lead boat, we could see them sitting in the cockpit: inviting your friends and relations for a holiday seemed to be a Panther Sailing thing. Their presence took Paul's attention off what the rest of us were up to, and while we personally considered this to be a good thing, that didn't apply to everyone. As we were about to discover...

Pasiphae had come in just behind us, so fast that she ran smartly aground just ahead of us with a resounding bang that made us wince. (Richard later described this as "just touching"!) A hurried reverse and a careful investigation proved that she had charged straight into a ledge of rock and stopped as if she had hit a brick wall – as in a way, she had of course. Richard retired, blushing, to deeper water and we all settled down again.

By this time it was well after seven o'clock. Two more boats were just coming round the headland into the bay, and a swift count of heads revealed a deficit of one, but Paul had gone below out of the evening chill to join his friends; with the coming of evening the wind was dropping at last and being replaced by a thin miasma of mist that lay just above the water, softening the focus of the view and pushing the temperature down.

We did the same. We were too tired to want to bother to row ashore to one of the tavernas we could still dimly see there, and Marina volunteered to make omelettes later on if somebody else did the washing up. Since Marina's omelettes are legendary, we agreed to this with flattering enthusiasm. Steve had discovered a packet of soup mix behind the larder unit, left by a previous tenant, and we decided to start with that. It was minestrone, I remember. Silly, the things that stick in your mind.

'Posh dinner,' said Marina, lazing on the seat and reaching for a book. 'But later on – much later. I feel as if I've gone over Niagara in a barrel!'

'Who was it said that the Med in June was calm, smooth and relaxing?' I asked her. 'Apart from Panther Sailing, that is…'

'When we were –' Marina began, but Steve interrupted, tetchily.

'I wish we knew what the forecast is. I don't like having no radio apart from the VHF. Not with this arsehole in charge.'

The said VHF was busy tonight, with plenty of chit-chat between Paul and his flotilla, on the pointless subject of whether or not one should dress for dinner in the local tavernas! Steve had left it on, I believe, just to see what would happen, he loved to be able to criticise Paul, whom he was coming increasingly to despise.

'Very comical,' he commented scathingly. The hard day was telling on him, too. The clever comments bounced back and forth over the air, accompanied by much giggling, but then, suddenly, there was an interruption.

'*Eleni, Eleni, Eleni,* this is *Circe,* over.'

They had to repeat themselves twice before Paul broke off his amusing conversation to reply.

'*Circe,* this is *Eleni,* over.'

'Paul, we're about a mile off the coast now, and visibility is down to about two hundred yards, we can't find the landmarks. Over.'

Circe, you should have been in two hours ago, what kept you?'

'Our anchor was fouled in the harbour at Hydra. It took that long to clear it. We had to dive for it in the end.'

'Well, get in as soon as you can.'

There was a brief pause, and then the social chatter began again. Jay made a sound of disgust, and Steve was clearly astounded.

'Is that all he has to say? Just a smart rap on the knuckles – public at that – for being late?'

'And where was Paul when they were stuck in the harbour?' asked Marina, with spirit. 'When we were in the Ionian –'

'Here we go,' groaned Jay.

'No, listen a minute. Our lead boat never left harbour until we were all clear.'

'And neither should Paul,' Steve agreed, forcefully. 'Him and his stupid half-a-mile of bloody chain! Asking for it –'

'Ssh,' I said, holding up a hand for quiet. *Circe* was on the radio again, with a further plaintive request for guidance, but nobody was taking any notice. Steve went up on deck and took a look round. The mist had thickened a little, nothing to bother us here at anchor but it would certainly be enough to obscure the shape of the land from out to sea.

'I've a good mind to get the anchor and go and fetch her in,' he said, but before he could do anything so provocative, the radio crackled into life again.

'Yacht *Circe, Circe, Circe,* this is motor vessel *Anatolikos, Anatolikos.* Come in if you hear me please. Over.'

Something jumped inside me. Even after my "serious talk" with Jay before breakfast, and a day spent uncomfortably wondering what Steve really did think about me, I couldn't control it. I gave a quick look towards Jay, but he was leaning forward, attention centred on the little drama unfolding on the VHF radio. In and around, the talk about dinner jackets, incredibly, continued unchecked.

'I hear you, *Anatolikos.* Oh... over. Sorry.'

'*Circe,* I have you on radar, you are about two miles south-south west of the entrance to Sounion Bay. I will talk you in on a compass bearing. Suggest you switch to Channel 9, now clear, and call me again. Over.'

'My God, this is unbelievable!' muttered Steve. 'Why doesn't Paul just shut them all up? It's outrageous, having to change channels in the middle of an emergency like that!'

But Paul was one of the offenders, of course. *Circe* had switched channels now, and Jay reached for the mike. 'I'll give the silly sod a piece of my mind he won't forget in a hurry!'

'Don't.' Marina reached out to lay a restraining hand over his. 'It won't do any good,' she added, apologetically. 'Only get us disliked. It isn't just Paul, you see, they don't understand.'

'Then someone ought to bloody well tell them!'

'Yes. But not us. And not now.'

Steve was guilty of borrowing a catchphrase from Marina. 'When we were out in the Ionian the other year, one of the boats got lost on the way to the barbecue – actually, they had followed the wrong flotilla, it happens from time to time when you get someone who won't admit they can't navigate. It was a quiet evening, with excellent visibility, but the Skipper took the lead boat out and searched around, radio and everything, until he found them and knew they were safe. He was gone three hours, and it got dark, and the hostess and the engineer had to manage the barbecue on their own, but none of us was allowed to have our fun spoiled. And that's the way it ought to be, it's what their job is all about. But this – this incompetent shambles –' Words failed him, but his tone was rich in disgust. Marina just touched his shoulder and got to her feet.

'I'm going to make those omelettes.'

I sat wondering if it had been Oliviero on the radio. Had it not been for what Jay had said earlier, I don't think it would have occurred to me, he had already come and gone, but Jay had given him an importance that our brief acquaintance hardly justified. It occurred to me, for the first time, that his excellent English might well be because he *was* English, although the name *Oliviero* sounded foreign. Perhaps he was a mixture, English mother, Greek or Italian father.

'Susie, you're dreaming again!' Jay accused me. "Susie" had always been his particular pet name for me and I had loved to hear him use it. Now, after this morning, it made me squirm, it sounded so patronising. Oh dear!

'I'm tired,' I excused myself. Steve smiled at me across the cabin table.

'We all are, it's been a tough day. I think we all deserve a sloe gin.'

None of us mentioned the most disquieting feature of the incident, which was that Paul had never realised *Circe* was missing, but I think it was in all of our minds as Steve assembled the glasses. We avoided the subject, and each other's eyes, and for once our pre-dinner drink was taken almost in silence.

The omelettes were predictably excellent, although we all agreed that the soup must have been down behind the larder unit for some time. While we were eating, *Circe* came in and anchored on the far side of the bay, and Steve at last relaxed. There was no comment on the radio, which we had left switched on now simply out of curiosity, nor any among ourselves. Presumably – *presumably* – Paul realised she was safely in, but sadly, it was more likely he was living it up with his friends in one of the tavernas.

And tomorrow, weak links and strong together, we were bound for the Windy Isles, in unsettled weather and with a Skipper who failed to take his responsibilities seriously.

It was certainly going to be an interesting cruise!

Day Six: 10th June

The weather was behaving very strangely for June, although Paul didn't seem to be losing any sleep over it. We on *Phaedra* were all disturbed very early on this morning by an ominous crunch and a shudder through the hull. Jay and Steve collided in the companionway as they rushed up on deck to see what had happened, to find that the wind had swung abruptly west, and although gentle in the dawn light, had been enough to swing *Phaedra* inshore. This, coupled with the rise and fall of the tide (it was about three days after the full moon, so it was a huge nine inches or so!) had been enough to make her just touch bottom on the shelf of rock on which *Pasiphae* had grounded last evening. She had swung back again now, but the water upwind was softly ripped once more, as another gentle gust came from the west. Jay looked at Steve and grinned.

'Should we rush to the radio, do you think, and shout *Eleni, Eleni, Eleni, help, help, help*?' he asked. Steve snorted in disgust.

'Stop talking rubbish and start that engine. I'll get the anchor.'

Marina and I, who had followed them on deck, went below again. There was no crisis and Marina began filling the kettle. The engine throbbed into life and we could hear the anchor rattling home; we motored a little way off shore, Steve dropped the anchor again and Jay killed the engine. End of drama. They came below looking rueful.

'Bloody stupid thing to happen,' said Steve. 'Fancy getting left by the tide in the Med! I'll never live it down.'

'Don't worry darling, we won't tell anyone if you pay up,' said Marina, teasing.

'We couldn't have expected a westerly,' argued Jay, unamused.

'The secret of good seamanship is to expect *anything*,' Steve contradicted.

Marina began quietly pouring boiling water onto coffee in four mugs. 'Did Paul see you?'

Steve gave a short laugh. 'Not him! He's still tucked up in his little bunk! His friend did stick his head up, and waved as we went past. That's all, though.'

Since we had inadvertently got up so early, it seemed a shame to waste the extra time. We decided that we would walk up to see the ruined temple up on the headland before breakfast, and pay our respects to Poseidon. This meant rowing ashore in the dinghy. There was nobody stirring on any of the other boats that swung quietly to their anchors in the bay and nor, surprise, surprise! was there anyone on the gate at the foot of the upward path. It was locked too, but we ducked under the barrier and climbed up the rocks instead. There was a wonderful view from up there, and the temple, though in ruins, was curiously impressive. I wandered away from the others as they walked around chatting and trying to find Byron's signature (reputedly on one of the columns). Jay was taking photographs, calling us all into a group, but I wanted to be on my own.

I stood on the edge of the high cliff and listened to the sigh of the sea, and tried to imagine the great god who makes the storms and the calms in his fastness beneath the waves... only his face was always the dark and lively face of Oliviero, and disturbed, I turned back to the others again. Marina was waving and calling.

'Sue! Hi, Sue! Come and be in this picture!'

Jay came to meet me, putting his arm about my shoulders and giving me an unexpected hug. Meeting him halfway, partly because I felt guilty, I tilted my head to smile at him. Marina and Steve looked pleased, no doubt taking the credit to themselves, but where was the harm?

I still loved him, of course I did, that was part of the trouble. He had been part of my life for twenty years, it was impossible to imagine what it would be like without him. It was just all so very difficult.

I heard the click of the camera shutter and knew that Marina had recorded the moment to keep. I felt a stir of an emotion I didn't recognise, a flutter of restlessness. I gave Jay's hand on my shoulder a quick squeeze and then ran forward, free... the word actually came into my head.

There is magic in Sounion, but I'm not entirely certain if it is good magic.

Steve, who is about as sensitive to atmosphere as the rocks we stood on, said that he needed his breakfast, and after a few more pictures we ran back, down the path this time, and ducked under the barrier. We had been up at the temple for nearly an hour, and there were people awake on the other boats as we rowed back to *Phaedra*, one or two of them splashing about and shouting in the cool water. Paul was on *Eleni*'s deck as we rowed past.

'I warned you you'd drag if you didn't put more chain out,' he told us.

'We didn't drag,' said Steve, resting on his oars. 'The wind changed and blew us onto the shelf.'

The wind had filled in properly now, settled in its more usual quarter, a light and steady breeze from the north west. Paul gave a sour, knowing smile.

'Oh rubbish, you dragged your anchor and drifted. Put more chain out next time when I tell you.'

Speechless with fury and scarlet in the face, Steve bent to his oars without another word. In fact, none of us spoke until we were once again safely on board *Phaedra*, and hopefully out of Paul's earshot. Then Marina said, tersely, 'He's a twit! Even if we had dragged, fancy contradicting the paying customers right out like that!'

'We didn't bloody drag!' said Steve, angry with her.

'I know that.'

'He called me a liar!'

I went below to start the breakfast. I supposed that I should have felt indignant too, but I was still too unsettled by the temple to have room for another strong emotion. And yet, what had happened up there? Nothing! Just the silly fantasies of an unhappy middle-aged woman with a crisis in her marriage, with almost grown-up children back home in the New Forest! But even so, I went to the mirror above the washbasin in the heads and peered at myself in its inadequate square. My own familiar freckled face peered back at me, surrounded with its mop of unruly curls in which incipient grey was kept at bay by a skilful hairdresser. A feather of fringe across a broad forehead, fair skin now reddened by the sun across the cheekbones. An interesting face, I had always hoped and believed, rather than a pretty one... and Poseidon was beautiful.

'That bacon is frizzling to a very expensive crisp,' I heard Marina say, as she jumped down into the little galley. 'Sue, Sue, where've you got to?'

I leaned back so that she could see me in the doorway. 'Just cleaning my teeth,' I lied.

Steve was still disgruntled when we sat down under the cockpit awning with our bacon, eggs and juice. He seemed to feel – and who am I to say that he was wrong? – that Paul had enjoyed the feeling that he had caught us out, after all the comments we had made about Panther Sailing's maintenance standards – or lack of them.

'He's afraid of us because we're not only obviously experienced, but prepared to criticise,' Steve said, discontentedly.

'Just don't let it spoil your holiday,' Marina advised. 'We needn't take any notice of him, there's loads of free sailing to come yet.'

'I think "afraid" is coming it a bit strong,' said Jay. '"Resents" might be nearer the mark.'

'Afraid of, or resents, what's the difference? He liked catching us bending, or thinking he had anyway.'

'In a way, you can't really blame him. A Skipper needs to be seen to be the boss, after all. He needs to be respected.'

'Paul,' said Marina sapiently, 'needs to be admired.'

How could such open admiration be rude?... but Oliviero/Poseidon, I somehow knew, had no need of it to bolster his self-esteem, he was already a complete person, maybe not perfect but with confidence to match. Paul, on the other hand, only thought that he was.

It was now more than time for one of us to go ashore for the briefing, which as usual was to take place in a handy taverna. It was Jay's turn, fortunately, and he set off in the dinghy while the rest of us went swimming off the back of the boat. Steve and I swam across to *Hippolyta* to visit with Sylvia and Janet, Bill and Ken having gone ashore to the meeting. They had enjoyed Perdika, they said, and although they were a little bit worried about the Cyclades, their holiday was being a success so far. They leaned over the transom to tell us about it, while we hung onto the boarding ladder. Last night's little drama seemed to have passed them by, probably they had turned off their radio in harbour, or gone ashore, or both, and neither Steve nor I mentioned anchor-dragging. Sylvia, in particular, needed all the confidence she could muster for the days ahead. But I knew without him saying it that Steve had now definitely settled in his own mind that *Phaedra* wouldn't be too far away from *Hippolyta* as we headed east, and although it would probably never be discussed, that Jay would feel the same. We left to swim back to *Phaedra* only when we saw Bill and Ken returning in their dinghy, and soon after that the fleet made sail for Kea, our next destination.

We ourselves were in no particular hurry. Kea was only twelve or thirteen miles away, and we had a hard sail yesterday. We lazed around on the deck for most of the morning, watching the others busily hauling up sails and starting engines. Someone called out to ask if we intended to stay there all day and Marina called back, 'Yes!'

Carol, Charles and Richard dropped by on their way back from a trip ashore, and were persuaded to come aboard for a drink. Steve, probably still smarting from his own experience and its repercussions, teased Richard about their arrival last evening.

'So, who ran aground then?' he asked, grinning.

'It was only a bit of sand,' Richard tried to tell us, but Jay and Steve greeted this with derisive laughter.

'Keep talking! But remember, we heard you – *kerblong*!' We all laughed, including Richard, and Carol changed the subject, asking if we had been up to the temple.

'It's well worth the money,' she assured us. 'You should go up there if you're not leaving just yet.'

'We already did,' Marina informed her, and added that we had seen it for free. Carol was indignant about this.

'You jammy devils! We paid 250 drax each!'

'You should get up earlier. We did.'

It was Richard's turn now to grin. 'Yes, we heard you had a bit of trouble first thing.'

There was a short, electric silence. Steve had gone tight-lipped and silent, and it fell to Jay to explain exactly what had happened. Charles and Richard were quite prepared to accept our version of events – after all, they had hit the same shelf of rock themselves, and could have no doubt that it was really there. But Jay hadn't mentioned to Steve that it had been brought up at the briefing, in Paul's translation, as an awful warning to the others to do as they were told.

'Father knows best,' said Carol, with a little shrug of her shoulders and a speaking look. Steve looked furious to think that he had been made to seem a fool in front of everyone, even though he hadn't been there to see it – or perhaps because he hadn't been there to defend himself, which on reflection, was probably a good thing. Jay assured him that he had told some of the others the truth.

'But the fact of the matter is, there are very few people on this flotilla in a position to criticise,' said Charles, more soberly now. 'Did you hear that little fiasco on the radio last evening?'

Jay gave a short laugh. 'I'd love to hear what our coastguards would say if anyone carried on like that back home! You'd be in grave danger of losing your licence, I should think!'

'But none of these, or very few anyway, have licences. Except Paul, of course. Presumably.'

Pasiphae's crew left soon after that to make sail for Ayios Nikolaos, via a suitable beach, but Marina said that we had eaten too many meals on board lately, and anyway, the bread was hard. We therefore all piled into the dinghy again and rowed ashore to a taverna on the beach, where we ate fried squid and the obligatory soggy chips and drank cold beer. And then, there was no putting it off any longer, we really had to set sail ourselves. Everyone else was long gone, lead boat and all.

Watching Steve's back as he rowed us out to the yacht, I wondered if he had been over-reacting earlier, or if Paul for some reason *did* see him as a threat. His qualification as Yachtmaster Instructor would appear on the booking form. Marina too, as I already mentioned she holds her Yachtmaster certificate. Jay has a Coastal Skipper certificate, I hold Day Skipper. It was perfectly possible that *Pasiphae*'s crew held similar, or the four young Canadians. If Paul had any sense, he would take full advantage of this, with his rookie flotilla to worry about in expert sailors' territory. But he wouldn't, of course, and he wasn't – worrying, that is. The fact that he was taking his present attitude, in every respect, made me begin to wonder exactly what our Skipper's qualifications actually were. It wasn't a comfortable speculation.

There is no clear dividing line, no equator dividing west from east, as you sail from the Saronic Gulf into the Cyclades, and yet I felt a shiver of anticipation as we sailed eastwards, towards our first rendezvous with the fabulous Windy Isles. Was it the islands, I wondered, as I lay in the sun at ease in the flubber, deflated again now and back on the cabin roof. Yes, there was something splendid about the very sound of them, but was it only that? Or would I maybe be wiser not to pursue that line of thought? *Anatolikos* was out there somewhere, and Delos was on our itinerary under the heading of free sailing – but if we ever arrived there ourselves, she would probably be long gone. She would have three or four days start of us, at the very least.

I couldn't get that young man, Oliviero, out of my head. He had come, subtly and without my realising it, to represent a challenge, not as a scalp for my belt, for I knew Marina had been right in her estimate of him, but as a yardstick by which to measure the viability of my marriage. For this, Jay himself was almost entirely to blame, he alone had set up Oliviero as the touchstone for my fidelity and happiness. So eager had my husband been to prove me at fault that he had succeeded in turning a brief, meaningless flirtation into something that was rapidly becoming graven in stone. It had certainly not been his intention. And then I found myself smiling, for if anyone was a scalp on a belt, it was me, on Oliviero's, and my presence there would probably startle that young man exceedingly. For a moment I felt tender and motherly towards him, immeasurably older and wiser. If I never saw him again – and I probably wouldn't – I would always remember him with kindness He had given me back something that I had, without really noticing it, long lost: self-esteem.

I sat up, and looking across the sparkling water, saw Kea, craggy and high, standing guard over the entrance to the Gulf of Petali, with other islands lying like clouds on the water in the heat-hazed distance beyond.

'Did you get a chance to ask Robin about this log?' Steve was asking Jay, for we were still apparently making phenomenally fast passage over the ground. Jay said that Robin had told him it might be possible to adjust it to register a more probable reading, and had promised to have a word with them about it in Ayios Nikolaos, where we were headed now, and the two of them began a technical discussion on the suggested modification. I suddenly felt an irrational wish to interrupt them, to make Jay take a good look at the beautiful scene around us and admit the siren quality of these islands, but he would never understand, and he would be someone else if he did. It was Oliviero who sat on deck, absorbed with a sketch book and a pencil.

But realistically, he had probably only been charting wrecks or designing a new and improved outlet pipe for the heads, or something equally prosaic. And I must put him right out of my mind. He was, and would remain, a completely unknown quantity and comparisons were not just odious but dangerous.

Ayios Nikolaos was a repeat of Aegina, with Paul and his radio making things complicated, and a very pointed request to Steve to lay out enough anchor chain, which didn't go down well at all. And it was a repeat in other ways, too, with everybody going ashore to spend the evening in separate groups or small cliques, with the lead boat crew sitting apart, smiling in a friendly enough manner if anyone came close, but making no move to encourage us. Only Sylvia and Janet made any real attempt to talk to them, perhaps seeking encouragement for tomorrow's long sail to Siros, although one or two of the others had queries – or would it be complaints? But Robin did come later on to the taverna where we sat at a table covered with empty plates and half-full beer bottles, and talked to Steve and Jay about the log, and about other things too and for the first time.

'There seems to be a bit of unrest among the tribes,' Marina remarked, artistically casual. Robin pulled an expressive face.

'Not surprising, when the office back home made such a pig's ear of everything. Of course, the girls in the office don't know the area, they don't understand. But it's made things very awkward.'

'Was your last flotilla with Panther Sailing?' Jay asked. Robin nodded.

'Their Ionian operation is a lot slicker than –' he began, and then bit his lip and gave a rueful grin. 'Oh well, you aren't stupid, I don't suppose. I'm not sure if I'm going to stay on, to be honest.'

'So what's the trouble over here?' Steve asked, but Robin obviously thought that he had said enough already and wouldn't be drawn. He would only explain that each area was under a different manager, answerable to a central office in Athens, whose chief was as often in England as in Greece. That wasn't actual criticism, simply information. He turned the subject neatly then and talked about the Ionian for a while, which pleased Marina and Steve, and then about sailing in general. He wasn't as knowledgeable as Steve or Marina, or even as Jay and me, but he had done a lot of dinghy sailing, had a working knowledge of bigger boats, and held a degree in engineering. He wanted to work on designing marine engines; big ones, for ships, not little sewing machines to put into yachts. He came alive as he talked, and smiled and laughed, and the shadow that Emmy – or something, anyway – had cast across his eyes was gone completely. Perhaps he hadn't known Emmy long enough for it to hurt too much, or perhaps, too, she and only she was behind his earlier remark.

Charles, Carol and Richard joined us later on, and the eight of us sat yarning under the stars late into the night. It was only much later, as I rolled into my bunk at last, that I remembered the little that Robin had said, and how he had stopped himself so abruptly, and wondered what he could have added to it had he chosen.

Day Seven; Sunday, 11ᵗʰ June

We awoke early again, and since we had plenty of time on our hands before Paul's nine o'clock briefing, decided to go ashore and once more have our breakfast in a taverna.

'All this hanging around in the mornings is wasting our holiday,' grumbled Steve. 'If only he'd have his briefing an hour earlier, we could all be out enjoying ourselves before half the day has already gone!'

'Perhaps he thinks we all want to have a lie in,' I suggested, but the suggestion was like a red rag to a bull. The concept of "having a lie in" when there is serious cruising to be done is not one that Steve will easily accept.

'We don't *all* have to be there,' he pointed out. 'He could at least give us the option.'

When they were in the Ionian, briefings had been at eight o'clock, generally over breakfast in a handy taverna, said Marina. They had been friendly occasions, and as a matter of course, complete crews had attended even at that hour, and certainly none of the skippers had ever complained. Jay and I were getting a bit sick of the perfections of their previous Skipper, admirable though he undoubtedly was. We laughed at her, I remember. She took it placidly, probably she knew herself that she was overdoing it, but Marina never allows such considerations to worry her. We could afford to laugh, after all. We didn't need Paul, if push came to shove we would manage very well without him. Us… and three other boats, maybe, out of the dozen of us. *Pasiphae*, the Canadians on *Penelope* and the man whose wife was recovering from a slipped disc operation, which effectively reduced the number able to cope alone to three-and-a-half.

I do not understand, in retrospect, why we laughed. It was too serious, and we didn't see, even yet, how much more serious it might become: an accident waiting to happen. Not even Steve, although he was concerned about *Hippolyta*, mainly because of Sylvia's obvious fear. Paul was a careless Skipper but be couldn't be blamed for everything, and presumably he wouldn't have been given the job if he wasn't ultimately capable of doing it. It was, we now knew, his second year with the flotilla, he and Emmy both. It had to count for something. So we reasoned, and looked at objectively, we had every right to do so. It was what we were all paying for, after all. Peace of mind, and help with problems: support, in fact.

We had time for a swift restock in the local supermarket ('if this is "super,"' commented Marina, looking around her, 'I should hate to see another kind!') after breakfast, and before the briefing, which should tell you something. Because we had eaten aboard at Sounion, and because we had been warned that Foinikas, where we were now bound, had very little in the way of shops, we went back to the quay eventually fairly heavily laden. There was a lot of cheerful activity going on as everyone prepared for sea, we had all got our second wind and were looking forward to the day's trip; it was to be another long one, thirty miles or more, but it would be fair sailing nearly all the way. I wondered fleetingly about Sylvia, for this one there was no dodging.

We left Ayios Nikolaos soon after ten, bound for Siros, Jay on the helm. It looked as if it would be a fast trip, there was a fresh breeze outside the shelter of the harbour, and quite a steep sea, waves of eight to ten feet, well spaced; *Phaedra* rode them easily enough. It was the very best kind of sailing, lively enough to be interesting but not so much as to be worrying. Steve was moving around the boat as usual, mending things and tightening bottlescrews, contented but still restless, humming to himself – by the time we returned her to Panther Sailing he had her tuned up beautifully. The log showed 28.6 knots, so Robin's recommended adjustment hadn't been wholly successful, no doubt that would be the next thing on Steve's list when we arrived in Foinikas. Marina sat up on the foredeck again, splashed with spray and dreaming into space, so that Steve had to keep stepping around her. I went below after a while to fetch the lunch we had already prepared before leaving harbour, and the larder unit rushed out and gave me an enthusiastic bang on the thigh. I kicked it back smartly and swore.

We all sat in the cockpit and ate bread and cheese and oranges, enjoying the superb sailing weather and taking turns on the helm as we ate. The prevailing north-easterly that blew up here in the northern Cyclades meant that it was a reach again once we had rounded the northern end of Kea. *Phaedra* lifted and swung over the waves, slithering down into the troughs as if she was on a toboggan run. Steve was on the helm now, he nursed her along, luffing into the puffs to gain a fraction of extra speed, and deliberately surfing down the waves, making the best of the conditions: we left him to it.

He was enjoying himself, and at least it kept him in one place. The sun shone, spray flew. Away across the water, we could see some of the others as distant grey triangles against the pale sky. I wondered aloud if one of them was *Hippolyta*, and how Sylvia and Janet were liking it. It was blowing around force 4 and rising, which is enough for beginners.

'Ken and Bill can handle this,' Jay said confidently. That was no doubt true, and true for Janet too, but Sylvia struck me as the kind that visualises possibilities too clearly, and she was completely ignorant about sailing which wouldn't help. She wasn't our responsibility, but I still couldn't help wondering; I liked her, and she was way out of her comfort zone here.

We made good time to Siros, five hours from Ayios Nikolaos to Foinikas, at an average speed of just over six knots (calculated, failing our log, by a process of simple multiplication and division!) and entered the harbour to find, as usual, that our lead boat was there ahead of us, anchored off the beach. The small quay was fairly crowded but we managed to squeeze our way in and moor bows-to, after all why row a rubber flubber if you don't have to? They are ungainly beasts at the best of times. Since our Skipper was still safely aboard his boat, we were able to do it without interference, although obediently mindful of his instructions we did drop our kedge the now statutory ten boat lengths away. It bit at once, and since *Phaedra* was still carrying quite a bit of way, the first knot in the line caught at Steve's hands and he nearly took a dive over the transom! Two other boats from the flotilla had followed us in and managed to find room on the quay, but the late comers had to anchor off with *Eleni*. These included *Hippolyta* so we had to wait to find out how they had fared today. It had certainly been boisterous, particularly towards the end, and one or two of the faces on the quayside were looking a bit green. We helped with warps and exchanged stories with other crews and then settled down with the second bottle of sloe gin.

Paul and Emmy arrived at the quay in a dinghy, rather too late to be of any use, and Jay invited them aboard. For the second time, they refused and Emmy smiled at us briefly and none too happily.

'She'd been crying,' Marina observed, thoughtfully, as their outboard-propelled inflatable shot them back across the little bay. 'Love's young dreamboat hit a rock, do you think?'

It wasn't long after this that the rattle of an anchor chain coming up carried to us across the water, and *Eleni*'s engine thrummed into life. She didn't appear to be going anywhere, just motored round in circles, raising and lowering her anchor. We could see Emmy labouring away on the foredeck, and Paul on the helm, but of Robin there was no sign, and the two friends, we already knew, had been left behind in Sounion to catch the bus back to Athens. Steve, lying back in the corner of the cockpit with his feet on the opposite locker, raised his glass in mock salute.

'Here's to energy and industry,' he said, and Marina responded as if someone had pressed a button, 'Hark who's talking!'

The lead boat crew were together again when we finally stepped ashore. There were no tavernas on the quayside at Foinikas, but a walk through the village brought us to the beach, where there were a couple (one calling itself a restaurant) and a small shop too. Pine trees grew along this beach, the moon shone through them onto silvery sand, it all looked very romantic. In the taverna recommended by Emmy at the morning's briefing, Paul, Emmy and Robin sat, for once, with the crew from one of the flotilla yachts. Paul was smiling, turning on the charm for the punters: Emmy sat staring at her almost untouched plate. Robin spoke quietly with his neighbour, except for Emmy they all seemed to be having a good time.

We chose to sit outside on a terrace festooned with coloured lights. The wind had gone down with the sun, and although it was cooler here than we had expected it to be in June, that wasn't necessarily a disadvantage and it was still pleasant. *Hippolyta*'s crew came to join us, they were pleased with their day and prepared to go on enjoying it; they really did make the most of things from start to finish, you couldn't help liking them for it. Sylvia had been sick, she told us, almost with pride, or not sick exactly, probably just plain frightened, she wasn't sure which (which bore out what I had thought before) and now they were safely ashore, she didn't care either. She wouldn't admit to not having enjoyed herself, but quite a lot of her euphoria seemed to be due to being safely back on dry land.

'It was really wild out there,' she told us, wide-eyed. 'Some of those waves must have been twenty feet high!'

'Here, pull the other one, it's got bells on!' said Jay, grinning.

'They were,' Sylvia insisted. 'When you looked down from off the top, it was easily twenty feet, wasn't it Jan?'

'You had different waves from us, then,' Jay told her, still grinning, but Sylvia stuck to it that her waves were twenty feet high. She confided quietly to me, later on, that she hadn't always enjoyed it.

'I like lying on beaches, Sue,' she said. 'Last year, we went to Tenerife, the four of us together, we shared an apartment and had a lovely time. But the men had set their hearts on doing this and Jan didn't care either way, she's lucky. She's happy whatever we do. Only, it's not really my thing, if you see what I mean. Lying on the beach and hitting the shops, and a comfortable bed to sleep in at night, that's me. Ken and Bill know how to sail, of course, but I couldn't help thinking this afternoon... what if it had blown up even more? They don't have the experience that Steve and Jay have. Or you and Marina, either.'

Poor Sylvia. I find it very difficult, as I suppose everyone does, to understand people who don't like what I love, but I do accept that they exist and have a point of view too, and I could see that the Cyclades were going to be educational for her, to put it charitably. But I didn't say so.

'You'll be fine,' I encouraged her. 'There's the lead boat to look after you, and we'll be around too. You can always talk to Marina and me if it gets on top of you.'

'I hadn't the heart to tell Bill how much I hated the idea,' said Sylvia.

Marina now broke in to ask if anyone knew what the lead boat had been up to this evening. 'Going round and round in circles like a hamster on a wheel,' she said. 'We thought at first they must have dragged their anchor, which would have served them right, but they went on and on, and round and round.'

Janet exchanged a glance with Sylvia.

'Well, we don't know for sure, because we hadn't got here then, but according to the Canadians, Emmy made a bit of a mess getting the anchor ever when they came in, and so Paul made her do it again, over and over, until she had it right.'

Marina thought this must have been a bit humiliating for Emmy, and said so. 'After all, nobody gets it right every time, even Steve nearly went over the side with the kedge when we tied up here! No wonder she was upset, poor girl.'

'Silly twat,' Steve muttered, not too loudly.

Through the door of the taverna, I could see the lead boat crew as the centre of an admiring crowd. Emmy was smiling again now, tilting back her head to say something to Richard, or was it Charles? Sylvia looked directly at Steve.

'Don't you like Paul?' she asked.

'He's all right.' Steve would still not be drawn into openly passing judgement. 'A bit pleased with himself.'

'Do you?' Marina asked, but Sylvia wouldn't commit herself either. To a certain extent, our Skipper was still surrounded by the natural respect due to his position, the real man hidden from view by the charisma that went with the job. People wanted to be able to defer to his judgement and trust him, and to find him likeable, and so they did. It was all part of the flotilla thing.

Emmy came out onto the terrace, hesitated, and then came over to us. She smiled. 'Is everything all right, did you have a good sail today?'

Jay pulled out a chair, inviting her to sit with us. 'Have that drink you didn't have time for earlier,' he said. This time she accepted, taking the offered chair and accepting a glass of wine, but she was still not really herself, there was a tautness about her. I thought that she was still on the verge of tears, although she forced a smile and made herself talk easily.

It was Jay who broached the dam, quite unintentionally, when our own experience of the day had been thoroughly discussed. 'How about you? Did you motor all the way or did you manage to have a good sail yourselves? Did you enjoy yourselves too?'

Emmy looked down into her half-empty glass. 'No,' she said precisely.

Steve floundered into the breach with all the finesse of an inebriated hippopotamus. He said, 'No, you didn't motor all the way; no, you didn't sail, or no, you didn't enjoy yourselves?' He paused then, belatedly remembering what we had been told, and ended lamely, 'We saw you had a bit of trouble anchoring.'

Marina tried to kick him under the table and caught my ankle instead. I winced. Emmy began to cry.

She didn't do it noisily, which would have been less unnerving, but simply sat there with the tears sliding silently down her nose. The men looked alarmed and Sylvia offered her a tissue.

'Come on, mop up,' she advised. 'It can't be as bad as all that.'

Emmy spoke on a low, hopeless wail. 'Nothing's gone right this year, nothing!'

And then, of course, it all came out as if the cork had popped out of a bottle. How she and Paul had sailed together on the Saronic gulf flotilla last year and everything had gone really well, but this year there had been nothing but trouble. She didn't seem to want to specify exactly what the trouble had been, whether personal or just general trouble, but two engineers who had either walked out or refused to sail with Paul came into it somewhere, and the last Cyclades flotilla was mentioned too, when, as on this one, there had been some discontent, but at least, she sobbed unguardedly, those people had been experienced sailors, not like this awful muddle! Anchoring was mentioned, and a big row, but by this time she was almost incoherent. She ended on a wail. '… and he hasn't spoken to me all evening.' She scrubbed at her eyes with Sylvia's tissue and began to pull herself together. 'I'm sorry, I shouldn't have unloaded all that onto you, you're meant to be enjoying a lovely holiday. I'm sorry.'

'Don't worry about it,' advised Janet. 'Are you two engaged, or what?'

Emmy didn't answer directly. 'We'd talked about going to the States together when the season is over.'

'And now?'

'I don't know.' She sniffed juicily. It made her seem heartbreakingly young. Poor Emmy.

Steve refilled her glass and she cheered up a bit and began to talk of other things. After a while Robin came over and took her away to deal with somebody's query about showers. When they had gone, we exchanged glances. The picture of Paul refusing even to speak to the poor girl wasn't a pretty one, but in all fairness, we only had her side of the story.

'This,' said Steve, speaking for us all, 'is a very strange carry-on indeed.'

'*Carry on Sailing*,' Bill suggested.

'A lover's tiff can happen anywhere,' argued Janet, but Jay said that it shouldn't happen between two people responsible for the safety of other people, and when Janet had thought it out, she had to agree that made sense.

There was one thing you could say in favour of this flotilla, I reflected over my wine, it did obliterate personal problems to a very large degree. With so many different things to worry over, I was getting spoilt for choice.

That was the moment that I realised that cynicism helped.

In the second that followed the realisation, panic swirled into my mind in a great wave. If I stopped caring, or pretended to stop caring, if I stepped back and took the cynical view of a mere onlooker, then everything would be lost. Emptiness would roll in to fill the space left by the loss of everything that gave meaning to my entire life. No husband, no marriage, no pride, nothing. Just a great aching space where all these things had been, and a home that would be no longer a home, for my two girls were already preparing to fly the nest in the normal order of things. I would be left with my share of the bricks and mortar, and a little money of my own that would keep me from being penniless, and I supposed I could get an unskilled job somewhere, if at my age I could find somebody who wanted me.

The unbidden thought followed on the panic, that I would survive. Better, quite possibly, than Jay would, although he didn't really want me any more.

But this, I could neither admit nor accept. He had to want me, he could not, after all these years, just put me aside for a cheap little nympho like Dawn. *He couldn't!*

Or perhaps he thought that he could, but so help me, I would fight first!

Wonderful stuff, wine.

And cynicism too, if you like.

'I'm pissed,' I remarked, setting down my empty glass.

'It's what holidays are for,' said Bill, and refilled it.

And somewhere out there on the wine-dark Aegean Sea, *Anatolikos* went about her business.

Day Eight: Monday, 12ᵗʰ June

The next morning I had a hangover, not surprisingly, and the weather was different. The sky was dull, with a thin skim of high haze, and for the first time (apart from the brief storm in Poros, that is) there were no distinct shadows. The forecast was supposed to be much like that of the previous day, with the possibility of rain later, but when we went on deck first thing there was no sign of yesterday's fresh breeze.

Today, we were free sailing, and the briefing was to be earlier than usual, for the lead boat wanted to get across to Mykonos: apparently early was OK, so long as it was for their convenience. Tomorrow we would all meet again on Tinos, but today was our own to do what we wanted. If we wanted to go to Mykonos too, sailing directions would be given and instructions on mooring up in the harbour, or there were bays where we could anchor off in safety, there was Delos to visit by ferry – ruins, for those that liked them. Delos itself is now a prohibited anchorage for yachts, but there were good anchorages quite near. Rhinia, for instance. Rhinia had its part to play in my life, had I but realised it.

Most of us, of course, opted for Mykonos, one of the showplaces of the Aegean, and the playground of the rich and famous. Some may have been influenced by the fact that our lead boat would be there, but it was the most tempting of the options on offer without that. We ourselves set sail as soon as the briefing was over, breakfast being eaten on the way.

The water was pearl-coloured as we motored away from Foinikas, and the air felt warm enough but somehow clammy. There were tattered strips of cloud caught on the highest mountains, and Steve looked at them thoughtfully.

'When we sailed in the Ionian, clouds like that were a bad weather sign,' he remarked. 'See those ragged streaks on the mountains when you're over on that side, and you can bet your boots there's going to be one hell of a blow later on.'

'I wonder if it means the same on this side?' Jay speculated idly, but Paul had said nothing about it, if so. Even the VHF, usually alive with unnecessary chatter and pointless instructions, remained silent apart from the odd burst of excited Greek. We discussed it for a minute or two. *Eleni* was the only boat that carried an ordinary radio, and Paul took the weather information from the early shipping forecast, broadcast in English at six o'clock, passing its relevant points on to us at the briefing later. Much as we failed to admire Paul as he might have wished, we didn't imagine that he would sleep through it, and take his weather reports from less informed sources. That would be going too far down the slippery slope of total irresponsibility even for him, surely, and anyway, it was June. The meltemi shouldn't blow for a month yet.

There wasn't enough wind to make it worth hoisting sail, and we chugged across the glassy sea under engine. Except for Steve, who was still on the fidget, we felt relaxed and at ease in the warm, still air. Steve was taking the opportunity to put a new whipping on the end of the main halyard.

'It's like sharing a boat with a hyperactive gerbil,' I remarked lazily, and Steve gave a burst of appreciative laughter.

'The old girl can still do with a bit of TLC,' he excused himself, and it was true, she was a perfect minefield of broken, missing or faulty bits and pieces.

'I wonder who is ultimately responsible for off-season maintenance?' Jay speculated aloud, but we were all feeling too laid back to recognise that he had just asked the million-pound question. We sat around making jokes and teasing Steve – we would have been better employed in studying the Pilot Book!

Hippolyta had left Foinikas soon after us and was hauling up behind us with her engine going full bore. We gave *Phaedra* a few more revs to shift her along a bit, the wind might fill in later, and when – or if – it did, we would make sail. We couldn't be bothered right at this minute.

Mykonos harbour is remarkable, among other things, for a very unusual quay; I don't want to bore you, but in view of what happened later I need to describe this in detail. Instead of running straight along in the normal way, it is a series of square indentations filled with rocks, alternating with square projections to which one, or at most two, yachts may tie up. It is oriented north-west/south-east, and approached from the south-west. On entering the harbour, Jay headed for the southernmost pier, but at the last moment he

125

saw the angle of the anchor warp from the next boat along and changed his mind, perhaps in response to a tap on the shoulder from a watchful guardian angel, who knows? We took the next pier, and *Hippolyta* slid alongside to raft up next to us, bows just clear of the lumpy rocks. They would have to get ashore via *Phaedra*, but we didn't mind that and if the whole flotilla came in we would need all the space we could steal. In continued obedience to standing orders, both our anchors were laid well out, although Mykonos has a smallish harbour compared to some, and enough boats could make a real cat's cradle of it as Steve didn't fail to point out, but this compliance didn't extend to making fast to the rings set in the quayside with a bowline, which would pull tight under stress and be difficult at best, impossible at worst, to undo in a hurry. Steve would be scrupulously fair over Paul's instructions but only up to the point where he considered that, given his wider experience of the sailing area, they might be justified.

'Silly nonsense,' I said, busy with round turns and half hitches. 'Someone should give him the *Ashley Book of Knots* for his birthday present.'

'Or lessons in elementary seamanship,' added Steve, less kindly. He and Ken began fastening springs from boat to boat to prevent us from surging together in any wash from passers-by. Jay meanwhile rigged the awning over the cockpit, for by this time, although the sun was still hazy, the sky had cleared and it had become very hot. Sylvia said there was some retsina in their cool box (icy cold is the only way to drink it), she and Janet, bikini-clad, climbed across to *Phaedra* with the bottle. Steve and Jay had fallen into conversation with some Germans on the quay, Ken and Bill had gone below to catch up on some sleep, and it was just the four of us who sat under the awning, ice-cold drinks in hand, looking out at bright water and the comings and goings in the harbour. Some fairly big ships, ferries mainly, came in and out, and nine of our own boats and the lead boat had come in by this time to moor up for the night. Three of ours, the two men on the boat moored to starboard of us told us, had gone to Rhinia to anchor off in a quiet bay there, including *Aithra*, who, with her uncertain engine, preferred to keep out of crowded harbours where possible. Even without them, by five o'clock there was no room for another boat on the crowded quayside; with ourselves and others we were rafted tight from end to end. Mykonos is a popular destination.

By this time the temperature had begun to fall at last, and since Steve and Jay had come back, we said a temporary goodbye to our friends and went ashore to explore this famous resort. It was quite a leap to get there, for the rocks lay along the bases of the piers too, and it wasn't possible to lie close enough to use the gangplank as we had in Hydra: we had to haul in on the mooring ropes as tightly as we could and jump for it one at a time. We walked along the road towards the main town, past a beach on which brown bodies lay supine under coloured beach umbrellas. In the middle distance, beyond the south quay, a row of Greek windmills stood out against the sky, glittering like salt in the clear light and looking, to be honest, a bit like salt pots too. And the town turned out to be not simply pretty, but every dream of the Mediterranean come true at once.

Along the harbourside, a wide area has tavernas and simple gift shops, sandwiched between mouth-watering goldsmiths' shops and others selling beautiful china and clothes, and behind this a maze of narrow little streets, just wide enough for two to walk abreast, had more shops, surprising vistas of water or mountains, incredibly beautiful flowering trees, hanging balconies, patient donkeys with panniers filled with vegetables and flowers... snow-white buildings, barrel-roofed out here as a protection against earthquakes and looking as if they were made of icing sugar, picked out in ultramarine... unexpected squares, tree-shaded, set out with chairs and tables for eating and drinking... Shutters clicked as we wandered around with our cameras, examining the wares for sale and absorbing the self-conscious charm of the place – for Mykonos is a bit self-conscious, proud of itself – they even whitewash around the edges of the paving stones! Jay posed elegantly outside a picturesque bar, and two passing Americans grinned as they went by.

'I wouldn't do that just there,' one of them said. 'It might attract attentions!' He used the plural deliberately, for that, of course, is another side to Mykonos; it reputedly has one of the highest gay populations in the Mediterranean.

Marina insisted on going into one of the goldsmith's shops to enquire the price of a particularly delectable bracelet, but it turned out to be solid gold and studded with real diamonds and emeralds, and cost about 300,000 drachmas. On the counter in the same shop was a woven basket of cheap silver rings for the holiday trade. Mykonos in cameo, the super-rich and exotic rubbing shoulders with the shoddy and commercial.

The famous Mykonos pelicans, that appear on many of the postcards here, posed for us obligingly alongside a caique conveniently unloading fish. It was almost too much to believe! And there were cats too, lots of them, hanging around hoping for someone like Steve to come along.

We bought a few small souvenirs, and as we carried them back to the boat we ran into Paul and Emmy, apparently communicating again, linked arm in arm and seeing the sights together on what was, for them, another day off. They stopped to speak to us, however.

'I'm glad we ran into you,' said Paul. 'The Port Police were down on the quay looking for everyone, they want to see all our ship's papers at half-past five.'

It was by then nearly seven o'clock, and we immediately felt like criminals. Paul only laughed.

'Don't worry about it. I haven't shown mine yet, either. Whoever goes, don't forget the crew's passports.' They wandered on casually into the town, and Steve, who takes being a skipper seriously on his own boat, even on a pleasure cruise with friends, remarked that our leader set a wonderful example of responsibility. After Sounion, Steve was on occasion openly rattled about Paul, taking on himself the worries about the weaker links in our flotilla chain that didn't seem to bother Paul at all. But that is another side of Steve, and one of the reasons, I suppose, why he is always so uptight for so long at the start of a holiday.

We had marked down a taverna by the water at the back of the town for dinner that night, where we had seen fish displayed in the cold tray outside; squid and mullet and swordfish, expensive here, but cooked over a charcoal grill too tempting to ignore. However as we went ashore, after Jay had been to report to the Port Police with all the necessary papers as instructed, we ran into Carol, Charles, Richard and the crew of *Hippolyta*, and one or two others whose names I never got to know properly, and we all ended up going into the town together.

As we walked in a straggle through the narrow streets, I found myself beside Sylvia, who told me that discontent was beginning to swell in the ranks. I wasn't entirely surprised.

'Under the circumstances, I suppose that was inevitable,' I said. She agreed.

'Several people are finding the long hours sailing too hard,' she said. 'They hadn't bargained for them – they thought it was going to be shorter trips and easier sailing.'

'That's partly Paul's fault – the easier sailing, I mean,' I pointed out. 'If he'd only have his briefing at a reasonable hour, people could get away in the morning when the winds are lighter – they fill in at midday out here.'

'That's what Bill says, but it isn't only that.' Sylvia sighed. 'If we could get away earlier, we'd arrive at places earlier too, and be able to explore properly, or find somewhere to go swimming. But as things are, we're waiting around half the morning, sailing all day, and only arrive in time for dinner, unless it's a very short trip.'

I agreed that this was disappointing, for we had grumbled about it ourselves, as you know.

'The last Cyclades cruise, they had complaints too.'

'Goodness, surely they didn't have a mix-up on that one, too!' I exclaimed.

'No, but they were unhappy with the distances, just as we are.'

This seemed strange to me – we had chosen this cruise *because* of the longer distances and stronger winds, which offered excellent sailing as well as interesting places to visit, but an awful lot of people, it now appeared, had chosen it simply because the Cyclades sounded romantic, and not bothered to mark off distances on the chart. On the other hand, the brochure hadn't stated categorically that the cruise was only suitable for experienced sailors, and possibly it could be argued that it should have. Marina, who had come up alongside and overheard Sylvia's last remark, said half-apologetically that we were having a great time, but it appeared that we were in the minority. I began to feel slightly embarrassed.

'Shut up about it,' I muttered in Marina's ear, as we walked. 'They'll think we're showing off.'

'We can't help it if they can't read a chart.'

'No, but we don't have to rub it in.'

She shut up then, but we were both left feeling a bit awkward.

Fortunately, Sylvia had gone on to a different track and was eulogising over the shops, which was an altogether easier subject.

The taverna that we now visited was crowded, and in order to sit all together we had to be inside. This was even an advantage in one way, for a tiresome little wind had sprung up as the sun went down and was eddying gustily around the square, picking up dust and blowing it around. It wasn't a proper taverna – more a cross between a taverna and a French restaurant – the food was good, but not strictly Greek, which suited those who spend their holidays abroad hunting the streets for fish and chips and burgers, but there was no squid or moussaka or meatballs in egg and lemon sauce to be had, none of the lovely barbecued fish to which we had been looking forward. On the other hand, it was a step forward for the flotilla to be at last beginning to get together, as advertised, albeit not everyone, and under our own steam. The lead boat crew had so far made no attempt to bring this about since their punch party the evening we arrived in Aegina. They were nowhere to be seen tonight, either, but since we were free sailing this of course was their privilege.

It was an excellent evening, a bit of an impromptu party, and we didn't leave the taverna until shortly before midnight. By that time, the wind had got up a lot. It was funnelling along the narrow streets in heavy gusts, whipping up twirling dust-devils to dance in the lamplight, and when we got back to the open quayside it was much stronger still. A heavy surge had started to come in through the harbour mouth, and the yachts were swirling about at their moorings, tugging at warps and dipping restlessly up and down: it was going to be difficult getting back aboard, particularly for the less athletic among us. We all stood in a group and looked up and down the quay, and some of us began to be worried. It didn't look too good. The wind howled like a banshee in the rigging above our heads.

'What do you think?' asked Richard. 'Ought one of us to walk back into town and see if we can find the Skipper? See what he has to say, after all, he's been here before.'

Jay, Steve and Charles nodded their agreement. Free sailing we might be, but Paul was the one ultimately responsible to the Company for the safety of us all, and in those sheltered streets he wouldn't realise, just as we hadn't, quite how bad conditions were becoming. Richard strode off, and the rest of us waited in an uneasy little group.

The holiday mood of the meal had evaporated, none of us had very much to say. One or two of the other crews came back onto the quay, saw our group, and drifted over to join us. I think we were all relieved when we saw Richard coming back.

'Did you find them?' called Jay, walking to meet him. 'What did Paul have to say?'

Richard waited until he was back with the rest of us before he answered.

'They're only just up in the town there,' he said. 'I found them quite easily, and I told Paul what was happening down here.'

'And?' asked Steve, when Richard hesitated. Richard pulled an expressive face.

'You aren't going to believe this. He laughed. I don't think he really believed me.'

'Is that *all*?'

'No. He said, "You're free sailing, it's nothing to do with me."' Richard shook his head. 'He doesn't intend to give us any advice even, let alone help.'

We stood around talking uneasily for a while longer, but without positive leadership from our Skipper it proved difficult to get anything decided. Jay and Steve did manage to get a search organised of our boats for spare warps, and with help from Ken and Bill fastened extra springs to hold the boats as far apart as possible, but that was about as far as anyone else was prepared to go.

'We ought to keep an anchor watch,' Steve said, but Paul's laissez faire attitude had rubbed off on some of us, and among the men, only Jay, Ken and Bill agreed with him. The four of them arranged a rota, two hours each through the night. Bill was on first watch and Steve elected to stay up and keep him company, and that settled, and since there was nothing else to be done, the rest of us turned in for the night.

It wasn't so quiet on board tonight. The surge, leap and twist of *Phaedra*'s hull was uncomfortable and we only slept fitfully. I daresay we weren't the only ones.

Day Nine: Tuesday, 13ᵗʰ June

At two in the morning, those of us on *Phaedra* who had at last managed to get to sleep were woken again by an almighty crash! I struggled out of a shallow doze to find that the boat was quivering from stem to stern, and that outside, the elements appeared to have run amok. The wind screamed like a wild thing in the night, and everything on deck was banging around, the boat leapt against her ropes as if she was trying to escape and flee from the chaos. Steve ran for the deck before he was fairly awake, dragging on jeans over pyjamas as he ran, but Jay must have been already out there for the space beside me was empty. Marina and I tumbled out into the main cabin together, not knowing what had happened, alarmed, confused, and only half-awake.

It was a struggle to find clothes on the jerking, bucking boat. Panties were the worst, fumbling at speed, both legs seemed determined to go through one hole, but in a little over two minutes I was racing up the companionway in Marina's wake, still with no very clear idea as to what had happened – or was happening, even – just the instinctive knowledge that something was very wrong indeed. As I reached the deck there was another of those terrible crashes, that sent me staggering as *Phaedra* was flung forward by the heavy surge, nudged ominously onto the rocks. Men were running up and down the quay: Jay was there, and Richard and Charles, Steve of course and Bill, all hurrying to haul the yachts back on their anchors, well clear of the piers and the treacherous rocks. Jumping ashore was a nightmare as *Phaedra* pitched and dipped like a mad thing.

It was even worse than it looked at first glance once we had time to look properly, for it was easy to see, now that we were on the quay, that the mooring ropes, made fast to rings set in the top of the quay, sawed continuously on the angular concrete edges of the piers, taut as violin strings or abruptly slackened and viciously jerking. Barely organised panic reigned in a darkness that was barely lit by the street lamps on the road above. Steve's voice could be heard above the wind, shouting instructions to those in a fit state to act on them. I am ashamed to say that it was mainly the very few women who had come ashore that were panicking, but in their defence, on the whole, they were the least experienced. Marina and I found a niche for ourselves, calming them down.

'What's happening, what's gone wrong?' somebody moaned.

'Where's Paul?' cried another.

Where, indeed?

'It'll be OK,' soothed Marina. 'The men will have it all under control in a minute, it's only the sea coming in through the entrance and breaking straight onto the quay. It'll be fine.'

I touched her arm. 'Don't speak too soon,' I said, under my breath. Marina looked where I was looking.

'Oh God,' she said, 'What a bloody awful night!' We began to run.

A couple of berths down from *Phaedra*, the last yacht in line had dragged her anchor – not one of ours I'm pleased to say, but she had springs attached to *Aphrodite*, who was. *Aphrodite* was occupying the berth that we had nearly taken ourselves, in what seemed now like another world than this cold, roaring darkness, and in her turn had springs across to *Ariadne*, in the berth between us, which Jay was even now swiftly undoing, for in the confusion that reigned on the quay, the stranger yacht had started her engine, hauled up her fouled anchor and *Aphrodite*'s together, cast off her bow lines and pulled out, dragging *Aphrodite* with her by the forgotten springs that had held them apart, but were now holding them inexorably together Tom and Sally, a young couple reputed to be on their honeymoon, fought to free themselves as they were forcibly uprooted from safety, but it was a losing battle. *Aphrodite*, with a full gale bearing the entire weight of the yachts on the quay down upon her, had nothing on her side but the slim chance of getting her engine started and getting away before she was pushed onto the rocks, and it was a chance that realistically had no hope of coming off. The trailing warps, belatedly thrown into the water just as they might have been of some use by the thoughtless skipper of the escaping yacht, wound themselves around *Aphrodite*'s propeller, and helpless at the mercy of the wind and no longer attached to anything, she ran onto the rocks beyond the quay. The other yacht made her way to a safer upwind berth without a backward glance for the trail of disaster that she had left behind her. It was, I believe, the worst display of bad seamanship that I had ever seen and remains so to this day.

Very few ordinary yachtsmen, thank God, ever witness a shipwreck, and it had never even entered my head that one could happen within hailing distance of the shore, in harbour, with a crowd of people standing by watching. Marina and I stood together on the quayside and, in utter disbelief, saw *Aphrodite* wallowing onto the rocks. Even over the storm we could hear her hull grinding on the sharp black teeth. We yelled for help, and people came running to join us, but all any of us could do was to stand there, sick and helpless. Steve was shouting something, uselessly, against the gale, his anger was a tangible element.

Someone ran for the Skipper.

Eleni was upwind of the rest of us, and the lead boat crew were all still soundly sleeping, oblivious to the emergency. At that end of the quay, of course, well upwind and in the lee of sheltering buildings, they were safer than any of us, as probably they had known they would be. While we waited for Paul and Robin to arrive, Steve tried to get a warp across but the wind kept catching it and whirling it away. We could see Sally's scared white face as she clung to the rolled jib, clutching uselessly for the flying end. She was so close that we could see the wetness of tears glittering on her cheeks in the lamplight.

'Please help us,' she pleaded. 'Do something, please – help us!' Her voice was a piteous piping between the roaring gusts. So close... but not close enough, there was nothing that could safely be done. Perhaps with a dinghy and an outboard, as the lead boat had, there might be a chance. Jay was trying to reassure them, yelling at the top of his voice to be heard.

'Hang on, Paul and Robin are on their way –'

Tom hung over the transom, dangerously far out, engaged in the futile task of trying to disentangle the warps from the propeller. He was so far over that he could easily fall if the boat lurched the wrong way, and Steve bawled at him to get back inboard.

Paul, Robin and Emmy came running. Emmy clutched Marina's arm, near to tears herself.

'I hate boats!' she cried, on an angry sob.

By this time, *Ariadne* was in trouble too, grinding her rudder on the rocks as the swell surged in, for she had come in stern-to, unlike most of us, because the water shallowed at this end of the quay.

Phaedra came next in line, but I tried not to think about that. The quay was alive with activity; people shouting, running about, fetching more warps, to no particular end, beyond seeming to be doing something – anything – to help. Marina, Emmy and I stood back and watched, for there was nothing we could usefully contribute. It was a time for brute strength rather than feminine guile, but we couldn't leave, held where we were by the horrible possibilities, and the chance that in the end there might be something we could do after all. Sally had begun to scream, open-mouthed. Paul yelled at her to shut up and Tom yelled back, angrily.

Chaos!

Steve cannoned into us in the dark, swearing.

'Why doesn't that bloody fool go and get his bloody outboard dinghy?'

'It's deflated,' said Emmy, in a small voice, but Steve had already gone. She began to sob openly.

'Hold on,' said Marina. 'The Mounties are on their way.'

A huge RIB with a powerful outboard and three men on board roared out of the darkness beyond the quay, searchlight blazing, and edged in on *Aphrodite*'s quarter. In spite of the lurching of the boats, we saw them heave one of their number unceremoniously aboard. Steve, by this time, was aboard *Ariadne* and Marina gripped my hand as he, too, was bundled hastily across via the RIB.

'Oh God... please be careful... Steve...'

I glanced at her and saw that her eyes were tight shut.

'It's all right, he's on board. They've taken a warp across.'

The powerful outboard stopped idling and grumbling and burst into its deep-throated roar again. Slowly, painfully slowly, *Aphrodite* was drawn off the rocks and slowly, slowly towed along behind the line of moored yachts to the empty ferry berth upwind of us. Paul, Robin and one or two of the other men hauled *Ariadne* back into her position by sheer brute force.

'It looks as if the fun is over,' I said, and touched Emmy's shoulder briefly. 'Come on, let's go and see the damage. There might be something we can do to help now.'

By the time we reached the ferry berth, Tom and Sally were being helped ashore. They were considerably shaken and Sally was quietly weeping.

'I'm never going on a boat again, never!' she wept, into Tom's shoulder. He put his arms around her protectively.

'It's all right, we're OK now,' he said, to the gathered crowd.

'Sally should be ashore for the night after an experience like that,' Jay said, to Emmy. She looked at him helplessly.

'But what could we do with them? Where would they sleep?'

Behind us, the town of Mykonos was still swinging away into the small hours, oblivious to near tragedy and high drama. Parties of revellers staggered laughing along the gale-swept quay, waving to us cheerfully as they went. Their laughter grated uncomfortably on the raw edges of a disaster so narrowly averted. There had been plenty of rooms to rent, I had noticed, in the far-from-sleeping town, at around 5000 drax a head – which is not a lot. I mentioned this.

The suggestion had a stiffening effect on Sally. She pulled herself together with a visible effort.

'I'm all right really. I want to sleep aboard.'

'You're safe enough in the ferry berth for tonight,' somebody said. An assured voice that knew what it was talking about, distancing itself from the general excitement. My stomach lurched and I peered at the speaker in the turbulent darkness, and then involuntarily across the harbour to the south mole. Clearly spotlit under the street lamps I could see the fat blue shape of a big motor vessel, that had certainly not been there when we went to bed. Beside me, a swift impression of a young face, dark hair, and taut, whiplash strength. Oliviero – *Oliviero*!

Charles was urging Emmy to take Sally, at least, on board the lead boat for the night, and Emmy hesitated, her indecision obvious. Sally settled the question for herself. 'I want to stay with Tom,' she cried shrilly, and threw herself back into his arms. He held her tightly and stared at us over her head, defensive and challenging.

'We'll be all right, but thanks.'

'Leave them alone,' advised Oliviero. 'The fun's over, no need to make a three act drama out of it.' He turned away, speaking to me as he went, although in that wild darkness I don't think he recognised me. 'A hot drink, well-laced with something, might help, don't you think?' I found myself nodding in agreement. It was the first really sensible suggestion anyone had made for some time.

He walked off along the quay towards the town. The big RIB I realised, had already gone, he must have been the one who was aboard *Aphrodite*.

136

'Who was that?' Jay asked, and I told him I thought it must have been someone off the boat on the south mole. Paul, who was close by, spoke with an edge to his voice.

'One of those bloody divers, was he? Bloody sauce!'

It was on the tip of my tongue to tell him that nothing had been said, or done, that night that he shouldn't have said or done for himself, but instinct luckily prevented me. Steve took my arm and pulled me away from trouble.

'Leave it, Sue. There were a few words while we made fast here.'

'What about?' I asked, with interest, for the field of possibilities was alarmingly wide. Steve laughed, without humour.

'It went along the lines of pig-ignorant fools who lead people into danger, just for a start,' he said. 'It appears that this gale was forecast.'

'But –' I stopped. Paul had said nothing about it. Was that so unexpected, by this time? Probably he hadn't even known, hadn't bothered to listen to the early forecast: somehow that was slightly worse than simply omitting to tell us, I wasn't sure why. I remembered the cloud tendrils on the mountain tops and what Steve himself had said, but I made no comment. It seemed best.

Ken came over to us, huddled into his anorak and looking weary and windswept.

'That German chap on the boat by ours is saying that if the wind goes round just a point or two, we'll all have to get out, the harbour won't be safe. He's sitting on deck in his oilies and life jacket, just waiting.' And with his masthead anemometer registering force 9, gusting 10, it transpired. But there's always one, I told myself uneasily. Show them trouble, and they'll predict crisis.

I can't answer for everyone else, but my heart gave a bump of alarm. To go out into strange waters in a panic, at night, and in this gale? And so many of us, and some of us so very inexperienced too. But looking at the situation objectively, if it had to be done, we would all have to do it. We could already see the potential danger, had even had it graphically demonstrated, and if we stayed in worsening conditions we could lose the whole flotilla.

Bill and Sylvia, incredibly, had slept through everything so far, and Ken went off to wake them up and tell them the glad tidings. *Phaedra*'s crew just stared at each other, too tired now to think constructively.

137

'Well,' Jay shrugged fatalistically. 'There's nothing we can do about it, except keep watch. You two –' he meant Marina and me – 'might as well get some rest while you can.' There was obvious sense in this. We made the dangerous leap back on board, worse than ever now that the boat lay further from the quay and was surging up and down so much, and went below. We had all decided already that if necessary we would abandon ship – the yachts were not our own, and were presumably well insured, and none of us felt like risking our own lives unless to save someone else's. Sail out – yes, if we had to, and if we could; face shipwreck in harbour, definitely not. Marina and I packed all our gear and put the bags in the forepeak ready to sling ashore, and then we went back to our berths, fully dressed, and lay down, shoes and all. But not to sleep. In spite of the shortened kedge warp, *Phaedra* was still plunging at the pier with a bone-shaking crash at intervals, and our adrenalin levels refused to fall.

Outside in the roaring darkness and the raging gale, the men patrolled the quay. The lead boat crew had, unbelievably, gone back to *Eleni*, presumably to sleep if they could, but by this time Steve had taken charge, and nobody needed Paul. Vigilance was necessary, indeed, essential. Every remaining spare warp – there were pathetically few – had now been collected up for use in an emergency. Janet and Sylvia, less used to boats than Marina and me, and therefore even more frightened, abandoned ship and went to sit out the night in a twenty-four hour bar and disco at the far end of the quay. It was to be a long, long night.

Morning came at last and the gale was still blowing, picking up clouds of the white dust from the quayside to add the final touch of desolation to a most un-summer holiday-like scene. We were still there, that was about all you could say, and another problem had arisen overnight. Jay and Steve had spent most of their time splicing ropes rubbed into halves on the hard edge of the quay, and apart from Marina and me, it now turned out that nobody else knew how to. Our feeble female fingers weren't strong enough to cope with the wet, tautly stretched ropes we would have to work with, and – yes, you've guessed it! – not one of our boats carried a marline spike, not even the lead boat. Splicing must be becoming a lost art, along with cave painting and spearing mastodons, judging by this pitiful showing! We were a bit startled by this discovery, and found it hard to believe. Steve and Jay found it depressing, they were already sick of the job.

Quite early in the day, Paul called a briefing. For once there were no dissenters and the flotilla assembled almost down to the last glum, anxious, punter, and sat around wondering what was going to happen next in this chapter of accidents and mismanagement. We were indoors – it was far too wild to sit outside – huddled over cups of coffee and thick slabs of peasant bread and jam.

'We'll make a run for it,' Paul announced. 'Head back for Siros, and sit out the gale there. Foinikas is a safe harbour in a north-easterly. If we leave quickly, we should make it in plenty of time.

'Plenty of time for what?' someone asked suspiciously, and another voice said, in patent horror, 'You mean, it's going to blow *still harder?*'

'Not until around midday,' sad Paul. 'We've time, if we don't waste any. Is everybody happy with that?'

What a question! There was a silence that seemed to grow and spread like fog. Nobody spoke, each of us waiting for somebody else to point out that charter boats aren't supposed to sail in anything over force 6 in Greek waters. Finally, Jay took the initiative, asking tentatively, 'Do the Port Police agree with that?'

'Oh, I haven't asked them,' said Paul, unbelievably.

Beside me, I felt Sylvia stir nervously. For her, it must have been a choice between the devil and the deep blue sea – the gale threatening to increase on the one hand, the Port Police gunning for us on the other. She wasn't a fool – that was most of her trouble, of course – anybody could see with half an eye that we were caught between a rock and a hard place, trapped in a bad harbour in a howling gale. But the fact remained that far from being a force 6, it was blowing force 8 with gusts up to force 9 this morning, and rising, and the Port Police had all our names from the night before – had probably asked for them, now we came to think about it, because of the gale forecast for the area. If we defied the Port Police, it wouldn't only be Panther Sailing who would find themselves blacklisted, but each one of us should we ever wish to sail in Greek waters again.

Typically, it was Steve who summed up the situation. We were all prepared to make a dash for it, he said, but not without permission, and a murmur of agreement ran around the room. Paul got to his feet.

'Right, I'll go and see them,' he said. 'Meet here again in half an hour.'

Nobody left. We all sat around uneasily, not talking much, just waiting. And of course the result was a foregone conclusion, we weren't allowed to sail. We were stuck in Mykonos until the gale abated.

We all began to drift back to the quay, uncertain what to do now, and Paul and Robin decreed that the morning be spent re-tying warps, checking anchors, fixing springs and making everything as safe as possible, most of which had already been done the previous evening while they took their ease in the town. Paul didn't know how to splice either, and nor did Robin. It began to look as if the term *a long splice* was going to take on a whole new meaning for Jay and Steve.

There was nothing for me to do, and almost of themselves, my feet took me strolling through the town, drawn like a magnet towards the south mole, with Marina yawning at my side. *Anatolikos* was still moored up there, but she looked as if she was preparing for sea, with men busy on deck coiling down warps and checking the lashings of her gear. Oliviero saw us, and climbed the short ladder from her deck to speak to us.

'Everything all right after last night's shenanigans?'

'Except that we're stuck here,' said Marina, making a face. He gave a not unsympathetic nod.

'You would be. What I'd like to know is what that Skipper of yours thought he was doing having you here in the first place. Everyone knows Mykonos isn't a good place to ride out a northerly. The Pilot Book even warns you about it.'

'He didn't realise it was coming,' I offered.

'Then he's an even bigger klutz than he looks. It's part of a well-established low pressure system that's been boiling up over Turkey all the week. It's all over Europe by now, I don't see how he could have missed it. Better make the best of it, you'll be here for a while yet.'

'What do you call "a while"?' Marina asked, with suspicion.

'Several days, anyway.'

'Thanks a bunch!'

He laughed at that. 'Oh, Mykonos isn't a bad place. You can

spend all your money and get drunk every night. If you need some advice, take a bus.'

Somebody called him then from the boat, and he said goodbye and swung back down the ladder, Marina and me already forgotten.

'Was that a new way of saying "on your bike?",' Marina wondered, speculatively.

'I wonder what he would have called Paul if he had been a fly on the wall this morning,' I said.

'I don't think we would have liked to hear. Paul certainly wouldn't.'

As we strolled back towards the town, I was aware of the thumping of my heart and a shortness of breath I hadn't experienced since I was a girl, that half-painful, half-delightful twisting in the gut that rightly belongs to first love... whatever was the matter with me? Almost as if she read my thoughts, Marina suddenly said, 'You and Jay seem to be settling down a bit.'

'Well, it's been easy, being on holiday and everything. And he's stopped jumping on me every time I open my mouth. But...' I paused, wondering what I had been about to say.

'Steve had quite a long talk with him last night. While they were splicing.'

'For what it's worth,' I commented, moodily, remembering another long talk that Jay and I had had, and wondering if he had said any of that to Steve. I did hope not. I could have added that there had been plenty of counter-distractions, but that was too obvious to waste words on. I had been trying to put the whole prickly subject on the back burner as I had resolved, for Marina and Steve were right, their summer holiday was no time for us to start fighting and disintegrating. If that was what we had been doing. I sighed again.

'Isn't it windy enough for you already?' asked Marina. 'Oh look – what wonderful sunhats! Do let's buy ourselves some!'

'They'll blow away,' I said, glad of the change of subject. The hats were enormous, striped straw with flamboyantly coloured flowers round the brim. I couldn't imagine wearing one on a boat, whatever the weather. Marina was unconvinced, however.

'Oh, the gale is bound to drop sometime!'

But not that day. It blew and blew, and the dust got into everything. We were all tired after our broken night, we sat yawning on the yachts all afternoon, or loafed around the quay listening to the three boats who had gone to Rhinia talking to *Eleni* over the VHF. They too had experienced a rough night of it, although nothing to compare with ours, and two of them wanted to find a quieter anchorage. Could they go round to Ornos Bay on the lee side of Mykonos island? they wanted to know. The Port Police, consulted by Paul, said that yes, they could, but on no account must they come into the harbour here. Some time later, one of them came on the radio to announce that they had arrived safely after a short, wet, hard sail.

'It's like a millpond round here!' the disembodied voice crowed gleefully, as we surged uncomfortably up and down against the piers. In the daylight, we had hauled out far enough to keep from crashing into them, but it was still an unenviable place to spend any length of time. Even *Aithra*, who had preferred to stay at Rhinia rather than risk sailing in these conditions with her dodgy engine, would be better off than those of us who were trapped here.

Aphrodite had to leave the ferry berth during the morning, she now lay against the south mole in the position vacated by *Anatolikos*, by this time long gone. She was a lot more comfortable than the rest of us, but looked rather lonely lying there. I wondered where the diving boat was bound and if we would see her again... and then stopped myself. That way, madness lay and I had enough problems already.

Marina and Steve had gone off into the town, and now returned with fresh bread that scented the whole ship deliciously, sizzling hot spanikopitia (spinach pies) for dinner, beautiful cheeses, fresh figs... perhaps Mykonos had its advantages after all. We had elected to eat on board tonight and turn in early, we all needed a good sleep. Your turn for the catering, Marina told me, but with what they had brought back it would be easy.

The gale was still roaring overhead. Early night or not, it was obviously going to be another broken one. Before we settled in for the evening, Jay and Steve went along to the lead boat to represent to Paul the desirability of organising a watch system for the coming night, so that everyone had the chance to get a decent amount of sleep.

'That's fine,' said Paul. 'Why don't you organise it?'

Even Steve, whose opinion of Paul had hit rock bottom by this time, blinked a bit at this, but obviously our Skipper wasn't going to bestir himself so they went from boat to boat trying to make up a rota. It was probably unfortunate that the gale chose this moment to have a temporary lull.

'Oh, it's dropping now,' one crew said.

'There's no need, we're OK now Paul's been round,' said another. A general feeling that the worst was now over seemed to prevail, and Steve even got snarled at by one of the skippers for checking his warps for chafe.

'Don't you touch that warp, it's all right,' he barked. It was already fraying slightly, but Steve simply shrugged and walked away. He wasn't looking for a fight, if the warp went, it went, and we could only hope we wouldn't all be swept away when the boat broke loose. Jay had gone off to find Robin, to see if any plastic piping was likely to be available to sheathe some of the warps where they crossed the edge of the quay, which would help. Robin promised to look in the bosun's store aboard *Eleni*, but he didn't sound optimistic. Even so, that was the most positive response they got.

We ate the spoils of Steve and Marina's shopping expedition, and after we had washed up, set about turning in for that early night we had promised ourselves. The wind had certainly moderated, probably to a steadier force 8 Steve reckoned, and even that was quite strong enough. He and Jay, despairing of any help, worked out a two-hour shift system between themselves and patrolled the quayside throughout the night. Ken and Bill appeared once or twice although they obviously saw no real necessity, but of our lead boat crew there was no sign.

It was another long night, full of splices. Watched over by Steve and Jay, Ken and Bill, quietly replacing warps and keeping everything secure, the flotilla slept peacefully.

Day Ten: Wednesday, 14th June

It has to be true, because I have proved it, that it is impossible to live with even the most depressing of problems all the time. In spite of the shadow hanging over my marriage and the anguish I felt whenever I thought about it or was reminded, I couldn't help enjoying Greece. But the problem was still there, under the surface, and kept sticking its head up like some horrible gorgon determined to bring me down.

Today turned out to be one of those occasions.

In spite of, or maybe because of, another disturbed night, we all woke up early, and to begin with, the day got off to a good start.

'I want to get some photographs,' Jay said. 'This early morning light is like nothing else. D'you want to come?'

The invitation was perfunctory, but at least it was there. As one of his original complaints had been that he was lonely, and by inference that I took no interest any more in what he did, I agreed to go with him, although I would sooner have turned over in my bunk and had another hour. If this was an olive branch, I should be failing myself as well as him to refuse it. He gathered his gear together, and we went up on deck to find that as the gale bit deep, the swell in the harbour was worsening, so that getting ashore was by no means as simple as it had sounded. We had to call Steve up to help Jay swing on the warps to bring *Phaedra's* nose in close enough for me to get ashore at all, and even them it was a hazardous business that involved a leap into space at the exact right moment at the top of the swirl, when the bow was well up, and an instant before it dropped away sideways again. Jay, whose legs are much longer, had less trouble, but even for him it was far from easy. Perhaps we should have been warned.

The gale was still blowing without remittance, but at least there was some sun this morning, and in the little twisty streets of the town it was possible – almost – to forget about the quayside dust and the lurching boats. But it wasn't as pleasant a walk as it had promised to be. Jay kept stopping to take pictures and then wandering off before I could get back to him. I knew that he would be like this, of course, because he always is, but today it seemed more than usually irritating and I even began to wonder if he was deliberately trying to lose me, except that he was the one who had suggested I came. I daresay that the constant battering of the gale and the broken nights, on top of the strain of our struggling marriage, had a lot to do with it, but I began to feel as if I had an over- wound spring inside me. We came perilously close to quarrelling, not once but several times, until at last my mood penetrated even Jay's absorption in his photography.

'What the hell is the matter with you this morning?' he snapped.

I leaned my elbows on a handy low wall and looked down at the harbour, now directly below, to avoid meeting his eyes. 'Lack of sleep.' I tried to speak lightly.

'Then why the hell didn't you stay in bed?'

'I thought it would be nice to be out together.'

'Then why behave like a stupid bitch, and spoil it?'

I took a deep breath. An apology was due. 'I'm sorry,' I said.

Jay began to put his camera into its case, a long-suffering expression on his face. 'We might as well go back, if you're going to be like that.'

'I didn't mean to spoil things for you. I've said I'm sorry. Let's go on.'

'I don't want to any more,' said Jay, with a scowl.

I swung round on him. *'I've said I'm sorry*! What more do you want, blood?'

Jay swung on his heel without answering and stalked off back the way we had come. I left the support of the wall, finding to my surprise that I was trembling, and walked a few steps after him.

'There's no need to go all the way back through the town. If we turn left at the end here, it must take us right down to the quay.'

'Rubbish!' he snarled. 'We're too far over! We came up this way, so it stands to reason we have to go back the same way.'

'If you want to walk round in circles all morning.'

'You always think you know best!'

'I nearly always *do* know best, when it comes to finding the way anywhere.'

But this was fighting talk, and Jay had taken enough. He turned on his heel and walked briskly off. I hesitated for a moment, tempted to go after him and try to make peace, but a niggling feeling that I had somehow been deliberately put in the wrong yet again prevented me, although for the minute it was hard to see how. I turned and went in the opposite direction.

Yes, I know. Kindergarten stuff. But it is this kind of childish squabble that is the real killer in a relationship, not the major brawls. If you quarrel over something worth the fight, at least you are standing on firm ground, but once you start bickering over nothing you are well into the mire.

As I had thought, the next turning took me back down to the harbour via a steep street with residential houses on either side, rather boring. As I walked, I reviled myself for my stupidity. This was no way to set about saving us from divorce, poor Jay was probably even more tired than I was after two nights spent splicing ropes in the dark. I could have been more understanding. If I wanted to save our marriage, I would need to try harder in future.

I was the only one who was trying at all.

The thought came from nowhere, and stopped me in my tracks with an involuntary cry of pain. And it wasn't true, it wasn't true! Since our brawl in front of Marina and Steve, Jay had been behaving like an angel.

Because we were in front of Marina and Steve?

I started to walk again, but more slowly, and for the very first time the thought went through my head, was it really worth it? If I had to fight so hard to stop in one place, could we ever go forward unless Jay helped? Wouldn't it just be easier to let it all slip away and begin again?

I didn't want to begin again. Some stubborn bit of me insisted on going on loving him. Oh, how simple everything would be, but for that!

I came out onto the road above the quay, and the gale, from which I had been sheltered between the houses, leapt at me in a cloud of stinging dust. Marina, I saw, was sitting on the deck, talking to Ken and Bill on the next boat, so at least I could be sure of help getting aboard. Of Steve, there was no sign.

'Hi,' said Marina, after I had made the perilous leap without accident. 'What have you done with Jay?'

'I left him,' I said without thinking, and her jaw dropped. 'No, no,' I hurriedly corrected myself, 'not *left* him, left him. Just left him up in the town. Where's Steve?'

'Asleep.'

I sighed, and spoke before I had thought out what I would say. 'Sometimes, I feel as if I've taken a one-way ticket to nowhere.'

'Then jump ship,' said Marina, watching me.

'If it were that easy.'

'You sound as if you wish it was.'

'To make it easy, I would have not to care.'

'Or to care about something else more.'

I stared at her. 'What on earth do you mean?'

'I'm not sure.' Marina frowned. 'I think, that there's nothing but grief in caring for someone who doesn't care back, and you might... well, just as well find something else to do.'

'Such as?' I sounded derisive. She didn't answer me directly.

'Look Sue... this is awfully hard to say, because Steve and I like you both so much, but I do think someone needs to say it. You have always cared more about Jay than Jay has cared about you. I don't mean he doesn't love you, I know nothing about that. I just mean that you have always given more than you have received. And there must come a time, surely, when you have to... well, stop. Stop wasting time. Stop wasting *you*.'

Some things are just so true that you can't argue with them. I sat down abruptly on the cabin roof beside her.

'You can't just stop loving someone.'

'No, I don't suppose you can.'

'You must think me a great fool.'

'Maybe.' Marina smiled at me. 'But I'll tell you what else I think, and that's that you're a bonnie fighter, Sue Starkey, sure as hell you are! Which is fine, so long as it's a fight you can win.'

'She isn't even worth it,' I said, unguardedly.

'They seldom are,' said Marina, and began to sing under her breath. '*The other man's grass is always greener, the sun shines brighter on the other side...*'

I wanted to weep, but I wouldn't do it in front of her.

'I'll put the kettle on,' I said. I wonder how many people that simple phrase has piloted out of the shallows.

'Tea, please, for me,' said Marina.

On my way back to the cockpit with the mugs, we were hailed by Ken.

'Steve around?'

'Asleep,' said Marina, for the second time, as she came to collect her steaming mug.

'We've just been talking to Paul.' Bill came to lean on the rail beside Ken, looking down at us across the narrow surge of white water between us. 'He's still on about making a run for it, and the girls are jumpy.'

On cue, Sylvia appeared in their cockpit behind them.

'At least we're in a harbour here,' she said, looking uneasy. 'It'd be an awful sail, even just round the corner to Ornos. I'd sooner stay here, even if it is uncomfortable.'

Steve's sleepy face appeared in the companionway, yawning.

'Don't worry Sylvia, the Port Police are on your side. It's going to blow hard for another twenty-four hours at least, according to the forecast, and it's stronger than ever now, too.'

Sylvia tried to smile, but I could see that she was already looking ahead to the end of that twenty-four hours. I tried to encourage her.

'It's all right, you know. The boat will take a lot of punishment.'

'It's not the boat I'm worrying about,' said Sylvia. 'I'm never going sailing again after this. Not ever.'

Sally had said the same the night before last. Panther Sailing were doing well!

'It'll be a long swim back to Ayios Giorgos,' said Jay, jumping down from the quay and looking at me very pointedly. I inwardly raged at his insensitivity – it wasn't the moment for *dear old Jay, everyone knows he's a tease*! He never knows when to shut up. I had never consciously criticised this side of him before, rather found it endearing on the whole. I found myself looking at him with new eyes and a dreary feeling of insecurity.

Paul and Emmy strolled past on their way to the town.

'We'll get away tomorrow,' Paul called, confidently, and added with a wry grin, 'Maybe!'

148

Steve yawned again and rubbed at his eyes. Jay asked, 'Has Paul made any comment on last night, at all?'

'I don't think he even realised anything happened,' said Steve, and laughed shortly. 'There'll be no medals handed out for this lot, you may be sure. There's some toast under the grill, come and get it before it burns.'

We still had no grill pan, of course. We made our toast on the base of an upturned frying pan, as best we could. It burned quite easily made this way.

We spent a long time over breakfast, all of us too tired to be hungry, picking at burned toast and drinking cup after cup of strong coffee or tea, according to taste. Steve began to wonder how *Aithra* was faring over at Rhinia on her own.

'They should have come across with the others. Paul should have seen to it. It's no place and no weather for them to be all by themselves.'

'I expect it was the state of the engine that stopped them,' said Jay. 'Jenny's one gutsy lady, but she's a fair-weather sailor, dinghies mostly, she admits it herself.'

'There's plenty of wind, but they could reef right down,' said Marina. 'It's not as if they have to come into a harbour. Just get to Ornos and sling the anchor over.'

'Dinghies are one thing,' said Steve. 'Anchoring under sail in a yacht – even without a gale – is rather different. I can't blame her if she didn't want to risk the chance, but...'

'Sylvia said that she stayed with the other two in case the engine failed completely,' I mentioned. 'If the wind dropped at least they could tow her, was the idea.'

'But they're in Ornos Bay now.' Steve's lips tightened. Marina swept the plates and mugs together into the sink.

'They'll be all right, so long as they sit tight. Better than roaring out with a green crew into a green sea, and the engine does go, they said so. Sort of.'

'"Sort of" isn't good enough in these conditions. I wonder what Robin had to say about it?'

'It's not up to Robin. He hasn't the time and he hasn't the spares. It's up to Paul to say whether she should have sailed or not. Presumably he thought they'd be all right where they are.'

'Paul!' said Steve, with such loathing that Marina looked surprised. 'He's in charge, after all.'

'You could have fooled me!'

'You can't worry about everyone, Steve. It's not our affair. And what could Paul do, anyway? He couldn't force them to come if they were afraid to. And now, let's not sit here all morning, let's go and do some serious shopping. Since we're stuck here, let's not waste it!'

'Good idea.' I seconded this attempt to lighten the atmosphere. 'I want to buy some presents for the kids, and send some postcards.'

'Oh, what the hell!' said Steve, getting to his feet. 'It's broad daylight, there's plenty of people around. If anything goes wrong, let them deal with it!'

Marina looked relieved, and shortly after, all four of us left the boat and headed for the shops. Jay was still not speaking to me, but Marina was being so deliberately vivacious – on Steve's account rather than ours – that I don't believe they noticed. I stole a glance at Jay's profile as he strode along beside me in stony silence. In his younger days he had been a very good-looking man, if a bit too aware of the fact; as he grew older he had become, if anything, more so – on both counts – but he had always been so nice, everybody agreed on that... and we had been through so much together, to sink now just because of a greedy little sexpot like Dawn seemed stupid. And whatever Marina chose to say, the answer wasn't simple. It was not, for instance, to be found in sun and sea and romantic evenings under the stars, or in a silly middle-aged woman's stupid crush on a handsome young man. Oliviero had gone without a backward glance, and Jay was still here. In body, at least.

I think I spared a fleeting thought for Oliviero then, for his life spent diving to the depths of the sea, exploring wrecks, seeing marvellous things... adventure, excitement, promise of new horizons... or what did I know about him, really? Perhaps he considered it as just a job of work. All that part of my life was behind me, if I had ever had it at all. What I had possessed until Dawn, what I wanted to keep, was my home, my family, my husband and the future we had both worked for... sailing together on *Foxtrot*, and time spent laughing and drinking with our friends down at the yacht club. Lovely holidays like this one, golden days of our sunlit summer. I had felt myself so fortunate only a short time ago. Jay and I had always been such friends, as well as lovers.

But now? Jay coming home every night, sitting with the newspaper while I prepared a meal, watching the news, watching his interminable snooker, going off fishing on his own half the night. Every Friday evening, come rain or shine, spent on my own while he went, as if it was some demanding religion, to the Rugby Club to play pool... Sunday afternoons at home spent watching him snoring, if I was lucky enough to have him there at all, slumped unattractively in an armchair, or a garden chair according to the season, while the hours of my life ran away like water down the plughole – *my* life, spinning away in waiting, always waiting for something to happen, for Jay to come home, to wake up, for the phone to ring, for the children to come...

I had never been discontented before. I had counted my life a happy one.

Had Jay, I wondered, before the advent of Dawn? Or had he been bored...

... *too*...

But that was surely tantamount to blasphemy.

When we had done enough shopping (too much, according to Jay and Steve), we all walked round to the south mole to visit Tom and Sally, who had by this time quite recovered from their frightening experience. They offered us coffee, but it was really too hot for warm drinks and after a while we drifted off again, into the teeth of the gale, looking for something to do.

'It's only a mile or so to Ornos Bay,' said Steve. 'Who fancies a walk? I'd like to see the place.'

Marina did, Jay and I didn't. The two of them went off together, promising to be back before too long, and Jack and I had a silent lunch together in a taverna. He spent most of it writing postcards, while I watched the world going by and felt dully miserable. When we left to go, he accidentally knocked them all off the edge of the table, and I bent to help him pick them up.

'I'll get them' he said, pushing me away, but not soon enough. I had seen her address and the opening words, *My darling*. I hardly even felt surprised, just deadly tired of it all.

He knew I had seen it. He shuffled the cards together and pushed them into the pocket of his sailing jacket, meeting my eyes defiantly.

'She's a neighbour, and a friend, dammit!' he exclaimed.

'I didn't say anything.'

'There's nothing to say. And you looked it.'

'Do you have to call her "darling"?' I demanded, suddenly angry. What kind of a fool did he take me for? Answers on a postcard, please.

'It's just a thing one says. Darling.'

'Don't,' I said. 'Don't, I can't bear any more!'

To my astonishment, this seemed to touch him. Or perhaps it was guilt. He reached out and stroked my cheek with his finger.

'Susie... there must be a way.'

'Not for her *and* me,' I said. He took the postcards out of his pocket, riffling through the sheaf to find it, and held it out to me.

'Tear it up. Go on. Tear it.'

'You do it.'

But he slipped it back into the pile.

We walked back to the quay, both of us I think unclear as to exactly what had just taken place. Some milestone had been passed, but no signpost. The gale blasted into our faces and my eyes were watering. I think they were. It was a really bloody day!

The crew of *Hippolyta* were sitting in their cockpit in company with a bottle of ouzo and some chilled beer, they saw us and called us aboard.

'It's sizzling here in the sun,' Janet said, moving up to make space for me. 'If only this horrible wind would drop, we could put up the awning and it would be lovely.' Both she and Sylvia looked strained and tired, but then, didn't we all? She sounded cheerful enough. Sylvia made a face.

'So-and-so wind! I suppose it will drop one day but even the thought of that is a bit like the dentist – something you know has to be got through but wish it didn't.'

'It'll be a doddle,' Ken assured her blithely. 'You'll see, Bill and I will look after you. And the lead boat will be with us all the way.'

'No sign of it dropping yet, so stop worrying until you need to,' Jay advised. 'Anyway, Bill's right, you know. It'll be a piece of cake.'

'He's Ken,' said Sylvia.

Jay went back to *Phaedra* soon after that, claiming that he had some sleep to catch up on, so I was the only one of the four of us who had a ringside seat for the next instalment of our catalogue of disasters. Ken had turned on the VHF; even in port the flotilla used it to communicate from boat to boat, and Paul had said nothing about it – in fact, he was as big an offender as anyone. At times it was like a seafaring version of *The Archers*. Bill and Ken were aware that Steve and Jay disapproved but they had never asked why, and Ken, at least, seemed to feel that they were making mountains out of molehills. This afternoon, however, brought a reality check.

'*Eleni, Eleni, Eleni*, this is *Aithra*.'

This was repeated once or twice with increasing urgency, and then *Ariadne* answered, offering to go into the town and look for Paul. Jenny's voice, distorted by atmospherics, said yes please, and we watched from the cockpit as one of the two youngish men who crewed our neighbour went ashore and strode off along the quay. After that nothing happened for a bit, then we saw Robin coming back. He went aboard the lead boat and a moment later his voice crackled over the radio.

'*Aithra, Aithra*, this is *Eleni*. What's your problem? Over.'

'*Eleni*, is there any sign of this wind abating? We've very little food left on board, and there's nowhere here to get any.'

'The forecast is at least another forty-eight hours before it drops below force 7,' said Robin. 'You'd better sail round to Ornos, Jenny, and join the others. You'll be all right there.'

'Our engine isn't reliable – you know that. And I'm not sure about sailing. Could you or Paul come to help us?'

'I'll have to ask Paul. Stay listening and I'll call you back. Over and out for now.'

Robin went ashore again, and we watched him running down the quay towards the town. Janet shivered.

'I'm glad I'm not on *Aithra*. What will Paul do, Sue, do you think?'

'Sail out and put Robin aboard I would think,' I said. 'That's what I would do.'

But not Paul, as we should have known. Robin came back shortly, still at a run, and called up *Aithra* again.

'*Aithra*, Paul says we can't come out because our anchor is fouled, and anyway the Port Police wouldn't let us back again and we need to stay with the rest of the flotilla. I'll call up one of the boats round at Ornos, they'll keep a watch out for you when you arrive there. You shouldn't have any trouble. Take in all three slabs and keep half the jib furled to balance her, you'll walk it I promise.'

'We're awfully close inshore. Suppose something goes wrong?'

'It won't go wrong,' said Robin, in as heartening a voice as I suppose he could manage, which wasn't very. 'Have everything organised and start her sailing as soon as your anchor's atrip, no worries. Just make sure you start on the offshore tack – pull the jib aback and the tiller hard over, and she'll pay off in the right direction as you bring the anchor aboard.'

'I wish you could come,' said Jenny, and I thought her voice shook a little. 'I've never anchored under sail.'

'You'll manage fine. Or you can stay where you are.'

'We've only got half a loaf, three eggs, and two overripe figs. Oh, and a tin of beans.'

'Better get it over with then. You know the drill. Just put it into practice. It works like the book, I promise you.'

'Oh God, Robin –' Even over the distorting radio, the note of near-panic in her voice was unmistakable this time. Robin heard it.

'Stay there,' he cried, suddenly urgent. 'Just stay there, Jenny.'

'How can we?'

Now Robin's concern showed clearly in his voice. 'Jenny, you've got to decide. There's some buildings marked on the chart, about two miles north of you. Perhaps you can get food there.'

'We've already tried. There's hardly anything.'

'Then I don't see that you've got a great deal of choice. But you must make your minds up quickly and let me know. Call me back, I'll be listening for you. Listening out for now, Jenny.'

'Thanks Robin, I'll call you. Oh – out.'

'Panther flotilla, Panther flotilla, please leave radio clear until Jenny calls back. Thank you.'

We had none of us heard Steve and Marina return, and had no idea they were there until Steve's furious voice from *Phaedra*'s deck made us all jump nearly out of our skins.

'What the blazes is going on? Where's Paul?'

'Up in the town somewhere, I suppose,' Bill said. Steve looked grim.

'Then I'll go and find the bugger! Surely to God he can get a boat to take him across to Rhinia? God dammit, I'll go myself – Jay'll come with me – where is Jay?'

'Sleeping.'

'Then I'll wake him up! I'll tell Robin and then I'll get organised.'

He turned and was gone, Marina running behind him. After a moment I climbed back across onto our own boat, but without help I couldn't get ashore. I stood on the bucking deck, holding onto the forestay. Steve had reached *Eleni* and I saw him jump on board, and Robin's head coming up out of the hatch. There was an argument with much arm-waving, then Steve turned and jumped back ashore to rejoin Marina, and after a brief word strode back into the town. This time, Marina didn't follow. She walked slowly back to the boat and stood on the quayside, looking at me.

'Robin is angry as hell,' she said. 'He couldn't say so, but he is. He said he'd go with Steve if Paul agreed, he's calling *Aithra* now.'

Paul and Steve came back together, and we could see from quite some way off that they were arguing furiously. Emmy trailed a few paces to the rear, looking acutely unhappy. We could hear their voices, but not the words, and the general impression was one of mutual rage.

A small crowd had gathered on the quay by this time, and Ken and Bill had helped me to get ashore. Paul strode into the middle of the group.

'Let's have no more of this hysteria!' he cried angrily, before he had even stood still. 'Jenny has only got to make a simple sail of a few miles, she's not got to cross the Atlantic! She's got a strong-handed crew, so why all the fuss? The other two managed it with no trouble at all!'

'The others are rather more experienced, and their engines worked,' retorted Steve. 'Good God, it's such a little thing to do – to take a boat over there and put an experienced crew aboard to help her! It wouldn't take half an hour! You can do it – we can't!'

'It's totally unnecessary.'

'You tell her so, then,' I suggested indignantly, and Paul said, by God, he would, and he went, and did. Not quite so abruptly. Just enough to make the poor girl feel stupid and inadequate. Being a girl of guts, as Jay had remarked, for if she hadn't been she would never have taken on the job of skippering a crew of complete land lubbers in strange waters, she naturally responded by saying that of course she could manage. End of incident, as far as Paul was concerned.

'I hope he sleeps well at night!' said Steve, bitterly. 'The only good thing is, if they get there at least they'll be all right in Ornos.'

'Good, is it?' I asked.

'Lovely,' said Marina. 'Sheltered as anything, with a marvellous beach, and tavernas, and even a shop – I wish we were there ourselves.'

The group was splitting up now, everyone drifting back to their own boats or towards the town. The general feeling seemed to be that Steve had made a fuss about nothing, but in one or two quarters I sensed that Paul had lost a bit of ground. Steve was too disgusted to care. He said, 'I'll tell you what, let's take a taxi and go over there for our meal this evening, then you and Jay can see it too. I want to get out of this place!'

And we would be in an excellent position to see that *Aithra* arrived safely, but he didn't say that. Carol, Charles and Richard came over to us as we were climbing back aboard. Richard said, but doubtfully, 'She will be all right, Steve. She's a pretty competent lass, done a lot of dinghy sailing, knows what's what and all that.'

'Not quite the same thing,' said Steve, but he did look slightly comforted.

'If nobody makes her think she can't, she'll manage all right,' Charles added his contribution. 'It's only a little trip.'

'Paul could easily have sent someone with her.'

'He didn't see any need. He should know, if anyone does.'

'Oh, should he? I wish I had your faith!'

'Come on, he isn't that much of a fool,' said Richard. 'He wouldn't actually endanger lives.'

'Let's hope he hasn't.'

'Pessimist,' said Carol. 'And talking of endangering lives, did you know we were on TV last night?'

'What?'

'Yes – they had a crew here yesterday morning, most of us were at the briefing but they spoke to one or two – the woman on *Persephone*, the one with the bad back, was one, and they took film of *Aphrodite* and that dive boat, and everyone heaving about on the piers. There was an interview with the Captain of the dive boat, and one of the archaeologists who's pretty famous, apparently, but it was all Greek to us, of course, because it was Greek television. We saw it on the news in the taverna where we had lunch, it was quite a surprise!'

'That'll be a thrill for Paul's head office,' said Steve, with grim satisfaction. 'Hope they trim his sails for him!'

'They might be as stupid as he is,' said Marina, but we didn't like to think so.

'No wonder Emmy looks so miserable,' I said.

We waited until Jay woke up, and then took a taxi across to Ornos. The interior of the island looked very barren seen through its windows. There were brown expanses of nothing much, scattered with poor-looking little houses and clumps of prickly pear; Marina said it had been like walking through a desert, but it was quite true what she had said about Ornos bay, it was lovely. So quiet... of course, the wind was still shrieking round elsewhere, but here in the bay it was warm and sheltered. There was a wide, sandy beach with people lying there in the sun or swimming in the smooth, flat swell that was all that found its way between the headlands, there was a fringe of beach-side tavernas that looked more than inviting, there was a small village, and even, as Marina had reported, a tiny shop of sorts.

'If only we'd known it was like this, I'd never have put into Mykonos at all,' said Steve. 'Handy for the town, too – it can't be more than ten minutes even on the bus. If only Emmy had thought to tell us, what suffering we would have been spared!'

'Emmy is only really interested in Paul,' said Jay.

The flotilla yacht *Hecate* and her sailing partner *Electra* lay comfortably to their anchors just offshore, and in our chosen taverna we met *Electra*'s crew of two pleasant, elderly couples out to enjoy themselves. Naturally, most of the talk was centred on *Aithra*.

'We tried to persuade Jenny to come with us, but Paul said the wind wasn't forecast to last and she was worried about their engine,' one of the women told us. 'Of course, the anchorage in South Bay is very sheltered, and we gave them our bread and some cheese in case. But she really did think she would get out today, and probably meet us all in Tinos.'

'Paul should have kept her under his eye with that engine,' said one of the men.

'Under Robin's eye, at all events,' said Marina.

'She ought to be here by now if she decided to come at all,' said Steve, his eyes straying towards the bay. Nothing moved on those smooth, sheltered waters but the odd swimmer cavorting along the edge.

'They'll be all right,' I said. Marina muttered something under her breath, too quietly for Steve to overhear, about "bad vibes", which I wished I hadn't heard either. Marina, as you know, can sometimes get very close to the target, if that's clairvoyance, perhaps she does have a touch of it.

'Is it very bad back in the town?' someone asked, and Jay and Marina launched into a horrific account of conditions on the north quay, with ropes chafing through and no sleep at nights, and all the boats surging up and down on the swell, until their listeners actually laughed it was so unbelievable in this quiet setting, and said they were glad they weren't there.

'We wish we weren't either,' said Jay, laughing with them, but he knew he had coloured in the details a little – as if the reality wasn't bad enough. 'As a matter of fact, perhaps we can improve things a bit tomorrow,' he added. 'I noticed as we drove across, there are an awful lot of abandoned motor tyres lying around. If we took some back with us, we could sheathe some of the ropes with them and help stop the rubbing. Robin did try to get some plastic piping, but couldn't; tyres might do just as well. Remind me to tell Paul, Sue, he can organise a collection, one or two people hired those little jeeps today.'

'Paul couldn't organise a Sunday School treat in a heatwave!' Steve said, and one of the women from *Electra* murmured, 'Neither could you, my dear man – all those overheated children, grizzling and fighting!' But she was smiling as she said it. There was no overt criticism of our Skipper here, but nor was there any rush to defend him. Interesting.

After a while, *Electra*'s crew went back to their boat for their supper, and Jay picked up the menu to order a meal for ourselves, but Steve was restless and walked to the edge of the terrace, looking out over the beach towards the water. After a minute or two, I went to join him.

'She'll be all right, Steve,' I repeated, for the second time. He said,

'If she left when she was told, she should have been here ages ago. It can't be much more than five miles, for God's sake, and it's blowing holy hell!'

'Perhaps she waited. Perhaps she hoped the wind would drop a bit.'

'Or perhaps she tried to take the Delos channel.'

'Oh, come on Steve! She may be a woman driver, but she isn't a complete fool!'

'She could have thought it looked more sheltered.'

'I bet it doesn't!' I said. 'More like the devil's boiling pot, I should think.'

'No bloody engine!' said Steve. 'And what else could go wrong on one of these damned deathtraps, Sue? Jackstay parted, or worse, a shroud gone?'

'Steve!'

'Oh all right, say it then. I'm being an old woman, but I've got a gut feeling about this one, something's wrong. She should be here. And we haven't even got a radio to know what's going on.'

Marina had the same feeling, but I didn't tell him that.

'We couldn't do anything about it, even if we had,' I told him, pragmatically. 'Come on Steve, snap out of it! You need food, that's what's the matter with you! Come and choose something to eat – and look, there's a cat for you!'

The scrawny little cat distracted Steve for a little while, but as we waited for our food to be brought – never a speedy business in tavernas where they cook to order over a charcoal grill – he was back on the prowl, muttering that it was getting dark now, and where the hell were they?

Deep shadows were gathering under the headlands and in the curve of the bay as the light began to fade from the sky. On the anchored yachts, pinpricks like stars broke out at the mastheads, in the windows lights began to glow. And then, just as our meal arrived, we saw at last the firefly dance of moving lights at the entrance to the bay, green first, and then green and red close together, and the dim shadow of a sailing boat outlined against the pewter gleam of the sky.

'She's here!' cried Marina, jumping to her feet and thus betraying her own anxiety.

We were all at the verandah rail now, peering across the now deserted beach towards the water.

'Making a pretty neat job of it too,' observed Jack. 'Full genny – no main. Good girl – good girl!'

Aithra came dancing in between the headlands, hit the smoother water and slid onwards. Her genoa flapped as she rounded into the wind, even above the overhead moan of the gale we heard the rattle of her anchor going over. The sail dwindled, vanished as someone pulled on the furling line.

'God!' exclaimed Steve, 'but I'm hungry!' He turned away, back to the bright-lit interior of the taverna and the expectant little cat.

A little later, as we sat over our wine, a loaded dinghy came ashore and a laughing group of young people came tumbling up the beach towards us. Jenny was in the van, as she reached the soft sand she fell on her knees, picked up a fistful in her two hands, and kissed it.

'Land, land!' she cried.

The four of us were already halfway to meet them, and they hailed us with delight, euphoric with sheer relief, it was obvious. There were six of them – odd, I had thought there were five – dancing on the sand like savages. Jenny flung herself into Steve's arms and hugged him like her dearest friend.

'What a trip! What a bloody awful trip!' But she sounded happy. The others crowded round us, all talking at once, so that nothing could be heard properly until Jenny, letting go of Steve, abruptly pulled the sixth member of their party into the light. 'And this is Oliver,' she said. 'He rescued us!'

'Stuff that, you didn't need rescuing.' Oliviero met my eyes, smiled warmly. 'Why, Sue! Hullo again.'

'You know each other?' asked Jenny, surprised.

'We've actually never been formally introduced before,' I said.

'Food!' One of the young men who formed *Aithra*'s crew pushed forward into the taverna, and he and Jay began to drag a table up to ours as the waiter hurried up to help with chairs – how different from the Panther Sailing Yacht Club!

'You must stay and eat with us,' said Jenny, catching Oliviero's arm, but he excused himself.

'I have to catch the bus,' he explained. 'Look, it's just come in, and there won't be another for at least an hour. You're all right now.'

'You could catch the next one.'

'I've things to see to in town. And I can hardly wish myself on friends for the night after midnight.'

'We can find a bunk for you,' Jenny urged.

'Kind of you, but no thanks. I'll see you again, maybe.' He said a hurried goodnight and ran off along the beach, turning once to wave. Everyone waved back, calling thanks, and then tumbled into the taverna to sit down, still laughing.

'So tell us what happened,' said Steve, when the decibel level had dropped a little and the other diners were no longer staring at us.

'What didn't happen?' asked Jenny, flinging her arms wide. 'God, what a fiasco! We got out of South Bay all right, it's a deepish, squiggly one, quite sheltered, so we didn't realise quite what it would be like outside. We put the slabs in the main ready, but we – I – decided to sail out with just the full genoa to keep it simple. We did what Robin said, and she paid off just like he said she would, then we hauled on the sheet and walked the anchor chain aft and fairly dragged the hook out of the ground when we got her sailing, and that was no problem. But then, when we got outside the headland –'

'– we really felt the gale then,' interrupted one of the others.

'– and some fool had ripped out the genny without keeping the furling line taut, and it was all tangled round the drum so we couldn't reduce sail –'

'– and while we were wrestling with that, and the boat was leaping up and down –'

'– the main halyard worked free and blew away and got all snarled up in the shrouds so we couldn't hoist the main either –'

'– and all hell broke loose –'

'– and Cape Podi was getting nearer and nearer –'

'– and her head wouldn't come round –'

'– and the captain panicked!' finished Jenny, happily, reaching for the bread. 'I sent one of the crew down to yell for help – well, anyway, to ask Paul what we should do – but he wasn't there, and then suddenly, like the answer to a prayer, this big motor boat came churning past and threw us a line, and towed us round the corner into the next bay, where we anchored again and untangled the drum, but of course, there was no way we could get at the main halyard without a bosun's chair. They sent a boat over to see that we were all right once everything had calmed down, full of dishy Greek and Italian men! Well, we were safe then, of course, but we still didn't have any food, and then one of them asked if we were with the flotilla that had been in Hydra and was now in the harbour at Mykonos, and of course, we said we were and he got very red in the face and made a noise like a blocked drain emptying.'

'Then we explained, of course, and he said something in Greek to the others, and they all began jabbering together,' someone else took up the tale. 'Yes please, Dave, I'd love some more wine –'

'They advised us to stay where we were.' The one called Dave took over the telling now, pouring wine with a generous hand. 'But of course, we were getting pretty hungry by this time. So that Greek chap who was with us just now offered to sail over with us and see we got here safely.'

'That was a dodgy one,' another young man cut in. 'We had no idea who he was, except that he was a diver – did I say it was a dive-boat? – hardly a glowing recommendation, given the circumstances.'

'Useful if we sank,' crowed Dave.

'And there was the question of salvage, of course, but we were already deep in over our heads on that one. So we had a hurried committee meeting and decided that the boat was Panther Sailing's and we were past caring if they lost her in a lawsuit, just so long as she didn't sink with us on board and it was our fault.'

There was a short pause, and everyone was suddenly sober. Then Jenny laughed again, and picked up her wineglass.

'So here we are! And Oliver was marvellous, he let me bring her the whole way and hardly said a word until it was time to light the sailing lights. Then I got paranoid about the Greek police and sailing after dark, of all stupid things after what we'd already gone through! He said they'd never know if we didn't tell them, and even if they did find out they wouldn't care, because they all know him anyway. Then of course, we asked "how come?" and although it was a bit like drawing teeth, he did tell us. He's been sailing to the Med five or six times a year as a delivery skipper, until last autumn when he decided to chuck it in and stay out here, and got a job with the divers – he's got all the necessary paperwork, and has actually worked as a salvage diver back in England for a short time, soon after he left university.'

'But you say he's a Greek,' said Steve, puzzled.

'Well, he's got a Greek name anyway.'

'Oliver?'

'Nankervis.'

The breath caught in my throat and I choked, for of course, Nankervis isn't a Greek name at all, for all it sounds as if it ought to be. Jay caught my eye across the table and grinned, more friendly than he had been all day.

'Your Greek be a Cornishman, me lover,' he said, putting on an exaggerated accent. We both love Cornwall and had spent many holidays there when the children were young, mainly in the same place so we had got to know people. And lately we had sailed there with *Foxtrot* which, as you know, was how we met Steve and Marina.

'Really?' Jenny sounded surprised. 'I thought all Cornishmen began with Tre, Pol and Pen. There's a rhyme – *by Tre, Pol and Pen ye shall know Cornishmen.* Or something.'

'Oh, they do – they do. Those of them, that is, that don't begin with Nan or An, or who aren't called Pascoe or Sincock or Carne and etcetera.'

'Well, there you go. You learn something new every day,' the lad called Dave said. 'He didn't sound like a Cornishman – not if that's what they really sound like.'

Which was true. Oliviero – no, Oliver – had no distinctive regional accent at all, which was one reason why I had been so sure he was foreign. My mistake. I had judged him by his company in the light of my own over-romantic wishful thinking and been wrong, but now, with this new knowledge, I wondered how I hadn't recognised that he spoke such good English because he *was* English – or Cornish anyway, which in Cornwall they claim isn't quite the same thing.

I preferred Oliviero, I decided, the romantic Greek, or maybe Italian, charmer of my daydream. Like "Emily", once the name was separated from its Italian form it was dull and old-fashioned. Oliver Nankervis was an entirely different person from the romantic Oliviero. Perhaps people called him "Olly" even. We once had a cat called Olly.

We went back to Mykonos an hour later, on the last bus; it didn't seem worth calling up another taxi, and anyway, it made an interesting experience. I remembered what Oliver had said about bus rides, but it seemed a long time ago. The bus set us down at the back of the town in a little square high above the harbour, and as we walked downhill we ran into Paul and Emmy. They greeted us cheerfully.

'The gale is going to blow until at least Friday,' Paul told us.

'Oh no, I'm sick of this wind!' cried Marina. She turned to Emmy. 'If we're all going to be stuck here another night, why can't we organise some kind of group meal, or a social event of some kind, to boost morale a bit? I think everyone would appreciate it, and it might cheer us all up.'

'That's a good idea,' said Emmy – why had she not thought of it for herself? 'I'll see what I can arrange, shall I?'

Jay mentioned motor tyres, and Paul said that he would get some collected up tomorrow. We left them then, and strolled on through the town back to the dust and noise of the gale-swept quay, to find Ken and Bill sitting on bollards, hoping no more warps were going to go before Steve got back. This is exactly how they put it, and I saw Jay scowl – he was having a bad day, one way and another. There was already a little pile of frayed and parted ropes waiting for our return, and only one, already mended, spare left

'Have you seen Paul?' Ken then asked. 'Only, there was a bloke down here earlier, looking for him. He wasn't very happy, we thought.'

'What was he like?' I asked, already guessing.

'Young. Dark hair. Ferocious.'

I was right, that could only be a description of Oliver Nankervis, no doubt getting fed up with rescuing Panther Sailing's clients from shipwreck. I felt unreasonably embarrassed, as if the implied criticism was aimed at me personally, and I think Steve may have felt the same, for he said, 'Paul has succeeded in making us all look stupid, it seems to me.'

We sat around in the cockpit for a bit, wondering if we had the energy to go to bed. Jay, who was suddenly back in his bad mood, wondered aloud what new disaster tomorrow would bring, and then Steve announced that he was going to turn in, since he would have to be up again in two hours time. Jay was taking first watch, with Ken, the splicing was waiting for him. Paul, I don't think, even realised that watches were being kept.

Ours was one of the few boats that it was possible to get directly on and off, and I lay awake awhile listening to the thump and scramble of the flotilla returning to its bunks. One or two of them called a quiet goodnight as they used us for a thoroughfare, but eventually even these noises stopped, and there was nothing to hear but the unending gale.

Day Eleven: Thursday, 15th June

During the night we woke up suddenly, all of us at the same time. We were so attuned to the weather by this time that the tiniest change was like an alarm bell. I lay for a while, listening, and heard somebody – Steve for a guess – walking about on the deck. The wind had swung just a fraction – and was it dropping at last? It still sounded blustery and wild, and the change was so subtle it was hard to pinpoint it, but it was there all right. And all was well. Apart from the watch keepers holding their wearisome vigil on the quay, we slept again until morning sunlight, spilling through the open hatches, woke us to another day.

Marina set the tone early, standing in the cockpit with her arms raised to the heavens, and yelling at the top of her voice, '*I hate this filthy dust*! *I shall never be clean again*!' Everyone in earshot broke into sympathetic laughter, for we all felt the same way. It wasn't worth putting on clean clothes, we had no facilities for washing anything and they were covered in dust within minutes of going outside. Our hair and nails were permanently full of it, and our eyes were developing pretty red rims. Escape was the one thing we all dreamed of, but it never seemed to happen.

But the wind had definitely gone round a point or two. Of that, there was no doubt.

After that little sideshow, the day settled down to being just like any other morning in Mykonos until well after breakfast, which, when we came to look back on it, was probably about right. We had become used to calm starts to our calamities, and today's was to be a humdinger!

The first unusual thing was Robin, coming aboard before we had even finished dressing, and asking for a lesson in splicing. It had apparently dawned on him for the first time last night that Steve and Jay were shouldering an unfair burden, and he apologised.

'It was such a slick operation, I never even realised it was going on,' he said. 'I should have, I'm really sorry... but there's been such a lot happening, I had other things on my mind.'

None of us asked what those were. He had dark shadows under his eyes as if he hadn't slept well, but then, none of us had done that for some time, and a restlessness that needed an occupation. Jay sat down in his underpants and gave him a lesson there and then, before sending him off with some rope ends to practice, Before he left, he gave us the glad news that the wind had moderated to force 7, and we might get away today, at least to Ornos. It sounded like the promise of heaven.

Force 7 it might be, but that is still blowing a hooley even so, and at the briefing, Paul only held out hopes that we might get away tomorrow, if today was being a bit too optimistic. Change was coming, he said – more truly than he could have known. So, back to the quayside.

'There was somebody here, looking for you,' Sylvia told Paul.

'What sort of somebody?' Paul asked, unconcerned.

'A man in a suit. He looked like some sort of businessman.'

Not Oliver, then. In any case, here came Oliver now, striding along with a face like thunder. He stopped in front of Paul.

'Are you in charge of this outfit?'

'I'm the Skipper, yes.' Paul looked wary.

'Good. I want a word with you. Will you have it here, or somewhere less public?'

Paul was immediately on the defensive. 'On what authority?'

'Does it have to be on any?'

Paul visibly hesitated. Oliver was a stranger to him, so far as he remembered, for he had only ever met him in the dark. Then he looked round the circle of his interested audience and back to Oliver's stormy face. Discretion won.

'You'd better come aboard my boat,' he said.

They walked away together with a yard between them, like two tomcats squaring up for a fight. Ken raised his eyebrows.

'So, what was *that*?'

'Nemesis, I hope and trust,' said Steve, grimly. He told *Hippolyta*'s crew about the events of last evening, it made a change to be first with the gossip. Several others gathered round to listen, too. One or two of them had heard Jenny trying to reach Paul, but of course, none of them knew why for nobody had answered her.

Emmy, who was still with us, looked at Marina and me unhappily.

'Can I come on board with you?' she asked. 'I don't think I'll be wanted on the lead boat.'

'Be our guest,' I invited. She jumped aboard and sat down in the cockpit with us, but, like Robin earlier, she was ill at ease. On the quay, the crowd had grown and we could see Janet and Sylvia talking to Carol and Richard with much animation and arm-waving. Everyone was looking towards *Eleni*, the tale of *Aithra*'s evening out was obviously losing nothing in the re-telling. Steve went below and made some coffee, the five of us on *Phaedra* sat drinking it, feeling awkward. At last, Emmy spoke.

'It isn't always like this,' she said, tentatively. 'It's the gale... and everything.'

Steve looked at her with surprising gentleness.

'It's a big responsibility. You need to take these things seriously.'

'We do – we try to, but it's all gone wrong this year. Everything!' She had told us that before, but this time there was a real note of desperation in her voice. Steve was sitting on the cabin top by now, his fingers busy with yet another splice.

'Emmy dear, the gale is only a small part of it. You must know that.' She turned her face away, and Steve went on, steadily. 'Broken or missing gear, faulty equipment, engines that won't work...'

'Oh, I know – I know! But we're only given so much to spend on each flotilla.' A tide of colour swept up her face. Steve reached for another rope and began deftly untwisting the strands.

'And anything over goes into the kitty?'

'No! Of course not!' But she spoke too loudly.

'That's a horrible thing to say, Steve!' cried Marina, but Steve was watching Emmy.

'Is it? I wonder if Emmy even knows. Who keeps the books, Emmy?'

'The manager in charge of the area... and the individual Skippers, of course.'

'Of course.'

Steve's fingers flashed at speed, weaving in the strands, making one long, serviceable rope out of several frayed pieces. His eyes flicked back to Emmy's face.

168

'Then either the whole organisation is criminally under-funded, or somebody's on the fiddle,' he suggested. 'Or alternatively, of course, the staff involved are so totally inefficient that they don't know how to tackle their jobs. Or even a bit of both, they can often go hand in hand. It isn't only this flotilla, the shore/flotilla seems to be the same, and it goes right on through – it began in Athens, as soon as we got off the plane.' He paused. 'I think Robin suspects the answers, don't you?'

Emmy said earnestly, 'Nothing like this flotilla has ever happened before. Truly.'

'I should hope not, indeed!.'

None of us said the words "knock-on effect" but I think all of us thought them.

She got to her feet. 'Here comes that angry man now, I think I'd better get back.' She hesitated, her eyes going from one to the other of us. 'I'm glad that you're here.'

She said no more, but leapt nimbly onto the deck and ran forward. Jay set his work aside to go to help her ashore, but Oliver reached the ropes first and hauled *Phaedra* into the quay, giving Emmy a hand as she jumped. She said something to him quickly, and ran off towards the lead boat, but Oliver stood up, dusting off his hands, looking at us.

'May I come aboard?'

'Be our guest,' said Jay, coolly I thought. Oliver chose his moment, jumped, and came forward to seat himself beside Steve, reaching for the pile of ropes without comment. He had a knife in his pocket, he unleashed a businesslike marline spike and set to work with competent swiftness. For a minute or two, nobody said anything.

I don't know how the situation would have developed, but it never had a chance anyway. Poseidon the god of the sea must have really had it in for Paul. You could see his point.

All the time we had been galebound in Mykonos the big inter-island ferries had been plying in and out as usual without causing more than a minor flurry or two, but now, a very large water tanker was coming in between the moles, apparently determined to go stern-on to the north quay. As we watched, fascinated, she dropped two enormous anchors right across all of ours – each lying, of course, the prescribed ten boat lengths out – dragged around a bit while she seemed to be making up her mind, drifted to a close twenty-feet or so off our collective transoms and came to a solid halt against the quay.

'Now that,' said Steve, 'is just what we needed to make things perfect.'

Oliver gave a smothered laugh. 'Yes, it's not really been your week, has it?'

'You must think we're all a load of idiots!' burst out Jay, resentfully. Oliver looked at him gravely.

'The right circumstances can make a fool out of anybody.'

But he had laughed first, and I could see that Jay had taken it personally. I said hurriedly, 'How are you going to get back with your boat?'

'She'll come in later and pick me up. But not right now, let's hope.' He gave his finished splice a quick tug to settle it in and went on, 'Are you making short ropes or long ones out of these sad fragments?'

'We haven't enough to spare to make decent warps, only emergency ones,' Steve told him. He picked up the splice and looked at it critically. 'Thank God for a proper sailor.'

Oliver raised his eyebrows before turning to sort through the heap for two more reasonably compatible pieces. 'Surely there's enough of those here?'

Steve gave an unamused laugh. 'So far as ropework goes, there's Jay and me, and as of this morning, our engineer. And Sue and Marina if we had a marline spike between us all. According to the inventory, there should be one on every yacht. There isn't, of course, Jay and I are making do with this spoon.' He tossed it in his hand; filched from our cutlery box, it looked a bit bent by this time.

'Jesus!' said Oliver, but he didn't sound altogether surprised by this time. He picked up his knife and handed it to me. 'There you are. You'll have to take shifts, I'm afraid.'

I climbed up on the cabin top and knelt to sort through the pile of ropes. He was so close to me that I could feel the warmth of him against my bare arm. I kept my face down, conscious of my colour rising, my skin tingling, and cursing myself for being foolish. Marina got to her feet and said she was going to see if the beer was still cold.

I sat, busy with my splicing, shoulder to shoulder with Oliver and wondered why he had chosen to come on board. To help with the ropes, perhaps? But how could he have known of the necessity until he was actually here? So, to wait for his boat then? But he could have done that more comfortably in any taverna in the town. To see me again? But that was absurd! Anyway, he was taking no particular notice of me now, but talking to Jay and Steve about the winds that blow in the Mediterranean, and of the barren islands of the Cyclades which he knew well, but of which we would see no more after this. It was obvious from the way he talked that he was a yachtsman of far more than even Steve's experience, a full-time professional with his eyes on blue water. A man that no woman would ever hold for long, for he was already deeply in love with the great oceans and the wide skies and the steady trade winds that blew in the great empty spaces between. My heart seemed to twist under my ribs and my throat ached. Too old, and married – of all women, I was not for him. I couldn't think what had come over me.

After a while Robin came and joined us, and Marina fetched out another can. Although he and I were slower than the other three, we very shortly had the whole lot done and neatly hanked ready for use. Because Oliver was there, none of us felt like asking what Emmy and Paul were doing, although I had seen them walking along the quay towards the town a little while earlier. Not entwined arm in arm as usual, there had been space for the gale to blow between them.

Oliver left once the ropes were done, collecting his knife and walking away with a casual, assured lope and no backward looks. Jay watched me watching him.

'Seems a nice enough chap,' he said distantly. 'Bit of a man's man.'

I wondered who he was trying to deceive, himself or me? Oliver Nankervis was a deeply attractive man, and whatever word might fairly sum him up, it certainly wasn't "celibate". But in the sense that he probably wasn't the type to marry and settle down, Jay was right. I turned to my husband, and on impulse reached up and kissed him. 'Aren't you all, at bottom?'

He kissed me back, but I felt a now-familiar reservation. Was I making a fool of myself, I wondered, trying to hold us together? Or was I making a fool of myself by yearning too conspicuously for a man probably at least twelve years my junior, or even more? Or did Jay simply sense my own confusion? I drew back and looked at him, a frown between my eyes that wouldn't smooth out.

'Jay?'

But he turned away, yawning. 'I'm going below for a kip before lunch. My eyes are all gritty.'

Like the wind itself, my thinking had almost imperceptibly swung a point or two. Confused and disturbed, I didn't realise that I was already looking at things from a different standpoint. I felt snubbed, and disappointed too, but there was no reason I could put my finger on.

By lunch time, there was mutiny abroad. The skipper of *Persephone* (I believe his name was Ted) told – not asked – Paul that he was putting his wife and his friend's wife ashore to take a taxi, and with Tom as extra crew was sailing round to Ornos Bay. He had borne enough, his wife had borne more than enough, in fact they were all fed to the teeth with the whole thing, and if Paul didn't like it, he could do the other thing. Paul didn't actually argue, but it turned out that there was a small snag. Their anchor was firmly caught by that of the water tanker, and there was no way that they could get it in. There was a brave attempt to do so – Robin even dived with mask, snorkel and fins to the bottom of the harbour to view the problem close up, but in the end, *Persephone* sailed without it. Paul brought the warp over and made it fast on our transom.

'We don't want to lose it,' he said.

'Thanks a million,' said Jay. We now had two fouled anchors, one on each quarter. Great!

Later still, fired by *Persephone*'s example, one of the others decided to follow suit. She, too, had to leave her anchor behind, and Paul brought this one to join the first, firmly attached to our transom by one of his all-purpose bowlines. Now we had three.

'Any idea when that tanker is due out?' Steve asked, and Paul said he thought around five o'clock. Steve and Jay quietly untied both spare anchor warps and re-fastened them with slip knots. Paul looked mystified.

'What are you doing that for?' he asked.

Steve had jumped ashore and was scouring up and down the quay. He shortly came back with what he wanted, and while Paul silently watched, buoyed the end of each anchor warp with an empty plastic bottle, well stoppered. Robin made another dive and came up shaking his head.

'She'll take both when she goes, and unless we're very lucky, a few others as well,' he reported.

Persephone came on the radio to announce her safe arrival in Ornos Bay. She had enjoyed a fantastic sail, Ted enthused, we should all come round and join them. We all foregathered on the quay yet again, and there was some talk of a mass exodus.

'The ladies could go across by taxi,' someone said. 'The men can sail the boats there a few at a time, no problem.

Marina was indignant about this. She said, 'Stuff that for a game of soldiers! Why should the men have all the fun?'

Janet and Sylvia looked at her as if she had run mad, as did some of the other women. Steve grinned. 'Sounds great. Jay and I'll escort the ladies, and Marina and Sue can take the ship round.'

Somebody laughed, until he realised that Steve meant it. In the event though, the only one of us who got away that afternoon was *Aphrodite*. Tom and Ted came back from Ornos on the bus and took her, with Sally aboard (no taxis for Sally, either) in order to make room on the south mole for *Anatolikos* who was heading in from the open sea. The water tanker kept the rest of us trapped. Paul was worrying about his flotilla's anchors. Perhaps he felt he had already created enough of a fiasco without losing every kedge in the fleet.

In spite of this, however, and in spite of the fact that he had told us the tanker was due out at five, he was later seen leaving the quay again, Emmy trotting faithfully beside him. Robin sat in our cockpit with us, more cheerful than we had yet seen him, waiting for action. I think he was glad to have a chance to prove that he, at least, wasn't a complete moron.

But five o'clock came, and the only thing that happened was that a youngish man dressed in a light business suit came down to the quay looking for Paul. He didn't seem at all pleased to learn that our Skipper wasn't there, and took Robin off with him to *Eleni*. Robin had looked considerably surprised to see him, we all decided, so obviously they weren't complete strangers to one another. Marina was the only one of us who actually saw the man leave; later on, she said that he didn't look as if he had enjoyed his visit. I might have seen him, for

I was in the cockpit with her, but I was looking across the harbour to *Anatolikos*, trying to kid myself that I wasn't watching for Oliver.

Those who read this will probably think that I was not only incredibly naïve, but stupid with it. If so, they have never been in the grip of this kind of fever. I hope they never will be, for it brings no happiness, only pain – and shame, for those who suffer it hurt not only themselves, but run a great risk of hurting others too. Look at me – I had everything to lose by it, for like the proverbial city set on a hill it cannot be hid, least of all from someone as close as a husband. Oliver, I was certain, had meant nothing like this to happen. A mild flirtation, a bit of harmless fun – how could either of us have known of the fire that would burn in me so consumingly as a result? There was no denying it, it had already gone beyond control and I knew it. It must burn itself out, and it was a toss up whether that flame would refine or destroy.

But at least I need not make Jay look a fool; I knew how that felt at first hand. If I was to suffer, it must be alone. I found the resolution at last to turn away and go below, to where Jay slept sprawled on the saloon cushions, snoring gently.

Maybe, if he had been awake... but then again, probably it was already too late by then.

I stood looking down at him. Jay – my dear, familiar husband, who no longer cared enough to look at me properly... anyway, what man ever sees his own wife clearly? And love and courtship begin marriage, they do not make it. It is affection, familiarity, shared experience ... trust... that do that. I was conscious of an urgent wish that he would open his eyes, smile at me, hold out his arms and tell me that he loved me, *show* me that he loved me, and save me from this wild wind that was blowing me away... away from him... away...

I was very tired, close to exhausted even, by so many bad nights and perhaps that was why everything seemed so clear and bright and inevitable, and why I didn't even have the strength to be frightened any more of what might come.

But Jay slept.

Late afternoon crept on and became early evening. A lot of the flotilla had gone off into the town, but, as Steve pointed out, with three seriously fouled anchors now attached to our boat, we were stuck where we were for now. Paul had no doubt known what he was doing when he tied them to *Phaedra*. Marina and I went ashore to see what we could find for an easy supper on board, and on our way past the beach, met up with Paul and Emmy riding on a small scooter. Emmy had an old motor tyre under each arm, they stopped to have a word with us.

'Everything all right?' Paul asked, just as if he hadn't made a habit of being somewhere else whenever it wasn't.

'Some man came looking for you,' I told him. 'Robin spoke to him. He'll tell you what it was about.'

Paul nodded, thanked us, and rode off with a wave that made the little scooter swerve dangerously so that Emmy nearly dropped one of her tyres. Marina rubbed her nose as she pensively looked after them.

'I wonder why he didn't do what we suggested, and get the others to collect them?' she speculated. I shrugged my shoulders.

'We know already he doesn't seem able to delegate,' I pointed out.' Marina sniffed expressively.

'He managed to delegate to Steve and Jay with no trouble. Anyway, that wouldn't matter so much if he only did the jobs himself.'

'Well, this time he is.'

We bought more of the wonderful hot cheese puffs, a fresh loaf and some sticky cake, together with more of the ripe green figs that taste of honey and some slices of unidentified sausage and then made our way back to the quay. On the way we met Janet, Sylvia and Carol. Obviously, it was Girls' Afternoon Out.

'Been shopping?' cried Janet cheerfully, when she saw us (I nearly said "gaily", but you don't use that word carelessly on Mykonos).

'Only food,' said Marina. Janet looked disappointed.

'But aren't you coming this evening? Emmy's booked almost a whole taverna for us.'

Nobody had bothered to tell us, but anyway we could hardly leave *Phaedra* under the circumstances. We told them this, but except possibly for Carol, they missed the point.

'Paul must have that in hand,' said Sylvia, with a confidence we wished that we could share. 'Anyway, someone said that tanker wasn't going out until tomorrow.'

'How early?' asked Marina, for nobody had told us that, either.

'I think one a.m was mentioned.'

'Well, we've got the food now. Anyway, we're all a bit tired. None of us has slept properly for the past few nights.'

Janet and Sylvia tried to persuade us, but we really had no heart for the proposed treat. Although Marina and I hadn't actually kept watch, we had been disturbed every few hours or so by our husbands going back and forth and we were shattered. And as it happened, we weren't the only ones to miss this group meal, Paul and Emmy weren't there, either. I'll tell you what happened. You'll never credit it – or come to think, maybe you will.

We arrived back at the quay laden with our shopping, to find Jack and Steve talking to the German skipper who had been calamity-howling on the first night of the gale. He was leaving for Tinos first thing in the morning, and had come aboard to thank them for their vigilant watch-keeping, and to present them with a bottle of Johnnie Walker. Black label, too! Some of the warps, we saw, had now been sheathed with bits of motor tyre where they crossed the sharp edge of the quay.

'Robin did it. We helped him,' said Jay. Nobody had really expected that Paul would.

Steve gestured upwind, towards *Eleni*.

'There's been a bit of excitement up there,' he said. 'That chap came back – the one who was here earlier – and met up with Paul at last. They've been standing on the deck, shouting at each other and waving their arms about. I think he might be the managing director from Athens, taking exception to our TV image.'

Marina climbed up onto the cabin top to see better.

'They're still at it,' she reported. 'Come on Sue – we wanted to go to the loo anyway. Let's go and see what's going on.'

'How can we?' I objected, but we went anyway. The nearest toilets here were in the place at the end of the quay where Janet and Sylvia had spent that first night. It was called The Yacht Club, like Panther Sailing's headquarters (not what we would consider a yacht club back home, but in this case anyway, a jolly, friendly sort of place for all that, in a Greek sort of way) and to get there, we had to pass the lead boat. Sadly for Marina, she had moored up bows-to, like most of us (you get more privacy that way) and all the action was taking place in the cockpit. All three of the crew were there, and the man in the suit was doing most of the talking, thumping on the deck with his fist to emphasise his points. Paul was red in the face, Emmy looked from this distance as if she was crying. Robin had his back to us, but the back looked wooden. As we approached, Paul turned abruptly and vanished below and Emmy let out a scream. 'No Paul, no! Paul please come back – *Paul*!' but then a belated sense of decency had taken us past and out of earshot.

'We'll walk back more slowly,' said Marina.

There was a queue for the toilets – we were all using them as a matter of course during the daylight hours, as there was no way our holding tanks could be pumped out in the harbour – and it was more than ten minutes before we were headed back. Things had moved on dramatically. Paul, carrying a big kitbag, solidly stuffed, was making his way forward along the lead boat's side deck, with Emmy scrambling behind him, yelling and sobbing, and the man in the suit was climbing up to follow them both. Robin alone remained in the cockpit, sitting with his arms folded and his face like stone. Marina caught my arm, but I was already slowing down.

'Paul!' Emmy shrieked. She had fallen onto her knees over a cleat on the foredeck. 'Paul, oh please come back! Paul!'

Paul flung his kitbag ashore and jumped after it, nearly landing on Marina. He brushed her aside without seeming to see her, shouldered his bag and began to walk briskly away. Emmy had stopped. The man in the suit was holding her arm, dragging her onto her feet and she scratched at his hand angrily with her fingernails.

'Let me go. I have to stop him!'

He dropped her arm, but she made no attempt to follow Paul. She stood there, sobbing wildly. We were so close that even above the gale we heard snatches of what she said, although she was no longer screaming. '...you can't... I'll go too... your silly flotilla then?'

The man in the suit looked round with a touch of desperation, and saw Marina and me standing there.

'Are you part of this flotilla?' he barked. Marina nodded,

speechless by this time. Emmy went on sobbing. Robin had got to his feet, but he wasn't doing anything, he just looked punch drunk. The man in the suit looked dazed too, as if events had moved faster and gone further than he had ever intended. He wasn't so very old – about our age, or less even – and although nobody could have said that he was panicking, there was a wild look in his eye. In the background, Robin began to laugh, an angry sound with no mirth in it. Marina said slowly, not believing her own words, 'Do we take it that we are now a flotilla without a Skipper?'

'Or a hostess!' wept Emmy.

'Of course not,' the man snapped, looking rather hot. 'Robin, here –'

'Oh no!' cried Robin, instantly. He added, more quietly, 'Look, I'm just an engineer. I know a bit about sailing, but not nearly enough to be a Skipper, particularly not here and now. I'm not going to pretend. Things are bad enough already.'

Emmy let out a howl of misery. I was aboard by this time, my arms round her, but she was beyond comfort, clinging to me as if I was a lifebelt and she, drowning. Marina said, 'Do you think it might be a good idea if we all went back to the cockpit? People are beginning to stare at us.'

She made the jump aboard to join the rest of us. Robin made some tea and we all sat in the lead boat's cockpit, drinking it. Emmy had calmed down a bit after a good cry into my T-shirt, which was now damp as well as dirty, but sat without speaking at all, and neither of the men seemed to know what to do next. Marina said, cautiously to Suit-man, 'What about you? Could you do it?'

'I'm like Robin, except that I'm just a pen-pusher, a mere weekend yachtsman. Ladies and gentlemen, I think we have ourselves a problem.' He grinned, suddenly and boyishly, but obviously, things were bad enough. 'Of course, Paul may come back when he's calmed down.'

'With all due respect,' said Marina, 'we're better off without him. He…' She glanced at Emmy and ran out of steam.

I said, 'There are several pretty experienced yachtsmen here – Marina's husband, and mine, and us too if it comes to it, and the three on *Pasiphae*, and there's a boatful of Canadians over in Ornos who seem to know their way around too... we could get the flotilla home safely between us, I'm sure.'

'Maybe that's what we'll have to do, if it comes to it – if we can sort out the insurance.' He looked unhappy. 'I have to find out exactly what's been going on before I can decide anything. You should never have been here in the first place, with weather conditions the way they were shaping up –' But he broke off there, perhaps feeling that he had said too much already. Emmy got to her feet.

'I'm going to pack,' she announced.

'Oh no, you're not!' Suit-man rose to his feet too, blocking her path to the companionway.

'Oh yes I am!'

It was like something in a pantomime. Suit-man must have realised it, for he pulled himself together and spoke more quietly. 'Things are bad enough, without you rocketing off like a hysterical missile!' He paused, and then added tellingly, '*Too*.' Emmy's mouth set in a stubborn line.

'If Paul loses his job, I don't want mine.'

'There's no "if" about it, my dear girl. He's lost it. Finish.'

Robin spoke quietly, and for almost the first time, 'Let's get the ships home safely, Emmy. You can leave then, without making bad, worse.'

'Oh, can she?'

Emmy stood irresolute. 'I don't even know where he's gone,' she said wretchedly.

'It can't be far though,' I told her. 'The island isn't big enough. Please don't cry any more.'

She was at the beginning of life, lucky Emmy. She had time to start a new page, not once but many times if need be. She couldn't know that though, she was too young... so perhaps it was poor Emmy after all, and lucky Sue, who was old enough to both know and to accept... accept that for her the book of life was half-written... oh shit! Why did this have to happen to poor Emmy?

Robin looked at his watch. 'I hate to interrupt this touching scene, but we have a group meal with the paying clients to organise right at this minute.'

'You get on and do it, then!' Emmy pushed past the director from

Athens, for it was obvious that was who Suit-man was, and this time he didn't try to stop her. She vanished below, and we heard a door slam somewhere beneath our feet.

'Christ!' said the director. He looked first at Marina, then at me. 'Look, can I ask you to keep your mouths shut about this until I've had a chance to think? We don't need any rumours going about and setting off a panic. I'm sure this whole thing can be sorted out somehow, and we'll get you home safely, I guarantee it.'

We were possibly safer without Paul, but neither of us said it a second time. We promised that we wouldn't breathe a word outside our own ship, and he looked relieved.

'I need to telephone my office. Perhaps we can get someone out here in time, there's four days yet before you have to be back. There's a shore/flot in their first week at base, I might be able to borrow their Skipper.'

I didn't think anyone would be too enthusiastic about spending another three or four days in Mykonos, but it didn't seem kind to say so. He went on, 'And now, I suppose, I had better see this Greek professor who stirred the pot to begin with.' He glanced across to where *Anatolikos* lay in her old berth on the south mole. 'This whole little affair is bidding fair to make ripples at government level if we can't resolve it now –' But there, he broke off again, said good evening to Marina and me and that he hoped we enjoyed our group meal, and left us.

'There goes a worried man,' said Robin, watching him.

'He needs to be,' said Marina. She looked at Robin uncertainly. 'Look, if it helps, Steve is a Yachtmaster Instructor. The Greeks would accept that as a qualification, wouldn't they? Just to get us safely back to Ayios Giorgos?'

Steve would enjoy running the flotilla, and would do it well, but it would hardly improve his already highly debatable holiday. I understood Marina's hesitation, but it seemed to me that it was a bit late for worrying about things like that. Robin looked doubtful.

'I honestly don't know. That professor is some really big bazooka, he could make a lot of trouble if he wants to. It could be the end of our whole operation out here if we don't play our cards right.'

Marina tried to look sympathetic, but it was impossible to avoid thinking that, the way Panther Sailing operated, it might be a mercy all round. But the excitement was over now, and back on *Phaedra* our supper would be getting cold. We said goodnight to poor Robin and left him standing there, Paul's mantle resting temporarily and uneasily on his unwilling shoulders.

This late in the evening, and with the gale still blowing, it was too cold to sit outside. Everyone else had gone ashore by this time, but the four of us sat in *Phaedra*'s cabin eating our meal and talking about this latest, totally unforeseen, development. Jay was of the understandable opinion that, taking the swings with the roundabouts, it was the best thing that could have happened.

'We can get back to Ayios Giorgos all right,' he said, reaching for the chart. 'If we can get out tomorrow, we can take it in reasonable hops, straight back the way we came, familiar harbours all the way. Nobody needs to be scared of that. Or perhaps they'll just ship us all back to Athens on a ferry and give us a refund.'

'Hope they give us a refund anyway, after the way we've worked for them these past few days,' grunted Steve. He had finished eating and now climbed up the companionway to the cockpit, glass of wine in hand, to have a quick check round to see that all was well. The big tanker looked as if she had settled in for the night. He stood there for a minute or two, looking across to the south mole, but there was no activity going on over there. If the unfortunate director was on board *Anatolikos*, he was causing far less of a stir than he had on the lead boat. But no doubt, a respected Professor of Archaeology had more self-control than Emmy or Paul.

Marina went to sit on top of the steps to be close to Steve. 'Isn't this fun?' she enquired, of the world at large – it is another of her catchphrases, as you may have noticed. Then she treated us to a First. 'Nothing like this ever happened when we were in the Ionian!'

Panther Sailing had scored a point at last!

Steve tilted his head back, as if listening.

'Ssh,' he said, 'Hear that? The wind's moderating, it's stopped howling in the rigging.' He took a couple of steps towards the transom and raised his glass, shouting suddenly into the diminishing roar of the gale. 'Here's to you, Poseidon! Give us a fair wind for Siros!' And he poured the last of his wine as a libation over the stern.

Day Twelve: Friday, 16ᵗʰ June

At one a.m, Steve and Jay were both on deck, but there was no sound or movement on the tanker, and Jay came back to bed, rolling in beside me with a grunt.

'Nothing doing. Latest guess is six a.m.'

But at six o'clock, again, everything was quiet. Steve, this time, came below with the news.

'Eight a.m.'

We were all of us up and ready for that, but we might as well have stayed in bed. They did.

'The man in the suit who came yesterday, he was from the office in Athens,' Sylvia told us, confirming what we had already deduced, but she added, which did rather surprise us, 'Paul has been called away suddenly illness in his family or something. Emmy is rather upset about it.'

I wondered if her inside knowledge stretched any further.

'What happens to the flotilla, then?' I asked. She looked doubtful.

'I suppose Robin will take us back,' she said.

Conscious of Steve grinning at my shoulder, I said diplomatically, 'I suppose it's an option.'

'The wind's going down fast now, anyway,' said Steve, with satisfaction. 'The gusts are still force 8, but generally it's well below 7. We should get away today, no problem.'

By ferry? I asked myself, but no doubt we should soon learn.

Standing orders were to attend the morning briefing in the usual taverna, and nobody had told us any different. It wasn't our place to spread alarm and despondency, in fact we had promised not to, so when the rest of the flotilla began to go ashore for breakfast and information, we went with them. Latest news of the tanker was that she would leave at ten o'clock, but anyway, we could see what she was up to from our waterside meeting place. Steve and Jay chose a table where they had a clear view, ready to leap to their feet at the first sign of her getting her anchors in.

None of our lead boat crew was there when we arrived, and discussion was rife as to what was going to happen now. Some people suggested openly that Steve was the man to take over the flotilla, but the more general opinion was that Robin would take us straight home to Ayios Giorgos, which was an interesting comment on his standing with the fleet. Whatever people thought of Paul, and nobody was saying very much, feeling sorry for his alleged personal troubles, Robin stood high in everyone's estimation, including our own. He had tried to do his job in very difficult circumstances, and none of us felt that we could have done any more. Torn between loyalty to his employers and their inadequate organisation, his had been in an unenviable position. But was it going to get any better now? We waited with as much interest as anyone to find out.

We sat, as was becoming habitual, with the crew of *Hippolyta*, and the sympathetic speculation of Janet and Sylvia about the supposed illness in Paul's family that had called him away so abruptly was becoming embarrassing. Jay wasn't helping either; he looked stormy and was unusually silent, a dark mood that seemed mainly directed at Steve, which made a change. To ease the situation and change the subject, Marina asked how the group meal had gone the night before.

'It was a bit of a non-event, really,' Janet told us. 'The taverna didn't really want to cater for such a big party, and so the service was awful. Then, of course, Paul and Emmy weren't there, and Robin was trying not to let us see that he was worried about something and not quite bringing it off.'

'And did you all sit together this time?' asked Marina. Sylvia shook her head.

'No. We all sat at separate tables again, here and there – some of us sat together, but only because we chose to ourselves. We were with Carol and Richard – and Charles, of course. We missed you.'

'We couldn't leave *Phaedra*,' said Marina. 'Steve and Jay were worried about that tanker leaving.' And three fouled anchors, but she didn't mention them.

'Do you think we really will be able to go today, Steve?' Ken asked, but none of us knew the answer to that. Steve only said, 'If we don't, we'll find ourselves pushed for time. We've only three days left, counting today, to get back in.'

'It's still blowing awfully hard,' said Sylvia apprehensively. Steve gave her a reassuring smile.

'It's dropping all the time now, it's blowing itself out. I can safely promise, everything will be fine once we know what we're doing.'

'Here's Emmy,' someone called, right on cue, and every head turned.

Emmy was coming along the harbour front from the direction of the south mole. She looked, even from a distance, desolate and unhappy, black smudged eyes in a face yellow-pale under her suntan. She was closely followed by – practically with – a noisy group of the multi-national divers from *Anatolikos*, including, I saw, Oliver, carrying between them an assortment of gear: a couple of canvas bags that had seen hard service and a toolbox. I remember that I wondered idly if they were off to dive for something, and if so where.

There was a dreadful sort of inevitability about the events of this holiday, which couldn't even be dignified by the name of coincidence, that led me on and on into uncharted territory that I had no wish to explore. I found that I wasn't even really surprised when the entire group stopped beside our taverna, the escort piled the baggage in a heap, and there was a lot of back-slapping and embracing before they turned and walked off, waving, back towards their boat, leaving Emmy – and Oliver – with us.

Emmy picked her way among the silent flotilla towards the vacant table where she, Paul and Robin generally sat, taking Oliver with her. He caught my eye as he passed our table, and I could have sworn that he winked at me. But perhaps I imagined it. I felt suddenly hot all over. Emmy said, 'You tell them – I can't.'

Oliver perched himself on the edge of the table, leaning back on his hands, and gathered everyone's attention simply with a look. He didn't seem wholly at ease, either.

'My name is Oliver Nankervis, ' he began. 'As you must know by now, your Skipper has had to leave rather suddenly.' He paused, obviously wondering how much we all knew, and a voice at the back of the room shouted unexpectedly, 'Hurrah!'

Oliver directed a steady look in the direction of the shout.

'Well, that's none of my business,' he said. 'What is my business, is getting you all back to base without drowning any of you and ruining your holiday yet further, which is what Panther Sailing have invited me to do.'

'But aren't you a diver, or something?' somebody asked, with understandable caution. Oliver smiled in the direction of the question.

'Fear not! First and foremost, I'm a professional skipper. But not, I must tell you, of a flotilla. I can offer you no social graces or frills, simply my help and guidance in getting back to Ayios Giorgos in one piece. Some of you won't need it. Those skippers will have to bear with me if I tell them things they already know. It's safer, given these conditions and with your varied experience, to be too careful than to take anything for granted, and this I'm sure you will all agree with.'

A murmur went around our group that I thought was not only agreement, but a measure of relief too. Mind you, he had yet to put his money where his mouth was. We waited in silence. Oliver said, 'I don't suppose someone would like to find Emmy and me some coffee? We've been argu – I mean, talking, near enough since dawn, and I don't know about her, but I'm dry.'

Three people, including Sylvia, rushed to attend to it. Oliver went on speaking.

'Today, we're going to Siros. We shan't be able to leave until that tanker has gone, but she's due out quite soon now, and with this wind we should make good time. I estimate that if she keeps to her schedule, we should all be safely in harbour by teatime, or soon after. In the meantime, I want all skippers aboard their boats, please, and all crews back on board by eleven at the latest. I shall go round to each boat individually and go over the chart with you and give you the sailing instructions for the day, and I would impress on you that what I say, goes – even if some of you consider me over-cautious. I have already told the company's representative that I won't take on an unknown responsibility unless I have absolute cooperation, is that understood?'

Everyone nodded, and the murmur ran round again, more widespread this time. Oliver said, with another of his engaging smiles that this time included everyone, 'Good, then we won't fall out. Robin has gone over to Ornos Bay to re-capture an escaped halyard and to hand out the orders for the day to those over there, but he'll be back before we sail. They will obviously get away before you. There'll be a lot of boats taking shelter in Foinikas, I think it probable we shall all have to anchor off, but if there is room on the quay, I'll try to be there to help you. And one last thing –' He paused. He deliberately collected Steve's attention, and his smile deepened. He was nobody's fool, Oliver. I had completely gone off my breakfast.

'Radio etiquette on this flotilla has been a bit slack, so let's get it straight. Don't use the radio unless I specifically call you, *unless,* and this is the only exception, you are in trouble of some kind. At all other times, please maintain radio silence but keep your ears open. And finally, Greek harbours are in general not bottomless, as I'm sure you've all discovered. So disregard what you have been told before and use your own judgement – as a guide, in most of them dropping your anchor three boat lengths out from a quayside is more than enough, anything over six is serious overkill. If you look at the chartlets which I'm told you all have in your sailing notes, you will see that they tell you the depths in the harbours on your itinerary and you can calculate from that information how much chain to put out, and thank God, here comes that coffee!'

A crowd swiftly gathered round Oliver and Emmy when they sat down to their coffee, all firing questions and eagerly talking.

'*The king is dead, long live the king,*' said Jay cynically, and Steve remarked that at least, on the face of it, this one was fit to rule, and we would see what we would see. After which profundity, he suggested we went back to the boat.

'Unless we need any more stores,' he added. 'You two women can see to that, and don't be late back on board.'

Marina said we could probably do with more bread, and we went into the town together for the last time. When we returned to the quayside some twenty minutes later, the flotilla was humming with activity, preparing itself for sea. Jay was on board *Phaedra* and Steve was on the quay talking to Ken and Oliver, he grabbed the warps as we arrived and began hauling in with Ken's help.

Jay stood on the foredeck ready to catch the bread as Marina threw it to him before, timing it to the swell, she jumped and landed safely, climbing over the rail laughing. It was now my turn to make that death-defying leap for the final time.

Perhaps it was the close proximity of Oliver that upset my judgement, or maybe it was just that old thing about the pitcher that went too often to the well. However it was, this time, for the first time, I misjudged the moment. *Phaedra* surged up towards me, I took a breath and leaped – a fraction of a second too late. I was already in

186

mid-air, only the toes of one foot in touch with the quay, when I saw to my horror the boat dip and swing away, and for one awful, endless second I seemed to hang poised above the rocks and the horrible swirling water... and serious injury, or even death. I don't think I even screamed – and then Oliver caught at my arm and yanked me back from the brink of disaster with a strength that sent me whirling straight into his arms. We both staggered back under the impact.

Our eyes met, mutually startled, and time stood still, holding its breath. For what seemed an eternity we stood locked together. I could feel his heart beating like a trip hammer, was close enough to count his eyelashes. I couldn't move, or do anything sensible – and then he slowly let me go, and nothing was ever going to be the same again.

He said, 'Not the best place to trip, really. Are you all right?'

I nodded, speechless.

'Take a deep breath and try again – come on Steve, all heave together – she'll come in nearer than that if we give it some wellie –'

He was kneeling beside Ken, his hands on the ropes. Under his shirt, the muscles rippled powerfully across his shoulders. Dizzy as much with the shock of revelation as with my near-death experience, I drew breath as he had commanded and slowly unloosed the fists that I hadn't even realised I had clenched. *Phaedra* dipped her nose preparatory to her next upward swing.

'Ready?' Steve called. '*Now!*'

And I was safely on board, clinging to the rolled jib with Jay holding my arms. I knew that even if we were kept here for another week, which God forbid, I could never make that jump again.

One long, mournful hoot came from the water tanker, and the brief incident was over. The next act of our island drama was about to begin.

Steve was on board before the hoot had fairly died away, and he and Jay raced for the cockpit to stand by the borrowed anchors, all ready to slip them if necessary. The tanker's winches began to clank and clatter, her engines began to throb. She moved out majestically across the harbour, winding her heavy anchor chain as she went, and the warps to our transom tightened expectantly. At this point, Steve and Jay wisely slipped the knots and stood holding the buoyed ends of the warps. As the tanker moved slowly out of her berth,

Jay called excitedly, 'I've got a bite, I've got a bite!' and leaned back against the pull.

'Let it go, you fool!' I cried, but he wouldn't.

'Not likely, I've not caught one as big as this in years!'

A cynic might have argued with that, remembering Dawn.

The rope began to thrum rhythmically. 'Don't be so *stupid*!' I cried, and Jay laughed and at last let go. There must be an unsuspected amount of stretch in your average rope, the buoy shot straight across the harbour like a missile, planing in a cloud of spray as it went. It might as well have been on elastic! Fortunately, there was nothing in its path.

The tanker, by this time, had both her anchors up. The one on the port side looked fine, but from her starboard bow there depended her own huge anchor, hung about like some futuristic Christmas tree with Paul's final legacy – chains and ropes and a fine selection of the flotilla's small kedge anchors! She turned in a disconsolate circle round the small harbour, trailing debris behind her, and came to rest just clear of the trots of fishing caiques lying off the southern shore. *Eleni*'s inflatable dinghy with its powerful outboard came zipping into view with Robin aboard – where had he appeared from? – and roared across to see what, if anything, could be salvaged, but as he tugged and struggled with the muddle hanging from the tanker's anchor, her captain suddenly realised that his ship was drifting aground and gave orders to drop the port anchor again. It roared, heavy and huge, straight past Robin's ear and even at this distance, he visibly changed colour.

'Reminds you of Mr. Bean,' said Steve, awestruck.

I glanced back over my shoulder at the quay, but Oliver had gone. Robin was heading back towards us, he vanished from our view behind the boats moored along the piers, and reappeared a moment later with Oliver on board as well, armed with a pair of heavy cutters Of course! Our lead boat was now equipped with a toolbox. They managed to rescue two anchors before a Greek caique got in on the act, passing a line to the tanker and preparing to pull her from her undignified position in the shallows. Steve covered his eyes.

'I can't look. Tell me when it's all over, and I'll see to the funeral arrangements.'

But that was the last straw, discretion was the better part of valour. I saw Oliver point towards the shore, and Robin sent the dinghy hurtling towards us out of harm's way. The caique fussed busily towards the harbour mouth, the towline tautening behind her. She looked extremely small for the task she had undertaken, and we all watched her futile endeavour with sympathetic fascination. Ken and Bill had hurriedly distanced themselves from their anchor – it was one of the ones hauled up from the deep by the tanker – and Steve, finding himself with a spare in his hand, passed it across to them.

'Here,' he said helpfully. 'Have this one, instead.'

The caique was soon forced to abandon her impossible mission, and after a short pause, one of the smaller inter-island ferries, that had been unloading its passengers in the ferry berth, chugged out to take over. This was a more realistic proposition, and we all felt that the drama must now be approaching its climax – and it was.

The captain of the tanker obviously felt that he had now done all that could be expected of him, and it was time to go and try to sort out the tangle in safer, deeper water. As the ferry struggled gamely, her engine thrummed full speed ahead, the propellers spun, and she pushed herself clear of the shore and majestically followed the little ferry seawards. From her starboard anchor, there still hung an artistic festoon of chain and several dangling anchors, and from the port anchor, elegantly draped over the straining towline, there now depended what appeared to be an entire trot, with one little fishing boat still attached and planing gamely alongside. A huge cheer went up all round the harbour.

There was no act that could follow that one, it was time to leave. Steve turned away from the view of the departing tanker and towards the rest of us.

'Right, that seems to be it. Now let's get ready for sea!'

It was still blowing hard, and outside the harbour we could see the whitecaps on the water. Mindful of the fact that our new Skipper seemed, so far, to be a lot more in touch with reality than our old one, Jay and Steve were anxious to demonstrate that they, too, knew how to run a tight ship. *Phaedra* was equipped with the anchor points to rig a running lifeline, but of course there was no suitable warp, and Steve improvised with the inboard end of the plaited kedge warp – by some miracle, we still had ours – running it right round the boat to take the personal lifeline clips if anyone had to go on deck while we were sailing. Jay showed Ken and Bill how to do the same on *Hippolyta*. While this went on, I was down below to make sure that all loose gear was safely stowed, and Marina was checking life-jackets and personal lifelines out of the hanging cupboard where they were stored. For once, Panther Sailing appeared to have got something right, for the life-jackets were virtually new and in good order, although the lifelines on the safety harnesses were only single-clip. Double are better – you can stay clipped to the ship's running line, or any other suitable anchor point, with one clip, while moving the other onto the next anchor point, or past the shroud, or other obstruction. Even with a running line, such as Steve had rigged, there are times when it is necessary to unclip a personal lifeline, and that's the moment that the accident happens. A lot of people don't bother with running lines, but if the anchor points are provided it's a sensible precaution in heavy weather. The wire safety rails are not necessarily up to the sudden strain caused by the weight of a full-grown adult being swept over the side – and in Panther Sailing's particular case, not unexpectedly, some of these safety rails were only of thinnish rope, not wire anyway.

We all bundled ourselves up in the lightweight wet-weather gear which we had brought with us, and Panther Sailing's life-jackets and lines, and sat around in the cockpit like so many men from Mars, waiting for Oliver. He had started his rounds at the upwind end of the quay, and so came to *Hippolyta* before us, but it didn't take him a minute to size up the situation.

'Rock'n'roll,' he said, running an approving eye over the preparations. 'That saves some time. If one of you comes aboard here, it will save still more.'

Steve and Jay both climbed across. The briefing was swift and concise: our new Skipper would disentangle us one at a time, starting at the leeward end of the line, and send us flying on our way to Siros. We were to take down two slabs in the main, and use only two thirds of the jib, maximum.

'That'll be plenty to handle, and you won't go that much faster by crowding on more sail, even if you can handle it, and I'd prefer the fleet to stay pretty much together until I know your individual experience better. There's a heavy sea out there. If the wind moderates still more during the trip, then it's up to you to decide whether to shake out a reef or not, but don't be foolhardy whatever you do. The wind is nor'– nor' east, it'll blow you straight to Siros on a reach, you couldn't have it better. Steer 270°, altering 260° here –' he indicated a point on the chart that, firmly anchored by willing hands at all four corners, still managed to flap on the cabin top '– off Kaloyeres Point. That will take you straight to the point *here*, and then you're in sight of the entrance to Foinikas. You've been there before, you should have no problems. Any questions?'

'Is it going to be terribly rough?' Sylvia asked.

Oliver would never make the diplomatic service! He laughed. 'Wet, windy and wild, I should imagine,' he said cheerfully. 'But at least it should be quick. Stay in sight of each other, and I'll be right behind you. No problem.'

Sylvia looked as if she had plenty of problems, but Oliver, highly competent yachtsman though he might be – obviously was – was too young and too inexperienced in the tiresome skill of living in harmony with others to read the signs. He wished us all a cheerful *bon voyage* and leapt across *Phaedra* and then onto *Ariadne* without a glance in my direction. I wondered if I had been wrong, there on the quay. But no… there are some things it is impossible to be mistaken about. This was one problem that wasn't going to get up and go away.

Whatever I felt, whatever divine madness had me in thrall, *Oliver felt it too and was equally in its grip.*

I couldn't believe it, but at the same time, I couldn't be wrong. Just for that one, never-ending moment as I stepped back from the brink of death, I thought that I had looked into his soul, and he into mine.

It took an age to get everyone disentangled, there were so many springs and warps, not necessarily attached only to the flotilla, and a lot of people just sat there like dummies waiting to be untied. Steve and Jay helped by unravelling as many as they could, starting from our end, while Oliver and Robin worked from the other, and at last we were all unsnarled and ready. It was time to be gone.

Ariadne was the first to leave, and as she pulled slowly away from the piers, Steve had our engine started. Marina was on the foredeck ready to take the warps, Jay prepared to bring the anchor inboard, I was on the helm. Oliver and Robin undid the well-spliced, ragged warps, coiling them, tossing them, leeward rope first then upwind, to Marina. I engaged reverse as Jay finally brought the kedge in and we moved slowly out from the quay. Then engine into neutral, slow forward – watch out for those rocks under the water – and we were at last under way for Siros!

I took *Phaedra* out of the harbour while the men got sail on her – and oh, it was wonderful to see that dusty quayside receding behind us! We cleared the mole and the wind hit her, she dipped and curtsied as she felt it and swung away over the sea that was pale-green and cloudy with turbulence, spray blowing like smoke in the wind from the wavecrests, headed for Siros heeled over in the wind and flying... flying!

"Ladies by taxi", indeed!

Oliver's *wet, windy and wild* proved to be a fair description. We were reaching through short, steep seas and it was quite a rough ride, with the occasional heavy slam as the bow overshot and came down heavily in a trough. Spray flew, like diamonds in the sunlight, and after a while Steve went below to boil a kettle for a hot drink, where the larder, which all this time had been sulking in its hole, seized the opportunity to fly out and catch him a triumphant bang on the thigh! Things were getting back to normal. Close behind us, *Hippolyta* sped amidst a silver cloud from her own bow wave. Jay was taking photographs again.

We had a marvellous sail back to Foinikas; the prospect of that pleasant, sheltered bay was half the joy of it! And at Foinikas we could have a swim – hooray! – wash away all the quayside dust at last, follow it with a freshwater shower, be clean again! And put on fresh clothes, and sleep the night through: oh, how wonderful that would be!

Eleni passed us just as we approached Foinikas; she had only one reef down and her full genoa, and she was going like a train, passing through the fleet like a knife through butter. Oliver was on the helm, as she swept through our lee we were close enough to see his hair blown about in the strong wind. He had his hands full. Emmy and Robin were sitting in the cockpit, and Emmy waved as they passed us. Perhaps she was cheering up. Lucky Emmy – Robin had to be an improvement on Paul.

And she had Oliver, as well.

If any of the three of them stayed with the flotilla after next

Monday... but that needn't worry any of us. We would be on our way home.

Oliver had been right about the number of boats taking shelter in Foinikas, and we did have to anchor off this time but nobody cared. We had all had enough of being tied to a quay to last us a long time yet. We enjoyed our swim and our showers, indulged in the anticipated luxury of clean clothes at last, and settled down in the cockpit with the last of the sloe gin. Down below, everything was in chaos, but we told each other that we could tidy up later. Marina said, with an impish grin, 'The cushions in our cabin have been flung about all over the place – it looks as if we've been trying out new positions!'

Jay laughed uproariously, far more than the remark merited, even though it was funny. I watched him and wondered how he could possibly be so insensitive as to sit there laughing while I was in such emotional turmoil. It seemed incredible that he didn't guess; after all, we were meant to be a couple, had been so for a long time now. Yet he could sit there, laughing with Marina as if all was well with the world, talking to Steve about our new Skipper being a vast improvement on the old one so far, and how he seemed quite a nice fellow into the bargain.

A nice fellow, little did he know! I was still having difficulty in taking on board the fact that he probably wouldn't really care, except in so far as his male pride would be affronted. Emotions are such complicated things.

'He'll soon dry Emmy's tears,' Jay was saying.

'You reckon?' Marina asked, with a quizzical lift of her brows.

'It's a cert! He'd eat Paul for breakfast!'

'Poor Robin,' I said.

'You reckon that, too?'

'All right, Cassandra,' said Steve, laughing. 'So what's your prediction?'

'I'm not predicting anything,' cried Marina, indignantly. 'I just think it's all a bit more complex than you think. For just one thing, Emmy was really in love with Paul.'

'He stood her up pretty abruptly last night – and there wasn't a sign of him this morning.'

'Poor Emmy, then,' I said.

'There, I'm with you.'

I wondered what else she had in mind. She had said *for just one thing*. You never quite know, with Marina.

We sat over our drinks until the light began to fade in the sky, relaxed in the knowledge that the worst had to be behind us now, that we would sleep undisturbed tonight, and that the flotilla was now recognisable as someone else's responsibility. Steve, I thought, looked shattered, he would be needing a second holiday to get over this one. Jay is different – he hadn't taken the plight of the flotilla so much to heart, nor assumed its troubles as his own in quite the same way. Jay is basically irresponsible, he always has been. He had enjoyed the feeling of people turning to *Phaedra* for advice, or even, in some cases, leadership, but for its own sake only. He had liked the... well, I suppose I mean the *admiration*, and been put out when Steve garnered more than Jay considered his fair share. He had not, like Steve had, looked beyond the immediate moment to a continuing obligation. In fact, I suddenly saw, he probably had more in common with Paul.

It was odd, the way I suddenly saw him so differently – so clearly. I had never considered him in quite this light, and yet, he hadn't changed in any way. Had he always been so centred on himself? He had, at times, really seemed to resent the way some people had said, "Ask Steve," or "Steve will know about that..." I shifted uneasily on my cushion. Doors were opening in my head that I would have preferred to stay closed. I had been married to Jay for twenty years; it was rather late to start wondering if I really knew him at all. And I loved him... of course I loved him. That was what all my worries were about.

Yet in the depths of my soul, the flame of my infatuation burned steady and clear, and old values, old conceptions, were purging away.

It was pleasant to be able to row ashore for a meal without feeling that we were betraying a trust. We landed on a convenient helicopter pad at the edge of the water, belonging, said Jay without rancour, to some rich git, and then Marina said, 'Have you got the ship's purse, Steve?'

'I thought you picked it up.'

194

'I haven't got it,' said Jay. 'Sue, you must have it.' I shook my head.

'Don't all look at me. I thought Marina had it.'

'God, what organisation!' Steve exclaimed. 'Toss you for who rows back for it, Jay.'

They tossed a coin and Jay lost, and climbed back into the dinghy. Marina said she thought the purse was on the saloon table, but if it wasn't, it might be anywhere. Steve called that we would wait in the taverna, out of the wind, which although it was now much less, and we were sheltered from it here, was still with us.

'You two go on,'I said. 'I'll wait here for Jay.'

I was aware of him already, under the shadow of the nearby trees, although I couldn't see him. Steve and Marina crunched over the shingle to the road and walked off, arm in arm, in the direction of the bright lights of the "restaurant" taverna where we had eaten before.

Oliver stepped out of the shadows and came towards me.

I moved towards him as if drawn on a string.

We met in a long, wordless embrace, and a kiss that sent the flame blazing through every nerve in my body. I was incandescent with desire, one great throbbing pulse of pain and light.

'This is plain stupid,' I said, breaking free at last. Oliver laughed.

'I was rather enjoying it.'

'I have a daughter nearly as old as you.' A bit of an exaggeration, but only a bit. He couldn't be much more than twenty-five, maybe -six but Sally was still a month or two short of nineteen.

'So what?'

His hands were still on my shoulders, his touch tingled through my spine like sparklers on firework night.

'But *why*?' I asked. I didn't really expect an answer, but Oliver gave me one just the same.

'A psychologist would probably say that my subconscious was searching for a mother figure, and for all you know, he would be right.'

'*Are* you?'

'I have more than enough mothers already. I have a stepmother, as well as the natural model.'

There was something in his voice that hurt me. I asked, without knowing why, 'Which of them brought you up?'

'My stepmother tried. I don't think she's proud of the result.'

I didn't ask him about his real mother. The "No Entry" signs were clear enough.

'And what would this psychologist have to say about me?'

Oliver said, deliberately, 'That you've grown bored with your husband, perhaps? And for all I know, he could be right there, too. Or of course, he could be wrong on both counts. I never did set much store by psychology, anyway.'

'I've been married a long time,' I said, not sure if I was offering defence or confirmation.

'Does it matter anyway?' Oliver asked. 'It won't last. It's just a williwaw.'

'A what?'

'A williwaw. A sudden gust that hits you from nowhere. It lays you on your beam-ends for a minute or two, and then it's gone.' He gave me a wry smile. 'And then you go down below to see how things are, and you find everything has flown out of the lockers and is lying in a heap on the floor... and it takes a while to put it all straight again.'

'But you do, in the end?'

'Of course. Things may not be in quite the same places, but that doesn't matter. However careful you were the first time, there's always something that could have been stowed better.'

'Don't things get broken?'

'Sometimes. Not if they were stowed right in the first place.'

'I see. But what do you do, while it's blowing?'

'Make the most of it, of course.'

I was silent. Ask a silly question... The possibilities were endless – and alarming. My heart seemed to have moved up into my throat, and its throbbing pulse blocked anything I might have wished to say. Oliver moved his hands up to my face, which didn't help, tilting it between his palms so that I looked up at him. He was a lot taller than me, about six foot, probably, maybe a little less. He kissed me, very gently this time, full on the lips.

'Don't look so worried. What can happen, after all? Even if I slept with married women, which I never yet knowingly have, where would we go? And anyway, I think it's going to rain.'

196

I said, finding my voice at last – or somebody's voice, it didn't sound like mine – 'We only have until Monday, and it's Friday now,' and heard the desolation in the words.

'Then on Monday, the williwaw will stop blowing.'

And I would never see him again. Angry tears stung behind my eyes. It was so unfair, I had never asked for it! And I would be hurt, most dreadfully, and maybe he would too.

Oliver slipped his arm round my shoulders and began to walk with me back towards the landing place. Out on the water, Jack was rowing for the shore, a dark blob on the luminous bowl of the moonlit bay. 'Don't think ahead,' he said. 'We have two days – don't spoil them. They'll be over soon enough as it is.'

The inflatable grounded on the shore and Jay scrambled out. Oliver took the painter and made it fast to a ring in the concrete slab, not with a bowline, as I noticed in a detached sort of way, but with a round turn and two half-hitches as we did ourselves. The three of us walked up to the taverna together, but it was Jay who had his arm, rather possessively, round my shoulders now.

Steve and Marina had found a table inside, it was still too draughty to be outside even though the wind was dropping all the time now. The crew of *Hippolyta* sat with them, and they had saved places for Jay and me. Jenny called across to Oliver as he came in with us, and he left then to go over to her; I felt ridiculously as if I had been wrenched in two. Just a williwaw it might be, but while it blew it couldn't be fought. I didn't, I thought stupidly, even dare to let go of the tiller to take in a reef. I could only hang on and let it blow me where it would.

'Marvellous sail, wasn't it?' said Ken, as we took our places.

'Marvellous! Such a relief to be away from Mykonos.' I heard my own voice, speaking banalities, and marvelled at myself. I sounded quite ordinary, and yet not ten minutes ago... Across the room, Oliver caught my eye and smiled, and looked away. At his side, Jenny bubbled happily with her youth and vivacity, her young crew and the four equally young Canadians all grouped around her.

Fantasy time. I must be barking mad.

'What d'you make of our new Skipper?' Sylvia asked me. I opened my mouth but no sound came out. Fortunately Jay picked up the question.

'Captain Bligh – thou shalt reef or be clamped in irons!'

'Be fair,' said Steve, mildly. 'He was right.'

'Oh, come on Steve! You or I, or even Marina and Sue, could have handled more than that. So could a lot of the others!'

'You know that, and I know that, but he doesn't know that. All he knows so far is that one or other of us has had to be rescued over and over again. What would you do, in his place?

'Well, I was grateful to him,' said Sylvia, firmly. 'I felt a lot safer, knowing that Ken and Bill couldn't go crowding on sail and tipping us over. At least we stayed reasonably level, even if we weren't breaking any records.'

Perhaps I had done Oliver an injustice. Maybe he wasn't as young in worldly experience as I had thought.'

'He's pretty gorgeous, anyway,' said Marina, as if that clinched it.

'Oh God, you women!' said Jay. 'Here they are again, all swooning over a pretty face as if it was that alone that made a seaman!'

'That wasn't fair!' I cried.

'Christ, it was only a joke!'

'A rather tasteless one. Women aren't such fools as you like to make out.'

'No?' He grinned at me. 'Confess it, Sue. Even you aren't totally immune.'

Even me? Whatever did he take me for?

'The whole subject is totally irrelevant anyway,' said Steve, interrupting firmly. 'I freely admit it, he's a man of a lot more seagoing experience than I shall ever get the chance to be; good God, he's a professional skipper! You don't get far in that game if you aren't good at the job, and what you happen to look like is neither here nor there.'

'He's so young,' said Janet.

'So were we all, once. Make no mistake about it, that's one formidable young man.'

'I wonder how he intends to get us home?' Bill speculated.

'We're supposed to have a race home from Perdika on the last day,' said Janet. 'It's our last port of call.'

'I suspect you may be lucky that you've already seen it,' said Steve, wryly. 'Siros to Aegina is one long trip.'

'How long?' demanded Sylvia, immediately worried. Steve narrowed his eyes, trying to visualise the chart.

'Seventy miles? A hell of a haul, anyway.'

Sylvia looked horrified. 'You mean, we've got eighty miles to go in two days?'

'All of that.'

'But –'

'This wind will blow us home,' Jay tried to comfort her. 'It'll be a reach all the way, if it holds. We'll waltz it!'

'That's rather what I was afraid of.'

Jay grinned. 'There ain't no other way to get there, lady.'

'This holiday has been a real bummer!' she exclaimed angrily. 'Never, never again!'

We finished our meal, and then Steve yawned and said that he, for one, was ready to turn in. We all got up to go and Oliver called across to us.

'Skipper's briefing at eight o'clock, please. Here.'

'Fine.' Steve raised a hand in acknowledgement.

We rowed back to *Phaedra*, but tired though I was, I couldn't get to sleep. I lay in the cramped darkness of our little after cabin, acutely aware of Jay breathing easily beside me, and the walls and roof seemed to close in on me. After a while, I scrambled as quietly as I could to the door and picking up my pillow, went out into the saloon. There was some spare bedding in the forepeak, I rolled myself up in it and lay on one of the saloon bunks, staring up at the rectangle of starry sky that showed in the open hatchway. It was only claustrophobia, I told myself. Of course it wasn't that I didn't want to be so close to Jay. He was my husband, my husband, my husband.

He was my past, and maybe – although it seemed less and less likely – my future. He wasn't my present.

My present was Oliver, that formidable young man who had been such a disappointment to his unknown stepmother.

He was very far from boring.

Why? Why? Why me?

… and Monday was so short a time away.

Day Thirteen: Saturday, 17ᵗʰ June

All through that night it was eerily quiet, give or take the occasional gentle patter of rain on the deck above my head. No lurching or banging, nobody running up and down the companionway during the dark hours. It was still blowing hard in the morning, nowhere near a gale but still hard enough, but the sky was clearing and here we were sheltered. The early morning sun was warm. It almost tempted us to go swimming again, but with a briefing at eight there was hardly time. We rowed ashore for breakfast with the shopping baskets; in spite of what we had been told on our first visit there was a little shop close to the taverna, where we planned to top up the stores. Marina and Steve had peered inside last night while they waited for Jay and me to join them. Frozen bottles of water, Marina had told us gleefully, and fresh bread after nine o'clock, she had ordered two loaves.

In the taverna/restaurant, the flotilla, looking a good deal more alert this morning, awaited the arrival of the new Skipper. Already, people were forgetting all the things that had gone so disastrously wrong and relaxing, enjoying themselves, making themselves believe that it hadn't been so very bad after all.

'Of course, we could have carried more sail yesterday with no trouble,' said Ken, with an expansive gesture of one arm that nearly knocked a passing waiter's tray from his hands. After he had apologised, Ken went on, 'The girls were a bit worried, but we could have handled it, no problem.'

Steve sat down and reached for the menu.

'It was pretty rough all the same, and he was right to be cautious. We had this out yesterday.'

'Oh, don't get me wrong, I'm not criticising,' said Ken, hastily. 'Still, I hope he isn't going to nanny us all the way home. Paul didn't.'

Paul hadn't done a lot of things, but none of us said so.

'Well, I hope he is,' said Sylvia, to me, under her breath. 'Bill is all right, but Ken likes to crowd on all the sail he can and have the boat sailing on her ear, and everything falls out of the lockers, and I have to close my eyes and think of... well, of England, actually. Dry land, you know, and nice firm houses. And I don't believe we go any faster.'

'You probably don't,' I agreed, but I didn't think she wanted a lecture on the optimum angle of heel in small yachts, and anyway I wasn't sure that I could explain it in words that would be understandable. It's one of those things that I have quite clear in my mind right up until the moment I try to define it. What she had said had reminded me of Oliver and the williwaw. I caught myself yawning, and rubbed my eyes.

'Didn't you sleep well?' Sylvia asked, sympathetically.

'Not very. I think it was too quiet.'

Oliver, Emmy and Robin were coming up the steps together. They looked very much at ease with each other, and even Emmy was managing the ghost of a smile this morning. Robin was actually laughing. The flotilla gathered round, cups of coffee and slices of bread spread with strange nameless jam in hand, to hear what was planned for the day. Oliver unrolled the chart he carried on one of the tables and called for volunteers to hold it flat – and here, I just mention that Panther Sailing had apparently never heard of chart covers. The chart of the Cyclades that we had on *Phaedra* was falling to pieces and going into holes with age and constant folding. It was probably no bad thing that we had never made it to Tinos, which had almost worn away completely in one of the folds.

'We have three different options today, depending on what you all want to do,' Oliver said, when everyone had drawn close enough to hear him. 'We've a long trip home however we do it, and two days to do it in. Also, of course, there are several things that you are entitled to expect on your holiday, some of which I understand you have already missed out on... for one reason or another.'

Emmy looked down at her feet, and Robin's mouth had a sardonic twist as he watched her. Poor Emmy, she wasn't in for an easy time of it. Robin must be as sore as a grizzly bear over all the disasters that Paul had orchestrated for him to share in, and Oliver's natural beauty and charisma weren't going to help if he really did fancy Emmy after all that.

'We're supposed to have a race on the last day, from Perdika and round the islands to home,' somebody said.

'That's covered by one of the options. Unfortunately, we can't cover everything. However, there's a rattling good wind again today, and if it stays in the same quarter we can leave now and go back to

Sounion, sail across to Perdika tomorrow for an early lunch, and race home more or less directly back to Ayios Giorgos, leaving Moni and Angistri to the north, in order to arrive by around four o'clock – if that's what you really want to do. There are alternatives.'

'How far is Sounion from here?' Sylvia asked Steve. 'I don't even want to *know* about racing!'

'A fair old sail,' Steve told her.

'About fifty miles,' said Oliver, overhearing. 'Kea's in the way, or it would be a bit shorter. Then around twenty-five to Perdika, and another eleven or twelve to home. But it wouldn't be much of a race. A reach pretty well all the way if this wind holds, just a matter of who blew along the fastest.'

'Won or lost at the start?' said Charles.

'Pretty much.'

'What else can we do?' asked Janet.

'We could go straight across to Perdika today. That's a long way, but there's a fair wind. Nine or ten hours sailing, a bit too much for some of you, probably. It's still quite lumpy out there, although the forecast is improving. Then you could have your planned race around Moni, Ipsili and Nira tomorrow.'

From the looks on the faces of the various crews, there was little enthusiasm for this option, although one or two looked keen on the race. Bill said, 'I don't know about everyone else, but we'd like it to be as easy on the crew as possible. I'm happy to skip racing if everyone else is.'

'No barbecue, no race, no bloody anything!' the disgruntled voice of Ted was heard to mutter at the back of the room. Oliver must have had ears like a bat, he picked him up smoothly.

'Which brings us to Plan C,' he said, with a smile in Ted's direction. He could charm the birds from the trees, that man. Ted melted like butter in the sun and smiled back.

'You've all had a rough ride,' said Oliver. 'Foul weather, a few bad disappointments, a lot of problems. Emmy and Robin and I were discussing it last night, wondering if there was still time to put even one thing right for you. We came up with this. If we scour the local shop for bits and pieces we could, if you so wish, sail to Kithnos today, which would give you another island, and bring up in a quiet bay that we know of for that barbecue that you missed out on earlier. How does that grab everyone?'

'We'd still have a long sail home,' said Bill, peering at the chart over Oliver's shoulder. 'Not much less than if we went from here to Perdika.'

'That's true, but there's two plus factors. One is a reduction of ten miles or so in the distance, that could be as much as two hours. The other is that the wind is moderating all the time now, and the sea will go down fast. It'll be an easier sail tomorrow than it will be today. If we start very early in the morning, we should be well on the way home before the wind picks up and starts blowing again around midday. But I do mean *early*. Talk about it among yourselves, and we'll take a vote on it.'

There was a babble of talk as everyone began discussing the various alternatives with the people nearest to them. Sylvia and Janet were sold on the idea of the barbecue and the long, but easy sail home without the pressures of racing, and most people seemed to feel the same way. Somebody asked, 'Will we find anything we can barbecue here?'

'Frozen chicken legs,' said Emmy sullenly, and Oliver said, 'You can barbecue corned beef if you really want to.'

'When you said we'd have to leave early,' Carol said cautiously, 'what does early actually mean?'

'That's the snag,' said Oliver. 'I would think, around seven… tomorrow's packing-up day, you'll need all the time you can steal.' He turned to Emmy. 'The floor is yours.'

I thought there was a warning behind the words – every nuance of his voice went through me with the brightness of a sword – and perhaps I wasn't imagining it, for Emmy forced a smile to her mouth although her eyes were tragic, with the dark shadows like bruises beneath them.

'We have to get back to Ayios Giorgos by around mid-afternoon to pack up,' she said. 'The yachts all have to be cleaned – I'll come round to show you how to do that – ('Saucy bitch!' said Steve, under his breath, for we have cleaned more yachts than enough in our time. Marina smothered a giggle.) – and you'll be packing everything you don't need for the night, ready to be off the boats at eight thirty on

Monday morning. All the inventories must be checked, and I'll be giving back your deposit cheques if there are no shortages or damages –'

'What about the damage done in Mykonos?' interrupted Ted, on a sour note. 'I hope we aren't going to be penalised for that. There's chips all down our stem from banging against that quay, just for a start.'

'Of course you aren't,' said Robin. 'Any damage due to the storm is down to the Company's insurers.'

'I'm very glad to hear it. None of us would have been there at all if we had been given the forecast!'

'And in the evening,' said Emmy, in a small, clear voice, 'we shall all be going to the Yacht Club for a group meal, and if we had been able to have a race, of course, there would have been the prize giving.'

'We could have a race,' somebody suggested, carried away on the tide of all this new enthusiasm. 'Of sorts, anyway. No official start line or anything, just whoever makes it home first.'

'Good idea – start any time after dawn,' said Steve.

'Ugh!' said Janet.

'Good idea,' agreed Oliver. 'So, what do you all want to do? It's time to decide – there's not a lot of time to spare whichever option you choose.'

A fresh buzz of talk broke out, but suddenly there was a new feel behind it. All through this holiday there had been a buzz of talk, but it had been dissatisfied, uneasy, disappointed. Now, when we were on the point of going home, it was as if the sun had come out after a fortnight of grey skies and rain. It wasn't so much Oliver's charismatic personality, although I don't believe he understood its potency himself, it was the feeling that we had, for the first time, that things were being planned and arranged for our benefit and enjoyment, that the success of our holiday was as important to Panther Sailing as it was to ourselves. Quite simply, we were no longer being short-changed, and everyone knew it.

The suggestion that we should compete to arrive home first – The Great Grain Race, somebody christened it, in a burst of creative imagination – had tipped popular opinion in favour of the barbecue. It was decided, with amazingly little argument, that we should each give a sum of money to Emmy, who would do the catering, rather than working on an every-man-for-himself system. The lead boat crew volunteered to concoct a fruit punch, any other drinks we would provide for ourselves. Oliver showed the various skippers where was the bay that he had in mind, but today he gave no further sailing orders.

'It won't be anything like yesterday,' he said. 'Nowhere near as bad. You all survived that. If you're not happy, have a word with me before you go, otherwise get yourselves there any way you like, bearing in mind always that a good seaman never takes unnecessary risks. Just be there by five for one final briefing, for whatever you may do, I am definitely *not* getting up before dawn!'

'Why, what time does Dawn get up?' Jay called. I muttered under my breath, 'You should know!' and Marina dug her elbow into me. Perhaps it was unworthy, at that. Oliver just grinned at him without answering, and the meeting broke up with laughter and anticipation, which made a nice change from gloom and trepidation.

We collected our bread and a couple of bottles of frozen water to help the cold box along until we got back to Ayios Giorgos, then rowed back to the boat to prepare for sea. The wind was still quite strong, and a lot of people, we noticed, were bundling themselves up in their heavy gear again, but we elected to favour a more laid-back approach. The sun was warm, the wind dropping all the time, the forecast good. We lay around sunbathing as we reached along in a brisk wind, over a softening sea, to Kithnos and the tiny, secluded bay of Episkopis.

It was like familiar old times, and yet it was not. The four of us were there together, as we had so often been before, sailing a boat and soaking up the sunshine, taking it in turns to go below to brew up coffee or tea, picnicking in the cockpit, talking together at ease, but all the time I was aware that things had subtly altered. Not for the others – not even for Jay – but for me. I no longer felt a part of them, but sat curiously detached on the sidelines, looking on. The centre of my world had shifted, it was no longer here on *Phaedra* but somewhere out there on that dark blue, foam flecked sea aboard *Eleni*. I knew it was foolish, that way led to nothing but heartache and bitterness and loss, but while my tide flowed strongly, while the williwaw blew, I had to go with them. Choice was quite simply not involved.

I couldn't resist stocktaking again, but now with a detached pragmatism that I would never have believed just a week ago. Of course, nobody gets out of marriage exactly what they expect, but what had we, in fact, expected? We had married very young, I had been barely nineteen and Jay only a few years older, but had we been content? I thought that probably we had, once, but the events of the last few months had opened the door on all kinds of dark, cobwebby places, where shadows filled the corners and light filtered only fitfully, and I found that I no longer knew with any surety when it had all gone sour. No doubt we both thought that we had done our best, but had we? A cold, inexorable feeling that it no longer mattered anyway couldn't help but grow in me, contrasting cruelly with the brilliant sunburst warmth of Oliver's williwaw. If that could be my future, I thought, it wouldn't be hard to walk away. But it wouldn't be – couldn't be.

But Oliver had looked at me, and if he was to be believed he had seen something in me worth loving. The ghost, perhaps, of the intelligent, ambitious young girl who had once been me, the one who had longed for excellence, thrown up everything for love, and apparently achieved – so far – only bare mediocrity. And if he could see her, why not somebody else?

I didn't want such a somebody. I wanted only Oliver, whom I could never have. There was nothing I could do to change that. I wished I could cry, for myself, for him, for Jay and our fading marriage, but of course it was out of the question. The comment it would arouse could never be countered, for how could I ever tell the things I had learned on this holiday, from the bitterness of understanding at last that I no longer really mattered to Jay, to the emptiness of Monday hanging over me like a storm cloud, and the future on my own that would one day have to be faced?

Everything was falling out of the lockers with a vengeance, and it looked as if quite a lot would get broken.

We had good sailing that day, so it was a pity I had let myself become so morbid – "menopausal" Jay would no doubt have said, although I hoped that was some way into the future yet. The further we got from Mykonos, the brighter even the weather seemed to become. By afternoon we had rounded the northerly tip of Kithnos and begun the seven mile run down towards Merikha, and Steve and

Jay had the chart out. It showed two biggish bays, Fikiadha and Apokriosis, and then just to the south of them, a narrow entrance like the neck of a bottle leading into Episkopis. There was a shelf of rock marked to the north, Steve said, we must be careful to clear it. Meanwhile, we ran easily now over a slow, lazy swell along the steep shore of the island, looking out for the indent in the coastline where the harbour of Merikha and our destination both lay. The cliffs were very steep and dark, it looked a forbidding place.

'That'll be it,' said Jay, pointing. He was on the foredeck keeping a look-out. The wind had fallen light now, and Steve switched on the engine to help us in. We rounded the headland into smooth water and a calm; the sails flapped, hung slack. Ahead of us, two other yacht from the flotilla motored towards the entrance to the bay, sails already stowed.

'Take the tiller, Sue,' said Steve. 'We'll get the sails off her as we go in. Just head *there* –'

I took the tiller and headed us in between the tall cliffs. Steve had smothered the engine until it was only just kicking the boat along, he and Jay bustled about, stowing the sails. Marina sat in the cockpit, looking about us with interest.

There was something about the place, don't ask me what – what Marina always referred to as "bad vibes", perhaps. I didn't like it much. I thought that it looked unwelcoming, as if it rejected the very idea of people coming here to make merry, and it was full of shadows, not light, so that I saw it as a picture of my own state of mind. The sun was still quite high in the sky, but even so the tall, dark hills shut it out. There were a few olive trees scattered along the shore, twisted and gnarled by exposure to the elements so that they looked as if they had been designed by some inspired surrealist. The few buildings to be seen looked poor and threadbare, and only a mule track led over the shoulder of the headland to the village of Merikha, and that was steep and narrow and looked hard going. There wasn't a soul in sight apart from ourselves. I felt a shiver down my spine, and wondered if it was just the effect of my own depression.

Much later on, Steve confided to me that he hadn't liked the place, either.

'There's been great hardship there,' he said, seriously. 'You could feel it in the air.' I wished that he had told me at the time, for the place gave me the crawls and it would have been nice to be able to say so, maybe laugh and be laughed at, exorcise it.

Quite a few of the flotilla were there ahead of us – we hadn't been hurrying – including the lead boat. A row of dinghies were pulled up on the beach, and a pile of dry wood had already been gathered on the foreshore. Steve remarked that it looked as if everyone had been very busy, but that he felt we were entitled to a break, and had anyone got the right time? I would have liked to go ashore, where I could see Oliver and Robin busy building a fire, but Jay wanted coffee and Steve agreed with that. Marina was leaning over the stern, throwing bits of bread to two little white ducks that had come to say hello, quacking loudly for handouts. They were proper little scavengers, those two! They greeted every boat as it came in, and never failed to get fed, not even by the gloomy Ted.

Steve had found another leak in our water system, and once we had finished our drink he began his incessant gerbilling again: really, it was providential in one way that Panther Sailing had such a poor maintenance record, it kept him entertained for hours! Jay said that he wanted to go ashore and take some pictures while the light lasted, but he didn't ask if Marina and I wanted to come with him. He climbed into the dinghy, promising to be back in half an hour to take Steve ashore to the briefing, and we were left high, and thanks to Steve and his fiddling with the pipes, not particularly dry. I wondered if Jay had done it on purpose.

We sat in the cockpit and debated whether to go swimming or not, but decided against it. Instead, Marina picked up a little box that had contained a pair of those wristbands designed to combat seasickness (actually they work quite well, but I have a theory that you have to believe in them first). The pictures on the label illustrated the various uses. They were very basic. Marina wrinkled her brows in a frown.

'*Does* anyone get sick watching the telly?' she asked me. I reached out and took the box from her to study it.

'It's meant to be a train, stupid!' I too studied the pictures for a bemused minute. 'How very awkward if you had a baby who was pram-sick.'

Marina shuddered. 'Don't even go there! Sue is everything OK with you?'

The suddenness and unexpectedness of the question made me drop the box. Marina being clairvoyant always makes me jump.

208

'Of course it is!'

She looked at me doubtfully. 'You could tell me if it wasn't. We've been friends a long time.'

I couldn't tell her, of course. Even the very best of friends, after what I had already said, would make the obvious reply if I confided that I no longer either loved or trusted my husband, but instead had fallen heavily for a handsome young buccaneer a good many years my junior. And surely too, even the very best of friends would be pardonably sceptical if I said that the... well, attraction, for want of a better word, was mutual. I know what I would have said, or at least thought, myself. And maybe I was a discontented, borderline-menopausal, middle-aged woman grabbing at straws, and Oliver a shallow charmer playing along with me for what he could get out of it.

Except that it was hard to see what he *could* get out of it. And the fact that he was not shallow.

It is so very hard to describe him. I looked at him with the eyes of love, but I am too old, I think, to be dazzled or deceived. For people like Jay, his looks were against him, but there was strength in his face, not weakness, and his charm was natural and not put on. He had a rare quality that I could neither name nor pin down, elusive and uncatchable as the meltemi itself; he was special – not just to me, but in himself. To define him is as hard as to define the colour of sunlight. I believed him when he said he loved me. Unfortunately, I also believed him when he said it was a stray gust from nowhere, soon to die. I ached with the need to confide in someone... but I said nothing at all.

Marina said, 'Oh well, if you don't trust me...'

'It isn't that,' I said. But it was.

Steve had finished messing around beneath the galley sink, and came on deck in his bathing trunks to go for a swim. It was almost five o'clock by this time, so it had to be a very quick one, and he was still down below dressing when Jay came back. He hurriedly threw on a shirt and was in the cockpit and over the side before Jay had time even to fasten the painter, leaving Marina and me once more on our own.

I decided to wash my hair. I had, for once, nothing to say to Marina, or she to me, and sitting on deck watching Jay and Steve on the shore, laughing heartily over some unknown joke with Oliver and Robin, as an occupation soon grew stale. I went below.

Washing your hair sounds like a simple thing to do, domestic and rather boring and hardly worth a mention, but nothing to do with Panther Sailing was ever quite as straightforward as it looked. The heads on *Phaedra*, as on all yachts of similar kind, were rather cramped, and unless you wanted to have a shower, which I did not as we were running low on fresh water, to wash your hair you had to use the basin. This could most conveniently be done if you could unscrew a leg and set it aside, but failing this option you had to shut down the lid on the loo and kneel on it with one knee. To complete this picture of an accident waiting to happen, I should add that this loo worked on a vacuum principle and had a seal ring round the lid, and on this occasion, Steve must have left the seat damp after his swim. You're probably ahead of me on this one...

I twisted myself into the standard contorted posture required and, washed my hair in about six cupfuls of our precious water supply, but when I untangled myself, I found that my weight, bearing down on the loo seat, had caused such heavy and prolonged pressure on the damp seal that it had clamped itself tightly closed. Nothing I could do would shift it. I got a fingernail under the seal after a little while, but instead of the usual *sssssh-plop* that signalled the release of the vacuum, I just got this very quiet, long-winded *hisssss*. I began to think that I was going to have to go and confess to Robin that I had hermetically sealed it, but at the last desperate moment it reluctantly let go.

'Whatever are you doing down there?' Marina called anxiously. 'Are you all right Sue? You've been simply ages!'

'Just slitting my wrists and mixing an overdose,' I called back, with admittedly black humour. Marina, at any rate, didn't find it funny.

'Don't joke about things like that,' she retorted, so crossly that I had to apologise. She gave me a very strange look.

I told Emmy and Robin about my mishap with the loo when we eventually got ashore, finding them together at last, and Emmy laughed the first really spontaneous laugh that I had ever heard from her. Robin grinned, and said that it was one more for the record book.

'Why, do you keep one?' I asked in surprise.

'Oh yes.' His grin grew broader. He looked amazingly different since Paul had gone from the scene. 'You wouldn't believe some of the things that go on.'

If Panther Sailing was involved that was possibly true, although after the last ten days or so I wouldn't have put money on it. But that came later. For the moment, I was still stuck on board with Marina waiting for Jay and Steve to come and collect us, which they eventually did. All things, so they say, come to he who waits, and we had certainly waited all right. They had Bill and Sylvia with them.

'Pity we've drunk all the sloe gin,' said Steve, regretfully, 'but there's still plenty of ouzo.'

Sylvia, yet again, had obviously not much enjoyed the day, although she bravely asserted that she had, but at least she was looking forward to the barbecue.

'Emmy must have cleaned that little shop right out,' she told us. 'There's heaps of food. It's going to be fun.'

'It's all been *fun* in a sort of a way,' said Marina thoughtfully. 'I've enjoyed it anyway – well, most of it. A lot of it... some of it.' We all laughed but we knew what she meant. Now that the worst was presumably over, we could afford to laugh.

'Even the night of the shipwreck?' Jay asked, teasing.

'*Which* shipwreck?' countered Marina. 'Well no, not those sort of things. But Mykonos wasn't that bad, in fact it would have been lovely if we hadn't been stuck on that awful quay. I swear that dust is still gritting in my teeth!'

'I just pushed all the clothes we were wearing into a plastic bag, and tried to forget them,' admitted Sylvia, with a shudder. 'They were absolutely black – quite disgusting!'

'Half the fun of sailing, that is,' Jack told her.

Out of the corner of my eye, I could see Oliver on the beach, doing something to the fire they had built, Robin helping him. There was a lot of activity going on ashore, in fact. Somebody was coming along the sand dragging what looked like a small dead tree, with a line of Canadians dancing behind whooping like idiots. I wanted to be there, but I was afraid to say so in case I gave too much away. I wanted to hear him laugh at me again, see the deep creases in his cheeks when he smiled at me, and the way his eyes narrowed in amusement. I wanted to learn him by rote, so that I could keep him in my heart for ever. Instead, I was sitting on the cabin roof with my shoulder touching Jay's, and fantasy and reality grated painfully together. I found myself hoping, traitorously, that Jay had him in some of his photos, then at least I could look at him from time to time. If looking could ever be enough.

The barbecue was timed to start at eight, and we didn't go ashore until then. The wind had died away to nothing and the night was still and warm as we rowed ashore. Although there was still a fading light remaining behind the hills, it was already dark in the enclosed bay. It was better in the dark, I discovered. Attention became focussed on the leaping flames of the barbecue fire, the barren hills and the ruinous buildings shut out beyond our private circle of warmth and firelight.

Th lead boat crew had brought two windsurfers ashore – every yacht carried one, but I haven't bothered to mention them as we had little chance to use them – and on these, they had set out an incredible feast, considering the lack of facilities they had encountered. There was a large plastic bucket containing a dangerously potent fruit punch concocted by Oliver and Robin from anything they could lay their hands on, of which we all had a glass on arrival. It was guaranteed to make any party go with a swing, although I suspected that too much of it might make the party swing a bit too far. Above the fire, they had wedged a big metal grating on which a huge array of assorted chicken legs and wings sizzled, scenting the air deliciously so that our mouths watered in anticipation. Emmy sprinkled it with wild thyme picked from the bushes around the edge of the beach, with squeezed fresh lemon juice and thick green olive oil, fragrant in the evening air. She had made a dip – goodness knows what of, tinned sardines seemed to feature quite heavily, and tomato ketchup and other more secret ingredients – and there were little salty biscuits beside it to keep us occupied while we waited for the chicken to finish cooking. Jacket potatoes, foil wrapped to keep them hot, waited at the side of the fire with plates of butter to melt over them; there was a big pan of ratatouille, bowls of grated cheese to sprinkle over it, a dish piled high with great slices of water melon, pink and cool. We spread rugs on the sand and sat down, all mingling together properly for the first time since our cruise had begun.

'And this is what they wanted us to miss!' said Carol, sighing with pleasure.

'But would it have been the same with Paul, do you think?' Jenny asked, her eyes straying towards Oliver as he bent over the fire. The firelight flickered over his face, making hollows of his eye sockets, throwing the elegant planes of his cheekbones into high relief. Not for the first time, he reminded me of some ancient god – not Poseidon tonight. Pan, perhaps, or Bacchus – one of the less reliable ones.

Or were those two one and the same? Jay would tell me, no doubt, but I didn't ask him. Then I looked suspiciously at my plastic cup of punch. It was well named, I decided, but what the hell! I tossed off what was left and went over to the fire for a refill.

'Hi,' said Oliver. 'Enjoying yourself?' His fingers touched mine as he ladled the punch into the cup, it was like being brushed by nettles. He bent his head close to mine. 'I love you, Sue, you're a lovely woman. Smile!'

'What is there to smile about,' I whispered, our heads close together now.

'Now. This moment. Today, yesterday, tomorrow. Didn't you ever hear that rhyme – *there's an old and cheery saying that will always get you through; never trouble trouble until trouble troubles you!*'

I wanted to cry out, *I'm married, there is no tomorrow for us* – but then I met his eyes and suddenly it no longer mattered. Not here and now, maybe not even tomorrow. And the day after that was a lifetime away, however brief that life would be. I did smile then, meeting his eyes, and our time hung suspended.

'Oliver!' Emmy came over to us. 'Oliver, I think the chicken's done, come and see what you think.'

I turned back to my friends.

Of all the evenings of that memorable cruise, this one was the best. It was as if nothing could go wrong: we ate, we talked, we watched the fireflies dancing among the olive trees. There was a great deal of happy laughter and joking and fooling around. Robin had brought an old cassette player ashore and some slightly dodgy tapes of Greek music, and as the night wore on and the levels in the various bottles dropped significantly, our lead boat crew taught us to dance a syrtaki with the fireflies, there on the sand. The moon hung in the sky above the steep cliffs, throwing her cold light down onto the scene. The dying fire spirted and crackled in a blaze of red embers that fanned out to rival the dancers under the olives, one glittering moment before they died... like my love... or like my marriage, making one final spurt before it was over for ever.

Jay was flirting with Jenny, he was taking no notice of me, and probably, tonight, I deserved that. In any case, it was no new thing. In the past, as you already know, I had thought it a simple reflex reaction that meant nothing, nor let it bother me, but Dawn, of course, had changed all that. Watching him now, I knew with chilly certainty that whatever happened in the future, however we might, or might not, cobble our marriage together, I could never trust him again. Could you, I wondered, live with somebody that you still loved and never trust them? For I did still love him in one way, that was the confusing thing. It was as if my wildfire passion for Oliver was a thing apart, happening to somebody else or running parallel, never to clash, so different that it wasn't even comparable. Was this, I wondered, through a haze of punch, one of life's great lessons? Looking back, I know that this moment was important; at the time, my great philosophical thought drifted into considering that this untrustworthiness, like his irresponsibility, had always been part of Jay – part of the price of being married to him. It had been quite a high price, taken all in all.

But that was getting me back into the realms of protective cynicism, and I wasn't sure that this was wise. I was aware that I was more than slightly drunk, and in danger of getting maudlin.

I got to my feet and stepped quietly away from the crowd, down towards the water. It was very still; the tiny waves along the shoreline curled, barely an inch high, and trickled around my toes. The water was as warm as new milk and silky to the touch. I didn't recognise what I was feeling... sadness, emptiness, but something more. An awakening, like the loom of the false dawn over the horizon after a long night at sea, the first herald of what is yet to come. That is the only way I can come anywhere near to describing the feeling, but it was real, more... and at the same time, less... of a breath of a promise than promise itself.

Oliver came towards me, a bottle in one hand, two filled plastic cups clasped precariously in the other. He held them out to me and I took one, unashamedly this time loving the warm touch of his hand against mine. Within the bright circle of the barbecue fire, there was talk and laughter, and a sudden burst of ribald singing. Here in the darkness there was silence, and the hush of the silken, tumbling wavelets around our feet.

We sat on the sand just outside the circle, but not so far away that people would wonder, our backs against the rounded flanks of a beached inflatable. We were at ease together, really talking for the first, maybe the only time, garnering knowledge that would be just another holiday souvenir, as useless as a kiss-me-quick hat.

'Whereabouts in Cornwall are you from?' I asked him, with idle curiosity. He looked surprised.

'I'm not. What made you think so?'

'Your name. Even if you don't live there now, your family must have once.'

'I think my grandfather may have done, back in the mists of time, but I've never been there, not even for a holiday. I'd like to, one day – but up until now, there hasn't been time.'

Roots wouldn't be important to him, I realised now. Silly me! I snuggled against his shoulder and he drew me close with a small sound of content.

'So what about you? Where do you come from?'

'We live in the New Forest. We keep a boat at Bucklers Hard, if you ever come into the Beaulieu River, you must give us a ring and drop in and see us,' Silly thing to say, I knew he never would.

'So I will.' But he knew it too.

I told him about *Foxtrot* and a little about the girls, but he didn't reciprocate with information about himself or his family. I learned only that he had been born in Dorset and had made his first delivery trip to the Mediterranean about six years ago. Although he had been to other places on the same errand, he said, it was the Mediterranean in general, and Greece in particular, that he loved best, and second came the Newfoundland coast. What would that contrast say of him to a psychologist? Of the time between his birth and his discovery of Greece, I learned nothing at all. I asked him if he had any ambitions beyond being a delivery skipper, or even a diver, but it appeared he hadn't thought that far ahead.

'I just take each thing as it comes,' he said lazily. 'Enjoy it, and when it's over, leave it and go on to the next thing.'

'Like me,' I said, before I could stop myself.

'Oh well...' he reached for the bottle, emptying the last of the wine into our two cups. The action hid his face from me. 'I'm not too good at commitments, Sue, not of any kind. I won't pretend, not even to you. Particularly to you. I value my freedom.'

He would, of course. And yet, it was an arid way to live, with no ties and no lasting affections. One day, even Oliver would be old.

'Have you no commitments at all?' I pressed, unable to visualise it.

'None.'

He hadn't said he didn't need them, I noticed, simply acknowledged his lack of them. I wondered, but did not ask, what it was that he was running from. There are true loners in this world – only a few – but one rarely meets them, and Oliver wasn't one of them. The way in which, in thirty-six short hours, he had brought this disenchanted and varied group of people together was the great give-away so far as that went. I wished that there was opportunity in which to get to know him better, already the sands of our time had run more than halfway through.

'Not even a girl somewhere?' I heard myself asking, jealously. He laughed then.

'A few. None that matters. And none like you.'

He had no need to say more, that was the way it was, always, between us. We had so brief a time – our love sent out its first shoots, flowered and was gone as swiftly as one of the blue moonflowers that twine the pergolas of the Greek tavernas. But while it lived, it was all fire and intensity, all total understanding, a mental uniting all the greater because circumstances dictated there could be no physical counterpart. Oliver was stronger than I. I would have gone with him into the olive groves and forgotten my marriage vows under the bright stars. Someone, I thought with a flash of perception, someone had hurt him, damaged him even, certainly made him the man that he was by that act of adultery. I could suspect it was his mother, but it could as easily have been his father and I would never know for sure. I knew then that I would never tell him what he had done for me, that if I met him at some distant future date, which was unlikely, I would never tell him who it was that had finally destroyed my fragile marriage.

And of course, it wasn't Oliver who had done so anyway. Our marriage had been destroyed from within over a long time, all Oliver had done was to touch the shell that remained so that it finally crumbled.

The party around the fire was breaking up. Footsteps crunched on the shingle, merry voices began calling, rounding up the crews who were by now so intermixed that they could have been a party of old friends. Oliver and I got to our feet and walked back to the fire. Jay was fooling around, dancing with Carol and playing the clown, Steve and Marina stood, arms entwined, on the sidelines. Under the cover of departure for the dinghies, Oliver's lips just brushed my ear.

'Goodnight, lovely Sue. Sweet dreams.'

I wanted to kiss him back, and wondered what people would think if I did. In the end, I kissed his cheek as if he was my son.

'You too. There's only tomorrow.'

'You have that wrong,' he told me. 'You should say, there's tomorrow too.'

Tomorrow would be another dreary "do" at the Yacht Club, another Us and Them evening. I hadn't asked, didn't really want to know, what would happen the day after that. If Oliver stayed with Panther Sailing, I wouldn't be there to see. If he did not, I wouldn't be any worse off. Panther Sailing, so far as I knew, had only asked him – were presumably paying him – to get us home. No, tonight had been our night, and it was already over.

Steve rowed us back to *Phaedra*, Jay wasn't drunk, exactly, but he had certainly enjoyed a very good time. He laughed a lot and made silly jokes. Marina sat perched beside me, looking down at her hands and saying nothing. Steve remarked that it had been a great evening, and not at all in Panther Sailing's usual style and only then did she look up.

'He's that sort of person,' she said, quietly.

'Who is?'

'Oliver Nankervis. He makes things happen. He's a catalyst. Like a hurricane passing through, nothing's the same when it's gone.'

Oliver said, a williwaw.

Jay laughed, too loudly, calling across the water to another dinghy close by.

'Great evening! We'll have another tomorrow.'

I heard Jenny laugh in reply.

That night, I slept in the saloon again, and Jay didn't offer to join me. Long after the others were asleep, I lay awake. I ached with longing, with sheer physical frustration, until a great shaking pain began and grew like a tight knot in my guts that threatened to break me apart, so that I rolled over and sank my teeth into the pillow to stop myself from crying out loud.

Day Fourteen: Sunday, 18th June

In spite of the after-effects of the barbecue, when we came on deck in the morning, three or four of the flotilla had already sailed, and several of the others were preparing to get under way. Steve looked at them with a jaundiced expression on his face.

'Such enthusiasm!' he said, without having any noticeably himself. 'Well, I don't think we have anything to prove, do you? I'm all for a quiet life.'

I thought Jay looked disappointed, perhaps he would have liked to race home, and even more, to get there first. My new discovery, that being liked or even admired was very important to my husband, nagged and reproached me. I should have recognised it in him a long while ago, but it was the situation created by Panther Sailing that had highlighted it, of course. A need to be admired was supposed to be an indication of inadequacy. Jay's seamanship wasn't inadequate, but perhaps his personality was? But nothing was going to alter the fact, painfully clear and possibly not only to me, that Jay called Steve a friend but was jealous of him because it was Steve, not he, who had attracted most of the attention in Mykonos.

I remembered him flirting hard with Jenny last night. I hadn't cared a scrap at the time, but now suddenly I saw it as a further attempt to make himself out no end of a lad. I caught myself wondering how Jenny had viewed it, and hoped that she hadn't thought him just a silly middle-aged man who couldn't keep his hands off pretty girls. She was well able to handle that kind of thing, as I already knew, but even so I didn't want anybody – by which I suppose I meant Oliver – to look at my husband in that light.

How odd it was to have lived with a man for twenty years, and suddenly to see him through the eyes of other people.

Orders for the day were to have cleared Episkopis by seven thirty, so we sailed before either Marina or I was up. Jay brought us tea in bed – we had been promised a lie-in, but the engine saw to that, of course, as soon as it started up. Marina came out of the cabin she shared with Steve and sat on the end of my bed to drink hers, she looked heavy-eyed after a short night on top of a good party, and had little to say for herself. I wasn't feeling exactly chatty either. Jay came clattering down the companionway and saw us sitting there, glum.

'What, have you two fallen out?' he cried, in a loud and cheerful shout. Marina winced.

'Go away, Jay. It's too early.'

He looked at her with a knowing eye. 'It *was* a good night last night, wasn't it?'

'It certainly was for you,' I told him sourly, before I had time to stop myself. Something – it could have been resentment if he chose to see it that way – showed all too clearly in my voice. He gave me a strange look.

'So? I wasn't the only one, was I? You were making a proper exhibition of yourself!'

My mouth dropped open in astonishment. '*I* was?'

'Sneaking off into the darkness with our Skipper, kissing him by the fire?' He grinned suddenly, but not wholly with amusement. 'I never knew you fancied a toyboy. Or was it the punch?'

'I'll punch *you* in minute,' I said.

'Give it a rest, both of you,' snapped Marina. 'Jay, you aren't being at all funny.'

'Why pick on me?' He pushed past us on his way to the heads, casual and unconcerned. He had only been teasing me, I now realised, winding me up. Was he that sure of me? Good old Sue, understanding, reliable, good little wife, who would put up with anything? With any humiliation? So that he could flirt with any pretty girl who came his way, but I was making a fool of myself if I sat talking to a younger man, was that it? Was that how everyone would see it? The questions poured into my mind, thick and cold as snowflakes.

'No,' said Marina.

'No, what?' I stared at her.

'No, it wasn't a bit like he tried to make out – was it?' She looked at me steadily. I wondered for a moment if she had read my thoughts, but she must simply have been following a line of her own. She added, for the second time, 'You might tell me, Sue. You know I won't gossip, not even to Steve, if you say so. And you don't get claustrophobia, whatever you say – do you?'

I pushed the sheet aside and swung my legs to the floor.

'I could do with another cup of tea, how about you? And then,

I'm going to get dressed.'

But I knew that I had told her more by that, than if I had simply admitted that I was attracted to Oliver.

When I got up on deck, I found that Oliver's predictions about the weather had been more than fulfilled, it was a glorious day for sailing. The wind blew steadily from the north west, the sea was flat, *Phaedra* was travelling like a train on a close fetch for Aegina. Scattered on the wide waters around us were other boats, all bound on the same course, but it was impossible at this distance to see who was who. Steve was on the helm, he looked relaxed and content. I looked at him with affection: Steve boasted a bit, maybe, but his boasts were not empty. He was competent, knowledgeable and OK, bumptious, but it was a very human failing, if a bit annoying too. Marina was fortunate, she would never find that she had spent half her life with a man who, if you turned him around, would prove to have no back, but just a sheet of blank cardboard... my own thoughts made me shiver. This was one holiday, I thought, that I would never forget until I died.

We had an uneventful sail back to Ayios Giorgos, the wind held and we made excellent time, arriving shortly after two o'clock. We were not the first, of course, that honour fell to *Penelope* ,the boat crewed by the four young Canadians, with whom we had never had much to do, since they were well able to shift for themselves. It was strange to sail back into that calm, blue bay and to see the white houses climbing up the steep shore, and the sun-soaked spread of Panther Sailing's Yacht Club. The beach was dotted with sunbathers, the bay was scattered with darting bright windsurfers and small sailing boats. It looked idyllic. Journey's end – but what a journey!

We slid inside the harbour mole, and there was Oliver on the quay, waving us to an empty berth. We went in stern-to, as we had been asked, and Robin and Oliver were both there to take our warps. There was no fuss, no panic, no half-heard, relayed radio messages, no criticism of where we had placed our anchor.

'Good trip?' Oliver asked.

'Terrific!' Steve was enthusiastic. 'Best sail of the whole fortnight! Pity we have to go home.'

As they arrived, people were gathering on the quayside, as were the ever hopeful dogs of accursed memory, not for any specific purpose (except for the dogs, whose purpose was the same as ever) but to exchange news of the voyage, to discuss "The Great Grain Race", to consolidate friendships begun on the moonlit beach last night. And also, as we discovered when we joined them, to mutter and grumble about the arrangements for our last night. Nobody, it appeared, wished for another night at the Yacht Club.

'It would be far nicer if we could have a really Greek evening to end on,' Jenny said, voicing the opinion of us all. 'One last taverna night – like the ones Marina has been telling us about, when they were in the Ionian.' She smiled at Marina as she spoke, the catchphrase had gone through the fleet like Greek tummy

'I suppose it's already been arranged,' someone said, doubtfully.

'We could *un*-arrange it,' I suggested. 'It's still early, there's probably time.'

Emmy came trotting along the quay, presumably to instruct us in the noble art of yacht-cleaning, and Charles and Richard grabbed her and put our proposal to her. She looked surprised, then dubious. Seeing a conference taking place, Robin and Oliver came across to see what it was about and to add their contribution. Unlike Emmy, they seemed to see no particular problem to having a last-minute change of plan, but they, of course, were not responsible for domestic matters. Nor did either of them have friends among Panther Sailing's Aegean staff, for what that was worth.

'It's too late to change anything now,' Emmy insisted. 'They'll have catered for us at the club.'

'They won't have started cooking yet,' said Robin. 'Anyway, the food will keep until tomorrow, they've got fridges and things.'

Oliver swept the whole question of the Yacht Club's catering arrangements aside.

'We'll ask Yianni what he can do for us,' he said. He and Yianni, who owned a vine-hung taverna right on the waterfront, were old friends it now transpired. Knowing what I now did of Oliver, that probably meant that Yianni would fall over himself to oblige, and so it proved, as Emmy told us when she came round to check the inventory while we were dutifully cleaning ship.

'We're all meeting at eight o'clock at Yianni's,' she said. 'There's going to be Greek dancing and things, it's all arranged.'

'What did they say up the road?' Jay asked, interested. Emmy said that they hadn't said very much at all, Oliver hadn't given them a chance, but she thought they had been a bit put out. She looked rather down-in-the-mouth herself. I wondered if there had been any message from Paul awaiting her, and if that was what troubled her, for last night she had seemed to be enjoying herself as much as anyone. I thought, probably not. Paul wouldn't want anyone around him who knew about his spectacular screw-up, so Emmy, too, would have reason to remember this trip, even if she didn't have enough reasons already.

At yesterday's evening briefing, Oliver had requested that every boat's crew should make a list of all the faults, shortages and damage that were to be found on board, and when we had packed as much as we could, cleaned below and scrubbed the decks clean of the very last traces of Mykonos, we sat down around the saloon table with a notepad and pencil. Steve wrote PHAEDRA at the top of a clean page and then looked around expectantly. There was so much to choose from, it was difficult to know where to begin.

'No boathook,' said Jay. 'That locker catch – the one that scarred us for life, that you threw over the side.'

'First Aid box,' said Marina.

'No grill pan,' I contributed.

Steve wrote busily.

'The hinges are broken on our cold box,' said Marina.

'And the cooling unit hasn't an outlet, so it doesn't really work properly anyway,' added Jay.

Steve was now scribbling rapidly. 'And it isn't connected to the foot pump, so it drains away into the bilge,' he said.

'That clip on the larder unit,' said Marina, rubbing her thigh which showed a dark bruise that we could all match.

'The end of the pipe to the bilge pump is loose,' said Jay.

'And the lights don't work properly in the forepeak, or the heads, or either of the aft cabins,' said Steve, writing. 'We've only done a botched job on them, just for now.'

'The cockpit air-vent leaks into our cabin when it rains,' said Jay.

'I cut my hand on the talurit splice on the mainsheet tackle,' said Steve, adding, 'So did Sue.'

'The bolt on the tiller extension is a good inch too long,' said Jay.

'It caught on my knee and bloody well hurt!'

'The log doesn't work,' said Marina.

We were well onto the second sheet now, and still going strong.

'The chart is falling to pieces –'

'– nobody knows how to work the holding tank properly –'

'– there was no sponge to dry out the bilges –'

'– and we only have four fenders instead of the six on the inventory –'

'Jesus!' said Oliver, from the companionway. 'However did you keep afloat?'

We all jumped. We had been so busy that we hadn't felt the boat rock as he came aboard. Steve looked up.

'Welcome aboard, Cap'n,' he said. 'Move up Marina, – make room for the boss!'

'Sit still, I haven't come to stop.' Oliver perched himself on top of the steps. 'I just came to see if you've finished your accident report yet. Some people seem to be trying to write a book.'

'Why "accident report"?' asked Marina.

'The sort that's looking for somewhere to happen.'

Steve tore off the closely written sheets and gathered them together. 'We could probably think of several more things, if we tried not-too-hard,' he said, 'but this makes a start.' Oliver took them and ran a rapid eye down the first one.

'What are you complaining about?' he asked. 'Panther Sailing would no doubt describe this as a well-found ship – you should read about some of them!'

Steve shuddered. 'No, we shouldn't! Are you going to try to put it all right before tomorrow? You'll never do it!'

'Or are you off diving again, and don't give a damn?' Jay asked. Oliver laughed.

'Who knows? This outfit might not want me when they hear my terms – at least three boats in this flotilla were unfit to put to sea, I won't take them again.'

So Panther Sailing had asked him, and he hadn't given an outright refusal. For the length of a Greek summer he would be where I could find him, within call if I needed him... except that wasn't in our contract, if we had a contract. *Oliver, Oliver, my dearest , my love...* Why do terms of endearment sound, even to the ears of lovers, so very trite? Why is there nothing new to say?

Oliver left, and Marina put the kettle on. We were almost out of coffee, it would just about last out until breakfast if we were careful; there was no point in buying any more.

The sands were pouring out now, pushing and bustling through the bottleneck of one last evening to pile in a heap of broken vows, empty dreams, bitter loss... I pushed the thoughts away. Tomorrow, this time, didn't belong to us, not to Oliver and me. There was only tonight left.

Yianni had done us proud when we assembled at the appointed time and place. He had pushed small tables together outside his taverna, to make one long, E-shaped table under the vines, and set it out with big bowls of Greek salad, saucers of houmous and tzadziki, plates of the coarse, hard peasant bread, carafes of red and white wine. On the pergola overhead, the vines looped and twined, with tiny bunches of ripening grapes mingling with the beautiful blue moonflowers. Marina looked at it all with a deep sigh of satisfaction.

'This is just how it was W3ITI,' she said happily. Jay laughed.

'I daresay young Oliver has seen a lot of flotillas in the course of his travels,' he said, with what I felt was unnecessary emphasis on the word "young".

Our lead boat crew circulated among us, greeting everyone, chatting a moment, binding the group together with invisible strands of goodwill. Ted was smiling, I saw him clap Oliver companionably on the shoulder. His wife looked pale, but happy – possibly because she could now look forward to going home. Jenny and her friends had joined up with the victorious Canadians in one boisterous group of younger people; they made an attempt to capture Oliver but, the perfect host, he wouldn't be trapped by any one group and moved on easily to the next. Emmy was beside him, determinedly smiling, forcing laughter. Robin was talking to Tom and Sally.

I don't know if Oliver had planned it, perhaps not, perhaps it just happened. When we had all sat down, the lead boat crew came round to take our orders for the main course, and it wasn't until that was done that they sat down among us themselves. Not all together, which made a Panther Sailing First, but wherever there was a space. Oliver ended up next to Marina, opposite to Jay, within touching distance of me. We didn't talk much, there was no opportunity; Steve and Jay monopolised most of the conversation, guiding it into talk of boats – our boats, not the flotilla's. Oliver refused to be drawn on the subject of Panther Sailing and the interest of Steve and Jay was fading fast now that our holiday was so nearly over, and it seemed that matters were in a fair way to right themselves. There would be letters written when we all got home, claims for compensation for Paul's shortcomings throughout the cruise, and particularly in Mykonos, but they were for later and no concern of Oliver's. So they talked of past cruises, and ones planned for the future; Steve picked Oliver's brains about the channel ports, and they compared hair-raising experiences in the traffic separation zones of the North Sea and the Western Approaches. Oliver had sailed very little in the North Sea, he was a south coast man of course, and Jay and Steve enjoyed telling him of mudbanks and shifting sands, of lightships and buoys that marked the vast expanses of water where even a ship as small as Steve's *Koala* dared not sail without a chart, even out of sight of land. The people around us listened, commented, and in some cases added tales of their own.

The prize-giving took place at the end of the meal. A china mug with the Panther Sailing logo for the Canadians was presented by Oliver with a speech that, under the circumstances, was a masterpiece of diplomacy, if short – needfully short, when you came to think closely. There were minor presentations to the boats that had come second and third. Ken, a little further down the table from us, called for a vote of thanks and three hearty cheers for our new Skipper and the rest of the lead boat crew, which was generously given and made the vine leaves shiver over our heads. Then, to our surprise, Ted rose to his feet.

'Unaccustomed as I am to public speaking,' he began, and there was a roar of approval from the flotilla that made the taverna's other clients turn their heads – again! He waited for the noise to subside and began again. 'Unaccustomed, as I say, as I am to public speaking, there is something that needs to be said on behalf of us all. It falls to me because, of all of us, maybe I have an apology to make as well.' He paused, and turned directly to Steve. 'Steve. If I was rude to you back there on Mykonos, I ask you now to forgive it. It was a bad time for us all, and perhaps I was unreasonable. We – that is, the rest of the flotilla as well as us on *Persephone* – are all agreed that without you there, things would have been very much worse than they were. We didn't appreciate at the time exactly what you, and Jay too of course, were doing, missing sleep keeping watches, splicing all those ropes, keeping us all safe, and we would like you to accept this small token of our appreciation and our thanks for all that you did for us.' He held out a bulging plastic bag. Everyone clapped and roared. Steve walked along the table to accept the offering, peered inside it, and burst out laughing. To the stamping of feet, he plunged in a hand and brought out a tangled handful of frayed rope, which he tossed into the air with a wild yell of triumph. Roaring turned into laughter as he dipped again into the bag, and withdrew a bottle of ouzo which he placed on the table before him.

Marina was laughing, but surreptitiously wiping her eyes too.

'Oh, I'm so glad,' she whispered to me, under cover of the noise. 'It was the only thing that was spoiling everything now – what Ted said back there in Mykonos. Steve was really hurt about it, although he said it didn't matter.'

Steve sat down with us again, grinning broadly. Jay muttered in my ear, 'All right so far as it goes, but he wasn't the only one!'

'Of course they mean you, too,' I whispered back. 'He said so.'

'Huh!' said Jay. 'The way Steve keeps shooting off his mouth, I doubt if anyone realises I did anything at all!' I looked down at my plate, embarrassed. It was hard on him, I suppose. Yes, it *was* hard on him. But the ones who succeed in this life, I have noticed before, are often the ones who don't hide their light under the proverbial bushel, for if you do that, nobody is going to go looking for it. And I would have liked him to be more generous. I would like to have been able to believe that his feet of clay at least stopped at the ankles.

The light died in the sky, the wine sank in the carafes. Yianni switched on strings of coloured lamps that hung among the vine leaves, attracting great moths that bumbled around in the leaves with a rustling sound. Greek music played, the talk and laughter swelled beneath the sound. The waiters began to pull the tables back from the centre of the forecourt, they threw aside their aprons and began to dance for us, the wild, exciting dances of Greece. Yianni swept Oliver to dance with them, you would never have guessed he wasn't born to it. Yianni's family, his wife, his daughters, came out of the dim regions in the back of the taverna and joined the dance. Black skirts swirled, white handkerchiefs fluttered, gold earrings caught the light and people began to clap to the beat thrummed out by the bouzoukis.

'It's magic,' breathed Marina. 'This is what Greece is all about, this is real, this is why I love it – this, and the smell of the wild thyme in the evening. And the cicadas too, only there weren't any this time. Sue, will you ever forget it?'

'No,' I said.

The rhythm was that of last night's syrtaki, the Greeks were pulling at the hands of the flotilla, tugging us, not unwilling, onto the floor to join in. Oliver was beside me, his hands held out to me. I went with him, dancing with him shoulder to shoulder under the coloured lights, his arm across my shoulders and mine about his waist.

I caught a glimpse of Jay, standing on the sidelines with a frown on his face, but then I remembered many occasions when I had sat, smiling politely, while he talked easily to some woman or girl and ignored me sitting there, and I shut him out of my mind and danced on.

As the night drew on, the music changed; modern dance music, foot-tapping disco or sentimental ballad, took the place of the rhythmic Greek country music. It was the turn of Yianni and his family now to sit and watch, which they did at the entrance to the taverna itself, nodding and smiling at the dancing throng. Oliver was teaching one of Yianni's pretty daughters to rock'n'roll, the floor cleared for them. She was a brilliant dancer, that girl, or she had done it before. One of the waiters was scowling, I noticed, and I wondered if he had an interest himself in the fair Yianoulla. Jay, beside me again now, grinned evilly.

'Your young friend will wake up with a knife in his back if he carries on like that,' he said. 'Greek girls don't.'

'Don't what?' I asked, although I knew perfectly well what he meant. He only grinned more widely and refused to answer.

'Have you seen Emmy?' asked Marina, on my other side. 'I haven't set eyes on her for ages.'

'The last time I saw her, she was dancing with Robin.' I had been glad to see it, it was nice to think that something might be going right for someone, although my interest in their affairs was only peripheral by this time.

Marina mentioned that had been a long time ago.

'Gone to the loo?' I speculated. She shook her head.

'I think she's sloped off somewhere. I saw her about twenty minutes ago, right on the edge of the crowd. She didn't know I was watching. I thought she was crying.'

'Poor Emmy,' I said, but there was nothing we could do. We were only birds of passage in Emmy's life, and I had no sympathy to spare for her. All my pain was for myself.

Oliver found me later, when the music turned sentimental and smoochy. He took me in his arms then and held me close, openly, as we drifted to the heart-wrenching melody of a sentimental ballad five years old. I could feel his body the whole way down my own, hard and supple and strong, desirous. His breath on my cheek smelled of ouzo. He hardly need to tell me how deeply he felt for me. I burned for him in return, and smiled the polite, company smile that might deceive the onlookers while we whispered to each other, there in public, the things that we could never dare say in private because of where it might lead. I knew then that we had now had all we would ever have, there would be no more. No touch, no kiss, no private speech. Just "goodbye" tomorrow as if we were barely acquaintances, and on into our own separate futures.

Partings so final are hard to take, and particularly so under the eyes of a crowd from whom all feelings must be hidden. I returned to my friends with a hard lump in my throat and pain like a knife in my heart, speechless. Marina took my hand and gave it a quick, wordless squeeze which nearly broke me in pieces.

Later on, unable to bear it, I wandered away from the party and along the quay to the beach that lay beyond the mole. There were lights and music in all the tavernas as I walked past, but the biggest roar of sound tonight came from Yianni's. If only the whole trip had been like that, what a wonderful holiday it might have been! I could understand now why Marina had been so enthusiastic all those long weeks ago, when we had first talked about a flotilla holiday.

The moon was past the full now, and it was shadowy on the beach. I walked along under the trees that fringed the road running behind it, not wanting to be seen in case someone called me back, wishing only to be on my own, to empty my heart, if I could, of this stifling hurt that restricted my breathing and made my eyes smart and my throat ache. I had to do it somehow. I couldn't go back to the close confines of a yacht's cabin feeling as I did without Jay and Steve, as well as Marina, knowing that something was wrong. I wanted to shout and scream, uselessly railing against the years that I could never call back, that separated me from Oliver and lay wasted behind me, but of course nobody can do that, and people would have thought I was a crazy woman if I had done any such thing. Nor, if I was honest, were they wholly wasted, I had our two lovely girls and to be fair, some very good memories, but they seemed very far away tonight. I could only walk and walk and walk, my footsteps soft on the sand, as if in the movement itself I might find peace of a kind.

Under the trees ahead of me, something stirred. The sounds from the quayside had died away behind me, I heard it quite clearly. The shifting of shingle, a caught breath like a sob, and a choked murmur, little more than a sigh carried on the soft night air.

'... there wasn't even a note. Nothing. He could have just written, couldn't he, even if it was only goodbye?' And then, after a pause, a broken whisper. 'We were going to go to America together.'

'If he's gone, he's gone.' I started. The voice was Oliver's, bracing and pragmatic. 'He knows where to find you, if you stay with the flotilla. Will you do that?'

'I don't know.' Emmy's whisper was tragic, on a rising note of pain I understood too well. 'There could be all sorts of reasons... he might get in touch later on... you know what the Greek post is like, and if I wasn't here...' There was a long pause, while I suppose all three of us accepted that was never going to happen, and then she said, more clearly, 'Are you going to stay?'

I could see them now, my eyes were getting used to the light. They were sitting close together under a low-growing olive whose branches tangled their way downwards towards the sand. I thought he had his arms round her, comforting her. Had he come to find her, or had he, like me, come out to be alone? Lucky Emmy, either way. He said, 'I expect so. For a while anyway, until they find somebody else to take it on. I enjoy a challenge.'

'If you do, I will.' She peered up at him in the dimness under the trees. 'It's something to do, and I suppose I have to – do something, I mean.' She gave a dreary little laugh.

'It'd help, if you do.' He stirred, drew away from her restlessly. 'Come on, dry your eyes. We have to get back to the party. We'll be missed.'

Emmy moved, leaning towards him. Her arms went round his neck, pulling his head down. Oh, poor Robin! I knew what was going to happen before it did, so that when they melted together in the shadows for a long kiss, I felt no surprise. But Emmy, who had started it, drew back first, her hands framing his face. I don't know what she had sensed in that kiss, but when she spoke, her voice was startled.

'You too?'

'Oh yes.' Oliver laughed, without mirth. 'Me too. Nobody is immune, you know.'

'I would have thought –' She broke off, embarrassed.

Oliver got to his feet. He stood still for a moment, his face turned towards me, listening. He couldn't possibly have seen me through the trees, but I had an odd feeling that he knew I was there. He said, '*Weeping endureth for a night, but joy cometh in the morning.*' I thought it was to me that he spoke. Emmy scrambled up to stand beside him.

'Holy writ is full of old saws like that,' she said, a challenge in her voice. Oliver slipped his arm through hers and moved her across the beach towards the surf line, away from me.

'New sores can find a lot of consolation in old saws,' he said lightly. Their footsteps clinked among the stones on the foreshore. I closed my eyes so that I wouldn't see them, walking away from me into a tomorrow in which I had no part.

He might very well sleep with Emmy before the summer was over, I realised that. They could take comfort in each other, what was there to stop them? She would probably forget Paul before the season was half over, blossom like a rose for Oliver and break Robin's heart, maybe, as Paul had broken hers, and never know it. Poor Robin.

And Oliver?

But I didn't know Oliver well enough to guess what he would feel, which was odd when I loved him so much.

Day Fifteen: Monday, 19ᵗʰ June

There was no howling in the night this time, but in the morning every gangplank had its dog, waiting to be fed! Sadly, there was very little to give them, but Marina unearthed a small tin of corned beef and opened it for them. Steve kindly informed me that I looked terrible, attributing this to too may ouzos at the party last night. I didn't disillusion him.

We had our final breakfast on board, finishing up the last ends of bread, butter and jam, put our bags ashore with the ship's laundry and had a last look round. Steve, gerbilling to the end, took the last of the paper kitchen towels to try to clean the windows, to leave *Phaedra* looking her best for the next crew. She had proved a characterless craft, with nothing to make us particularly attached to her, but we wanted to leave her in as good order as we could, even if Robin and Oliver failed to get through the monumental list of faults we had handed them. We had to drag him away before he had finished to his satisfaction, for the coach had arrived to take us to the airport. I took one last look at the bland scene of so many dramatic events, and followed Jay across the gangplank to the shore for the last time.

We loaded our own luggage, there is no point in expecting anyone to do it for you in Greece, they are always far too busy shouting at each other, and climbed aboard the coach. The lead boat crew waited to bid us goodbye, shaking hands and wishing us a good journey. Oliver kissed Marina on the cheek as she reached him, and moved on naturally to do the same to me, only somehow his kiss landed on my lips. He said nothing, however. I climbed onto the coach after Marina, feeling sickish and heavy-hearted, and sank into the seat beside Jay, who had kindly left me the window side. It was on the opposite side of the coach from the door, I had seen the last of Oliver as he of me. My eyes stung, painfully. It seemed so cruel, to have to drive away and leave him in that sunlit place. I bit my lip until I tasted blood, salt on my tongue. The coach shook as its engine burst into life, the door closed with a sigh. Past the heads of the people in the seats on the other side, I caught a last glimpse of Oliver, Emmy and Robin, waving beside an enormous pile of dirty linen, and then we were off. Goodby *Phaedra*, goodbye Ayios Giorgos, goodby, goodbye my heart's darling, my love, Oliver…

'Isn't this fun?' I heard Marina cry, predictably.

As the coach went round the first twist in the switchback road, I looked back. There below us was the blue, clear water of the enclosed bay, the village, the quayside. There were the boats, tied up stern-to as we had left them, like a row of piglets beside a sow, waiting for the next lot of adventurers to take them to sea. There, somewhere, was the lead boat crew who had brought us safely back from the brink of disaster, but if they were still on the quayside it was too distant to make them out. But they wouldn't be, of course. For them, there would be no time in which to remember. In a week, a fortnight, they would probably have forgotten our names.

'What's this?' Jay asked me.

I turned back to him. 'What's what?'

'In your basket. I don't remember you buying that.'

I glanced down at the basket at our feet without much interest. Lying in the top of it was a slim cylinder of white card, taped about with sticky tape. I had never set eyes on it before, but I knew with certainty how it come there and my heart missed a beat. I picked it up, squinting down inside it. There was a blur of colour, nothing I could recognise.

'Oh, it's nothing much. Just a last-minute souvenir.'

Jay had lost interest. He leaned across the aisle to talk to Steve. I fingered the roll of card, wondering. I had no idea what it was, no intention of finding out here and now. When I was home, perhaps, in some private place, then I would look. I tucked it safely down under the side of the basket where it was hidden from view and couldn't fall out accidentally. I was aware of it as if it had been fluorescent even though I could no longer see it.

Athens airport was crowded and hot. We sat in groups or pushed our way through to the Duty Free shop, talked of our experiences and speculated on what the outcome would be, for this holiday wasn't ending with a tidy cut-off, as they usually do.

'Would you have missed it, now that it's all safely behind you?' Steve asked Sylvia. She looked thoughtful.

'I don't know. I shan't be doing it again in any kind of hurry.'

'It isn't always like that,' Marina assured her, and no doubt was about to add that it hadn't been like that When they were in the Ionian, but Janet forestalled her.

'Do you think Robin will have any luck with Emmy now? When she's had a chance to get over Paul?'

'Not with that Oliver around,' said Jay, grinning. 'Robin doesn't stand an earthly!'

'Don't you be so sure.' Marina looked knowing. 'Emmy's on the hunt for a husband, whether she admits it or not. That's why she's out here in the first place. She's not got a hope in hell of getting Oliver. She might just settle for Robin, in the end. I hope she does, he's a better bet than either of the other two.'

'More soothsaying?' asked Jay, derisively.

'Call it an educated guess'

'So, what about Oliver?' What do you soothsay for him?' asked Janet.

'I don't *soothsay*, as you call it, anything at all,' said Marina indignantly. 'Oliver…' She looked at me, and shivered suddenly.

Steve said, 'You can't be cold, surely?'

'A goose just walked over my grave.' She smiled, but it didn't reach her eyes.

'About Oliver?' Sylvia insisted. Marina looked vague.

'Oh… he'll go far, and make his own destiny.' But I couldn't say if she truly saw it, or if she was just saying something to shut Sylvia up. Sylvia might have pressed us for more, for fortune-telling is fascinating even if you don't really believe in it, but at that moment a couple who had been looking at us and talking with their heads close together, obviously discussing us, pushed their way through the crowd to join us.

'You must be from the Cyclades flotilla,' the woman said, smiling. 'Did you have a good time?'

'The last two days were the best,' said Janet, speaking for all of us.

'Were you the flotilla that got stuck in Mykonos in the gale?' the man demanded. We said we were, and they looked at us in something approaching awe.

'We heard all about it,' the woman said. 'There was a terrific row at the Yacht Club – one of the directors came over from Athens, and Jimbo – he's the manager – nearly had a nervous breakdown on the spot! There's going to be an enquiry, or something – at least, that's what we heard.'

Interesting.

'So there jolly well should be!' retorted Steve.

They naturally wanted to hear all about it, but I left it to the others to tell them. I had other things to think about.

Did Marina guess the truth? I wondered. And if she did, would she ever let me know that she did? I had no idea, any more that I knew if what she had said just now was clairvoyance, in which I didn't wholly believe, or simply her own opinion. And what was I going to do now? The holiday was over, things were going to have to be faced. There must be many marriages like mine, held together by habit and convenience, grown meaningless with the years. I had made the best of it for a long time now, should I – could I – go on doing so, or would I now find the courage to make the break? And if I did find the courage, what would happen to me then?

'... of course, we'll never know who the real culprit was,' Steve was saying. 'It's like dry rot, it's gone through the whole organisation, but it must have started with someone – this Jimbo of yours, perhaps.'

'But he seemed so nice!' cried the woman.

'I expect that Genghis Khan seemed nice to his house guests,' said Steve, adding cynically, 'Particularly if they were paying.'

I couldn't concentrate. I didn't care any more about Panther Sailing, or Emmy and Paul, or Robin's frustrated intentions, even though if he really had any he must be almost as unhappy as me and perhaps I should have had some fellow-feeling. Quite suddenly, I had seen enough of Greece. I just wanted to be home.

Of the flight to Gatwick, there is nothing to be said. It was just a flight, like any other. I stared out of the window at the clouds for most of the way, aching with misery and wishing I could fast-forward the next few reels of my life and come out in some sunnier place. At Gatwick, more goodbyes had to be said. Goodbye Carol, Charles and Richard. Goodbye Tom and Sally. Goodbye Sylvia, Bill, Janet, Ken, maybe we'll see you later on this year. Goodbye Ted, and we hope your wife feels better soon. Goodbye, goodbye... and goodbye, Marina and Steve.

Marina hugged me tightly.

'You didn't really have a good time, did you?' she said. 'I'm so sorry, Sue.'

'I'm sorry if it spoiled your holiday, but I think it did us a service. A lot of things are clearer than they were. Perhaps we can talk now, and really get somewhere.'

'We like you both, so much.' She had said that once before. She hugged me again, and kissed me. 'We're always there if you need us, Sue. Whatever. Always. Remember, won't you?'

Steve was shaking hands with Jay, more earnestly than seemed on the surface necessary. He turned to me, and like Marina, enfolded me in a bear hug.

'Keep in touch, Sue. Let us know how things go. And keep smiling.'

And then the long road to the south unwound ahead of us.

I stood in my own familiar bedroom with the luggage at my feet and emptiness in my heart, looking with eyes that hardly saw at the contents of my basket, strewn carelessly across the bed. Outside the windows the sky was grey, promising rain. The sunburn on my arms tingled, reminding me of other days, other places... my face, when I caught sight of it in the dressing table mirror, looked like Emmy's, pale and shadowy. Nothing seemed truly real any more.

I picked up the little cylinder of white card that Oliver must have tucked into my basket as he kissed me goodbye, and with fingers that shook a little, at last broke the seal and unrolled it. A piece of thick cartridge paper sprang out and flipped onto the floor. I stooped and picked it up, spreading it out on the top of the chest of drawers.

It was a water colour painting of the harbour at Hydra. Unlike most watercolours that you see, delicate and pretty, this one was in-your-face brilliant with colour, full of light and vibrant life. Whatever Oliver could or could not do, he could certainly paint pictures. The little town climbed skywards around the deep bowl that encapsulated all the memories, all the heartbreak, all the unexpected, delicious, agonising joy of that strange holiday... and in the bottom right hand corner were three initials, written small. O J N, and beneath them a line of figures that gave the day, the month and the year in which my marriage effectively ended.

236

HAMPSHIRE

In the years that followed

I have re-read that last sentence, and it isn't quite true. Jay and I stayed together for some years after that bittersweet summer holiday, although things did eventually get to the pitch where they could continue no longer. I did try – it seemed so silly to end a marriage of such long-standing because of a man so much younger, with whom I never made love, and whom I would never see again, even though something had died when we got home, in both of us now. Some pretence that we had kept up for years had ceased to be necessary, so that it was as if a curtain had at last been drawn aside, letting light into shadowy corners. Things had become clear that up until then, it had been possible to ignore, for I had finally come to accept, not without pain, just how long it was since he stopped loving me. I didn't understand any more why he had stayed with me so long unless he, like me, had been afraid of what would follow if we stopped pretending. We were no longer even friends, if we were honest, just a familiar habit: we had nothing left to say to each other. If it had not been for the children, I think we would have parted then and there.

Sally must have been thinking about that day down at the Hard, when Jay had been so unaccountably missing. She and Stephanie had obviously talked it over, and I think that Sal would have been prepared to be philosophical about it; university had taught her a thing or two outside her chosen subject. But Steph, three years younger and just feeling her feet in the race to grow up, was devastated. We had teenage tantrums and sulks and tears at the bare idea that her home might be breaking up, and it brought both of us up short to consider. This wasn't just about us. It was about our children.

There was another factor in play, too, although I am a little ashamed to admit it. My short, abortive fling with Oliver Nankervis had brought Jay up all-standing. He hadn't expected it, *he* was the one who did things like that, not good-little-housewife me. When he suggested that we try to put it all behind us and try again for the sake of our children, I hadn't the fight left in me to refuse. Where would I go, anyway, if we parted? What would I do? There seemed no point in upsetting Steph just when she was about to sit those all-important A-levels, so when Jay said, 'Let's give it another try, Susie. For the children,' I agreed.

I'm not actually certain why I did that. Dawn seemed to have disappeared from the scene while we were in Mykonos, but Jay still worked late, so maybe she hadn't after all; the difference was that so long as he wasn't blatant about it, I didn't care. And I did still love him, in a way that was more than half habit, but I had recognised that whatever way that was, it wasn't enough. Now that I had loved Oliver, and been loved in return for however brief a time, I wondered if it had ever been enough. If that was so, if Dawn ever got her claws out again, I would have no right to hold him – to hold us both – to this barren nothingness whether for the children's sake or my own. And as it certainly wouldn't be for my own, why would I bother?

So we stayed together a while longer because I had no heart for change with Oliver gone, and Jay had no opportunity, and for the children, and that's the dreary truth.

During the long months after we returned from the Aegean, I wondered a lot about what set the williwaw blowing in the first place, and I have reached the conclusion that the chemistry between Oliver and me was both real and relevant, but that somehow, we were not synchronised with each other, if that makes sense; our time was out of step. We were needy for each other, true – out of loneliness, out of betrayed trust, who will ever know, or cares even? Need it was that bridged the gap, but need was nowhere near the whole of it, that alone could never have made such agonisingly painful magic. I believed that one day, should he ever marry – and I must admit it was difficult to imagine him ever settling down – Oliver would choose a girl recognisably like me, and that if ever I meet another man that I can love, he will have many of the qualities that make Oliver who he is... if another Oliver can possibly exist. I daresay that he had as many imperfections and faults as anyone else, but the truth is that circumstances didn't conspire to show them up. He stays in my heart and in my memory as invincible and strong, capable, tough and yet essentially vulnerable. He cannot possibly have been so perfect, I know this, of course I do. It is very suitable that he, who valued freedom so highly, should have been the catalyst that set it within my grasp.

Marina had that right, at least. A catalyst is exactly what he was. He loved me lightheartedly, and in doing so, he gave me back myself.

Of course, I feared the loneliness that I knew would be coming eventually, once the girls had left home if not before... but the essence of living is change, and I had to believe that something would happen to fill the void that separation, and I supposed eventual divorce, were going leave. I had no idea what it was likely to be, but that would be the challenge. The future would at least be mine again, and it might not be Jay's choice that made it so, for I didn't really want mere quiet companionship and a lot of lonely evenings as a permanent thing, I had realised that now. I wanted a life, and there has to be a limit to what you sacrifice for your children once they have independent lives of their own.

I said just now that I knew I would never see Oliver again, but strangely enough, I had been proved wrong. One night, some months after our return from the Aegean, I did see him – oh, not in the flesh, but on the West of England News. It gave me a shock, seeing his dear face so unexpectedly. He looked well, but seemed like a stranger. He was to sail round the world later on in the year, heavily sponsored, to raise funds for the hospital in his home town. It wasn't his own idea, some big wheel in the local business community set it going, but it was the kind of thing that Oliver would enjoy, he was made for wide solitudes and adventure. He was to go single-handed, non-stop, not in a conventional monohull but in a big cat, making an attempt on the world record. It was a crazy thing to do. Crazy, and dangerous, but he was certainly going far, and I have no doubt, following his destiny.

'Why look – there's lover-boy again, Sue!' cried Jay, looking at me out of the corners of his eyes.

'I can see,' I said, and he grinned.

'Shall we take *Foxtrot* down to Falmouth when he sails?' he asked 'Maybe Marina and Steve would like to come.'

Falmouth was where he would be setting out from; there would be a crowd of small craft gathering to send him off royally on his long voyage, but I didn't want to be among them, and I said, 'Where's the point? We'll see it all much better on the telly.'

'As you wish,' said Jay, still grinning. 'We can go and meet him if he gets back, instead.'

I didn't like that "if", but then, that's why he said it. And I didn't think Oliver would expect us to be there either, but I didn't say so. The news flash changed to something else, and the moment passed.

He hit the headlines again a year later, with an MBE in the New Year's Honours List. And then again, later that same year, but I can't bear to think about that. During these arid years, we did take another flotilla cruise with Marina and Steve – two, in fact, one in the Sporades and one in Croatia, although not with Panther Sailing. They were without incident and very enjoyable, but I thought Marina looked at me once or twice while we were among the Dalmatian Islands, with a question in her eyes which I ignored. By this time, there were too many questions that she might have asked.

I do not know what I would have done had another man, not Oliver of course, but someone who cared for me in the same magical way, drifted into my orbit during the next few years, particularly after both the girls had married and flown the nest for good, as they inevitably did in time. But he didn't. What happened was Billie, and Billie was to Dawn what a great white shark is to a river pike.

HAMPSHIRE

March/April 2004

I must have sat there for a long time, just staring at the computer screen, because the screen saver woke up, and a cloud of coloured bubbles took over from my dilemma. Not that it *was* much of a dilemma; if I wanted to keep my picture, I had to take a huge step into the unknown.

You see, I had thought that Oliver was dead. Right up until Maurice Hardacre had said his name, I had believed it, and now, I suppose, I have to tell you why.

About seven years ago now, Oliver did a very brave, but totally insane thing. He was walking up a street in his home town of Embridge quite late one evening, when he apparently heard a woman screaming for help in an alley that ran parallel to the street he was on. He ran through a passage between two houses and found a girl being attacked by a gang of drunken young louts, and being Oliver, waded right in. The girl escaped scatheless.

Oliver did not.

The local papers were full of it, even the nationals gave it a column; Oliver was still News at that time, although he had faded from the full limelight after his MBE. So I knew, from reading about it, that he was on a life-support system, not expected to live. And if he did live, they said, he would never walk again. The word "quadriplegic" was mentioned, and then it all died down. Our flotilla holiday in Croatia intervened, and by the time we got back from that, it might never have happened. I assumed, heavy-hearted, that he had died, and tried to be glad for him, because he would of all things have hated being paralysed. From that day to this, I had never heard his name mentioned. I never followed up on it. I preferred to remember him as he had been in Greece, young and adventurous and utterly amazing, and anyway, it was no business of mine.

But then, although as I told Maurice Hardacre, Jay and I collected pictures in a small way, we had only been able to afford to speculate with pictures by promising local artists: anyone whose "early" work would fetch £80,000 was way, way out of our league. I found myself wondering what his present work would be worth.

At that point, I pulled myself together. There was one way to find out, and I had to get on with it or risk losing my last, precious link with him. The screen had come back to life on its own by this time; I clicked on "Go".

Well, Oliver certainly hadn't died. The search came up with various prestigious Art Galleries in various cities about the world, and also the sort of galleries that sold pictures, where his work was either on display or for sale, but there was no biography, no contact point. One or two of the galleries gave prices for the works they held for sale, my head spun. How had that wild young adventurer metamorphosed into a painter just one of whose works would finance the purchase of a small house? Or even a not-so-small house in some instances. There were details of up-coming exhibitions, one in New York, one in Sydney. If there had been one in London, I would have gone to it.

What would someone do who wanted to commission a painting from him? Presumably he did take commissions. Not that I could even remotely afford to do such a thing, but there must be a contact point in there somewhere. I wondered about this for some time, but my courage failed before I did anything about it. Maybe it would all turn out to be a damp squib anyway.

No such luck.

Jay was on the phone the minute he received the valuation sheet.

'What a wonderful piece of luck! Well done you!'

I knew perfectly well what he was talking about, but I said anyway, 'What are you on about?'

'That picture you bought,' he said, impatiently. 'You know – you picked it up in Ayios Giorgos just before we sailed, that painting of the harbour in Hydra.'

'I didn't buy it,' I told him. 'It was given to me.'

'What, by lover boy? Come on Sue, pull the other one, it's got bells on! You told me you bought it.'

Had I? I didn't think so, but I couldn't really remember, it was so long ago. I knew I had tried to cover my tracks, but not with an outright lie, surely.

'I didn't buy it, I just told you. It's mine, my personal property.'

'No it's not. You bought it, with *my* money. That makes it ours, not yours.'

'No it doesn't. I didn't buy it, and if I had it wouldn't have been with your money.'

That was a mistake.

'Oh? Then whose money was it, then?' he asked.

I drew a deep breath and counted to ten.

'Nobody's. I told you, it was a gift.'

'Then it was a gift to both of us. Why should he give it to you, just because you had a silly schoolgirl crush on him? Grow up, Sue!'

I said nothing, I was too angry and didn't dare. After a minute, Jay said, in a more conciliating tone, 'OK Sue. I'll buy your share off you, the full £40,000, no arguments. Billie rather fancies having an original Nankervis over the mantelpiece, she's a bit of an art buff.'

She would be. The thought of that cow having my picture made me feel sick.

'Sorry Jay,' I said. 'My *share* is worth the full £80,000, and it's not up for grabs.' And then I put the phone down before I said something that I would be really sorry for. After a few moments, it rang again, and I glanced at the number on the caller ID and let it ring.

I had to think. And think fast, if the predatory Billie had her claws out. If I wanted to keep my picture I had to find Oliver, and I had no idea how to track him down. I knew so little about him, and I was pretty certain that his family, even if I could locate them in his home town over there in Dorset, wouldn't tell me anything. He had no public face, only a catalogue of pictures, and his private face was just that: private.

I needed help, someone who knew the art world as I did not, and I knew the very man. I took his card out of the box beside the phone and rang Maurice Hardacre.

He was in the auction room, his secretary told me, and would be until lunchtime. I left a message for him to ring me and sat down to think this out. I felt pressured and a little frightened. I had no provenance for my picture, Oliver was off the map, and Jay and Billie together were formidable. She, particularly, was used to getting exactly what she wanted, and I knew already that I was no match for her.

I think it's time that I introduced you to Billie.

Jay first met her when she came to his office wanting him to design an extension for her country house in the Forest. She had just divorced her second husband – or possibly he had divorced her, it wasn't clear – and she had a handsome settlement burning a hole in her bank balance and lofty ambitions. Her first husband, I later discovered, had died under slightly suspicious circumstances and left her a lot of money too, so she wasn't short of a bob or two. It was obvious quite early on in their acquaintance that she quite fancied adding a highly thought-of architect to her collection, particularly as he was something of a looker and making good money. It didn't bother her that he was married. The other two had been married when she met them as well. And Jay was far from averse to being sweet-talked by a leggy blonde fifteen years his junior.

I wouldn't have minded had Jay been open about it; our marriage was heading for the rocks anyway, had been for a long time now. I would simply have taken to the boats and left him to founder in his own time. But Jay, as you may have already realised, likes to deal in humiliation, and he left me to find out about his new romance from a third party. When I taxed him with it, he said one or two things that I found unforgivable and I told him to get out, which was a mistake since he then pointed out that he was the householder, and if anyone got out it would be me. Fortunately, at this point Billie invited him to join her in her own far more prestigious residence, so he put our house on the market and told me I could caretake until it was sold and *then* get out and take my damn cats with me, and started divorce proceedings before I had time to get to a solicitor.

This, of course, was exactly what Billie was aiming for.

'She'll marry him and then, after a decent interval, she'll take him to the cleaners too,' Marina, in whom I had confided, prophesied, but I had already worked this one out. Billie, as you must already realise, had a certain reputation, not unlike Dawn before her but more deadly because she did her research better, only Jay was too besotted to notice it.

'Just so long as she doesn't kill him, like she did the first one,' I said, callously.

'That's slander,' Marina said, with a certain admiration. I pointed out that no, it wasn't, if it was true.

But of course, I would never prove it, and maybe it wasn't true. Just as I now couldn't prove the picture of Hydra was mine, even though that *was* true.

'Will you really stay in that house until it's sold?' Marina went on to ask, and I told her, no I wouldn't. Not if the divorce went through first and I had enough money to get out and still go on eating.

'You must get a job,' she said. 'You can't be beholden to that traitor!'

'I intend to, but whatever it is, it won't put a roof over my head. I've been a wife and mother all my adult life, he can pay out for that, for I've had small thanks. That's not being beholden, that's being fair. And I'm not *completely* broke, either.'

Steve had nothing to say. He had liked Jay, and found himself in a difficult position. Another loss.

'It'll all sort itself out,' Marina said, trying to comfort me. 'What happens to the boat?'

'What do you think?'

She was silent. After a moment, she ventured, 'How are the girls taking it?'

'Steph is very upset, she was always Daddy's girl. Sal is more philosophical. But they both have husbands of their own now, they'll just have to grin and bear it.'

'You sound very hard.'

'I've spent the best years of my life trying to hold things together for them. They haven't been easy, Marina. Now it's my turn.'

'Don't bite my head off, I'm with you all the way! But I'm sorry about Steph.'

'She'll learn to live with it. And it isn't fair for her to blame me, Jay did it. I at least tried, he didn't.'

'Does Steph hate you for it?' Marina asked, soberly.

'No,' I told her. 'She hates her Dad.'

'Umm,' said Marina, thoughtfully. It brought me up short, and I listened again to what I had said.

'Steph doesn't blame me...' I said, slowly. The recognition of this made me feel a lot better. I squared my shoulders, although Marina, at the other end of the phone, couldn't see me.

'Attagirl,' she said, so she must have understood. 'Get out there and fight your corner – and good luck with the great white shark! Don't get eaten.'

No, I thought now. I wouldn't. But I hoped Maurice Hardacre would be able to come up with something or that might be an empty boast.

He phoned back at lunch time, apologising for not being there earlier although it was hardly his fault. 'Problems?' he asked.

'You guessed. I need some informed advice, I thought you might be able to help me.'

There was a pause, while he presumably thought about this. Then he said, 'I have an hour for lunch, perhaps we could meet over a sandwich and discuss things in comfort? I imagine this is about that picture.'

'It is. And that would be lovely.'

'I generally lunch at the White Lion, it's handy for the auction rooms. Twenty minutes?'

'Can you make it half an hour?' I would have to get my skates on; we live – I live – some way out of the town.

'I'll see you there, Mrs. Starkey.'

The auction rooms were on the outskirts of town, fortunately, and I made it to the White Lion in twenty-five minutes but it's lucky there were no speed cameras on the way. Mr. Hardacre was already there. He smiled when he saw me, and asked me what I wanted to drink, handing me the bar menu as he ordered . When I had chosen, we sat down together at a small table and waited for our lunch to arrive, and it didn't really feel as if I was lunching with a business associate. He was a pleasant man to be with: we talked about things that were easy and uncontroversial, the weather and the signs of the coming spring in the Forest, but when our light lunches arrived and we were no longer likely to be interrupted, he got down to business.

'Right, Mrs. Starkey. Tell me the worst. Your husband is making an issue of that picture?'

'He says it was given to both of us.'

'And you still maintain that it wasn't?'

'I most certainly do.' I took a sip of my orange juice. 'The trouble is, I don't know how to track down Oliver Nankervis. He seems to live only a virtual existence, with no actual reality. I don't know how to break in past the barriers.'

250

'Oliver Nankervis? How could he help? Does he know the man who gave it to you?'

He assumed it was a man: nice. I said, 'Oliver gave it to me himself.'

He was silent, watching me carefully. Then he said, 'Well, well,' and took a mouthful of his ham roll.

'You see the problem,' I said.

'To be honest, I don't know what I see.' He smiled at me. 'However, no problem is insuperable. I take it you had no joy on the net? That surprises me.'

'I had lots of joy, but none of it led anywhere. Lot of galleries, a couple of exhibitions on the other side of the world, nothing personal.'

He chomped on a few more mouthfuls of ham, obviously wondering if I was in my right mind or deluded, and if I *was* in my right mind, where this was going. Finally, he said, 'If what you say is true, and I have to admit I can think of no real reason to doubt you, then somehow we need to get a message through to him. That may not be as impossible as it looks. There must be lines of communication, and we only have to locate the right one.'

I liked that "we". I began to feel better: it was amazing, I had found, how much my skirmish with Jay had upset me. He went on, thoughtfully, 'Oliver Nankervis's career was launched by the Ladbourne Gallery in London. I know Gifford Thomas a little, although he is more or less retired now. If the situation was explained to him, I daresay he might undertake to be an intermediary.'

'That would be marvellous. Do you really think he would?'

'We can but ask. I see no reason why he should refuse. You only need a letter, after all, to confirm what you say. Something you can produce in court, if it should come to that. Let's hope it won't.'

'Then may I leave it to you? I think it may be quite urgent.'

That quiet, careful look again. 'I shall be delighted to help you,' he said courteously.

We finished our lunch, and then he had to leave. I drove home more sedately than I had on the outward journey, to find on my arrival that there was a flashy red car in the drive, and the front door was open.

I parked outside, since I would have to move anyway to allow my unwelcome visitor to depart, and walked quietly up the drive to the door. There was a set of keys in the lock that I recognised: I removed them and put them in my bag. Then I went to the door of the sitting room, also open, and stepped inside.

Billie was over in the corner by the window, her back to me and her hands on the frame of my picture. I said, 'Get out of here, before I send for the police,' and was astonished at the icy coldness of my own voice.

Billie swung round startled, but quickly regained her poise.

'I have a perfect right to be here,' she said coolly. 'This is Jay's house. He asked me to get this picture safe before you did anything silly.'

'Before *I* did?' I was outraged. 'That picture is mine, not his, and certainly not yours. Now, would you like to leave before I make that call?' I had my mobile phone in my hand, and I would use it too. She knew that, I could see.

She would have taken it had I not come back, I knew, but she was too canny to snatch it and run now. I could see calculation in her narrowed eyes, a dawning suspicion that there might be a chance I was in the right here, and she wasn't going to take any risks. She had only Jay's word, after all, and perhaps she already knew how much that was worth.

'There's no need to take that attitude,' she said haughtily. 'Jay only wanted to look after it while this whole question is settled. He says that it isn't properly insured, and should be in his safe.'

'How thoughtful of him,' I said, standing aside to allow her to pass through the door. She made no move to do so. I added, 'And do please tell him that I upped the insurance as soon as I found out its value. So there's no need for him to worry. And assure him I shall take proper precautions against theft. By anyone.' I thought for a minute there that she was going to argue, but she didn't. She said, 'Very well. I'll do that.'

She walked past me without hurry, and didn't say goodbye: I don't think I would have said it either, in her shoes. But at the front door, she paused, and turned back to me, where I still stood in the doorway of the sitting room.

'Please may I have my keys back?' She held out her hand imperiously. I didn't move.

'They aren't your keys. They're Jay's, and I can return them to him myself.' Maybe. 'Please shut the door as you go out.'

When I had watched her flash car reverse erratically down the drive and vanish out of sight, the first thing I did was to ring the insurance company; better late than never. Then I took the picture from the wall, wrapped it carefully in a pashmina, and tucked it into a small canvas shopping bag someone had given me for Christmas. Then I phoned the auction rooms again. My heart had begun to thump hard against my ribs and I felt curiously unsteady. How dared she, how *dared* she! And how dared Jay, too, sending her here to steal my picture!

Once again, Mr. Hardacre was conducting an auction, but this time I didn't wait around. I locked and bolted every door and window, then picked up the bag with the picture in it, and headed off to wait for him in the waiting area outside his office. His secretary, a pleasant woman, obviously saw that I was upset and brought me a cup of tea, and after a while I began to feel rather foolish but I went on waiting anyway.

I had to wait for well over an hour. His secretary brought me a newspaper to read.

By the time he appeared, I had calmed down a little, but all the same he took one look at me and said, 'I just have to deal with the sales, and I'll be with you. Would you prefer to wait in my office?'

I said I would, as people were beginning to come into the wide corridor to pay for their purchases and pick up the receipts so they could go and collect them, and I felt rather exposed. I picked up my precious shopping bag and the paper and he ushered me in and invited me to sit down.

I waited again.

'Now then,' he said, bustling in after another half hour had passed, 'tell me the worst. What's happened now?'

'I got to my house after lunch with you, and found my husband's bit of stuff trying to run off with my picture.' My voice broke, as much at Jay's treachery as Billie's presumption, and I bit my lip. I hadn't meant that to happen.

'I see.' He sat down behind his desk and looked at me thoughtfully. 'That picture means a lot to you, doesn't it? I don't mean just it's value.'

'Yes,' I said, and he didn't press it. Instead, he said, 'Why have you come to me now?'

I reached down and picked up the little shopping bag, setting it on his desk where he could see it.

'I want you to look after this for me. Until we can get it sorted out. If she gets her hands on it, I know I'll never see it again.'

'I see,' he said, again. He reached out for the phone on his desk, pushed it away again and pressed the buzzer for his secretary. She popped in like a jack-in-the-box, obviously scenting drama.

'Yes, Mr. Hardacre?'

'Get me the Ladbourne Gallery on the phone will you, Moira, please. I don't have the number handy in here.' She vanished again, and he pulled the bag towards him and looked inside before glancing at his watch and shaking his head over some private thought. 'The best place for this is in a safe deposit at your bank,' he said. 'It's too late now, they will be closing before you can get there. I'll put it in our safe for tonight and then you can pick it up from here tomorrow –' he broke off as the buzzer went on his intercom and his secretary's disembodied voice said, 'The Gallery is on the line now, Mr. Hardacre.'

He picked up his phone and had a short conversation about someone called Mr. Thomas, before putting it back on its rest and turning to me. 'Gifford Thomas is out of the Gallery today, he'll be in on Thursday. He will ring me then.'

Thursday was two days away. I swallowed, and said nothing. Maurice Hardacre said, 'Mrs. Starkey, I am beginning to think that I owe you an apology. I should never have insisted on putting this picture on the valuation sheet.' He touched the bag lightly. 'It was given just to you, wasn't it?'

'Yes,' I said.

'I'm not going to ask awkward questions, don't worry. But I do feel that I have created a problem for you and that I have injured you thereby, and feel it incumbent on me to sort it out if that is possible.'

'Thank you.'

He smiled at that, or rather, he grinned at me; it lightened his expression and took five years off his age. 'I think you should rather beat me round the head with your handbag, Mrs. Starkey. But be assured, I shall do my best to put this right. Now, let's get this treasure into our safe for the night.' He scrabbled in his desk for a luggage label, and wrote my name on it before tying it to the handles of the bag, binding them together, and took me with him to see it safely stowed away in a big, impregnable-looking safe in a cupboard in another office. I hated seeing it go out of my possession, but it was better than having Billie or Jay stealing it. Possession is nine tenths of the law, they say, and if Gifford Thomas, whoever he was, wouldn't play ball, I could easily lose it altogether. I thought, rather wildly, about private detectives, but it seemed a bit extreme.

'Now then,' said Mr. Hardacre, when we had returned to his office. 'I'll write you a receipt for that, and then I recommend that you go home and relax in a nice hot bath. And as soon as it can be arranged, I suggest that I come with you and we put this treasure into my bank, rather than yours, so that there is no chance of your husband talking his way in to get it. Not that I think he could, but there's no point in making things too easy for him.'

I said, foolishly I know, 'But don't you have to work?'

'I shall consider it as a work project, seeing that I put you in this situation. And I can slip out for half an hour provided there are no auctions. I'll let you know when.' He smiled, and I found myself smiling back at him. It must have given him courage for he said, 'Mrs. Starkey, I know it's rather short notice, but I wonder if you would care to have dinner with me this evening? There's a rather nice Greek restaurant opened up in the town, and I know you're a bit of a Hellenophile. No strings. Just a simple evening out with a friend.'

I hesitated, but then thought, well, why not?

'Thank you, I should enjoy that. It would make a lovely end to a rather gruesome day.' And also, if I wasn't there, I might manage to miss Jay's inevitable phone call, but obviously, I didn't say that. He looked pleased, and we made an arrangement that he would book a table and pick me up at seven o'clock.

I felt calmer as I left for home, and when I got there, the first thing I did was to hang a framed photograph of the girls in the empty space on the wall, before taking Mr. Hardacre's advice and going upstairs for a nice long soak in the bath, which calmed me even more. Then I got out, wrapped myself in a fleecy bathrobe, and sat on my bed with my mobile to ring Marina. The landline phone rang twice in the half hour that I was talking to her. I ignored it. I could guess who it would be.

It was the first that Marina had heard of my picture's history, although she had obviously seen the picture itself when she and Steve had visited. She had never studied it closely, and had no idea either that Oliver had painted it, or that he had given it to me, and she was rather indignant that I had kept it a secret.

'Why did you never say? I thought we were friends!'

'There didn't seem a lot of point. Nothing is so dead as a dead holiday romance.'

'Well darling, I know you won't agree with me but you were well out of that one! What a handful he would have been! Although he was rather gorgeous…'

I said, 'Did *you* know he was a famous artist now?'

'*Is* he? No, I didn't, I'm not much into art, but come to think, it doesn't surprise me all that much. You know who his mother is, I presume?'

'No.'

'She's that sculptress, Helen something… Macken? I expect it's in his blood.'

'How do you know that?' I asked, and was horrified at the pang of jealousy that shot through me.

'It was in the papers, darling, when he rode into the Valley of Death like the Six Hundred.'

I hadn't read them. I felt guilty now, as if I should have gone with him through that torment every step of the way – for what good it might have done. I said, 'Anyway, it turns out it's now worth a fantastic sum of money, and Jay wants half of it. Or none of it, but the picture instead so that his floozy can hang it on her wall and boast about it.'

'Jay really is under the influence, isn't he?' said Marina, almost admiringly. 'What a woman! What a bitch! So what are you going to do? Ask Oliver to vouch for its provenance? That could be interesting.'

'That's what I shall have to do, if I want to keep it,' I said. 'Only thing is, he's harder to track down than the proverbial needle in a haystack.'

'That figures.' She paused, and then put into words what I had been trying not to think, 'I wonder how he came out of that mess? If he's a painter, he obviously wasn't totally paralysed. Unless he's one of those amazing foot-and-mouth artists, but they aren't generally famous, of course.'

I said nothing.

'When we went on that cruise out of Split, I thought you couldn't know about it. You didn't say anything. But you did know, didn't you?'

'Yes,' I said.

'Oh, Sue! Why *didn't* you say?'

'What would have been the point? It had been years even then.'

'I didn't say anything because I didn't want to ruin your holiday if you didn't know already.'

'Thank you,' I said, uselessly.

We talked for a while longer, and then she said, 'You know, Sue, it's time you got yourself a life. You don't even *want* Jay back, and time is ticking past. Get on a dating site or something, see what you can find, live a little before it's too late. But be careful,' she added, belatedly.

I laughed: I felt better after chatting with her. It pleased me to be able to tell her, 'Actually, I'm being taken out to dinner tonight.'

Her blank silence was hardly flattering, but she pulled herself together nobly. 'Well, good for you. Who is he? What does he do? How long have you known him? Come on, tell all!'

Well, she deserved it, didn't she? I told her about Maurice Hardacre, and how I had met him, and she seemed pleased.

'An auctioneer, what fun! Will you go to sales and things with him?'

'Marina, I hardly know him yet. Let me sort out my own life, I'll be sure to let you know if anything interesting happens. Tonight is just dinner. OK?'

It was her turn to laugh now. 'Sorry, Sue. Only Steve and I do so want you to be happy again. What are you planning to wear?'

'Old jeans and the sweatshirt I do the gardening in. What do you think?'

'Smart but dull, knowing you. Put on something pretty and feminine, and two fingers up to Jay!'

I hate to admit this, but after she had rung off, I went to my wardrobe and opened the doors, searching the hangers for something pretty and feminine to dazzle Mr. Hardacre. What did I have to lose, after all? And Marina was quite right, my fiftieth birthday was heaving up on a distant horizon and Jay had already wasted at the very least ten years of my life. I didn't want to spend what was left of it alone.

The phone rang again before Maurice Hardacre arrived to pick me up. I looked at the caller ID just in case it was one of the girls, but yes, it was Jay. I left it. It was almost seven o'clock by now anyway, I didn't have time to argue with him.

The Greek restaurant was charming: it had pictures of islands and harbours and Greek churches on the walls, one of which I recognised from Mykonos. There was bouzouki music and lovely Greek food, and my companion was pleasant and considerate, such a change! He asked me to call him "Maurice" and I told him to call me "Sue", and we sat over a bottle of Mavrodaphne and some succulent, thyme-scented, spit-roasted lamb with lemon roast potatoes, sharing reminiscences of a country that, it turned out, we both loved. He didn't pry, and ask me how I came to know Oliver, and I didn't tell him, but there were plenty of other things to talk about. He liked sailing too, although he didn't own a boat of his own these days.

'I used to race in dinghies,' he told me. 'Too old for that now, and my wife wasn't keen. Sometimes, I still miss it.'

'What, dinghy racing?' He saw I was laughing at him, and smiled.

'I think I've gone a bit past that. But sailing generally, yes, I do miss it.'

'I think I will, too,' I said soberly. I hadn't thought about that so far, although Steve and Marina would no doubt invite me from time to time. I hoped they would. He saw the shadow cross my face.

'Well, the years catch up with us all eventually. And you never know what's round the corner.'

'We're not old,' I told him. 'In our prime, us.' He couldn't be more than a few years older than me, maybe less, maybe not as old as Jay, even.

As the wine sank low in the bottle, he told me about his wife. She had died about three years earlier, from breast cancer. He still missed her, he said, but he didn't think she would want him to mourn for ever. She had been a great one for looking forward to whatever the future held , only she had never been lucky enough to have one. He looked sad, but not desolate. He said that his wife had left him with many happy memories, and his only regret, a useless one, was that she was no longer there.

I caught myself looking at him with more attention than I had paid him before. He was a solidly built man, not over-tall, with a strong, square face and all his hair still – dark, crisp, and lightly peppered with grey, very personable altogether in a chunky, outdoors sort of way. I found myself wondering if he played golf, he looked as if he might. Then I realised that he was looking at me with equal attention, and I wondered what he saw. An ageing woman with uncontrollable hair? A deserted wife, an object of pity? I felt uncertain. Jay had done a thorough job on my confidence.

He drove me home just after ten o'clock, and when I invited him in for more coffee (we had already drunk quite a lot) he refused, saying he had to work tomorrow, but he would ring me on Thursday when he had spoken to Gifford Thomas. We parted with a sedate kiss on the cheek, and I walked into my house and the phone was ringing again.

Jay was furious. The delay in venting his rage had simply stoked it to explosion level.

'Where the hell have you been? I've been trying to get you all evening!'

'Out,' I said. 'I'm not at your beck and call, you know.'

'WI night, was it?' he asked, with scorn. I bit my lip. Not hard enough.

'No. With an attractive man.' I bit it again, harder. He laughed.

'Come on Sue, pull the other one! What attractive men do you know?'

'You might be surprised,' I told him. This time, the laugh had a sneer in it.

'I certainly should. Is that why you stole my keys? For Mr Attractive?'

'I didn't *steal* them, as you put it. I simply reclaimed them from a woman who had no right to have them in the first place! What were you thinking of, Jay? I came home to find her trying to steal my picture.'

'She wasn't stealing it. She suggested she should collect it and bring it to me so I could put it in the safe here. It's worth a small fortune, Sue, don't you understand that?'

'It isn't your picture, it's mine –'

'– ours –'

'Mine. It was a gift to me.'

'Oh, come on Sue, give it up! Get real! Why should he have given it to you? I know you were having a middle-aged fantasy, but he certainly wasn't! He had the hots for Emmy, everyone could see that! And a right fool you were making of yourself, too, you were the joke of the week only you were too dumb to know it!.'

I took a deep breath. I had no intention of hunting that hare, he was only trying to rile me, but it stung just the same. I said, 'We aren't going over that old ground again, Jay. You had no right to give your keys to that woman, and you know it.'

'I had every right. It's my house, if you remember.'

'It's *my* home, at the moment, and I don't want your tacky bit of stuff in it, and certainly not to steal things behind my back! Is that straight?'

'She wasn't stealing it. That picture is ours, not yours.'

'No it's not.'

'Prove it then. I bet you can't.'

I started to reply, but for the second time, managed to stop myself from rising to his bait. I said nothing, therefore, and after a minute Jay said, 'Anyway, I want my keys back. You had no right to take them. Billie will be over tomorrow to pick them up, and you'll give them to her if you know what's good for you.'

'Threats now, Jay? If you want your keys, come and get them yourself.'

I slammed down the phone before he could reply. I had been feeling relaxed and happy when Maurice brought me home, now I felt like an over-wound spring. I threw myself down onto the sofa and glowered at the opposite wall, thinking how glad I was that the picture was safely locked away at the auction rooms for the night. I wouldn't put it past Jay to come roaring round now, trying to railroad me into parting with it by shouting the odds to intimidate me.

He had never been like that in the past, I caught myself thinking. He had been a lightweight maybe, but a good companion, fun to be with, a great father to the girls. We had a good life, and if he had strayed as I supposed by this time he must have, he had done it discreetly. Up until Dawn. Dawn had been the watershed.

Or so I thought. Perhaps I was the fool.

I stood up at last and began to tidy up before going into the kitchen to feed the cats, who were feeling neglected and told me so. I cuddled each of them for a minute or two for our mutual comfort, and then I prepared for bed, not that I expected to sleep. I checked the locks on all the doors yet again, and for the first time in years, I set the burglar alarm. It didn't feel good, but Billie's cool intrusion into my home had freaked me out. I picked up the book I was currently reading and headed for the stairs.

Tomorrow, I resolved, I would finish packing away my personal possessions and get them out of the house. I didn't trust Billie, and worse, I no longer trusted Jay.

It had been such a pleasant evening until I picked up the phone. I should have left it, but I hadn't put it past him to ring me again at midnight if he felt like it. As I cleaned my teeth, I looked at my reflection in the bathroom mirror and saw my face, stressed and angry, and as I spat toothpaste with unnecessary violence into the sink, I came to a decision.

Sorry Marina. No more men.

The next day I was on eggshells from the moment I woke up, wondering if Billie really would come to get Jay's keys, and what I would say to her if she did. I wasn't going to give them to her, on that I was resolved. She had no right to them, and I hated the idea of her having free access to my home and my possessions, but she was perfectly capable of making a very unpleasant scene, and further eroding my relationship with Jay. We had parted fairly amicably, by mutual consent, it was only since Billie had put her oar in that we had started having all these horrible rows. I thought about that as I packed up the last of my books and other things that belonged to me – presents, received over the years, things that I had brought into our home on my marriage, mementoes of the girls when they were growing up. There were some items of furniture too, one or two good pieces that I had inherited from my grandparents: if they were gone, there would be no argument, and who knew what the acquisitive Billie might take a fancy to next?

It was only after I had packed everything except some clothes suitable for the coming warmer weather and a couple of books to read that it occurred to me to wonder where, exactly, I was going to put everything. Originally, Sally and her husband had agreed to store my stuff in their garage for as long as it took for me to find a place of my own, but they hadn't expected their space to be invaded this soon, and also, they lived fifty miles away. Gordon had a truck, but he wasn't going to drive it a hundred miles between finishing work and going to bed, and I couldn't ask it of him.

I thought about this for most of the morning, and Billie didn't appear.

She still hadn't appeared by the time evening came, and I could ring Sally, and the constant expectation of seeing her car on my drive had jangled my nerves all over again.

Naturally enough I suppose, Sal thought I was over-reacting, although she was sympathetic about it.

'That awful woman!' she said, with heartening indignation. 'Whatever was Dad thinking about to send her on his dirty work?'

'He – or more likely she – was thinking of a picture by a famous artist that's worth eighty thousand pounds,' I told her, cynically.

'I looked him up on the net,' said Sal, and she wasn't talking about her father. 'He's a really big banana in the art world, that Nankervis man. Are you certain that picture *is* really yours, Mum?'

'Oh, don't you start!' I exclaimed, and she apologised.

'Sorry Mum. Only Dad seems just as certain that it belongs to you both.'

'Well, he's wrong.'

'I'm sure if you can prove it, he won't push it,' she said. I wished I shared her certainty.

I mentioned my boxes of personal effects and the furniture to change the subject, and Sal was perfectly happy about it.

'Only, Gordon won't be able to get over to collect it for a couple of weeks. We're away this weekend, and the one after we've got people coming to stay. Will you be all right with it under your feet for that long? Maybe you should find someone else to store it for you if you really think it's that urgent, but I do think you're letting it all get on top of you, you know.'

'I don't actually think your father is going to descend on it and spirit it away as community property, if that's what you mean,' I said, although by this time I wasn't entirely sure – or at least, not about Billie anyway. I had some nice things, and she obviously had an eye for the good stuff.

'Of course he wouldn't, Mum, don't be silly!'

'I'll see what I can work out,' I told her. 'Maybe I can pay somewhere to store them temporarily.'

'Good, Mum. Let us know, we can come down next month, no problem.'

I rang off. Still no Billie.

I spent an uneasy evening with the telly, expecting to hear her imperious ring on the doorbell at any moment, and by this time another consideration was beginning to edge into my head.

Oliver.

Tomorrow, Gifford Thomas, whoever he was, would speak to Maurice. Maybe he would. And if he did, would he agree to bother such a famous artist (apparently) with what would seem such a small problem? And if he did, to take speculation a dangerous step further, what would Oliver say? Don't remember any Sue Starkey? Something like that? Perhaps Jay was right, and I had imagined the whole thing and he wouldn't know what I was talking about. Perhaps that awful beating-up had damaged his brain and he really *wouldn't* remember.

I began to feel sick.

I slept badly, but eventually Thursday came.

Maurice rang me from his office, very formal in front of his secretary, calling me "Mrs Starkey" again. The news wasn't good.

'I've spoken with Gifford, Mrs Starkey,' he said. 'Bad news, I'm afraid, although not the worst. Oliver Nankervis is out of the country for the next couple of weeks, over in Australia for an exhibition in Sydney.'

'I saw about that on the net,' I said, my heart sinking. A couple of weeks seemed like a year in prospect, with Jay and Billie nagging on at me all the time and the outcome in doubt.

'Yes, well, it's unfortunate, but there's nothing we can do about it. We shall just have to wait until he returns. If you can spare the time this afternoon, perhaps if you came over here, we could put the picture in the bank out of harm's way? Then your husband can still make things awkward for you, but he can't get his hands on it.'

'You're being very kind,' I told him, with gratitude.

'If you remember, I did say that I feel responsible for the situation. So let's try and keep things neutral over the next fortnight, and see what happens then. Yes?'

I agreed, and we made an arrangement for me to be at his office at three o'clock, and he rang off, and I sat there with my heart thumping. Another two weeks! And no guarantee that there would be a happy ending at the end of them. I was finding it difficult to breathe. How did Oliver, that free spirit that I remembered – thought I remembered – so well, allow himself to become so famous? I would have thought it would be the last thing that he would want.

Or perhaps he hadn't wanted it, perhaps it had just happened. A talent such as he appeared to have belatedly discovered in himself probably couldn't be hidden easily, and maybe he had needed the money. I thought about him for a while, but came up with emptiness. I had loved him, but never really known him. I could have read him all wrong.

We put the bag containing the picture into a safe deposit box that afternoon, and then Maurice, abandoning his formality, said, 'Come along Sue. We deserve a cup of tea after that, don't you think? Pity it's not later, or we could have gone to the White Lion.' He took my arm and steered me in the direction of the nearest café, where we sat over a pot of tea and a plate of buns and tried to make a plan of campaign to cover the next few weeks. Maurice had allied himself firmly with me; I don't know what it was that had pushed him off the fence, maybe something this Gifford Thomas had said, but he was definitely in my corner now.

'Your husband can't do anything now without a period for reflection,' he pointed out. 'The picture is in my bank, not yours, and he has to make his claim to both of us before we do anything. And believe me, the way you look this afternoon, I don't feel inclined to accommodate him.'

'Why, how do I look?' I thought I had covered most of the ravages, but he cocked a knowing eye at me. I remembered that he had been married.

'Shattered. Did you sleep at all last night?'

'Better than I would have if the picture had still been in the house,' I said. 'I keep listening for her car on the drive... it's like some kind of slow torture: will she come, or won't she?'

'You should get yourself a job and get out of the house,' he said, firmly. I said, without really thinking, 'So I will, when I've got the rest of my things safe. If a middle-aged woman with no qualifications can find one, that is."

Maurice studied me for a long moment, until I began to feel uncomfortable. I was about to mention it, when he said, 'What things, exactly?'

'Boxes of books. China. Some good pieces of furniture my Grannie left me. The clothes I won't need for the summer.'

'Van load or lorry load?'

'A decent sized van would do it. My son-in-law was going to collect it in his truck, but I've kind of jumped the gun.'

'They really have got you on the run, haven't they?' He sounded angry, and I said, 'I think it's more her. She's a very strong woman, Jay wasn't like that before. Far stronger than him, and greedy.'

'Don't feel sorry for him,' Maurice advised. 'He volunteered, presumably, he wasn't pressed. Well, that's not a problem; I can get a couple of the men to moonlight with one of the auction room's vans, but it's too late to ask them to do it tonight. Do you have somewhere to put it all?'

'Not yet. I thought I could pay to put it in store somewhere.'

He considered me, obviously thinking; you could almost see the cogs revolving. Then he said, 'I have a double garage with only one car in it these days. It's perfectly dry, and has a good lock, and we could cover your things with dust sheets to protect them. It won't be for ever.'

'You don't want to be bothered –' I began, but he cut me short.

'It's no bother, Sue. It'd be a pleasure to help you.'

There was a short silence. I thought he was probably still feeling guilty over his insistence on putting the picture on the valuation sheet, and I decided not to argue but to accept his offer gracefully. So I said, 'Thank you then. It would be so kind of you if you don't mind.'

I was doing a lot of thinking just lately, and most of it was wide of the mark.

'I don't mind,' he said.

We parted then, and I drove back to the house – I could no longer consider it my home, I realised. Billie had invaded my stronghold and I would never be wholly at ease there again. I wondered: I did have a little money of my own, inherited along with the furniture. It wasn't enough to buy in today's market, but perhaps I could find somewhere to rent and move out completely, and leave Jay to worry about it. After all, he was the one insisting it was *his* house, even though it had always been our joint home and I had run it for him for nearly thirty years. I didn't have to be an unpaid caretaker; if he could do a runner, so could I. I could put the cats in the cattery if necessary, at least for a while, although they would probably hate it. Come to that, I had friends who would give all three of us sanctuary if I asked. So far, I hadn't, not wishing to appear needy.

I still didn't wish to appear needy.

I stopped at a newsagent and bought a local paper, and took it home to study the job columns and the "To Let" advertisements. By this time, I realised, the only thing I would miss by leaving was our dear old dog's grave under the apple tree. It was time to get a life, Marina was quite right, and I was sick of waiting on Jay's convenience.

True to his word, Maurice turned up with two men and a van the following evening.

'Any sign of Bully Billie?' he asked, as he climbed out of his car.

'No.'

'War of nerves. Take no notice. Now then, show us the loot and let's get it loaded before she turns up and catches us at it. You can come with me and follow it home so you know where it's gone, and then I'm taking you out to my local pub for a steak. Or they do good fish and chips, if you prefer.'

I liked the sound of fish and chips, and I have no objection to being ordered about by people who have my interests at heart so long as they don't make a habit of it. I helped carry things out to the van, the men loaded it, and then I set the burglar alarm, locked up, and we drove away in convoy.

'I don't really know why I did that,' I remarked, thoughtfully.

'Did what?' Maurice negotiated a turn into a green lane.

'Set the burglar alarm. Jay knows the number anyway, and if he wants Billie to get in again, I'm sure he'll not hesitate to tell it to her.'

'Change it.'

'I don't know how,' I confessed, and he said he would do it when he took me back.

'Well thank you, but that might not be the best idea.'

'Why not?'

'Because it is his house as well as mine, maybe more than mine, and eventually I shall have to give him back the keys.'

He was silent for a moment.

'I shouldn't really ask this, I know, but how is the divorce progressing?'

'Slowly. My solicitor is pushing for half the value of the house, his is arguing that as I never helped pay the mortgage, I'm not entitled to it. I don't want alimony, I'd feel like his pensioner. I just wish I could tell him to take his money wholesale and push it down his tarty friend's throat.' That hadn't come out quite as I meant. I looked down at my hands.

'Has his solicitor been informed about the painting?'

'I don't know. If he has, I expect I shall soon hear about it.'

Maurice slowed to turn after the van through a wide gateway, and didn't look at me. 'You know you can always come to me if you need. No, I don't mean money,' – as I opened my mouth to speak – 'I mean for friendship. Advice. Support. All those things. And now, here we are. Home, sweet home.'

Maurice owned a pleasant thatched cottage – well, more of a house, really – with a long barn adjacent, on the edge of the town, nestling in the fringes of the Forest. The barn, he told me, had been converted into a flat for his late mother, but since her death some years ago had stood empty, or been used by friends for holidays.

'It's all too big for one person, really, but I can't bring myself to sell it,' he said, as we got out of the car. 'We had good times here, Christine and I: our children grew up here. It's hard to sell all your memories.'

'But you don't really, do you?' I asked. I had no choice about selling mine, but then a lot of those, at least recently, and so far as the house was concerned, weren't necessarily happy. 'You carry them with you. Tucked away in your heart.' Where Oliver was, and the dog would be. I pulled a face at my own sentimentality, and Maurice grinned when he saw it, although he didn't know the reason of course.

'I shall do it eventually, I expect,' he said. The men were opening the back doors of the van, he took out a remote control and opened the garage from where we stood. 'I'll give you the spare,' he said, so casually that I knew it must be the one his wife had carried. 'You may need to get in for something.'

The furniture was unloaded, safely stacked in a corner of the big garage, and wrapped in dust sheets. The garage felt perfectly dry and I knew that my possessions would be safe here, even Billie would never track this hiding place down. I don't know if I really believed Jay would send her burgling again, but I did feel easier in my mind when I had settled up with the men and the van had driven off, and Maurice and I got back into his car and drove to the pub. He hadn't asked me into his home: I had a feeling that he was trying to keep a distance, but as much for my sake as his own, and I would need to think about that. Too much of a gentleman to rush me before I was even divorced? Didn't want to give me ideas? I shook my head, without meaning to, and out of the corner of his eye he saw me do it. Without removing his attention from the road, he said, 'More problems?' and I replied, 'Life is full of them,' and then we reached the pub and the fragment got lost, thank goodness, in parking the car and making our way inside.

The fish and chips were excellent, and the pub dining room had a pleasant view out over the darkening Forest. We talked, from mutual choice I think, about casual things that interested us both and didn't step on each other's private ground, and finally left just before ten o'clock, and he drove me home. This time, he did come in for a coffee, which we drank in the kitchen with a cat each on our laps, since it was the only downstairs room that didn't look slightly decimated by my removal of strategic ornaments and pieces of furniture. Tomorrow, I would need to have a re-shuffle to hide the gaps and make the place look properly furnished again. We parted with another demure kiss on the cheek, and I reset the alarm, fed the cats, checked the locks on the doors, and went upstairs to my lonely bedroom.

I was in the sitting room the next morning, pushing furniture around to hide the gaps, when there was a long ring on the doorbell, and when I went, half-expecting Billie again, it was Jay, fuming on the doorstep. Saturday, of course. He had no doubt just left his office after his morning's work, taking me in on the way back to Billie, and he was furious. He pushed past me without ceremony, took a quick look round, and had turned on me before I had time to draw breath.

'So she was right!' he exclaimed. I took a step back: I didn't mean to, my feet did it on their own. He looked angry enough to hit me.

'Who was, about what?' I asked, taking another circumspect step backwards. He followed me, closing the gap in menacing mode.

'Billie said she drove past here last night and saw men loading a van from the auction room with furniture!' He swept his arm around him in a wide gesture that nearly caught me on the upper arm. 'And I see she was right! What the hell do you think you're playing at, Sue?'

Busy Billie again. Was the woman spying on me? Had he told her to?

'Check round,' I said steadily, although my heart was on the thump again.' You won't find anything missing that doesn't belong to me.'

'How can I be sure of that? You've already taken that bloody picture!'

'That was mine too. And you must *know* what should still be here.'

He obviously didn't, or not for certain. I saw his eyes flicker, but he came right back onto the attack.

'You had no right to touch anything at all until the house is sold!'

'On the contrary, I have every right to put my own property wherever I want.'

He glared at me. 'Maybe I should do the same. Then you'd be in the shit, wouldn't you?'

'Oh, don't be silly,' I said. Not the best answer.

'Anyway,' he said, 'I've put this house on the market with a second agent this morning to get it sold as quickly as possible – a nationwide one, not just local. That's at least one way to stop you stealing the light fittings!'

'I beg your pardon?'

'And I beg yours, madam Sue! And now, I'll have my keys back, please. I need them for the new estate agent, so you can't hang onto them any longer.'

'Of course,' I said, deliberately calm. 'I never said you couldn't have them, you only had to come and ask.'

'You said you wouldn't –'

'I said I wouldn't give them to Billie,' I interrupted. I went over to the desk – his desk – that stood against the wall and took the keys from the top drawer. 'Here you are. And if you give them to that woman again, I'll be taking legal advice!' I nearly threw them at him, and to my astonishment he hesitated, and said more placatingly, 'Come on, Sue. It needn't be like this.'

'You began it,' I said, smarting.

He took the keys and slid them into his pocket without looking at them.

'I'll tell the agent to ring and let you know when he's coming to check things out. Mind you're here.'

'I have no reason not to be, so long as he chooses a convenient time,' I said. I didn't tell him I was looking for alternative accommodation. Why should I? He hadn't warned me he was trying to hustle the sale of the house. I thought he would go then, but it seemed he still had something else on his mind. He said, 'How about some coffee?'

We went into the kitchen together, and he sat down at the table where Maurice had sat last night while I put the kettle on and found mugs. I wondered what he would say, but when it came, it didn't amount to much.

'We can do better than this, Sue,' he said, spooning sugar into his mug and not looking at me. 'We don't have to fight all the time. It's upsetting Steph, and where's the point? We agreed to split up, we don't have to fight about it.'

Steph has always been his pet. I said, 'I'm not trying to pick a fight, Jay. It seems to me that you're the one doing that, but I'm not making an issue of it. I'll be happy to declare an armistice if you do.'

He was silent for a minute, and I sipped my coffee and watched him think it out. Finally, he said, 'I'm sorry if it seemed like that. But when you took that picture –'

'– my picture.'

'You say that, but you know it's not true. You can't prove it either way, after all. I think it's ours, and I'm quite prepared to split with you. It must be just about the most valuable thing we own. You must see that.'

'*We* don't own it,' I pointed out. He looked at me sadly.

'We're going nowhere on this one, are we?'

'No. Sorry.'

He sighed. 'There's no doing anything with you, is there? Look, I know you're sore about Billie, but –'

'Excuse me?'

He went red. The conversation foundered.

He left soon after.

Well, I thought, that got us precisely nowhere. And if he was sending yet another estate agent to value the place, I had better get it into order for personally, I couldn't wait to be shut of it now. We had already had one or two people round to see it, but no firm offers, I hoped that Jay's new plan might work and would do everything I could to help it on its way.

Stephanie phoned that evening. Steph is the younger of our two girls, and had always been the most vulnerable. She still adored her Dad, in spite of what I had said to Marina, which I didn't resent since Sally was more of a Mum's girl so that was fair. When it came down to it, both of them loved us both, but maybe not quite equally. So what? But what Steph had to say this time made me furious, although I did try not to take it out on her. And to be fair, it was true that Sally

271

knew more of what had been going on, and had for years now, than had ever been shared with her younger sibling.

After exchanging the usual pleasantries and enquiries after my health and happiness, she got right down to business.

'Dad is very upset.'

'No, he's not. Dad is very pleased with himself,' I told her. 'He's made his choice, after all. I had mine thrust upon me.'

'Oh Mum! I know, and I'm sorry. But that isn't what I meant. He says you've... well, taken something that maybe you shouldn't have. He asked me... well, to speak to you about it, see if I can make you... well, see sense about it.'

'I see,' I said. I took a moment to control a sudden spurt of rage. How dared he involve our children? How *dared* he? I drew a steadying breath. 'You used that word three times there, Stephie darling, and it isn't *well* at all. I take it, this is about my picture?'

'*The* picture. The one that turned out to be so valuable.'

'Steph,' I said, 'you must believe me when I say that picture was a personal gift to me, only. It's Dad that wants to believe it wasn't. Or more likely, Billie.'

'That obnoxious cow!' exclaimed Steph, with heartening warmth. I felt a bit better. 'I expect she's egging him on, of course, she would. But Dad doesn't tell lies, and he's quite certain it belongs to you both... I always thought it did. Not that I ever took much notice, it was so small and hanging in a dark corner too. It isn't as if you particularly valued it, Mum.'

'If you put watercolours in bright sunlight, they fade,' I told her. 'And it would have looked pretty silly above the mantelpiece anyway. And I did value it, Steph. I do. More than you'll ever know.' I didn't add that her father told lies faster than a dog could trot; let the poor child keep some illusions.

'Well, OK, but it did belong to both of you, it hung in our house. Can't you come to some agreement over it? If you really want it, he's said that he'll sell you his half, whatever Billie says...'

My attitude about the picture, I realised, was becoming graven in stone. I said, tiredly, 'Steph darling, for what business it is of yours, I have no reason to buy what's already mine. Leave it darling. You'll only get hurt if you let yourself get caught in the middle.'

'But can you prove it's yours?' she asked, just like everyone else. 'He says you can't, and you can't because it isn't, and if you can't...'

I was getting weary of her inability to finish a sentence. Poor Steph, he had no right to use her to blackmail me – emotional blackmail, but blackmail all the same. I said, 'I may be able to, Steph. Stay out of it darling. Please.'

She wouldn't let it go, and when she finally rang off I put the phone down with actual relief, an odd emotion when you have been talking with a beloved daughter. I felt drained, trapped and threatened. I went and sat in my re-arranged sitting-room, that didn't feel like mine any more, and wished for the first time I had never set eyes on Oliver Nankervis.

But having done so, I couldn't rub him out. He was part of what made me the person that I had become.

A disturbing influence. A maverick. A catalyst. Call him what you will. I had a dreary conviction now that I would never see or hear from him again, but I resolved that I, not Jay, would arrange the sale of the picture if it had to come to that, and I would make sure neither he nor Billie knew where it ended up at auction: Maurice would help me with that. Jay could have the money, if he set so much store by it that he would drag our children into the disagreement, but Billie would never get her grubby, thieving hands on my picture!

On Monday, my solicitor told me that I would be better advised to remain in the house until it sold. Apart from the fact that it would sell better if it was lived in, if I moved out, his solicitor might try to argue that I wasn't entitled to the full fifty per-cent since I already had a place of my own and Jay was lodging in someone else's house – I did like that word "lodging". He didn't suppose for an instant that Jay would get away with that, but it was better not to risk it and there was every chance that he would try. Reluctantly, I agreed. Then I ran the picture problem past him, and he shook his head.

'If you can't prove sole ownership, it remains community property,' he said. Nothing new there, then. I went home depressed, and rang Marina, who was out. Then I went and looked at the calendar, restless for something to do. We would be well into May before Oliver returned from Australia. Even if he got in touch with me straight away, a lot of things could have happened by then. He might not get in touch at all. He probably wouldn't. He was a famous artist, I would be very small potatoes to a full-blown celebrity.

Jay thought he had never really cared a damn for me, and had said that people had found it funny that I thought he had. I felt so beaten down by this time that I was prepared to believe that might be true.

Without my furniture and all the personal possessions that defined me, the house felt empty and not a bit like home. I fidgeted around in it, and was even quite pleased to see the new estate agent when he arrived. He walked around, looking at everything with that measuring way they have, and making notes on a pad with his lips pursed thoughtfully. He said that although property in the New Forest area held its value well, it wasn't the best time to be selling, then shook his head and mentioned a valuation figure that made my hair stand on end.

'But in the spring, we do get a lot of prospective buyers,' he said, tapping his chin with his pen. 'It depends if any of them are prepared to pay that much. We shall just have to wait and see, and hope for the best. You only need one serious buyer, after all.'

He went, and so low had I come that I was quite lonely when he had gone.

Nothing got very much better after that over the next two or three weeks. Maurice took me out to dinner a couple of times, and we had a day out together one Sunday and picnicked in the Forest, and the machinery for Jay's and my divorce ground steadily onwards. We had a date for the hearing now; I was sorry in a way but in another, I couldn't wait. One or two people came and looked over the house: they seemed to like it well enough, but we still had no firm offers. I began to wonder how long I was going to be trapped here. I saw nothing of Billie and very little more of Jay, which suited me. The word "picture" was never mentioned.

And then, everything blew up together.

The 16th of May. A date I will never forget as long as I live.

It all began with a letter from Jay, that arrived in the post a few days earlier. He had consulted with his solicitor he said, and his solicitor was of the opinion that he could obtain an injunction to make me produce the small watercolour, valued at £80,000, by Oliver

Nankervis and include it with the rest of our communal property. I had failed in the interval – a whole month, he pointed out – to establish my sole ownership, and time was running out. If he had to obtain an injunction to reclaim property that was half his in the first place, the cost would of course be deducted from my settlement. Perhaps I would be good enough to let him know what I decided to do as soon as possible.

The letter had Billie stamped all over it. No doubt she had helped him to compose it.

It seemed oddly dismissive that he hadn't bothered to come round and discuss it with me. I wrote him a letter back telling him, in essence, to get lost.

Not long after that, the fateful 16th, he arrived on the doorstep after work, Billie at his side, and literally forced his way in. Not that I would have stopped him, but I might have had a go at stopping her. They stood in the hallway and glared at me, and the walls seemed to shrink inwards. Two against one wasn't fair. To try and open out the space a bit, I invited them into the sitting room. Jay stalked in past me, saying 'I don't need an invitation to go into a room in my own house!' and Billie oozed after him with a pitying smile.

'Now then,' said Jay, when we were all seated, 'I've had about enough of this, Sue. What have you done with that picture? I went to the bank to see if you had it in a safe deposit box, and they denied ever having seen it!'

'Good. You had no right to do that.' Thank you, Maurice.

'I had every right, and you know it!'

I was sick of this argument and said nothing. Billie said, in a gentle, reasonable voice that made me want to hit her, 'Come on Sue, don't be foolish. Jay will get an injunction, and you'll have to produce it then. We're prepared to be reasonable, we've already said that we'll give you the full value of your share and no arguments.'

'What's with this "we?" I asked. 'And please keep out of this, it's nothing to do with you.'

'Billie wants to buy the picture, so it is something to do with her,' said Jay, in the same quiet, reasonable way that made me want to hit both of them now. I took a steadying breath, and for some reason thought of Maurice again. Why wasn't he here when I needed him?

'Two things are wrong with that statement,' I told them. 'One is that it isn't for sale, and the other is that if it was, I'd burn it rather than see it in her hands.'

'Still sentimentalising over it, are we Sue?' asked Jay, with a nasty smile. 'Our little middle-aged fling with a chancer who forgot about you the moment you climbed onto the bus? If he gave it to you, why isn't he rushing to say so? He's had enough time.'

'You can sneer all you like, but it doesn't alter the fact that it was given to me, not to us.'

'Rubbish, Sue! Sentimental bollocks!'

Deadlock.

'Look Sue,' said Billie, wading in where angels feared to tread again, 'I can understand how you feel, but isn't it better that the picture should be out on display where people can enjoy it, rather than hidden away where only you can look at it? It's stolen goods, you can go to prison for that. Be sensible.'

My jaw dropped. I was speechless at her sheer effrontery, and looked, uselessly, to Jay for defence. He looked back at me solemnly and said nothing. I asked, 'Are you going to let her get away with that?'

'It's true, Sue.'

'You've been having a bad time,' said Billie, solicitously. 'You should go and see your doctor you know, he can give you something to calm you down: it's not your fault, it happens with all women your age. Then you'll think calmly again, and I know you'll see the sense in what we're saying then.'

'You're quite unreasonable about that damned picture,' said Jay, not helping.

'*I* am?' I asked him. Then I turned to Billie. 'Thank you for your solicitude, but I am not losing my marbles, thank you. And now, will you please both get out of here and leave me in peace? The ones who are trying to commit a theft are you. Now go!'

Jay bounced to his feet. 'All right, you asked for it! You can't support your claim, and anyway, I'm still pretty sure that you told me you bought it, and I shall say so. I daresay other people heard you, too. Steve says he might have.'

'"Might have" isn't good enough – if that's even true. Which it isn't, because I didn't.' I wished I was sure about that, but even if I had said it, it hadn't been true. It had been given to me. My uncertainty must have shown in my face, for Billie laughed, or rather, she giggled. Jay swept her up and headed for the door with one final shot.

'We'll see how you like it in court!'

Slam! I thought the house rocked with the force with which he closed the front door. I heard the engine of his car revving madly as he reversed down the drive, and I swear there was a clunk as he hit the stone gatepost, but I couldn't summon the spirit to cheer.

If Jay had convinced Steve that he had heard me say that, I could be in trouble. I imagined being in court, and what Jay would say about my "middle-aged-fling", and I knew that because I couldn't actually recall what I told him about the picture when he found it in my basket, my uncertainty would show in my face and in my voice. I began to shake. This was turning into a complete nightmare.

I would have to ask Steve. If Jay was lying again, I could discredit him, couldn't I? Steve would go into court and deny it, he'd do that for me.

I reached out for the phone to ring Marina, and as I touched it, it began to ring.

I snatched it up without thinking. Number withheld, one of those nuisance calls trying to convince me I'd won a holiday somewhere, or had a virus in my computer: well, I was in just the mood for them! I said furiously, 'Whoever you are, and whatever you're selling, I don't want to know! Now get off my line because I need to use it!' and an unfamiliar male voice that I half-remembered but couldn't place, said, 'Sue? Sue Starkey? Or do I have a wrong number?'

I nearly had a heart attack on the spot, I swear it. I said, in a voice I didn't recognise, 'Who is this?' and he said, 'Oliver Nankervis. Giff Thomas said you needed my help.'

I burst into tears, I'm ashamed to say. I cried so hard for a minute or two that I gave myself hiccups, and so when I had pulled myself together enough to speak, what I actually said was, 'I'm so -*hic* – sorry – *hic*. I've had a – *hic* – morning Are you -*hic* – still -*hic*?'

'Take a deep breath and hold it for a minute,' advised Oliver. 'There – is that better?'

'*Hic*,' I managed.

'OK, so it's not. Go and get a glass of water. I'll hang on.'

Getting the water gave me a chance to pull myself together, but I can't say I made the best of it. I tried drinking out of the wrong side of the glass as my mother used to tell us when I was a child, but only succeeded in nearly choking myself to death. Then, afraid that he might get tired of waiting and ring off, I carried the glass back to the phone and picked it up again.

'Are you still – *hic* – there?'

'Yes. And so, it appears, are the hiccups. Can you manage to tell me what this is all about?'

'How long have you got? – *hic*.'

'As long as it takes,' he said, calmly. 'No need to rush it, I'm not going anywhere.'

'*Hic*.' I took a sip of water. It helped a little this time, and I managed to say. 'I'd just had a row with Jay when you rang.'

'Bad timing, sorry. Go on.'

I didn't have to give him all the gory details, but I desperately needed to unload onto someone and he was there. Between hiccups I managed to tell him about the picture, and about Jay's threats to take me to court, and the acquisitive Billie. I don't know if I got it absolutely straight, it sounded incoherent even to me, but Oliver took it on the chin anyway.

'Why should he make a fuss about the picture? It isn't his. It's yours.'

If he had been in the room, I would have hugged him! Instead, I said, 'But I can't prove that – *hic* – and anyway, he swears I told him I bought it.'

'Did you?' He sounded interested.

'Not that I remember. But I could have – *hic*. I had to explain it some-*hic*.'

There was a silence, while he presumably thought about it. Then he said, 'Well, I don't see that you have to worry about it. I can give you provenance, which is what you need. Isn't it?'

'*Hic*.' I took another sip of water.

'In fact, I shall be happy to give him so much provenance that he chokes on it!' He sounded hearteningly angry. 'Why ever did you stay with that wanker so long, Sue? He was bound to drop you in it eventually!'

'Well, I'm not staying with him any longer. The divorce hearing is next month.' I added "*hic*" as an afterthought.

'Well, good. I'm happy to hear it! Now then, we'd better get you sorted out before they arrest you. Can you bring that picture down to me, here?'

'I don't know where – *hic* – is, do I?'

'I realise that. Have you a pen and some paper handy?'

'*Hic.*'

'I'll take that as a yes, shall I? Ready? Then write down this address…'

CORNWALL

May 2004

Maurice drove me down to Cornwall the following weekend, and I didn't bother to tell Jay that I was going there. I certainly wasn't going to tell him why: let him waste his money on getting an injunction if he wanted to. I had told him often enough that the picture was mine.

Maurice had been furious when I told him what had happened, and leapt immediately into the arena, scowling and demanding why I hadn't called him straight away.

'I'd have seen the buggers off!' he said, inelegantly, and it would have been unkind to point out that it was he that had got me into the mess in the first place, so I didn't. Instead, I told him about Oliver, and his request that I take the picture down to him in Cornwall.

'Cornwall is a long way,' said Maurice. He looked at me, and hesitated visibly before saying, 'You won't get there and back in a day, not comfortably. Whereabouts in Cornwall are we talking about?'

'He lives on the Helford River,' I said. I showed him the address and he went very quiet for a moment. I waited.

'That's a long way down,' he said. Then he added what sounded like the ultimate non sequitur. 'You watch cookery programmes on the telly, do you, Sue? This place, St. Erbyn, is a gourmet heaven shaping up to rival Padstow.'

'Is it?' I had thought the name of the place vaguely familiar, but I had been too stressed out at the time to pick up on it. Now, I did. 'Oh yes. That Cornish chef – the fat one, who makes you laugh and charms the birds from the trees – and then cooks them, probably, in a succulent sauce. I know him. Well, not *know* him, obviously, but I know who you mean.'

'Two Michelin stars. Yum!' He hesitated again, looking almost shy. 'Suppose I drove you down, and we spent the weekend? Presumably you have someone who can see to those furry monsters of yours? You need a break. We wouldn't get a table in his main restaurant, but I know he has a second one in the village somewhere, more of a bistro really, we might get a table there. We could get rooms at his pub, I expect. What do you think?'

I hesitated now, and he added, 'I'm not suggesting I come to your meeting with Oliver Nankervis. I get the feeling that's private between the two of you.' He looked a question, but didn't ask it outright and I didn't take the bait. He let it pass, and I liked him all over again for that.

There was something to be said for his suggestion, I thought. I liked Maurice, as I have just said, and it would be pleasant to have a weekend away with a friend, and the cats would survive a couple of nights in the cattery, they always went there when I wasn't home. And there was also a vague apprehension that I felt about Oliver himself, which I had tried to bury somewhere but hadn't succeeded in doing.

You see, I had truly loved Oliver, as if I need to say it again. For however short a time, he had been the sun in my morning, the cream on my strawberries, the song in my heart. He had been young, strong and beautiful, and the whole world had been his playground. But what was he now? I knew so little. I knew that he had been kicked almost to death in a dark alley, I knew that he had lain on the edge of that death for some time. I knew, or deduced, that he wasn't totally paralysed but I didn't know how far his recovery from that dreadful attack had gone. Was he in a wheelchair? Damaged, disfigured, embittered perhaps…? He had sounded quite normal on the phone, but face to face…? If any of those things were true, I knew that I would be deeply grieved. I wouldn't want to be alone, I might need a friend to confide in, to weep on even. I hadn't been able to ask him. I had to take it on trust.

The question was, was Maurice someone I would be able to confide in, and cry all over?

'Are you sure you want to go all that way for me?' I asked, temporising.

'I wouldn't have offered otherwise.'

I gave in. 'All right, then. If you're sure.' I really liked the idea of not going all that way on my own, now I came to think about it. Maurice looked pleased.

'I'll ring the pub then, book a couple of rooms.' He looked at me. 'We could go down on Friday after I finish work, come back Sunday evening, make the most of it. It's beautiful down there at this time of the year.' He hesitated. 'No strings attached. OK? Not unless you want them.'

I didn't know what I would want, until I had seen Oliver. I didn't really know what I felt about him now, but I did need some sort of ending before I could move on. I said, 'No strings,' and we exchanged a smile.

And now, here we were, in his car and well on the way to Cornwall, the shopping bag with the picture, still wearing its pashmina, safely at my feet. I had arranged with Oliver that I would go to his studio around eleven o'clock the following day and the very thought of that appointment dried the inside of my mouth and made it difficult to swallow. I hadn't even told Marina where I was going, and if anyone wanted to see the house over the weekend, Jay would have to do the honours, or ask the estate agent. Or bloody Billie. I didn't care any more.

'We'll stop in Truro somewhere for dinner,' Maurice said, as we drove. 'Or Falmouth, maybe. I believe they do bar meals at the pub, but it'll be a bit late to eat by the time we get there. Have you ever been there before? I never asked you.'

'I've been up the Helford in a boat,' I said. 'We anchored off Helford Passage, and you could sort of see St. Erbyn from there, but it's up a creek. I think we probably saw the pub as we sailed past – right down on the water. The road goes past it on a causeway, we saw cars.' It seemed like another life. Marina and Steve and *Koala* had been sailing in company with us, that would have been on the cruise where we first met them. Happy days! Days before Oliver, he would have been delivering yachts to the Mediterranean round about then. I added, 'I think it was before that chef, Mawgan Angwin, moved in. The place looked half asleep.'

'I doubt if it does now. I've never been that way at all, by land or sea, so I'll be interested to see it. We had holidays in Cornwall, but always up on the north coast.'

We compared notes on Cornwall for a little while, and it was comfortable. Then we stopped in Falmouth for dinner, and while we waited at our table for our meals to arrive, Maurice said, 'I know it's not my business, Sue, but are you going to tell me about your connection to Oliver Nankervis? Because I feel... unease in you, and I think you should tell me why that should be.'

I twirled my wineglass and watched the red wine, spinning.

'Oh... we met, briefly. We fell in love, it was like a whirlwind. He called it a williwaw. Quick, intense, and gone.'

'And that's why he gave you the picture.'

'Yes. Hydra is where we met.'

He said, without censure, 'He must be many years younger than you.'

'Twelve,' I said, and added, 'I think,' because I realised I didn't actually know. 'About that. It didn't seem to matter at the time. It wasn't going anywhere, we both knew that.'

'But you haven't forgotten it,' he said. It wasn't a question.

'No... I suppose I might have, if my marriage had been stable.'

'If your marriage had been stable, it would never have happened.'

I muttered, 'That, and the fact that until you told me different, just a few weeks ago, I thought he was dead. That kind of preserved him in aspic.' Then I blushed, for what I had meant to say, of course, was "amber". He gave me a grave look, and said, 'Then it's more than time you met him again, and got him out of your system,' and I thought there was something else after that, but he said it so quietly that I didn't catch it. It had almost sounded like "then we might be going somewhere," but I knew I must have misheard that. Whatever it really was, he didn't pursue it, and immediately changed the subject to something else. I wondered why he had asked his original question at all, but then, I have always been a bit of a fool where men are concerned. If you have read this far, you will know that already.

The Fishermen's Arms, when we finally found St. Erbyn in the maze of lanes on the south bank of the river, was lovely; a typical Cornish pub, white and sprawling beside the water, with its adjoining restaurant, the famous *An Rosen Gwyn*, or White Rose in English, beside it at an angle. This, which had once been a row of terraced cottages, was connected to the pub by a new extension that filled what had once been the space between them: here there was the reception desk, and here we discovered that the receptionist had misunderstood Maurice on the phone, and had given us a double room, not two separate ones. If it had been Jay in such a situation, I would have suspected a deliberate "mistake", but Maurice simply looked embarrassed.

The young woman who had come to answer the bell on the reception desk, unattended at this hour, was most apologetic.

'I do not know how Shirley came to do this,' she said. She was foreign, probably Polish or something I thought, and very concerned. 'There is no other room available for tonight, we are full with the sailing, and people who do not wish to drink and drive at a weekend.' She wrinkled her nose in perplexity. 'This room is twin beds, or I could ring and see if there is two rooms in a hotel nearby.'

The twin beds made the decision for me. Maurice had been working all day, and then driven all the way from Hampshire, he looked tired. I said, 'Look, don't worry. We're both grown-up, and we can manage for tonight, we can always look the other way. And maybe tomorrow there'll be another room available.'

She looked from me to Maurice, not sure what she should do, and Maurice said, 'That's fine with me if it's OK with you, Sue. I just want to get my head down.'

'I could speak with Mr. Angwin,' she said, doubtfully, her eyes turning in the direction of the doors into the restaurant. I could imagine what a busy chef would have to say about such an interruption and felt sorry for her. Maurice must have felt the same, for he said, 'No, don't bother, it's really quite all right. Just show us the room. And please, don't worry.'

Still looking worried, she took a key from behind the desk and led the way to the stairs, explaining as she went that she and her husband lived on the premises, and were the caretakers for the night hours. 'I am Gosia, he is Roger. We are here to help after the bar closes, if you have problems. More problems.' She smiled then, and stopped outside a door on the upstairs landing. 'Here is the room. I hope that you will be comfortable.'

When the door had closed behind her, Maurice and I stood and looked at each other, and I saw the laughter that was bubbling up uncontrollably in me reflected on his face. He sat down on the end of the nearest bed and gave way to it, and I stood giggling just inside the door. It was at least half embarrassment, of course, but it cleared the air.

'This is certainly going to be a weekend for you to remember,' he said, when he had regained control of himself. 'Oh, Sue, I am sorry. I promise I didn't do it on purpose.'

'I never thought you did,' I said. I lifted my suitcase onto a chair and snapped it open, placing the precious shopping bag on the floor beside it. 'Will you have the bathroom first, or shall I?'

'Shall I? I shall probably be quicker, if you're anything like Chrissie. I never did know what she did in there for all that time.'

While he was in the bathroom, and he wasn't noticeably speedy either, I looked around the room. It was pleasant enough, not very big but presumably it was once part of a cottage, so you couldn't expect acres of space. I went across to the window and peered out into the darkness: the river must be out there, or the creek anyway. Coming up through the floor I could hear faint sounds from the restaurant below, but it wasn't intrusive. I stood there looking out at lights shining on the road, a half-lit hedgerow and the water just glinting in the moonlight over to the right. This was Oliver's world, it felt strange. Then Maurice emerged from the bathroom, yawning, and asked, 'Do you snore? I should warn you, I do.'

I drew the curtains and turned back to the room, smiling without quite intending it or knowing why. 'I'm sure I do, everyone does. Except Jay, of course, he always swore he didn't, but there was quite often this phantom pig in the room with us.'

'Your turn in the bathroom,' he said, grinning appreciatively, 'I'll say goodnight now, in case I'm asleep when you come back. I'm shattered!'

'Goodnight then.' I kissed his cheek and he kissed mine, and as I went into the bathroom he was climbing into bed. He slept in just shorts, I noted.

When I came out, he was fast asleep. I stood looking down at him for a minute, thinking how vulnerable people look when they sleep, and then got into my own bed and turned out the light.

In the morning, the receptionist was on duty when we went downstairs to breakfast, full of apologies.

'I'm so sorry,' she said, when we stopped at her desk to ask where breakfast could be found. 'What an awful thing to do! I know just how it happened, and I can only apologise and promise you that my boss will skin me alive!'

'Don't worry, we were fine,' said Maurice. 'If you don't tell him, he'll never know.'

'*She*'ll never know,' said the girl. The nameplate on her desk announced her as Shirley Pengelly, and I remembered the Polish girl saying the name "Shirley" last night. 'I'll see if I can manage a second room for tonight, but I have to look at the bookings, or maybe I can fix you up somewhere else.'

'Don't worry, if you can't give us another room,' I said, 'We like it here. Although – just as a matter of interest – how *did* it happen?'

She blushed. 'There was someone with me when the phone went, and the computer was busy doing a print-out; I just wrote down the name and "two bedrooms, Fri/Sat" on a piece of paper, only I left the "s" off and then later, when he'd gone, I read it as "two-bed room." I'm really, really sorry, and you're being so nice about it.'

'Just direct us to breakfast, and we'll forgive you anything,' said Maurice, hungrily. She gestured to a door marked "Snug".

'It's served in there. Enjoy.'

We did, and when we had finished up the last slice of toast between us, we wandered out into the sunshine and walked up through the village, looking at everything with interest. It was a typical Cornish village, slate roofs, grey stone and whitewashed walls. There were a couple of tourist shops, a gallery selling pictures and pottery and a small farm shop that sold home-made jams and chutneys, proper knobbly vegetables with the earth still on them, and home-made bread and cakes, and at the top of the hill, a small supermarket and post office, and the Rosebud Café & Bistro – café during the daytime, bistro after seven o'clock. Maurice had managed to get a table for eight o'clock tonight, we looked forward to it. Then we walked back down the hill on the other side of the road, past rows of terraced cottages that must back onto the creek, and then we were back at the pub, and it was time to get the picture from our bedroom and for me to keep my appointment.

Oliver had given me instructions as to how to find his studio.

'Turn right along the foreshore towards the river mouth,' he had said. 'It's easier than driving down and then having to get out again. There's a second smaller creek joins St. Erbyn creek; the footpath from the foreshore will take you up over the bank and down into a lane. The studio is the first building you come to; there's a flight of steps up the side. Just come up them.'

It sounded simple enough.

Maurice came with me along the foreshore. I carried the precious bag and he strolled along beside me: there was plenty to look at. Our way ran past a large white building with a lawn covered with boats – Wayfarers, Lasers and Optimists, I saw, one or two were out sailing off the beach, but I supposed Saturday must be changeover day: most of them were parked on the grass. There was a large boathouse carrying a signboard reading PHOENIX SAILING SCHOOL, and there were two or three people on the lawn, busy sorting out the boats, including I noticed, the young Polish woman from last night sitting on a rug under trees, with two small, dark-haired children and a heap of toys. The lower half of the building appeared to be a chandlery, the top half had a balcony and french doors to the right, and windows on two storeys to the left, and a staircase running up from the ground to the balcony. We had to walk under a sturdy wooden jetty with steps down to the end of the lawn: the same notice was fixed to the side of it, and three yachts were moored at the end. Except for the jetty, which I vaguely remembered, and the boathouse, it was all new since my last visit here. If there had been a house, and I thought there might have been, the present building wasn't it.

'Looks prosperous,' commented Maurice, as we walked past. 'Ever fancy teaching sailing, Sue? You must know a bit about it.'

'I just enjoy *doing* it,' I said. 'I don't think I'd want it as a life, even if I was still young. And I imagine it falls off a bit in the winter, and I'll need an all-the-year-round job, even if it isn't full time.'

'Yes. I might be able to help you with that,' he said, thoughtfully. 'We'll talk about it when we get home. Right now, we're on holiday.'

As we passed under the jetty, three older children thumped along above our heads, shouting, and I thought about the girls doing stuff like that when they were on the verge of being teenagers, and felt sentimental. And then, we ran out of foreshore, and the footpath curved away up the bank ahead of us. I felt sick, suddenly.

'This is where we part company, I think,' said Maurice, coming to a stop. 'Unless you want moral support?'

'No. But thank you.' I hesitated. 'What will you do, while I'm gone? I don't know how long...'

'Walk around a bit, I expect, and then go and sit and relax in the sunshine outside the pub. I'll be in the bar, or just outside, when you get back.' He patted my shoulder. 'Off you go, then. Good luck.'

He crunched off back along the shore, and I took a deep breath. I was on my own.

The footpath led over the top of the bank and down into a lane, as advertised, hitting it on a right-angled bend. To my right, it ran steeply uphill, presumably back to the road: straight ahead, it ran along the bank of a narrow creek, nothing but mud at present since it was low tide. The bank had been built up with high stone revetments to which one or two boats were tied, lying tip-tilted on the mud flats, and a couple of swans and a heron walked around looking for lunch: there were small squares of garden between these revetments and the lane. The opposite bank was all woodland, sloping steeply upwards. On the landward side of the lane was a row of five or six houses, some with garages or boathouses, dreaming in the May sunshine against another notable rise in the ground: they were of assorted design and size, probably a hundred years or more old. What Oliver hadn't mentioned was that there was an aggressive clump of greenery in the right-angle of the lane, and I had to pass this before I saw his particular house at all.

Grey stone, double gable, steps to the front door. A car parked in a parking area just beyond. Between the house and the greenery, a double garage, or possibly a boathouse – or both, maybe – set back a little with a balcony over the top, a glass wall backing it, french doors standing open to the warm day. And a flight of steps running up the side of the wall with a sign at the bottom: STUDIO and an arrow pointing upwards. I was relieved to see them, for if nothing else they told me that Oliver hadn't ended in a wheelchair. I'm not sure I could have borne that.

I didn't really know what I felt now, either for or about Oliver; there was a lot more to resolve than the provenance of my picture. I took a deep breath and set my foot on the first step.

The steps ended on a square landing and a stable door, top section folded back against the inside wall. I paused here, with my hand on the lower half, looking in, conscious of an impulse to turn and run. All I could see was a bench running along the back wall of the room, with a fridge, a cupboard and an electric kettle at the far end, a sink in the corner, and the beginning of another bench running along the return wall. And pictures. Three of them that I could see, one large unframed oil painting propped against the wall opposite, two smaller ones in what I believed these days to be gouache, recognisable cousins to my vivid little watercolour, hanging beside it. No doubt there were more, further along the wall.

But what pictures these were! Oliver had come a long, long way since he had painted the harbour on Hydra, and that was very, very good. But these leapt off the wall, full of light and emptiness, ships and sea and smooth, rolling waves that seemed about to break and flood the room. And love. That was what hit you first. The pictures were painted with such love that they made the tears sting behind your eyes, for it was love for something that was now irretrievably lost, only I didn't quite understand that straight off.

'Are you going to stand there all morning, or are you coming in?' asked Oliver, and I pushed the door open and stepped inside and saw him in the flesh for the first time since that quayside parting at Ayios Giorgos.

He was sitting behind an L-shaped table, that had obviously been custom-made for the built-in sloping easel was at exactly the right height for the high-backed swivel chair in which he sat. The return section, to his right, was cluttered with tubes of paint and pots of brushes and other paraphernalia of his craft, and above, a north-aligned skylight shed light onto his work. He wore a scruffy, paint-spattered shirt open over a white T-shirt that it might have protected had he done up the buttons, and faded jeans, and was just setting down a brush to swivel the chair to face me, pushing himself to his feet using the arms.

'Sue,' he said, and held out his hands to me. I put the bag with the picture on the bench, and placed my own straight into them, and we took stock of each other, a careful mutual scrutiny. It was such a curious feeling, seeing a man I had loved so much and thought to be dead for so long.

The straight dark hair and the grey eyes with their flying winged brows were the same, but there is a very narrow line between being slim and being downright thin, and I reckoned Oliver was right on it. And those eyes that I remembered so well had a bruised look to them that some might have called romantic, but which I associated with kidney problems. I had a friend once who died of kidney failure, I recognised the look. He was still a very good-looking man, but there were lines on his face that had no right to be there at only thirty-five, give-or-take, that pain had written there, and an edge to him that had never been part of the carefree adventurer of the past.

'You were doing that when I first saw you,' he said, and gave me a crooked smile.

'Doing what?' I asked, bewildered.

'Sizing me up. 'Do you like what you see this time? – no, don't answer that. It's good to see you, Sue.' He dropped my hands and reached for the bag. 'This the body? Let's sort it out, and then we can sit down and talk properly.' He picked it up and carried it across to the far bench, and watching him, a lump came into my throat. Oliver had always been so graceful, supple as a cat and tuned to a hair. Now, although he moved freely, he didn't move smoothly; he seemed to me to lift his feet from the hip, rather than solely from the knee as most people do, and it gave him a slight lurch. I had known that there would be differences in him from the man I remembered so well, but I hadn't really thought what they might be. The wheelchair was as far as I had got.

He was unwrapping the pashmina now, and lifted the picture out onto the bench, looking at it critically. 'Not bad, for an amateur. Do you mind if I take the back off? I promise I'll put it back properly.'

'Do what you like, just so long as you don't hurt it.'

He grinned at that, and looked more like the man I remembered. 'I shan't. Here – take a look at this while I operate.' He passed me a long white envelope, unsealed, and reached for a small knife lying on the bench. Curious, I lifted the flap and drew out two sheets of paper. They were identical, so I read the top one, which had been sworn before a Commissioner for Oaths and declared in legal-sounding language that the painting of Hydra harbour, signed with the initials OJN and dated the ninth of June 1995 had been a personal gift, only to Susannah Starkey and was therefore her own property, to dispose of or keep as she wished. It had been signed on both sheets by Oliver, and by two witnesses: *Carl Colenso, Journalist* and *Małgosia Hickling, Secretary*. It would cook Billie's goose very nicely, thank you. I wondered inconsequently whether *Małgosia* was "Gosia" from last night. The other name rang a faint bell, but I couldn't pin it down out of context.

'My father had it drawn up, he's a solicitor,' said Oliver, deftly stripping the tape from the back of my picture and not looking at me. 'We made two copies, so you can give one to your husband's solicitor, and file the other as proper provenance for your heirs, or alternatively, for if you ever decide to sell it.'

'I shan't,' I said.

'Good.' He pulled away the last of the tape and lifted out the backing board, exposing the back of the picture. 'There's a pen around somewhere, can you pass it to me, please?'

I found it under a magazine, and handed it to him, and watched as he wrote on the back of the painting itself: *This picture was given with my love to Susannah Starkey in June of 1995, so that she could look at it whenever the days got dark in the future and see the sunlight and smile again. Oliver Nankervis, May 2004.*

I was so touched that I didn't know what to say, so that what I actually said was banal in the extreme. 'How did you know that my name was Susannah? Most people assume it's Susan.'

He was gently fitting the backboard back into the frame, not looking at me, but there was a laugh in his voice. 'I was the Skipper, remember? No secrets were hidden from me! Pass me that tape, will you?'

I passed him the reel he indicated, and watched him tidily seal the back once more. Then he reached for a smaller reel at the back of the bench, peeled off a sticky label with his name and the address of the studio, and stuck it half on the tape and half on the backboard, signing his name again beneath it and adding the date before tossing the picture right-side-round in his hands and giving it back to me. 'There you are, madam. You can put it back to bed now.'

'Thank you.' I wrapped it carefully in the pashmina and stowed it, with the envelope, back in the shopping bag. Oliver shrugged himself free from his scruffy work shirt, screwed it into a ball, and tossed it onto the bench among the shreds of tape.

'Now we've got that out of the way, coffee, or would you prefer a beer?'

I wasn't driving anywhere, after all and the day was warm. 'Beer would be lovely,' I said. He took two pint glasses from the cupboard and handed them to me.

'You take those, I'll bring the beer.' He opened the fridge, and nodded towards the open french doors. 'You'll find a table out there. Go and sit down, I'll be right behind you.'

We sat in the sun on either side of a wooden table overlooking the mud in the creek, and Oliver poured beer, sparkling into the glasses, and at first, we found nothing to say. Eventually, to break the silence, I said, 'How was Australia?'

'Hot. Full of kangaroos. And that's not what we need to talk about, my Susannah. You were crying your heart out on the phone the other night. How did you ever let things get to such a pitch? You should have dumped that cocky bastard the moment you got back to England. I thought you were going to, or I don't think I could ever have let you leave.'

I was startled at his vehemence, and it made me defensive.

'Oh... well, what happened seemed to have made him think... and then there were the girls to think about, Stephie still at sixth form, and Sally just coming up to her degree year... I suppose we just slipped back into the old groove. To be honest, I hadn't much heart for a major breakdown of the family right then.' I ended, before I could stop myself, 'I think I left it all with you.'

'Know the feeling,' he said, a little to my surprise. He saw my face, and went on, 'You undervalue yourself, Sue Starkey, do you know that?'

I had felt for a moment there that I had wandered into a bog, but now my feet were on firmer ground. I said, trying to laugh about it, 'I imagined you spending the rest of the summer making whoopee with Emmy. *Didn't* you?'

'No, I did not. For one thing, Emmy didn't stay with the flotilla for very long after you left. A couple of weeks, and she gave in her notice and went home. For another, and more importantly, I had no wish to, even had she stayed.' I said nothing, and after a minute which he spent turning his glass and watching the beer spin round and round, he said, 'And now? Do you have somewhere to go, something to do? A life ahead of you?'

'I shall get half the value of the house when the divorce goes through, and I have a little money of my own too. I can get a job. And yes, I shall have a life.'

'Promise me that.' He looked me straight in the face for the first time since we had sat down.

'In so far as it's down to me. Yes.' It was his turn to say nothing, and I went on, taking the war into the opposing camp, 'And did *you* stay with the flotilla?'

He shook his head. 'I stayed six weeks, until they found a replacement, but my heart wasn't in it either, and for a similar reason. Everywhere I looked, I saw you... I went back to Embridge in the middle of August, and made trouble – as usual.'

Embridge was the Dorset town in which he had grown up. He hadn't called it "home", I noticed. I asked, 'Whatever did you do?'

He said, precisely, 'I started an ill-advised affair with my sister's best friend, and threw a fox into the hen-coop.'

I hadn't associated him with siblings, he had always been a one-off in my mind. I said, 'I didn't know you had a sister!' before I could stop myself. He seemed happy to be given an opening to side-step his confession, and grinned at me.

'I have, and I haven't. Susan is my step-sister, Deb is my half-sister.'

So I had been right, he was a one-off. 'And which of them did you upset that time?' I asked.

'Susan. It generally is.'

'Did you care about her friend?' I wasn't sure that I really wanted to hear the answer.

'No. I just thought a bit of a fling might help, but it didn't. Unfortunately, Joanna took it too seriously.' He looked down, hiding his expression from me, and then back up to meet my eyes. 'So I did what I usually do, and when the chance came up, I ran away. As far as I possibly could. Like round the bloody world, to escape the pair of you!'

'I'm sorry,' I said, and I was. Oh, not for me, I'd gone past that long ago, when I had thought him dead – for the unknown Joanna, but far more, for Oliver himself.

'Oh well, it's history now. And as it turned out, it was the best thing I ever did.' He hesitated, oddly ill-at-ease, and I had to prompt him in the end.

'So? You can't just stop there.'

He said slowly, as if picking his words with care, 'The day I sailed into Falmouth, a lot of people turned out in a whole flotilla of small boats and yachts to cheer me in... including a boatful of pressmen, chugging alongside and shouting questions, taking pictures, being a general nuisance... and then a photographer shouted out that there should be a pretty girl in the pictures and one of the journalists picked up his girlfriend, who was along for the ride, and… well, threw her at me, to put it bluntly. Bloody good thing I had quick reactions in those days, if she'd gone down between the boats, she'd probably have been crushed.' He fell silent, and I prompted him for the second time.

'Go on.'

He said, simply, 'I knew the instant I put her down safely and got a good look at her, that she was the one for me.' He paused, and then added, helplessly, 'She had your ridiculous hair.'

I instinctively put up my hand to my hair, still wildly curly and uncontrollable after all these years, and all my attempts to subdue it, and I don't know where the words came from, but I knew they had to be said, not just for his sake but for mine too.

'It's all right Oliver. I'm not here to ask more of you than you've already given me. I don't want to open old wounds. That's all in the past and even if I wanted it, which I don't, we can't go there.' I added, meeting the problem head-on, 'So did you marry her?'

'Six weeks later. Everyone thought she was mad, but that was nearly eight years ago, and here we still are… in spite of everything.'

So she had stood by him. I didn't know her, but I loved her for that.

'As a matter of fact,' said Oliver, forestalling any comment that I might have made, 'you may have met her. She manages that pub you're staying in – I'm presuming you're down at the Fish?'

I laughed outright at that. 'Is she the one who skins people alive if they slip up?'

'What? Who said that?'

'I told him about the mix-up with the room, and I thought he gave me a measuring look when I mentioned Maurice, but he made no direct comment, merely remarking that it sounded like something in a bad sit-com, adding, 'I hope he behaved himself.'

'The perfect gentleman.' Was I just a tiny bit sorry about that? I hadn't been, last night, but now I wasn't sure. A silence fell between us. We sat there in the sun, drinking beer, and if I hadn't cared for him so much in the past, I might have said nothing. But something wasn't right here, and I knew it: there was a question I wanted to ask, and I had no right to ask it but I did anyway.

'Do you still go sailing?'

There was a silence when I swear the birds stopped singing in the trees. Then he said, very quietly, 'I thought you just said you didn't want to open old wounds.'

I had been right, there *was* something here.

'Well, do you?' I persisted. I thought he wasn't going to answer me, but eventually he said, 'I have done, a couple of times. With my stepsister's partner.'

A couple of times... in all those years? My heart clenched.

'And? That isn't a proper answer, Oliver.'

He turned on me, suddenly fierce. 'Listen Sue, it's none of your business! I told you, a couple of times. Leave it now.'

I met his swirl of anger with a bumping heart but I wasn't going to give in. The pictures in the studio behind me were crying out to me, and their voices held tears: I could hear them now, almost see them running down the canvas and paper on which they were painted. If what had once been between us had any value, if the williwaw had not blown in vain, this was the time to start picking up the debris on the cabin sole.

'Those beautiful pictures –' I said, but he cut me short.

'That's all that's left, Sue. Memories. That's all I have from all those years, and yes, if you want to know, it hurts me, and badly! It was my life, and it's gone, and it was my own bloody stupidity that threw it away, and I live with that. OK?'

'Some people would call it heroism,' I said.

He said nothing.

I said, treading on eggshells, 'Is there nobody you can talk to... nobody who understands? Your sister's partner, maybe, you go sailing with him...' I let the sentence trail away into silence. Something in his face forbade continuing.

There was a long, long pause between us, not a comfortable one. When Oliver spoke again, he seemed to have changed the subject completely.

'Do you follow ocean racing at all, Sue?'

'Jay does.' I wasn't sure where this was leading. 'I always find it rather... *big*, somehow. You never really see much action, except on the stopovers. I can't work up any enthusiasm.'

'But do you remember, about five, six maybe, years ago, a boat called *Orb Technic* winning the Round-the-World Race?'

'Yes, I do. Jay was very excited about it at the time, she set up some kind of record, didn't she?'

'She did, and unlike mine, it still stands.' He paused, and gave me a wry smile. 'Carl was on board. He was the tactician.'

It took a minute for the significance of this to sink in.

'This is your sister's partner we're talking about?' He moved his head slightly in what could have been an affirmative. I suddenly remembered the signature on the provenance he had given me, and the slight *ding* of familiarity rang a loud, unignorable bell. 'Carl Colenso,' I said. 'He wrote that novel about ocean racing – last year, it was a runaway best-seller. He won a prize with it... oh shit!'

'Oh shit. Exactly. He has done all the things that I have done, except screw up trying to be a hero and ending up with one kidney missing and a bloody great titanium rod up his back. He could do it all over again tomorrow.'

'Oliver, I'm so sorry.' I reached across the table and covered his hand with mine. He didn't move, and I didn't know what to say.

After a minute or two, he turned his hand over so that it gripped mine, and said, so quietly that I could hardly hear, 'You're right, my wise Susannah. I would like nothing better than to be able to talk with him... to anyone who had been where I have been, and seen the things I saw... who might understand what this... this emptiness feels like. Do you know why I don't – can't?'

'Tell me,' I said.

'Carl lived his father's dream, because his father was dying. And when he died, and Carl was unable to save him, he did a stint with sailing for the disabled to – to make amends, I suppose... and so, I can't, *can't* –' He broke off, and then finished, on a note of desperation. 'And I did it all to myself. Just like I always do.'

Well, I had done it all to myself too, I thought wryly. I now had to resolve it as best I could, and I wondered if, all those years ago, some prescient and merciful deity had thrown me in his path and conjured that brief whirlwind of passion just for this, and then dismissed the idea as ridiculous. But I couldn't leave it, I felt it to be too important. And Oliver didn't have to bring it up, he could have shrugged off my original question with some light dismissal, and I would have believed him. Probably.

I had a feeling, unsubstantiated but definite, that he had shrugged it off many times before and got away with it.

Why me? is the eternal plea of those who find themselves in the shit.

'I think you're looking at it from the wrong side,' I said, as calmly as I could manage. The look he gave me would have shrivelled ice, but I was determined to see this through now I had started it. 'You've just told me two things about Carl Colenso that you don't seem to have seen for yourself: he has great compassion, and he has experience that could help you get back, at least to some extent, into something you loved. You don't have to throw *everything* away, Oliver, that's just being pigheaded. Or are you too proud to be helped?'

'I don't want his pity.'

'I doubt if you have it,' I told him. 'I read that book, it was written by an intelligent man. He knows what you are. Believe it.'

For a moment there, I saw such fury on his face that I almost dropped my glass, but I managed to meet the look, and after a moment he spoke, although the anger still rang in the words.

'Now you're sounding exactly like my mother, and I told you once before, I have more than enough mothers already. In fact, I have even more now – I have a mother-in-law and a godmother too, all of them nagging at me for my own good, so don't *you* start!'

I said, with a tranquillity I didn't feel, 'Well, you started this off by nagging at me.'

He glared at me for a second, but I could see that something, at least, had struck home although I wasn't sure exactly what. Then he visibly relaxed.

'OK, if this is the time for home truths, Susannah Starkey, let me tell you one. You let that bastard treat you like shit! You let him humiliate you in front of other people and if I hadn't been the Skipper I would have happily punched his arrogant face and thrown him overboard! You're still letting him do it, you should have heard yourself on the phone! And I'll tell you another thing. If it had been remotely possible on a small island with all those people about, I would have sunk all my scruples about married women and taken you into the olive groves and shagged you until the stars fell out of the sky! You are worth a million times over what you award to yourself!'

I think we both felt it then, the last soft breath of the williwaw as it finally died away for ever. We were left looking at each other, and I thought that we had each of us, now, given to the other a gift of great value. The problem, and this for both of us, might be in accepting.

Oliver spoke first. His hand was still in mine, but no longer gripping with pain or maybe fury but relaxed and friendly. He said, 'Right, now we've got all that out of the way, I think we've maybe reached the time to say goodbye to the past. It's blown itself out. Hasn't it?'

'Yes,' I said, and felt oddly choked. It was what Sal had said about the house that had been the family home for so many years, but somehow, this hurt even more.

'Rule a line under it,' said Oliver, but gently. 'I'll think about what you said, and thank you for that – it probably needed saying. But you must do the same.'

'I will.' I withdrew my hand and joined it with its fellow in my lap. I would never see him again after today, I thought, and although I knew that I no longer loved him with that unrewarded passion that had brought us together, I also knew that I would miss him now that he had come back into my life, however briefly, with a fierce intensity that might burn away to embers in time, but would never die away to ash.

I had never even thought that he might be married. How silly!

'However,' said Oliver, 'I see no reason why we can't be friends. I would like you to meet my lovely Chel, and my amazing miracle daughter. I would like to meet this Maurice and run my critical eye over him. I hope that whenever you come to Cornwall in the future, you'll have St Erbyn on your itinerary.'

I was amazed at the wave of warmth that swept over me when he said that. He was deliberately building a new relationship over the grave of our old love, and I felt tears sting behind my eyes. I said, 'I'd like that,' and felt foolishly inadequate.

'Keep in touch,' he ordered. 'I'll maybe see you down at the Fish this evening, if you're still there. Carl too, I daresay, he and Susan often drift in on a Saturday night. *You* can run *your* critical eye over him and see if you agree with your own estimation of him.'

'We're eating at the Bistro. It depends how late you drink.' I added, 'Maurice wanted to take me to *An Rosen Gwyn*, but there wasn't a hope. No table for months!'

I thought we were now just making conversation to cover the emotion of our parting, but Oliver surprised me – again.

'Oh, we can fix that. Leave it with me, I'll see to it.'

'Good gracious! How? Coming the great artist? I don't see it.'

'Good, because I never do.' He grinned at me, more like the son I never had than the lover I had just relinquished. 'No, there's a table in the far corner with a potted plant sitting on it. In special circumstances, the plant will take itself somewhere else.'

'And your connections with the management will persuade it to move for us?' Maurice would love it, I knew, but I still didn't wholly believe in it. The Restaurant was famous, the waiting list for tables, notorious.

'It's a done deal. Mawgan is my brother-in-law, he'll do it for me.'

'What?' I stared at him, blankly. 'Good God, Oliver, is your entire family in this little village?'

'Just about.' He made a face. 'Come to Cornwall to get away from it all, and they all come flocking behind – no, it wasn't quite like that. Deb was here first, she runs the Sailing School you passed on your way here. She found this house for us when Chel and I needed a place with a studio. Susan and the children came down on holiday and forgot to go home when her marriage broke up, and Mawgan and Carl are both Cornish, so they were here already.'

'Good heavens!' I got to my feet, it was time to leave. 'Well, we would really appreciate it if you can do that for us.' It sounded absurdly formal under the circumstances.

He had risen too, and we moved together back into the studio, with its walls filled with wonderful pictures and my shopping bag, which I picked up on our way to the door leading on to the steps. In the doorway, we both paused and turned to each other. I had been going to say a simple goodbye, but Oliver took me unexpectedly into his arms and held me to him without speaking, and my own arms went round him practically of their own accord, the precious bag dangling from my fingers. We held each other so for a long moment, and it was a very long time since anyone had held me so close, and with such affection, but at last he let go and stood back, and where there had been that irrational, mutual love between us there remained a new friendship, warming the empty space where it had once filled the whole horizon.

'Goodbye, but just for now then, Sue. I'll see you again, I hope.' He meant it, I saw.

I said, 'I look forward to it.' I took one last look at those pictures, and turned to go, and he didn't wait to watch me. I think he was probably back with his painting before I was back on ground level. I wondered if he would actually take my advice, and found I had no idea, any more than I had any idea if I could take his.

So that was that, and of course I was sorry, I had loved him and held him in my heart for a long time, and to a certain extent I probably always would, but there was an upside too. I was free, as I realised he had been for many years now, and my step was light as I walked along the lane to the top of the footpath, headed back for … what had he called it? The Fish, that was it! Headed for the Fish.

She was coming up the footpath as I reached it, and I had to stand aside to let her pass. I knew who she was immediately, for yes, she had my ridiculous hair, only hers was red, not brown. She carried a small, dark-haired child of about eighteen months on her hip; one of the two from the rug, I thought, and wondered who the other one belonged to. She knew who I was too, and why I was there, for she smiled as she stepped past me and said, 'Thank you. Everything all right?'

I found I wasn't certain exactly what she had thanked me for, although on the face of it, it was letting her and the child pass, and replied, 'Yes thank you.' We exchanged a smile, hers had real warmth in it, I hoped mine did too.

'I expect we'll meet again, properly next time,' she said, and then added, 'He's waiting for you in the bar. Have a lovely day.' She walked on, and the little girl with straight dark hair and grey eyes waved a chubby fist at me and I stepped onto the footpath.

Oliver's wife. Oliver's daughter. His present, but I was his past now. I hoped she loved him as I had, but I didn't envy her one bit; as Marina had so rightly prophesied years ago, she had her hands full! For a short, shocking moment I imagined that free spirit I once knew, living among his family, painting his pain onto paper and canvas, unable to speak to the one person who might have understood, and then the stones of the foreshore crunched under my feet, and my heart rose like a bird as I started out over them

Ahead of me was all the rest of my life, and Maurice, I now realised, had plans for it. I wondered pleasurably what they would turn out to be and how far-reaching they were, and I walked with a new belief in myself to where he sat waiting for me in the bar.